Raves for Tanya Huff:

"If you enjoy contemporary fantasy, Tanya Huff has a distinctive knack, one she gives full vent in her detective mystery, *Blood Trail*. There's a strong current of romance . . . a carefully thought out pattern of nonhuman family life . . . an unexpected serious theme that helps raise it above the crowd . . . funny, often lighthearted and highly entertaining . . . more than just another 'light' fantasy."　　　　　*—Locus*

"No one tickles the funnybone and chills the blood better than Tanya Huff."　　　　*—Romantic Times*

"Huff tells a great story, but never takes herself or it too seriously. She consciously borrows elements from other books as well as movies, comics and mythology and combines them with her own great imagination to make a thoroughly satisfying story."　　　*—SF Site*

"Huff is one of the best writers we have at contemporary fantasy, particularly with a supernatural twist, and her characters are almost always the kind we remember later, even when the plot details have faded away."　　　　　　　　　　　*—Chronicle*

"The author of the 'Blood' novels has once again proven herself a master of urban fantasy."
　　　　　　　　　　　　　　—Library Journal

"This story is a gruesome romp through mystery, horror, and the occult. The author takes it seriously enough that it succeeds, but she also injects some delightful humor."　　　　　　　　*—Voya*

THE BLOOD BOOKS, VOLUME 3

BLOOD DEBT

BLOOD BANK

Tanya Huff

DAW BOOKS, INC.
DONALD A. WOLLHEIM, FOUNDER
375 Hudson Street, New York, NY 10014

ELIZABETH R. WOLLHEIM
SHEILA E. GILBERT
PUBLISHERS
http://www.dawbooks.com

Contents

Introduction

I never intended to write *Blood Debt*. As far as I was concerned, the story I was telling ended with *Blood Pact*—that was the ending I'd been aiming for right from the beginning. And then, after a while, I realized that I had something more to say, that I wanted to explore Vicki's new life and how things were different now.

One major difference is that Henry is settled in Vancouver and Vicki and Mike have to come to him. This change meant they no longer have a man on the inside—the Vancouver Police Department might owe Mike some professional courtesy but nothing else. If there's trouble, they're on their own. Granted, if there's trouble, they're often causing it but you get my point . . .

Because the Blood books were as much about the relationship between the three protagonists as they were about the metaphysical or the mystery, and because in *Blood Debt* I had wrapped those relationships up definitely, there will be no more Vicki Nelson books. I have now said everything I have to say about these people. This is it. The end.

Well, except for the collected short stories, which we are calling *Blood Bank*.

"This Town Ain't Big Enough" is a direct sequel to *Blood Pact* and is referred to in *Blood Debt*. Given what Vicki has become, the title pretty much explains the entire plot.

"The Cards Also Say" also takes place between *Blood Pact* and *Blood Debt*. In a way, *Debt* couldn't have happened like it did without this story since the blue van Vicki is driving in *Debt* makes its first appearance here.

"What Manner Of Man" is a look at Henry's past. I'm a huge fan of Georgette Heyer's Regency novels and was thrilled to be able to dip into the time period. The names of those who aren't actual historical characters were taken from classic vampire stories.

"The Vengeful Spirit of Lake Nepeakea" was inspired partly by a sales pitch I endured at a Florida timeshare and Michael Bradley's fascinating book, *More Than A Myth: The Search for the Monster of Muskrat Lake*. Bradley not only killed any romance surrounding the Loch Ness Monster but convinced me to stay out of deep water lakes.

"Someone to Share the Night" was written for a theme anthology called *Single White Vampire Seeks Same*. No, really, it was. I swear to you, I wouldn't make up a title like that. I adore the last line of this story.

"Scleratus" is another story about Henry's past. This one, however, is a little darker than most of the others. The story spring-boarded off one of Henry's flashbacks in *Blood Price*.

"Another Fine Nest" involves Vicki and Mike with giant intelligent blood-sucking bugs in the Toronto subway. And once you know that much, everything else just kind of drops into place . . .

"Critical Analysis" is essentially a locked-door murder mystery. Well, not a traditional locked-door murder mystery perhaps, but then the person solving the mystery is a vampire, so that kind of goes without saying.

"So This Is Christmas" is the story original to this book and is a direct result of my having to write a story at Christmas time. Originally, the part of Scrooge was to have been played by Mike Celluci but a page in I realized that just didn't work so Vicki, definitely the more cynical of the two, stepped into the breach. You can thank me later for deciding against Tiny Tony.

BLOOD DEBT

For Sean "Sebastian" Smith,
who not only mapped out the
city but brought it to life.

One

"How are you feeling?"

The young man attempted a shrug but didn't have the energy to actually lift his shoulders. " 'M okay," he muttered, watching the doctor warily. The incision throbbed, and he was too tired to take a piss without the huge orderly holding his pecker, but he wasn't going to tell the doctor that. Some people said he had authority problems. So what.

He had his money; all he wanted now was a chance to spend it. "When can I go?"

"Go?"

"Leave," he growled.

"That's what I came in to tell you." Her face expressionless, she stepped away from the bed. "You'll be leaving this afternoon."

"When?"

"Soon."

When she was gone, he swung his legs out from under the covers and carefully lowered them to the floor. Straightening slowly, he released the rail and stepped forward. The room whirled. He would have fallen except that a beefy hand wrapped around his arm and effortlessly kept him upright.

"You walk too fuckin' quietly, man," he said, turning to face the orderly. "Damn near scared me to d . . ."

The last word got lost in sudden pain as the fingers tightened.

3

"Hey, man! You're hurting me!"

"I know." Something glittered in the depths of soft brown eyes, something usually buried beneath an expression of unquestionable docility.

The setting sun brushed molten gold over the waves of English Bay, gilded a pair of joggers on Sunset Beach Park, traced currents of gleaming amber between the shores of False Creek, shone through the tinted glass on the fourteenth floor of the Pacific Place condominium tower and into the eyes of a young man who sighed as he watched it set. Nestled between the mountains and the Strait of Georgia, Vancouver, British Columbia, enjoyed some of the most beautiful sunsets in the world—but that had nothing to do with the young man's sigh.

Lifting a hand to shade his face, Tony Foster stared out the window and counted down the minutes. At 7:22 P.M., his watch alarm began to buzz. Pale blue eyes still locked on the horizon, he shut it off and cocked his head back toward the interior of the condominium, listening for the sounds that would tell him the night had truly begun.

Lying in a darkness so complete it could only be deliberate, Henry Fitzroy shook off the bindings of the sun. The soft sound of the cotton sheet moving against the rise and fall of his chest told him he had safely survived another day. As he listened, the rhythmic whisper became lost in the heartbeat waiting in the room beyond his bolted door and then in the myriad noises of the city beyond the walls of his sanctuary.

He hated the way he woke, hated the extended vulnerability of his slow return to full consciousness. Every evening he tried to shorten the time he spent lying helpless and semiaware. It didn't seem to do any good, but the effort made him feel less impotent.

He could feel the sheet lying against his skin, the utter stillness of the air. . . .

And a sudden chill.

Which was impossible.

He'd had the air conditioner disconnected in this, the smallest of the three bedrooms. The window had been blocked with plywood, caulked, and curtained. The door had flexible rubber seals around all four sides—not air-tight by any means, but the cracks were far too small to allow such a rapid change in temperature.

Then he realized that he wasn't alone.

Someone was in the room with him. Someone with no scent. No heartbeat. Fleshless. Bloodless.

Demonic? Possibly. It wouldn't be the first time he'd faced one of the Lords of Hell.

Forcing a sluggish arm to move, Henry reached over and switched on a lamp.

Sensitive eyes half closed—even forty-watt bulbs threw enough light to temporarily blind—he caught one quick glimpse of a young man standing at the foot of his bed before the faint, translucent image disappeared.

"A ghost?" Tony propped one leg on the wide arm of the green leather couch and shook his head. "You're kidding, right?"

"Wrong."

"Cool. I wonder what he wants. They always want something," he added in answer to the question implicit in Henry's lifted red-gold brow. "Everyone knows that."

"Do they?"

"Come on, Henry. Don't tell me in four-hundred-and-fifty-five odd years you've never seen a ghost?"

One hand flat against the cool glass of the window, the other hooked in the pocket of his jeans, Henry Fitzroy, bastard son of Henry VIII, once Duke of Richmond and Somerset, remembered a night in the late 1800s when he'd watched the specter of a terrified young queen run screaming down the hall to beg her king once more for a mercy she'd never receive. Over two hundred years before, Katherine Howard had attended his wedding to her cousin Mary. He hadn't gone to hers—her marriage to his father had occurred four years after his supposed death. Made a queen in July, 1540, she'd been beheaded in February, 1542, nineteen months later.

She'd been young and foolish and very likely guilty of the adultery she'd been charged with, but she hadn't deserved to have her spirit trapped, replaying over and over the soul-destroying moment when she'd realized she was going to die.

"Henry?"

"Whatever he wants," Henry said without turning, "I doubt that I'll be able to give it to him. I can't change the past."

Tony shivered. The centuries had gathered about the other man in a nearly visible cloud, wrapping him in a shroud of time and memory. "Henry, you're freaking me out."

"Am I? Sorry." Shaking off his melancholy, the ex-prince turned and managed a wry smile. "You seem somewhat nonchalant about being haunted."

Glad to have him back, Tony shrugged, a trace of the street kid he'd been lingering in the jerky movement. "He's haunting you, not me. And besides, between living with you for the last two years and dealing with the weirdos at the store, I've learned to take the unexpected in stride."

"Have you?" Not at all pleased with being compared to the weirdos at the video store where Tony worked, Henry's smile broadened, showing teeth. When he heard the younger man's heartbeat quicken, he crossed the room and wrapped an ivory hand around a slender shoulder. "So I've lost the ability to surprise you?"

"I didn't say that." Tony's breathing grew ragged as a cool thumb traced the line of his jaw.

"Perhaps not exactly that."

"Uh, Henry . . ."

"What?"

He shook his head. It was enough to know Henry

would stop if he wanted him to. More than enough, considering he *didn't* want him to. "Never mind. Not important."

A short while later, teeth met through a fold of skin, the sharp points pierced a vein and, for a time, the dead were washed away with the blood of the living.

The warm evening air lapping against her face, Corporal Phyllis Roberts cruised along Commissioner Street humming the latest Celine Dion hit and tapping her fingers against the top of the steering wheel. Although the new Ports Canada Police cars had air-conditioning, she never used it as she disliked the enclosed, spaceship feeling of driving with the windows rolled up.

Three hours into her shift, she was in a good mood. So far, nothing had gone wrong.

Three hours and fifteen minutes into her shift, Corporal Roberts stopped humming.

Turning into Vanterm, as of this moment her least favorite of the harbor's twenty-seven cargo and cruise ship terminals, Corporal Roberts squinted to make out the tiny figures of three men dwarfed by the bulk of a Singapore-registered container ship. The pole lights that turned the long wooden pier into a patchwork of stacked containers and hard-edged shadows washed away features so thoroughly she was almost on top of them before she recognized one of the men.

Leaving her cap in the car, she picked up her long, rubber-handled flashlight, touched her nightstick, more out of habit than any thought she might have to use it, and walked toward them. "You night-loading, Ted?"

Ted Polich, the shortest of the three longshoremen, jerked a balding head upward at the gantry crane that loomed over the dock like a mechanical bird of prey. "Controls have stiffened up and the son of a bitch is jerking left. We're trying to get it fixed tonight, so it doesn't slow loading tomorrow."

"God forbid," the corporal muttered. A huge increase in Pacific Rim trade had the port scrambling to keep up. "Where is it?"

"Up by the bow. It's caught in one of them eddies between the dock and the ship." Falling into step beside her, Polich shoved his hands in the pockets of grimy overalls. "We figured they'd send the city police."

"Sorry. You're stuck with me until we know for sure you saw what you said you did."

"You think we made it up?" asked one of the other men indignantly, leaning around his companion to glare at the cop.

Corporal Roberts shook her head and sighed. "I couldn't possibly be that lucky."

She wasn't.

Bobbing up and down in the narrow triangle between the bow and the dock was the body of a naked man, his back a pale, flesh-colored island, the strands of his hair sweeping against it like dark seaweed.

"Shit."

Polich nodded. "That's what I said. You figure he's a jumper?"

"I doubt it." While they did occasionally get jumpers off the Lions Gate Bridge, they hadn't had one yet who'd stopped to take his clothes off. Pointing her flashlight beam at the water, she slowly swept the circle of illumination over the corpse. Bruises, large and small, made a mottled pattern of purple against the pale skin. Not very old—*and not going to get any older,* she told herself grimly—he hadn't been in the water for long.

"Funny what makes some of 'em float and some of 'em sink," Polich mused quietly beside her. "This guy's skin and bones, should'a gone right to the . . . God damn it! Would you look at that!"

The other two longshoremen crowded in to see.

Flung forward, Corporal Roberts tottered on the edge of the pier, saved at the last minute from a potentially dangerous swim by a muscular arm thrust in front of her like a filthy, cloth-covered, safety rail. Breathing heavily, she thanked Polich and snarled a warning at the other two.

As they backed up, too intent on the body in the water to be properly penitent, one of them muttered, "What the hell could've happened to his hands?"

Sunset the next night occurred behind cloud cover so heavy only the fading light gave evidence that the sun had set at all. At 7:23, Tony turned off his watch alarm and muted the inane conversation filling in a rain delay for a Seattle Mariners' home game. Who wanted to hear about a shortage of organ donors when they were waiting to watch baseball? He never *dreamed* he'd miss Fergie Oliver. Leaning back in his chair, he glanced down the hall, listening for the first sounds of Henry's return and straining to hear the rattle of ghostly chains.

As the sun released its hold and his senses slowly began to function, Henry sifted through and ignored a hundred familiar sensations. An impossible breeze stroked icy fingers across his cheek. He willed his arm to move and switched on the lamp.

The ghost stood where it had the day before—a nondescript young man, needing a haircut and shave, dressed in jeans and a T-shirt. Its edges were indistinct and although Henry could see writing on the shirt, he couldn't make it out—whether because the writing hadn't fully materialized or because the items on the dresser behind the ghost's semitranslucent torso distracted him, he wasn't sure. As far as Henry could remember, he'd never seen the young man alive.

He half expected the specter to vanish when he sat up, but it remained at the foot of his bed. *It's waiting for something.* If a noncorporeal being could be said to have posture, the ghost's stance screamed anticipation.

"All right." He sighed and leaned back against the headboard. "What do you want?"

Slowly, the ghost lifted its arms and vanished.

Henry stared a moment longer at the place where it had been and wondered what could have possibly happened to its hands.

"It had no hands at all?" When Henry nodded, Tony chewed his lower lip in thought. "Were they, like, cut off or ripped off or chewed off or what?" he asked after a moment.

"They just weren't there." Henry took a bottle of water out of the fridge, opened it, and drained it. The growing popularity of bottled water had been a godsend; while blood provided total nourishment, all living things required water, and the purifying chemicals added by most cities made him ill. Bacteria, his system ignored. Chlorine, it rebelled against. Tossing the empty plastic bottle in the recycling bin, he leaned on the counter and stared down at his own hands. "They just weren't there," he repeated.

"Then I bet that's what he wants—vengeance. They always want vengeance."

Raising an eyebrow at Tony's certainty, Henry asked just where he'd acquired his knowledge of what ghosts always wanted.

"You know, movies and stuff. He wants you to help him take revenge against the guy who took his hands."

"And how am I supposed to do that?"

"Jeez, Henry, I don't know. You worked with Vicki; didn't she teach you nothing?"

"Anything."

Tony rolled his eyes. "Okay, anything."

Vicki Nelson, private investigator, ex-police detective, ex-lover, vampire—Henry had worked with her for one short year before fate had brought them as close together as was possible with his kind and then had driven them apart. He'd been forced to change her to save her life and forced, by the change, to give her up. Highly territorial, vampires hunted alone. She'd returned to Toronto and her mortal lover. He'd made a new life for himself on the West Coast.

Had she taught him anything?

Yes.

Did any of it have anything to do with handless ghosts?

No.

When he repeated his thoughts aloud for Tony's benefit, he added, "One thing she did teach me is that I'm not a detective. I'm a writer, and, if you'll excuse me, I'm going to go write." Not entirely certain why memories of Vicki Nelson always made him so defensive, he headed for his computer, waving at the television on his way through the living room. "Your rain delay seems to be over."

Half an hour later, having realized that the expected staccato clicking of keys hadn't yet begun, Tony pushed open the door to Henry's office. Standing on the threshold, he noted that nothing showed on the monitor but a chapter heading and a lot of blank screen.

"This spook really has you spooked, doesn't it?"

"Why do you say that?" Henry asked without turning.

"You're just sitting there, staring at your hands."

"Maybe I was deep in thought."

"Henry, you write bodice rippers. There's a limit to how much deep thought is allowed."

Seventeen years a royal duke, over four hundred and fifty years a vampire, it had taken Henry a while to recognize when he was being teased. Once or twice, Tony had come close to not surviving the adjustment. Lifting his gaze from his hands, he sighed. "All I can think of is, why me." He laughed, but the sound held no humor. "Which seems a little self-centered since I'm merely being haunted and was not the one killed and mutilated." Pushing his ergonomic chair away from the desk, he spun it around and stood. "I need to get out. Be distracted."

"Great." Tony grinned. "Bram Stoker's *Dracula* is playing at midnight at the Caprice."

"Why not." Enjoying Tony's poleaxed expression, Henry turned the young man about and pushed him gently out of the doorway. "I hear Gary Oldman is terrific."

"*You* hear?" Tony sputtered as Henry's inarguable touch moved him down the hall. "You heard it from me! And when I told you, you told me that you never go to vampire movies—*that's* why not."

"I changed my mind." Unable to resist, he added, "Maybe we can get a bite while we're downtown."

The elevators in the Pacific Place towers were as fast and as quiet as money could make them. With his fingertips resting lightly on the brushed steel doors, Henry cocked his head and smiled. "It sounds like Lisa's shredding the character of another cabbie."

Tony winced. "Man, I'm glad she likes *us*."

As the chime announced the arrival of the elevator, the two men stepped away from the doors.

"Hello, boys." One gloved hand clutching the arm of her paid companion, Lisa Evans grinned a very expensive and perfect grin as she shuffled into the corridor. The gleaming white teeth between glistening red lips added a ghastly emphasis to the skull-like effect created when age finally triumphed over years of cosmetic surgery. "Heading out for a late night on the town?"

"Just a midnight movie," Henry told her as Tony stopped the doors from closing. He scooped up her free hand and raised it to his lips. "And you, I expect, have been out breaking hearts?"

"At my age? Don't be ridiculous." She pulled her hand free and smacked him lightly on the cheek, then turned on her companion. "And what are you smiling about, Munro?"

Not the least bit chastised, Mrs. Munro continued to smile down at her elderly employer. "I was just thinking about Mr. Swanson."

"Swanson's interested in my money, not these old bones." But she preened a little and patted the head of the mink stole she wore over a raw silk suit. Once the mistress of a Vancouver lumber baron, she'd made a number of shrewd investments and parlayed a comfortable nest egg into a tidy fortune. "And besides, I'm not interested in him. All the good men are dead." Sweeping a twinkling gaze over Henry and Tony, she added, "Or gay."

"Miss Evans!"

"Chill out, Munro. I'm not telling them anything they don't know." Companion chastised, she turned her attention back to the two men. "We've just come from one of those tedious fund-raising things they expect you to attend when you have money. Organs, I think it was tonight."

"Organs?" Henry repeated with a smile, fully aware that Lisa Evans enjoyed those tedious fund-raising things where her checkbook ensured she'd be stroked and flattered. He also knew that if she was vague, it was deliberate—no one made the kind of money she had without knowing exactly where every dollar ended up. "Musical or medical?"

"Medical." Heavily shadowed eyes narrowed into a look that had been known to send a variety of CEOs running for cover. "Have you signed an organ donor card?"

"I'm afraid they wouldn't want my organs."

The look softened slightly as she leaped to the conclusion he'd intended. "Oh. I'm sorry. Still, while there's life, there's hope, and medical science is doing wonders these days." She grinned. "I mean, it's a wonder I'm still alive." Pulling her companion down the hall, rather in the manner of a pilot boat guiding a tanker into harbor, she threw a cheery, "Don't do anything I wouldn't do," back over her shoulder.

"Well, that leaves us a lot of leeway," Henry murmured as the elevator door closed on Mrs. Munro's continuing shocked protests.

Tony sagged against the back wall, hands shoved in his pockets. "Until I met Miss Evans, I always thought old ladies were kind of vague and smelly. Maybe you should send your ghost over to her."

"Why?"

"If all the good men are dead . . ."

"Or gay," Henry reminded him. "Suppose he turned out to be both? I'd hate to get on Lisa's bad side."

The thought of Lisa Evans' bad side brought an exaggerated shudder. "Actually, I've been meaning to ask you; how come you're so friendly with everybody in the building? You're always talking to people. I'd have thought it would be safer to be a little more . . ."

"Reclusive?"

"Big word. I was going to say private, but I guess that'll do."

"People are afraid of what they don't know." Exiting into the underground garage, they walked in step to Henry's BMW. "If people think they know me, they aren't afraid of me. If a rumor begins that I am not what I seem, they'll match it against what they think they know and discount it. If they have nothing to match it against, then they're more likely to believe it."

"So you make friends with people as a kind of camouflage?"

Frowning slightly, Henry watched Tony circle around to the passenger door. "Not always."

"But sometimes?"

"Yes."

With the car between them, Tony lifted his head and locked his eyes on Henry's face. "And what about me?"

"You?"

"What am I? Am I camouflage?"

"Tony . . ." Then he saw the expression in Tony's eyes and realized that it hadn't been a facetious question. "Tony, I trust you with everything I am. There're only two other people in the world I can say that about, and one of them doesn't exactly count."

"Because Vicki's become a vampire?"

"Because Michael Celluci would never admit to knowing a . . . romance writer."

Tony laughed, as he was meant to, but Henry heard

the artificial resonance. For the rest of the night, he worked hard at erasing it.

She'd seen the article too late to do anything about it that night, and the wait had not improved her temper.

"Is Richard Sullivan on duty?"

Startled, the edge on the words having cut her memory to shreds, the nurse checked the duty sheet. "Yes, Doctor. He . . ."

"I want to see him in my office. Immediately."

"Yes, Doctor." No point in protesting that he was cleaning up an unfortunate bedpan accident. Immediately meant immediately and no later. As she paged him, the nurse hoped that whatever Sullivan had done, it wasn't enough to get him fired. Orderlies willing to do the shit work without bitching and complaining were few and far between. Besides, it was difficult not to like the big man; those puppy dog eyes were hard to resist.

"What do you know about this?"

Sullivan looked down at the article and then up at the doctor. Denial died unspoken as she read his answer off his face.

"This *is* one of ours?"

He nodded.

"Then what part of my instructions did you not understand?"

"It's not that I . . ."

"Or do you not enjoy your job? Is it not everything I told you it would be?"

"Yes. I mean, I do. And it is, but . . ."

"You are *not* supposed to be showing initiative, Mr. Sullivan."

Their relative sizes made it ridiculous that he should cower before her temper, but he did anyway.

The ghost was wearing a Cult and Jackyl T-shirt, a local band that recorded in North Vancouver. Henry was a little surprised it wasn't a Grateful Dead T-shirt. He'd often suspected the universe had a really macabre, and pretty basic, sense of humor. Its arms still ended just above the wrist. Again, it seemed to be waiting.

Tony believed it wanted vengeance.

I suppose that's as good a theory as any, Henry reflected. He sighed. "*Do* you want revenge on the person who took your hands?"

Impatience adding a first hint of personality to translucent features, the ghost slowly faded away.

Henry sighed again. "I take it that's a qualified yes."

The apartment was empty when he emerged from his room. After a moment, he remembered it was Saturday and Tony would be working late.

"Which is probably a good thing," he announced to the lights of the city. He wondered if the ghost expected him to begin by finding the hands, and if he should be looking for the remains of flesh and bone or an ethereal pair quite possibly haunting someone else.

When Tony returned home after midnight, he was in his office with the door closed, deep in the complicated court politics of 1813 and more than a little concerned with his heroine's refusal to follow the plot as outlined. Dawn nearly caught him still trying to decide whether Wellington would promote her betrothed to full colonel and he raced for the sanctuary of his bed having forgotten his spectral visitor in the night's work.

"This is becoming irritating; do you at least know who has your hands?"

The ghost threw back its head and screamed. No sound emerged from the gaping black hole of a mouth, but Henry felt the hair lift off the back of his neck and a cold dread wrap around his heart. While the scream endured, he thought he sensed a multitude of spirits within the scream; all shrieking in unison, all lamenting the injustice of their deaths. His lips drew off his teeth in an involuntary snarl.

"Henry? Henry! Are you okay?"

The ghost's face, distended by the continuing scream, faded last.

"Henry!"

It took him a moment to realize that the pounding wasn't his heart—it was Tony, banging frantically on the bedroom door. He shook himself free of the lingering uneasiness and padded across the room, the carpet cold and damp against his bare feet. Releasing the bolts, he called, "I'm all right."

When he opened the door, Tony nearly fell into his arms.

Eyes wide, panting as though he'd just run a race, Tony pulled back far enough to see for himself that Henry was unharmed. "I heard . . . no, I felt . . . it was . . ." His fingers tightened around Henry's bare shoulders. "What happened? Was it the ghost?"

"I'm only guessing, but I think I asked it a question with a negative answer."

"Negative?" Tony's voice rose to an incredulous squeak and he let his arms drop to his side. "I'll say it was *negative*. It was bottom of the pit, soul-sucking, annihilation!"

"It wasn't that bad . . ."

"Maybe not for you!"

Concerned, Henry studied Tony's face. "Are *you* all right?"

"I guess." He drew in a deep breath, released it slowly, and nodded. "Yeah. I'm okay. But I'm gonna stay right here and watch you dress." Propped up on one shoulder, he sagged against the doorframe, too frightened to be tough, or independent, or even interested in Henry's nakedness. "I don't want to be alone."

"Do you want to know what happened?" From Tony's expression, it was clear that he hadn't needed to ask. While he pulled on his clothes, Henry described what had occurred when he'd tried to get more information from the ghost.

"So, you can only ask one question and if the an-

swer's yes, it disappears quietly, and if the answer's
no, it lets you know how disappointed it is with you."

"Not only how disappointed *it* is," Henry told him.
"When it screamed, I sensed a multitude of the dead."

"Yeah? How many dead in a multitude, Henry?"

"This is nothing to joke about."

"Trust me, I'm not laughin' inside." Tony followed
Henry into the living room, dropping gracelessly onto
one end of the heavy leather sofa. "Man, game shows
from beyond the grave. You mind if I turn on some
lights? That thing's still got me kind of spooked."
When Henry indicated he should go ahead, he
stretched back, flicked on the track lighting, and cen-
tered himself in a circle of illumination. "At least we
know two things. It *does* want revenge, and it *doesn't*
know where its hands are."

"What of the others?"

"Can we maybe deal with this one ghost at a time?
I mean, why borrow trouble."

Tucked into a pocket of shadow on the other side
of the room, Henry sighed. "I'd still like to know,
why me?"

"Like attracts like."

Brows drawn in, Henry leaned forward, bringing his
face into the light. "I beg your pardon."

"You're a vampire." Tony shrugged and stroked the
tiny, nearly healed wound barely visible against the
tanned skin of his left wrist. "Even if you're not a
supernatural creature, even if all you are is biologi-
cally different . . ."

"*All* I am?"

"Henry!"

Henry graciously indicated he should continue although his lip remained curled.

"Look, there's a whole shitload of myth about you.
Okay, not you specifically, but about your kind. It's
all around you . . ." He spread his arms. ". . . like a
kind of metaphysical fog. I bet that's what the ghost
is attracted to. I bet that's what pulls him to you."

"Metaphysical fog," Henry repeated. Shaking his head, he leaned back in his chair. "Did you talk like that in Toronto?"

"You needn't get so damned superior!" His relaxed posture gone, Tony jabbed a finger in Henry's direction. "It's a perfectly valid theory. Or have you got a better one?"

Surprised by the young man's vehemence, Henry admitted he didn't, but before Tony could continue, he cut him off with an uplifted hand. "Something's happening in the hall."

Tony's scowl deepened. "I don't hear any . . . shit." There was no point in continuing. Henry was already at the door.

He'd heard the ambulance attendants. As he stepped out into the hall, they were rolling the stretcher out of apartment 1404. The tiny figure under the straps lay perfectly still, one thin hand dangling limply off the side. The attendants were performing CPR even as they rushed toward the elevator, but Henry knew Lisa Evans was irretrievably dead.

He barely managed to keep himself from leaping back and snarling as Mrs. Munro clutched at his arm.

A few moments later, after bundling the sobbing companion into his car, he was speeding toward St. Paul's Hospital after the ambulance while Tony passed Mrs. Munro tissue after tissue from the box in the glove compartment.

The emergency room doctors took very little time before they agreed with Henry's diagnosis. They, too, had seen death too often to mistake it.

"She was very old," Dr. Zvane told them softly.

"There's older!" Mrs. Munro protested. Tony handed her another tissue.

"True." The doctor shrugged, and knuckled weary eyes. "All I can say is that it was her time. We did everything we could, but she'd gone on and had no intention of coming back."

Gripping Henry's hand hard enough to crack merely

mortal joints, Mrs. Munro sniffed. "That's just like her. You could never get her to change her mind once she'd made it up."

She'd stopped crying by the time she got back into the car. Although Henry had offered to drive her wherever she wanted to go, she'd asked to be taken back to the condo. "I have to get my things. My daughter will pick me up there.

"We were watching *Jeopardy,*" she continued, able to talk about what had happened now that it was officially over. "It was the championship round. Miss Evans had just shouted out, *'Who is Captain Kirk?'* when all of a sudden, she sort of whimpered and clapped her hands over her ears. She looked like she'd heard something horrible except I didn't hear anything at all. The next thing I knew, she was . . . gone."

Henry met Tony's eyes in the rearview mirror. It was obvious they were thinking the same thing.

"I don't think he's doing it deliberately."

"I don't care. He is responsible for that old lady's death, and I say he can go handless into hell."

Back in his circle of light, Tony shivered. Henry's voice had cut through the distance between living room and bedroom like the distance didn't exist, and every word had held an edge. When he appeared a moment later, Tony took in his change of clothes— his face and hair seemed luminescent above all that black—and asked, although he didn't really need to, "Where are you going?"

"Hunting."

It was almost impossible not to respond to the ghost's anticipation.

"You can stand there as long as you like," Henry growled, "but I am *not* going to help you."

The ghost threw back its head and screamed.

An unseen, unheard chorus of the dead screamed with it.

*   *   *

"I thought you weren't going to ask it any more questions!"

"I didn't." Henry stared down at the city, listening for the sound of a siren, his fingers splayed against the glass, the muscles rigid across his back. "I told it that it could expect no help."

"It didn't seem to like that."

"No. It didn't."

They stood together in silence, waiting for the sounds of another death.

Finally Tony sighed and threw himself down on the sofa. "Looks like we got lucky; nobody old enough, close enough. Tomorrow night, why don't you say nothing at all."

It waited. And it waited. When Henry tried to leave the room, it screamed.

They watched the ambulance arrive. They learned that the Franklins' baby died in its sleep.

"Babies. Man . . ." Two years ago, Tony had watched an ancient Egyptian wizard devour the life force of a baby. The parents walked on, completely unaware that their child was dead. He still had nightmares about it. "This is blackmail."

"Yes. And it has made me angry." The plastic cracked in his grip as he picked up the phone.

Swallowing nervously—Henry's anger could be as terrifying as silent ghostly screams—Tony managed a partial smile and asked, "Calling the Ghostbusters?"

"Not quite. I've decided this is not a job for a romance writer."

"Well, I guess not, but . . ." He let his next question trail off when Henry activated the external speaker on the phone. After two rings, an answering machine clicked on.

"Victory Nelson, Private Investigations. There's no one here to take your call right now. Please leave a message after the tone. . . ."

TWO

Detective-Sergeant Michael Celluci closed the heavy metal door quietly behind him and stepped cautiously into the shadowed apartment. A dim fan of light that spilled out from the office under the loft was swallowed up by the sixteen-foot ceiling in the main room. The building had been a glass factory before a recession had emptied it and urban renewal had filled it again with barely serviceable living space for the fashionable fringe of Toronto. The majority of the tenants dressed exclusively in black and most were involved in some way with "the arts"—although some of those ways were pretty peripheral in Michael Celluci's not at all humble opinion.

His soft-soled shoes making no sound on the rug that defined a right-of-way along one wall, he moved toward the light.

"So what about the guy you can see? What's he, the union representative?" The silence defined the response. "I'm sorry. I *am* taking this seriously. No, I am. Ask it innocuous questions until I get there." The old wooden office chair creaked alarmingly as it was tipped back on two legs. "Ask it things you *know* it'll have to answer yes to."

Just under the edge of the loft, an arm's length from the chair, Celluci stretched out a hand to grab a sweatshirt-clad shoulder. Just before his fingers closed on fabric, they were captured in an unbreakable grip.

The woman holding him flashed him a disdainful

nice try and kept talking into the phone. "Look, how hard can it be? Did you used to be a man? Are you dead now? Were you once alive?"

Were you alive? Celluci mouthed as she pulled him around the edge of her chair and pushed him down onto a corner of the cluttered desk.

Brows lowered, she acknowledged he'd heard correctly with a single nod, then tried to reassure her caller. "It doesn't matter that they're stupid questions as long as it answers yes. I'll be there as soon as I can. I'll . . ." Sighing, she settled back with an expression Celluci recognized—the first time he'd seen it, they'd both been in uniform, and it had been aimed at him. There could be only one explanation for it now; the person on the other end of the line was actually daring to give Vicki Nelson advice.

She'd never taken advice well. Not when she'd been in uniform and considered herself God's gift to the Metropolitan Toronto Police. Not when she'd made detective. Not when retinitis pigmentosa had forced her to quit a job she'd both loved and excelled at. Not during the time she'd been a private investigator. And not since the change.

If I didn't know, he thought, watching her features shift from impatience to irritation, *I'd never realize what she was.*

She looked much the same, only a little thinner and a lot paler. She acted much the same, having always been overbearing, arrogant, and opinionated.

All right, so she didn't used to drink blood. . . .

"That's enough!" Irritation had become annoyance and, from her tone, she'd cut off a continuing monologue. "I'll be there as soon as I can, and if you're not home when I arrive, I'm heading straight back to Toronto." Hanging up as the last "oh" left her mouth, she turned her attention to Celluci and said, "Henry has a ghost and would like me to get rid of it for him."

Cold fingers touched the back of Celluci's neck. "Henry Fitzroy?"

"Himself."

"Isn't he still in Vancouver?"

Silver-gray eyes narrowed as she gazed up at him. "He is."

"And you've just agreed to travel clear across the country to take care of his . . ." In spite of everything they'd been through—in spite of demons, werewolves, mummies, and the reanimation of the dead, in spite of vampires—his lip curled. ". . . ghost?"

"I have."

"And since you've presented it to me as a *fait accompli,* can I assume anything I have to say becomes irrelevant?"

Her brows drew in slightly. "This ghost is scaring people to death, Mike, and it's going to keep doing it until someone finds out why and stops it. Henry isn't trained for that kind of an investigation." When he opened his mouth, she lifted a hand in warning. "And don't you dare say I'm not either. I'll be stopping a killer. It doesn't matter that he's dead."

No. It wouldn't. But the ghost had little or nothing to do with his reaction. He leaped to his feet and pushed past her, out of the office and into the main room where he'd have floor enough to pace. "Do you know how far it is to Vancouver?"

"About 4,500 kilometers."

He stomped to the door and back again. "Do you realize how short the night is at this time of the year?"

"Less than nine hours." Her voice added a clear indication that she wasn't pleased about it either.

"And do you remember what happens when you're caught out in the sun?"

"I barbecue."

Hands spread, he rocked to a stop in front of her. "So you're going to go 4,500 kilometers, in less than nine-hour shifts, with no sanctuary from the sun? Do you have any idea how insanely dangerous that is?"

"I've been thinking about buying a used van and making a few minor modifications."

"A few minor modifications," he repeated incredulously, trying to bury fear with anger. "You'll be a sitting duck all day, no matter where you park—a charcoal briquette just waiting to happen!"

"So come with me."

"Come with you? As a favor to Henry-fucking-Fitzroy?"

She got slowly to her feet and glared up at him through narrowed eyes. "Is that what this is really about? Henry?"

"No!" And it wasn't; not entirely. "This is about you putting yourself in unnecessary danger. Don't they have PI's in British Columbia?"

"Not ones who can deal with something like this and no one Henry trusts." She smiled, a little self-mockingly, then spread one hand against his chest and added, her words slowed to the rhythm of his heartbeat, "I don't want to become a charcoal briquette. I could use your help, Mike."

His mouth snapped shut around the remainder of the diatribe. The old Vicki Nelson had never been able to ask for help. When Henry Fitzroy had given her his blood, he'd changed her in more than just the obvious ways. Celluci hated the undead, romance-writing, royal bastard for that.

"Let me think about it," he muttered. "I'm going to make coffee."

Vicki listened to him stomp into the tiny kitchen and begin opening and closing cupboard doors with more force than was strictly necessary. She drew in a deep breath, savoring the scent of him. He'd always smelled terrific; a kind of heated, male smell that used to make her incredibly horny whenever she got a whiff of it. Okay, it still made her horny, she corrected with a grin. But now it also made her hungry.

"Don't you ever throw your garbage out," he snarled.

"Why should I? I don't create any of it."

He hadn't needed to raise his voice. She could've heard him if he'd whispered. She could hear his blood pulse through his veins. Sometimes she thought she could hear his thoughts. Although he might be honestly concerned about the dangers of travel, when it came right down to it, he didn't want to go to Vancouver with her because he didn't want to do Henry Fitzroy any favors. Neither did he want her to go to Vancouver, and thus to Henry Fitzroy, without him.

Finishing off the bit of bookkeeping she'd been doing when Henry'd called, Vicki saved the file and waited for Mike to make up his mind, wondering if he realized she had no intention of going without him.

That Henry was being haunted by a ghost who played twenty questions with deadly results didn't surprise her. Nothing much surprised her anymore. *There are more things in heaven and earth . . .* She'd had it printed on her business cards. Mr. Shakespeare had no idea.

That Henry had called, wanting to hire her to solve his little mystery, *had* surprised her. He'd been so definite when they'd parted that they'd never see each other again, that they couldn't see each other again.

As though he'd been reading *her* thoughts, Celluci chose that moment to come back into the office and growl, "I thought vampires were unable to share a territory."

Vicki's chin rose. "I refuse to be controlled by my nature."

Celluci snorted. "Yeah. Right." He took a swallow of steaming coffee. "Tell that to the vampire who used to live here."

"I was willing to negotiate," Vicki protested, but she felt her lip curling up off her teeth. The *other* vampire had taunted her with the death of a friend and claimed downtown Toronto. When Vicki had finally killed her, she'd felt no regret, no guilt, and no need to tell Detective-Sergeant Michael Celluci the full details of what had happened. Not only because of what he was—not only because he was human— but because of who he was. He wouldn't have understood, and she didn't think she could stand it if he looked at her the way he'd sometimes looked at Henry.

So she'd told him only that she'd won.

Now she changed her incipient snarl into something closer to a smile. "Henry and I will manage to get along."

Celluci hid his own smile behind the coffee mug. He recognized the tone and wondered if Henry had any idea of how little choice he was about to have in the matter. He didn't want Vicki going to Vancouver, but since she'd already made up her mind, he couldn't stop her—nor was he suicidal enough to try. Since she was going, regardless, he didn't want her going alone. Besides, he'd enjoy watching his bloodsucking, royal bastardness get run over by Vicki's absolute refusal to do what was expected of her.

"All right. You win. I'm going with you."

". . . things are slow right now, and I've got the time."

Inspector Cantree snorted. "You've always got the time, Detective. I'm just amazed you actually want to use some of it."

Celluci shrugged. "Something came up with a friend of Vicki's out west."

"A friend of Vicki's. Ah." The inspector stared into the oily scum on top of his coffee, the heavy stoneware mug looking almost delicate in his huge hand. "And how is Victory Nelson these days? I hear she's been dealing with some strange cases since she got back in town."

Celluci shrugged again. "Someone has to. At least if they're calling her, they're not calling us."

"True." Cantree's eyes narrowed, and the look he shot at the other man was frankly speculative. "She never struck me as the type to get involved in this paranormal, occult bullshit."

Celluci only just stopped himself from shrugging a third time. "Most of her work's the same old boring crap. Cheating spouses. Insurance fraud."

"Most," Cantree repeated. It wasn't quite a question, so Celluci didn't answer it.

Inspector Cantree had narrowly escaped becoming the enchanted acolyte of an ancient Egyptian god. The others who'd been caught up in the spell had created their own explanations, but he'd insisted on hearing the truth. As he'd never mentioned it again, Celluci remained unsure of how much he'd believed.

The memory hung in the air between them for a moment, then Cantree brushed it aside, the gesture stating as clearly as if he'd said it aloud: *Forty-seven homicides so far this year; I've enough to deal with.* "Take your vacation, Detective, but I want your butt back here in two weeks ready to work."

"Vicki, we will never make it to Vancouver in *that.*"

"I know it doesn't look like much . . ." Hands on her hips, Vicki swept her gaze over the grimy blue van and decided not to mention that it'd probably look worse in daylight. It looked bad enough under the security light in Celluci's driveway. ". . . but it's mechanically sound."

"Since when do you know anything about *mechanically sound?*"

"I don't." She turned and grinned at him, meeting his eyes and allowing power to rise momentarily in hers. "But nobody lies to me anymore."

Because it had been used for deliveries, the van box had no windows to cover. Vicki'd had a partition with wide rubber gaskets installed behind the seats and another just inside the rear doors.

"You got it done fast enough, didn't you?" Celluci brushed at a dusting of sawdust at the base of the front barrier and frowned at the inner bolts that ensured there'd be no unwelcome visitors. "What happens if there's an accident and I have to get you out?"

"Wait until sunset and I'll get myself out."

"There's no ventilation, and it's likely to get hotter than hell in there,"

She shrugged. "I doubt I'll notice."

"You doubt?" His voice started to rise, and he

forced it back down, the dark windows in the surrounding houses reminding him that the neighbors were still asleep and very likely wanted to remain that way. "You're not sure?"

"I'm sure that I won't feel it. Other than that . . ." There were a number of things about being a vampire she was having to discover as the situation came up. Henry had taught her how to feed without causing harm, how to gently change the memories of those who provided nourishment, and how to blend with the mortals who walked the day, but he'd never taught her that swimming was out of the question because increased bone density caused her to sink like a rock—scaring the shit out of the lifeguard at the Y. Nor had he mentioned what traveling all day in the back of an enclosed van might do. "The SPCV suggests leaving a rear window rolled down a bit and parking out of the sun."

Celluci stared at her in confusion. "The what?"

"The society for the prevention of cruelty to vampires. It was a joke." She patted his arm. "Never mind. What do you think of the bed?"

He peered past her shoulder. The bed had padded sides ten inches high. "It looks like a coffin without a lid. I'm not using it."

"Suit yourself, but remember who's driving nights while you're sleeping." She mimed steering around a corner and did a fairly good impersonation of tires squealing against the road.

As Vicki's driving style hovered between kamikaze and Montreal cabbie, Celluci shuddered and checked his watch. Unfortunately, if they planned on leaving before daybreak, they didn't have time to fight about either the bed or Vicki's driving—and if he couldn't do anything about the latter, he certainly wasn't going to insist on removing the padding from the former. "Let's get going, then. It's four-twelve and sunrise is in less than forty-five minutes." When Vicki lifted both brows, he pulled a battered paperback out of his back pocket. "*Farmer's Almanac.* It's got sunrise and sunset for the whole year. I decided it might be best to be prepared."

"For what?" Vicki drew herself up to her full five-feet ten, her expression dangerous and purely human. This argument, or variations on the theme, long predated the change. "What's the matter, Mike? You still think I can't take care of myself?"

"Not between sunrise and sunset," he reminded her mildly, refusing to be drawn.

Vicki deflated. Unfortunately, he was completely and absolutely and inarguably correct. She hated that—not so much that he was right, but that it left her no room for argument.

And he knew it. Eyes crinkling at the corners, he shoved the book back into his pocket.

Stepping forward, she brushed the overlong curl of dark brown hair back off his forehead and murmured, "Come evening, however, no one messes with me."

Lying in the coffinlike bed, vibrating along with the van's six-cylinder, no-longer-entirely-to-company-specs engine, enclosed in a warm darkness so deep it draped over her like black velvet, Vicki could feel the sun. The flesh between her shoulders crawled. Two years a vampire and she still hadn't gotten used to the approach of the day.

"It's like that final instant, just before someone hits you from behind, when you know it's going to happen and you can't do a damned thing about it. Only it lasts longer. . . ."

Celluci hadn't been impressed by the analogy, and she supposed she couldn't blame him—it didn't impress her much either. While he'd pulled the van up under the security light and methodically checked for pinholes that might let in the sun, she'd almost gone crazy with the need to get under cover. He hadn't listened when she'd told him she'd already checked, but then, he'd always believed she took foolish risks.

Risks, she took.

Foolish risks, never.

Okay, hardly ever.

Wondering why she was suddenly doing numbers from *HMS Pinafore,* she licked her lips and tasted the memory of Celluci's mouth against hers. He'd wanted to wait for sunrise before he started driving, but Vicki'd insisted he start right after she closed herself up in her moving sanctuary. She didn't think she could cope with both of them waiting for . . .

. . . oblivion.

At that hour of the morning, traffic was heading into Toronto, not out of it and, for all its disreputable appearance, the van handled well. Fully aware he would not be able to explain the apparent corpse in the back should he be stopped by the OPP, Celluci drove a careful five kilometers over the limit and resigned himself to being passed by nearly every other car on the highway.

"Get your picture taken," he muttered as an old and rusty K-car buzzed by him. Unfortunately, the new Ontario government had recently pulled the photo radar vans, insisting they'd shown no positive effects. Celluci had no idea where the idiots at Queen's Park had gathered their information, but in his personal experience, the threat of the vans had kept paranoid drivers actually traveling at slightly less than the limit.

He stopped at Barrie for breakfast and a chance to stretch his legs. A tractor trailer accident held him for an hour just outside Waubaushene and by the time he stopped for lunch at the Centennial Diner in Bigwood, he'd heard Sonny and Cher sing "I Got You Babe" on three different oldies stations and was wondering why he was putting himself through rock-and-roll hell for Henry-fucking-Fitzroy.

"I should've tried harder to talk her out of it." He yanked a tasseled toothpick out of his club sandwich. So what if there were no PI's on the West Coast Fitzroy could trust? "How's he supposed to make new friends if he never talks to strangers?"

"Is anything wrong?"

Celluci manufactured a smile and tossed it up to his teenage waitress. "No. Nothing's wrong." Watching her watch him on her way back to the kitchen, he sighed. *Great. Not only does he expect Vicki to risk her life traveling across three quarters of the country, but now he's got me talking to myself.*

On the flyspecked radio above the pie rack, Sonny Bono once again declared his love in the face of everything they said.

"WaWa?" Knuckles on her hips, Vicki rolled the kinks out of her shoulders. "Why WaWa?"

Celluci shrugged, eyes appreciatively following her movements. "Why not WaWa? I thought you might want to see the goose."

"The goose?" Slowly, she turned and peered up at the nine-meter-high steel sculpture silhouetted against a gray sky streaked with orange. "Okay. I've seen it. I hope we're not sharing the high point of your day."

"Close," he admitted. "How're you feeling?"

"Like my body spent the day bouncing around inside a padded box. Other than that, fine."

"Are you, uh . . ." He broke off in embarrassment as a car pulled into the small parking lot and a pair of children exploded out of the back and raced up the path toward the bathrooms.

"Hungry?" Stepping into the circle of his body heat, she grinned. "Mike, you can say *hungry* in front of kids—they'll assume I'll be having a Big Mac, not Ronald MacDonald."

"That's disgusting."

"Actually, it's given me an appetite."

He grabbed her upper arms, halting her advance. "Forget it, Vicki, I'm too old for a quickie in the back of a van." But his protest had little force, and after the kids and the car disappeared, he allowed himself to be convinced.

It didn't take much.

Twenty minutes later, as they climbed up into the

front seats, Vicki reached out and caught a mosquito about to land on his back. "Forget it, sister," she muttered, squashing the bug between thumb and forefinger. "He gave at the office."

"We're just past Portage la Prairie?" Celluci looked up from the map of Manitoba with a scowl. He hadn't slept well, and the thermos of coffee Vicki'd handed him when he'd staggered out of the van could peel the residue off a garbage truck. He drank it anyway—after fifteen years drinking police coffee, he could drink anything—but he wasn't happy. The last thing he needed to be told was that they'd gone considerably past the point where he'd expected to take over. "You must've been doing between a hundred and twenty-five and a hundred and thirty kilometers an hour!"

"What's your point?"

"Let's start with the speed limit being a hundred kilometers an hour and take it from there. It's not just a good idea," he added sarcastically, fighting to refold the map. "It's the law."

Vicki clamped her teeth down on a complaint that a hundred K to someone with her reaction time was ridiculously slow, and merely shrugged. Her opinions didn't make the speed limit any less the law. If he'd suggested she'd been driving unsafely, then she could've given him an argument.

Leaning back against the van, she stared out at the farmland surrounding the gas station parking lot. With the station closed and the only illumination coming from the stars and Celluci's flashlight, it seemed as though they were the last people alive in the world. She hated that feeling and she'd felt it for most of the night as she'd sped away from Lake Superior toward Kenora and the Ontario/Manitoba border. At 3 A.M. even Winnipeg was a little short of people up and about—except for a sleepy clerk at the 24-hour gas station/donut shop where she'd filled the van and two transients spotted sleeping in the shelter of an overpass. She'd cut through the middle of Portage la Prairie rather than take the Trans-Canada Highway loop around, but it was still too early for anyone to be up and about.

Used to living, and hunting, among three million people, at least one million of whom never seemed to sleep, the isolation made her feel vulnerable and exposed.

"Give me that." She reached down and snatched the partially folded map out of Mike's hands. "All you have to do is follow the original creases. Why is that so difficult?"

Vulnerable, exposed, and in a really bad mood. Meeting Celluci's astonished glower with a half-apologetic wave of the map, she growled, "All this scenery is beginning to get to me."

Recognizing that on a perfectly straight, completely flat stretch of road no one was going to drive at one hundred kilometers an hour, the speed limit through Saskatchewan was one hundred and ten. Almost everyone did one twenty. Considering his cargo, Celluci compromised at one fifteen.

A lifetime's worth of wheat fields later, at 7:17 P.M. local time, he pulled into a truck stop just outside Bassano, Alberta, and turned off the engine, wondering if there was a Sonny and Cher revival going on he hadn't heard about. If he had to listen to "I Got You, Babe" one more time, he was going to have to hurt someone. Parking the van so that Vicki could exit without being seen, he walked stiffly across the asphalt to the restaurant. Sunset would be at 8:30, so he had little better than an hour to eat.

Soup of the day was beef barley. He stared down into the bowl and remembered all the meals he and Vicki had eaten together, all the gallons of coffee, all the stale sandwiches grabbed on the run. All at once, the thought that they'd never again go out for dim sum, or chicken paprikas, or even order in a pizza while they watched *Hockey Night in Canada* left him feeling incredibly depressed.

"Is there something wrong with the soup?" A middle-aged woman in a spotless white apron peered down at him with some concern from behind the counter.

"The, uh, the soup's fine."

"Glad to hear it. It don't come out of a can, you know. I make it myself." When he couldn't find an immediate response, she shook her head and sighed. "Come on, buddy, cheer up. You look like you've lost your best friend."

Celluci frowned. He hadn't exactly lost her. Vicki remained everything to him she ever had been, except a dinner companion and weighed against the rest that shouldn't mean much. But, right now, it did. *I thought I'd dealt with this. . . .*

He barely noticed when the waitress took the empty bowl away and replaced it with a platter of steak and home fries.

Vampire, Nightwalker, Nosferatu—Vicki was no longer human. Granted, she'd made a commitment to him in a way she'd never been able to before the change, but, given immortality, how important could the few years of his life be?

The rhubarb pie tasted like sawdust and he left half of it on the plate.

Shoulders hunched and hands shoved into his jacket pockets, he headed back across the parking lot toward the van. Vaguely aware he was wallowing in self-pity, he couldn't seem to stop.

When the van's engine roared into life, it took him completely by surprise. Standing three feet from the front bumper, Celluci stared through a fine film of bug bodies smeared over the windshield and into the smug face of a young man in his late teens or early twenties. He didn't realize what was happening until the young man backed the van away from him, cranked the steering wheel around, and laid rubber all the way out to the highway.

The van was being stolen.

Instinct sent him racing after it, but halfway across the parking lot, the fact he didn't have a chance of catching up penetrated and he rocked to a halt. He checked his watch. 8:27.

Vicki would be awake in three minutes.

She'd know immediately that something was wrong, that he wasn't driving. She'd pull open the partition behind the seats . . .

. . . and their young car thief was about to be in for one hell of a surprise.

Watching the grimy back end of the stolen van disappear into the sunset down a secondary road, Celluci started to laugh. His only regret was that he wouldn't be there to see that punk's face when Vicki woke up. He was still laughing when the waitress met him at the door of the restaurant, a worried frown creasing the smooth curves of her face. "Wasn't that your van?"

"It was." He grinned down at her, feeling better than he had in hours.

"Would you like to use our phone to call the police?"

"No, thank you. But I would like another piece of that delicious rhubarb pie."

Completely confused, she followed him across the restaurant and watched wide-eyed as he dropped onto a counter stool. She shook her head as he looked at his watch and snickered. He'd seemed like such a nice man and although she was glad to see that whatever had been bothering him obviously wasn't bothering him any longer, she couldn't understand his attitude. "But what about your van?"

The corners of Celluci's mouth curved up as he reached for a fork. "It'll be back."

Something was wrong.

Vicki lay in the darkness and sifted through sounds and scents and sensation.

The van was still moving. Celluci had insisted, for

safety's sake, they be parked at least half an hour before sunrise and sunset. Somehow, considering the completely unnecessary fuss he'd made over it, Vicki doubted he'd changed his mind. Either he'd lost his little book, he'd been unable to get off the highway, or he wasn't the driver.

The smell of the engine—gas and oil and heated metal—laid over the lingering scent of Celluci clinging to the padding of the bed made an enhanced sense of smell next to useless. The three little pigs could be driving, and she wouldn't be able to sniff them out.

Kneeling next to the plywood barrier, she filtered out the sounds of internal combustion and heard a stranger's heartbeat.

She growled low in her throat. Resisting the urge to crash through the barrier and rip the stranger's heart out, Vicki silently pulled back the bolts. Anger wouldn't get her the answers she needed. Anger wouldn't discover what happened to Mike Celluci. *First, I get some answers . . .*

To the young man behind the wheel, it seemed as though one moment the passenger seat was empty and the next there was a woman sitting in it, smiling at him. Her smile was terrifying.

"Pull over," she said softly.

More frightened than he'd ever been in his life, he braked and swerved onto the shoulder. By the time he fought the van to a standstill, his heart was pounding so violently, he could barely breathe.

"Shut off the engine."

He whimpered as he turned the key. He didn't know why, but he couldn't prevent the sound from escaping. When cool fingers grasped his chin and forced his head around, he whimpered again.

"Where is the man who was driving this vehicle?"

Her eyes were impossibly silver in the twilight. He didn't know what the rest of her looked like because all he could see were her eyes. "He's, he's at Ruby's Steak House. Maybe five miles b-b-back."

"Has he been hurt?"

Although not an imaginative young man, he had a sudden flash of what was likely to happen should he answer in the affirmative. His stomach spasmed, and his throat worked.

"If you puke," she told him, "you'll eat it. Now answer my question."

"He was f-f-fine. Really." When she seemed to be waiting for more, he added, "I looked b-b-back and he was laughing."

"Laughing?"

"Yes, ma'am."

Frowning, Vicki released the young man's jaw. Why would Celluci be laughing? She'd never suspected that he considered grand theft auto to be amusing. *Okay, he stopped for supper and someone stole the van. Why would he think that was funny?* Then she looked up at the streaks of gold and rose lingering on the horizon. All of a sudden, she got the joke.

If Ruby's Steak House was only five miles back, this poor sucker had driven off with a sleeping vampire moments before sunset.

When she noticed him fumbling with the door latch, she grabbed his arm. "Not so fast," she murmured, the threat softened but still there. "What's your name?"

"K-Kyle."

He was really quite attractive in an unshaven, outlaw sort of way. Slender but with nice muscles. Pretty blue eyes. Her gaze locked on the pulse in his throat. "How old are you, Kyle?"

"T-twenty-two."

Old enough. She let the Hunger rise.

Kyle saw her smile change. Almost understood it. Her face was very pale. Her teeth, very white.

"Actually, I think young Kyle's decided to give up stealing cars."

"Oh?" Celluci grinned at her profile, just barely visible in the pale green glow from the dashboard lights. "What makes you say that?"

"Well, I think he came to the decision when I pointed out how lucky he'd been."

"Lucky?"

"Sure. When he took this van, all he got was me." Vicki turned to face her companion, allowing the van to speed down the highway momentarily unguided. Her eyes gleamed, and her voice made promises for later. "I merely reminded him that another time, he might drive off with something . . . dangerous."

Sunrise the next morning was at 4:56, Pacific Time. At 4:30, Vicki pulled over onto a deserted scenic view and stopped the van. Driving west through the Rockies, she'd gained an hour of night. Since they'd left home, she'd gained three, but this would be the last. They'd crossed into British Columbia during the night and would reach Vancouver before evening. From now on, sunrise and sunset would occur in the same time zone.

Twisting around in the driver's seat, she stared into the shadows of her sanctuary. Celluci refused to sleep with the front partition up and she supposed she couldn't blame him, although the song of his blood behind her was a constant distraction. Considering the demands of the road as it passed through two national parks and crossed most of a mountain range, it was fortunate that, having fed deeply from young Kyle, she'd been able to keep most of her attention on her driving.

Sleep smoothed out the lines and shadows layered onto his face by fifteen years of police work and he looked much younger than his thirty-eight years.

Thirty-eight.

He had a scattering of gray hair at his right temple.

How many years were they going to have? Fifty? Forty? And what was she going to do for the rest of eternity without him? Facing immortality, she found herself mourning his inevitable death while she continued to live. Henry had warned her about falling into that kind of fatalistic despair, but it was a hard warning to remember while listening to a mortal heartbeat pounding out its few remaining years.

Oh, for God's sake, Vicki, get a grip! Leaning forward, she grabbed Celluci's shoulder and shook him hard.

"Wha . . . !"

"Sunrise in twenty minutes, Mike. I'll leave you alone to put your face on." Getting out of the van, she walked over to the railing and stared up at the Rockies. Rising in majestic silhouettes against the gray, predawn sky, they looked so definitively like mountains they almost looked fake.

Now this is immortality, Vicki acknowledged. *Next to these hunks of rock, I'm just going to live a little longer than average.* She heard Mike walk around from the other side of the van and said, "I left a message on Henry's machine when I stopped for gas. He knows we'll get to his place today."

"Yeah? Will he still be there?"

Eyes narrowed, she pivoted on one heel. "Why wouldn't he be?"

"Oh, I don't know. Perhaps *he's* willing to recognize his limitations." Three nights on the road, had left Celluci tired and stiff and not all the glories of a spring dawn in the midst of some of the most beautiful scenery in the world were going to make an impression until he had a piss and a coffee.

"He'll be there."

"What makes you so sure?"

"I told him not to leave."

Should've seen that coming, he muttered silently, following Vicki to the van. He caught her wrist as she lifted her hand to rub the back of her neck. "Did it ever occur to you that Henry Fitzroy knows better than you do what it means to be a vampire?"

She turned within his grip although they both knew she could have easily broken it. "Maybe he does, but Henry Fitzroy doesn't know what it means to be me, and I'm not buying into his territorial imperative crap."

Because he could see the doubt in her eyes, he let it go. They'd find out soon enough.

When he heard the bolts shoot back and the front barrier move, Celluci threw the last of his burger to a gull patrolling the strip mall parking lot and rolled up the window. He couldn't see anyone in earshot, but the last thing they needed was an eavesdropper.

The silver of her eyes flecked with lingering gold from the setting sun, Vicki's gaze swept past him. "Where are we?

"Cariboo Street, east end of the city. I thought you'd like to be awake when we arrived."

Vicki stared out the front window, across Vancouver, toward the ocean, toward Henry Fitzroy. Then she looked at Mike Celluci, *really* looked at him.

He had the strangest sensation that no one had ever seen him so clearly, and he could feel himself beginning to sweat. Just when he thought he couldn't stand another minute of it, she smiled, reached out, and brushed the long curl of hair off his face.

"Thanks. That's pretty perceptive for a guy who tapes *Baywatch*."

Three

Eyes narrowed, Henry glared at the handless ghost at the foot of his bed. His movements rigidly precise, he folded back the sheet and sat up. If he released even a fraction of the tight grip he maintained on his rage, it would surge out in a stream of angry accusation and another innocent would die.

He watched and waited, hoping the spirit would tire of meaningless questions. When it became obvious it hadn't, when it began preparing to scream, Henry snarled, "Was your mother a woman?"

Translucent features twisted into an annoyed frown, but it obeyed the rules and quietly vanished.

"Man, that is one pissed-off spook."

Henry paused, one hand on the bathroom door, and turned toward the hall corner where Tony lounged against the wall. "You could feel it?"

"Feel it?" Tony snorted, covering his fear with bravado. "I could almost see the waves of pissed-offedness radiating out from your room. I just, you know, wondered if you were okay."

"I'm fine. It can't actually affect me."

"Uh-huh. And that's why you just crushed the doorknob?"

Opening his fingers, Henry dropped his gaze to the unrecognizable piece of brass protruding from the bathroom door. "Perhaps I am a little . . . irritated. I'm sure I'll feel better after a shower." He took a half a step forward—one bare foot on tile, the other on carpet—and paused. "Don't you usually work Saturday evenings?"

Tony took a deep breath, lifted his chin, and met Henry's gaze square on. "I traded shifts," he announced defiantly. "So I could be here when Vicki arrived."

Red-gold brows rose. "To protect her from me?"

"Maybe." Expecting anger, and knowing how dangerous that anger could be, Tony would have preferred it to the undercurrent of amusement he could hear in Henry's voice. "Or to protect you from her."

Realizing that he'd hurt the younger man's feelings, Henry sighed. "I appreciate the intent, Tony, I really do, but for your own safety, if anything happens, anything at all, don't get between us. While I would never intentionally harm you, I'm not sure how much intent is going to count."

"Then why did you stay? You're ready to go to the cabin, you could've been gone when she got here."

"If I was gone when she arrived, Vicki'd never believe that two vampires are incapable of being together. She'd continue to think that I'm overreacting, that a response innate to our natures can be overcome." His eyes darkened and an aura of ancient power seemed to gather about him—in spite of the green velour bathrobe. "By remaining home for the first part of the night, by actually meeting with her, I'll prove my point in the only way she'll accept."

Tony nodded slowly. Having known Vicki since he was a fifteen-year-old street kid, the explanation made perfect sense. "I bet she was the kind of kid who stuck beans up her nose."

"I beg your pardon?"

"You know." His voice lifted into a shrill falsetto. "Now, Vicki, don't stick beans up your nose."

Henry grinned. "No bet."

"So you stayed to prove a point?"

"That's right."

"Not because you wanted to see her again?"

"Vampires do not maintain attachments after the parent-child bond is broken." Henry's tone ended the discussion. For added emphasis, he stepped into the bathroom and emphatically closed the door.

The knob fell off and bounced down the hall.

Bending to pick it up, Tony fitted his fingers into the creases Henry's fingers had made. *Don't get between us,* he repeated silently. *Yeah, like I'm in the habit of getting between The Terminator and the mother alien. . . .*

Michael Celluci watched Vicki pacing back and forth in the elevator—three steps back, three steps forth—and kept his mouth firmly shut. More than anything, he wanted to know if she'd even considered the possibility that Henry might be right. Unfortunately, although the words were pressing up against his teeth, he couldn't ask because, from her expression, she obviously had.

"His scent is all over this building," she muttered, nostrils flaring.

"Don't tell me he's been pissing in the corners."

Her teeth seemed longer than usual as she snarled, "That's not what I meant."

"It was a joke." When she whirled to glare at him, he spread his hands. "Just trying to lighten the mood."

"Oh." The bell chimed for the fourteenth floor. She spun back around to face the door.

Following her out into the hall, Celluci shook his head. "No need to thank me." As their names had been on a security list at the door, they'd been waved right through without needing to buzz up and so had no idea of what they were about to face. Given Vicki's reaction so far, if Henry had been stupid enough to stay home, it was going to be an explosive evening. He found himself wishing he'd brought his gun—although whom he intended to shoot, he had no idea.

"She's coming." Henry turned to face the door and Tony thought he looked like a cat, watching the shadows for movement no one else could see. A moment later, three evenly spaced raps that unmistakably said, *This is the police,* shattered the expectant silence into sharp-edged little pieces.

"You'd better answer it." Hands locked behind his back, Henry made his way to the far side of the living room. "I think it might be best if I kept my distance."

Almost afraid of cutting himself on the shards of anticipation, Tony walked to the door, took a deep breath, and threw it open.

Celluci, about to knock again, lowered his hand.

Vicki, who'd been staring down the hall, spun around.

Had Tony not spent the last two years sharing living space with a vampire, he'd have fled, screaming. As it was, he swallowed hard, tried to keep his legs from buckling, and forced his mouth into what he hoped was an approximation of a smile. "Yo, Victory. You're lookin' good."

The fear in his voice penetrated. There were a great many people whose fear Vicki rather enjoyed, but Tony wasn't one of them. *Let's just prove Henry's point for him, shall we?* she snarled to herself as she struggled for control. *I will* not *be dominated by blind instinct!*

Tony, watching the silver fade out of her eyes, exchanged a wary glance with Celluci, who added an infinitesimal shrug. Before either man could speak, however, Vicki found her voice.

"I just spent four days on the road, I need a shower, and I look like shit, but thanks for lying." She cocked her head and looked him up and down—to Tony's surprise the inspection didn't make him feel like a rare steak. "You, on the other hand, are looking good. You've filled out, got some color . . ." Her brows dipped down. ". . . but your hair's too short."

"It's the style," he protested indignantly, rubbing a palm over his close-cropped skull.

Vicki sighed. "Tony, it didn't look that good on Keanu Reeves either. Now then, you going to invite us in, or are you going to leave us standing in the hall?"

Ears pink, Tony stepped out of the doorway. "Sorry."

"As much my fault as yours," Vicki admitted. Looking appreciatively around the entry—Henry'd bought the Pacific Place condo after she'd returned to Toronto—she nodded toward the colonnaded arch. "Living room through there?"

"Yeah, but . . ." As she disappeared, he let his voice trail off and glanced up at Detective Sergeant Michael Celluci. During his years on the street, they hadn't exactly gotten along, but judging from the detective's expression, tonight the past had been buried under their common present.

"Is he in there?"

Tony sighed. "Yeah."

"Why, if he believes in this territorial imperative thing?"

"He wants to prove a point."

Like Tony before him, Celluci understood. "I can't say as I blame him. Let's hope we all survive it."

They walked together into the living room, each hoping that the silence had to be a good sign.

Henry stood with his back to the window, the lights of Granville Island beginning to pierce the dusk behind him. Head up, arms crossed over his chest, he wore a blue silk shirt, faded jeans, and white running shoes. His lips were pressed into a thin line. His eyes were dark.

Vicki stood by the ultramodern dining room table, the fingers of her right hand pressed hard against the green glass top. Head up, her left hand opening and closing by her side, she wore a blue silk shirt, faded jeans, and white running shoes. Her lips were drawn up enough to show the points of her teeth. Her eyes were silver.

Standing at the edge of the room, Tony could feel the tension building. In a moment, without a word being said, it would build past the breaking point. When that happened, he didn't have the faintest idea of what he could do to prevent the inevitable violence or if he'd have the courage to do it even if he knew. How would they fight? Would there be bloodshed? Wouldn't vampires instinctively refuse to waste so precious a resource?

Beside him, Celluci swept a cynical gaze over the room, snorted, and said, "I see you guys've got a uniform. What's next? Team jackets and baseball caps?"

Tony shot him a startled glance and faded back just far enough to use the detective's bulk as a shield.

The tableau broke. As Henry snarled and stepped forward, Vicki's sense of the ridiculous pushed past her instinctive responses. She stared at Henry's clothes, then down at her own, and snickered. "Christ, we look like a set of undead Bobbsey Twins."

Nostrils flared, Henry stopped and turned to face her again.

His aborted charge had brought him away from the window. Smile twisting into a snarl, Vicki backed around the table. "Don't stand so close!" She didn't want to attack, but she didn't think she'd be able to stop herself if he came any closer. She fought to see past instinct, to the lover, to the friend, to the teacher who'd taught her to survive within the parameters of her new existence, but the knowledge of what they'd once been to each other kept getting lost behind what they were.

"This is my territory, Vicki." Henry took a step closer, graceful, deadly. "Not yours. You do not tell me what to do in *my* territory."

"At least they're talking," Celluci muttered to no one in particular. "That's an improvement."

The vampires ignored him, and Tony fervently wished he'd shut up.

A muscle jumped in Vicki's jaw. "You asked me here!"

"You insisted we could work together," he reminded her mockingly.

"We could if you'd stop this Prince of Darkness bullshit and back off!"

"I'm not doing anything, Vicki. I am older than you.

I am more powerful than you. You can only see me as a threat. You can't help but respond."

"And what do you see me as?" she growled, anger provoked by the implication that he didn't see *her* as a threat.

"Something to be removed." His brows drew in and his voice grew scathing. "I do not wish my hunting ruined by a child."

Vicki dove up and over the table, almost before she'd decided to attack. Her hands reached for Henry's throat and grabbed only air. She spun around as she landed, but, off balance, she had no chance to block Henry's blow. He threw her against the far wall and was on her, fingers dimpling her throat before she hit the ground.

When Tony moved forward, a large hand closed on his shoulder and pulled him back.

"No," Celluci said softly. "Let them work it out."

Startled, Tony stared up at the detective. He couldn't believe that Michael Celluci was allowing this to happen, but although he was frowning, neither the larger man's gaze nor his grip wavered.

Her shoulders under Henry's knees, her throat in his hands, Vicki froze, caught in his eyes and recognizing defeat.

"We cannot work together," Henry told her, all the posturing gone from his voice, leaving it flat and tired. "And as you must remain here to do your job, *I* am leaving. I've borrowed a cabin on Grouse Mountain from a friend. I'll leave immediately and return when you've solved the case." His eyes never leaving hers, he released her throat and stood.

"So you're proved right." Vicki got slowly to her feet, one hand supporting her weight against the wall. "Happy?"

He sighed and one corner of his mouth twisted into an almost smile. "Actually, no."

"Stay here," Celluci murmured, finally releasing Tony's shoulder. "Keep an eye on her, but don't go near her until she's calmed down."

"Do I look stupid?" the younger man demanded,

wide-eyed and twitchy from the adrenaline buzz. "Where are you going?"

"I need to talk to Fitzroy."

"About what?" Then he followed the line of Celluci's gaze to where Vicki stood, eyes closed, breathing heavily, the fingers of her left hand sunk knuckle-deep through the leather upholstery of the couch. "Oh. Never mind."

When Henry attempted to leave the condo, black canvas case slung over one shoulder, Celluci was waiting at the door. He stopped with most of the entry between them. Any closer and he'd have to look up at the much taller man. "You have something to say, Detective?"

"You did that on purpose."

"What?"

"Provoked a fight. You knew that she had to attack you, or she'd never be convinced you were right."

"That's very perceptive of you, Detective." Henry studied the other man's face, not entirely certain of what he saw. "Are you going to tell her?"

"I haven't decided. But I'd like to ask you something: what if you were wrong?"

Henry frowned. "Wrong?"

"From what I understand, this is something new in the history of . . . uh . . ."

"Vampires?"

Celluci flushed. "Yeah. Vampires. For the first time, two of you are face-to-face and not fighting over territory because Vicki doesn't *want* your territory. What if you could've worked something out?" He spread his hands and stepped away from the door. "Now, you'll never know."

"Now, you'll never know."
The detective's words rang in his ears as Henry made his way down to his car. Vicki's scent remained a distraction, in the elevator, in the underground parking. It was the scent of another predator in his territory. It was also the scent of a women he'd loved.

Unfortunately, instinct kept insisting they were two different people.

He slid into the BMW and rested his head for a moment on the steering wheel. The difference in the scent that surrounded him and in the scent he remembered only served to remind him of how much he'd lost.

It took all of his strength, gathered and refined for over four hundred and fifty years, to drive away.

Leaving another vampire in control of his territory.

Leaving Vicki.

Tony showed them quickly around the apartment, then pulled his roller blades and helmet out of the hall closet. "It's getting late and I, uh, gotta go." When Celluci's brows went up, he looked uncomfortable and said, "I'm staying with friends. Henry thought it would be safer, since Vicki's not used to waking up to a blood scent."

"I'll still be here."

"Oh, yeah. I, uh, guess he figures you can take care of yourself."

"He's got it all figured out, doesn't he?" Celluci snorted. He watched Tony watch Vicki as she walked over to stand by the window and stare out at the city. It was the position Henry used to favor back in Toronto, and Celluci could tell by the recognition on Tony's face that it was still a position Henry favored. Maybe it was just a vampire thing—surveying territory, the hunter taking the high ground—but he hated it when Vicki reminded him of Henry.

"Henry's used to getting his own way."

It took a moment for Celluci to realize that Tony's quiet statement was a reply to his rhetorical question. Before he could think of a response, Vicki turned from the window.

"You will be here tomorrow sunset, won't you?" she asked, her preference clear.

Startled but pleased, Tony nodded. "If you're sure you want me."

"The last, and only time I was in Vancouver, I

wasn't paying much attention to the city." Wasn't paying much attention to anything except controlling the Hunger—she could remember the blood but little else. "If we're going to lay this spook, we're going to need someone who knows his way around."

"There's a whole bunch of street maps and stuff on the dining room table," he began, but Vicki cut him off.

"All a map'll tell us is where the streets are, not what they're about." She folded her arms and leaned back against the glass. "Unless that high school diploma came with a blindfold and earplugs, I can't believe you don't know what's going on out there. You were my best eyes and ears on the street, Tony."

Although he still looked pleased, he shrugged apologetically. "I'm not on the streets anymore."

"You still see things. You still hear things. And you have a gift for connecting the dots."

"For what?"

"For finding a pattern in apparent chaos."

"Really?"

"Yeah. Really."

Ears pink, he shoved aside the compliment, attempting, unsuccessfully, to hide how much it meant. "You want order out of chaos? Try being around Saturday afternoon when the Friday night videos come in. Look, I really gotta go, but I'll be back tomorrow sunset. A list of all the stupid questions Henry asked the spook's on the table with the maps. The number where I'll be staying and my work number's on the bulletin board by the phone. It's great to see you again, Victory." He grinned, and some of his old street-kid cockiness showed in the expression. "You too, Detective."

He paused at the door, roller blades in one hand, helmet in the other, backpack hanging from one shoulder. "Henry doesn't like me keeping much food around, but there's frozen stuff in the freezer and a little store downstairs on the parking level if you're hungry. He's open until midnight."

"Frozen stuff?" Vicki asked incredulously.

"Not for *you*, for Celluci." He snickered and closed the door.

Attempting to banish a vision of Red Cross blood bags, tagged and stacked and frozen solid, Vicki went back to the window and its view of the city. Of Henry's territory.

"So." Celluci propped one thigh on the back of the sofa. "Care to tell me why all the buttering up?"

"What are you talking about?"

"Vicki, this is me. Cut the crap."

She shrugged without turning. "We need him. Tony knows the city. Knows more than we do, anyway."

"And?"

"And maybe I didn't want to lose him, too. Henry is . . ."

"Different?"

"No. He hasn't changed, I have. I know how I used to feel about him—it's all there, but I can't reach it. Friend, lover; they're just words. When I look at him, they don't mean anything. Henry was right, Mike. He was right and I was wrong, and on top of everything else . . ." Her words took on a familiar emphasis. "On top of everything else, I hate being wrong."

Celluci touched the holes Vicki had made earlier in the green leather and decided not to mention his conversation with Henry.

Although his sunglasses blocked most of the light from oncoming traffic, Henry gladly turned off onto the unpaved access road and away from the constant irritation. Dropping his shades on the passenger seat, he leaned back and shook the tension out of his shoulders. He slowed slightly when, after a particularly vigorous dip in the road, his oil pan gently scraped against a protruding piece of the mountain.

He'd bought the 1976 BMW new, had coddled it through the salted winters in Toronto, and had no interest in replacing it. Most Vancouverites seemed to share his attitude. Since moving to B.C. he'd been constantly astonished by the number of twenty-year-old cars on the road—many with the original paint job still factory fresh. These were cars that back East had hit the junkyards long ago or were maintained by loving collectors but here, on the West Coast, were still being driven daily. Once or twice, while looking out at the city, Henry'd almost forgotten what decade it was.

He slowed still further as a raccoon, apparently indifferent to tons of speeding steel, crossed his headlight beam in a stately waddle. Familiar with raccoons as urban animals, it surprised him to see this one so far out in the country. They were all over Vancouver, were tame enough in Stanley Park to beg for handouts, and Vicki'd even had a family of them living in the attic of her three-story apartment building in downtown Toronto.

Vicki.

He should've known his thoughts would eventually circle around to her.

What if you were wrong?

Now, you'll never know.

It's better this way. The steering wheel creaked under his grip. *If I'd stayed and I'd lost control, I could have killed her.*

Or she could've killed you, murmured a little voice in his head, reminding him that Vicki had already killed for territory during the short time she'd walked the night.

It had been a fight she shouldn't have won, not against an opponent so much older and more experienced. But then, Vicki excelled at turning conventions upside down.

Henry had been told, had believed, and had lived by the belief that, when the parent/child bond faded, vampires had no further contact with those they had changed. Vicki had used the conveniences of the twentieth century—the telephone, faxes, e-mail—to wipe out something he'd taken as a given for over four hundred and fifty years. She phoned him, she faxed him, she sent sarcastic monologues by e-mail, she remained in contact and didn't give a damn about what vampires did or did not do.

In spite of everything, because Vicki had refused to have it any other way, they'd remained friends.

"At a distance," he added, carefully easing the car down a rutted lane. "Physical proximity is something else again."

You maintained control, the little voice pointed out. *You were angry, but that was all. If you hadn't provoked her, maybe, in spite of her youth, she could've maintained control as well. She believed that she could, and you know that with Vicki that's usually enough.*

Now you'll never know.

"Shut up!" With a savage twist, Henry shut off the engine and sat staring out at the small cabin illuminated by his headlights. A pair of windows tucked up under the eaves seemed to stare mockingly back at him.

"What's done is done," he muttered, turning off the lights and stepping out into the night. He would stay at the cabin until Vicki had solved the case and, by removing himself to a new territory, would, at the very least, not disrupt her concentration. With innocent lives relying on her abilities, this was not the time to test traditional boundaries.

By appearing to him, the ghost had made him responsible for the deaths it caused. Created Duke of Richmond and Somerset at six, Henry had been raised to take his responsibilities very seriously.

Celluci stepped out of the shower, into the towel Vicki held up for him, and sighed contentedly. "I needed that."

"I know." She flicked a drop of water up into his face. "You were beginning to get a little ripe."

"I thought you liked the way I smelled."

"You like the smell of leather, but you don't walk around with a cowhide up your nose." A fingertip traced damp circles in the hair around his navel as, eyes half closed, Vicki drew in a deep breath. "Trust me. You smell a lot more appetizing now."

He tried to catch her hand, but she easily avoided his grab. "Vicki, I really need a good night's sleep in a bed that isn't moving."

"So you want me to stop?"

He gasped as she widened the circle. "I didn't say that." A moment later, out in the hall, he dug in his heels and murmured, "Not in Fitzroy's bed." A moment after that, as Tony's bed rocked under their combined weight, he wrapped a hand around her jaw and moved her head away from his body. "If you bite it off," he growled, "you won't get to play with it any more."

Tony had the master bedroom and in the lights spilling in through the wall of glass that separated them from the city, Vicki could see as clearly as if the lights in the room were on. She slid out from under Celluci's arm and sat up, moving the pillows so that she could lean comfortably against the wall. "It's strange being here."

Celluci's "Why?" was a nearly inarticulate murmur as he rolled onto his side.

"Because I fought for the territory and lost, but Henry's the one who left." Drawing up her knees, she wrapped her arms around her lower legs and frowned out at the night. "I don't want this territory, but I feel like I've won it. Except that I didn't. Henry won. But I'm here. Is this making any sense?" She didn't bother waiting for a reply. "It feels like there's something missing, but I don't know what. It feels wrong, but I don't know what it needs to make it feel right. Oh, God." She let her head drop onto her knees. "I'm writing country music again. I hate it when that happens."

His breath warm against the skin of her hip, Celluci muttered something that might have been sarcastic.

"Mike?" She reached out to shake him, paused, hand

in the air, and changed her mind. *He needs to sleep. I'll just get dressed and take a quick look at what Vancouver has to offer.*

But she didn't.

Fingers lightly stroking his hair, she wrapped up in the familiar comfort of his life and let the night go by without her in it.

"We have another match."

"So soon?" He frowned at the papers spread out over his desk, at the manicured symmetry of his fingernails, at the phone. He enjoyed working late, having the office to himself; usually, it meant he remained undisturbed. "Isn't that dangerous?"

"Dangerous? In what way?"

"In that it might lead to discovery."

"I've told you before, the timing is totally random. I have no control over when the matches occur. Either it happens, or it does not." The voice emerging from the tiny speaker managed to sound totally neutral about either option. "But if that new list you sent me is accurate . . ."

"It should be. I paid enough for it."

". . . then I have a young man on file who fits one of your prospects."

Drumming his fingers against the polished mahogany, he weighed the options. "And you think he'll accept?"

"When approached the right way, they always accept."

"Yes, of course." He cut her off before she could say any more. He didn't want to know about the donors; they weren't his concern. "Very well, make him the offer. When he accepts, let me know immediately so I can begin negotiations with the buyer."

By the time dawn made its presence felt, Henry's car had been carefully locked away in the shed and all signs of his habitation had been erased from the exterior of the cabin. It was unlikely the day would bring company, but surviving for over four hundred and fifty years had taught caution first of all. Should anyone happen to wander down the narrow dirt track, the cabin would appear deserted. In Henry's opinion, he had less to fear from vandals than from neighbors; vandals seldom wandered so far from the beaten path.

With decks cantilevered out over the edge of a cliff, the cabin managed to be both isolated and directly above a food supply. While the friend who owned the property complained bitterly about how the Valley Breeze Family Resort had lowered property values in the area, Henry personally appreciated the view. Every pastel cabin nestled at the foot of the cliff held at least one meal.

"And why shouldn't I have a couple of weeks in the country?" he asked himself grimly as he locked the porch.

Because you're a vampire. Because this is not your territory. Because another vampire hunts in your territory. Because Michael Celluci might be right. . . .

"And that . . ." Teeth snapped shut around the words. ". . . is exactly why I'm staying where I am."

It was a petty resolution—he'd long grown past the need to lie to himself—but it effectively derailed the circling arguments.

The walk-in closet off the master bedroom had, unfortunately, been lined with cedar. Breathing shallowly through his mouth, wishing he'd brought some of Tony's laundry to cut the scent, Henry secured the door with a piece of two-by-one and lay down on the camp cot he'd set up earlier. As an added precaution, he'd draped a theatrical blackout curtain over the garment rack to fall around the cot like an opaque mosquito net.

The last time he'd spent the day in a closet had been right after the death and disappearance of Vicki's mother. Then, as now, he'd made it as risk free as possible.

All at once he frowned, trying to remember the last risk he'd taken.

He was vampire.

Nightwalker.

Prince of Darkness.

So why did life suddenly seem so middle class? So safe and bland?

Every risk he'd taken in the last few years could be directly linked to Vicki Nelson.

The bedding had been changed, but Henry's scent still coated the room. Instinct battled the need for sanctuary, and need won although her hands were shaking as she bolted the door. This wasn't the first time Vicki'd spent the day in another's sanctuary, but as her last experience had occurred right after she'd used a bank of tanning lights to turn the previous occupant into charred bone and ash, she didn't feel she had much basis for comparison.

The memories Henry's scent evoked warred with the reactions instinctive to her, to their, nature. She attempted to calm the latter by thoroughly searching the room.

"See?" It took an effort, but she kept her voice low—there was no point, after all, in yelling at her own subconscious. "There's no one here. No one in the closet. No little tiny competitor in the drawers. No one under the bed."

With sunrise reaching out for her, she folded the covers down and slid between the sheets. Listening for the comforting sound of Celluci's heartbeat, she . . .

Celluci slept soundly until just after eleven and stayed in bed for another hour after that because he could. In spite of Henry Fitzroy, this *was* his vacation. When he finally got up, his head throbbed and he ached in places he couldn't remember using. A comfortable bed seemed to have given the four nights of abuse on the road a chance to catch up.

Another long hot shower helped.

The coffeemaker and coffee he found on top of the fridge helped more.

"You want to bring North America to a stop?" he snorted as the aroma began to fill the kitchen. "Kidnap Juan Valdez."

He filled a mug from a Seattle PBS station, lifted the stack of newspapers out of the recycling box, and carried everything into the living room, where he made himself comfortable in one of the two huge leather armchairs.

The sooner they got rid of the ghost, the sooner he and Vicki could spend some time actually vacationing. At the very least, the sooner they could go home.

"And where there's a ghost," he muttered, snapping open the oldest of the papers, "somewhere, there's got to be a body."

Cedar?

It took a moment for Henry to realize where he was. When he did, he grimaced. Up until this moment, cedar had been a scent he'd enjoyed. "No wonder moths stay away from this stuff."

Awakening hadn't brought new insight. The mortal mind might find solutions during sleep but, with eternity before them, vampires were forced to deal with their problems night after night. During the day, their subconscious minds shut off with everything else.

Even before he extracted himself from the folds of the blackout curtain, Henry knew his problem hadn't changed. Anger propelling him up and off the cot, he pulled the chain that turned on the closet light.

With so little space, they were nose to nose.

Eyes watering in the sudden glare, Henry snarled, "Are you following me?"

The ghost silently disappeared.

Four

Senses extended, Vicki sifted the darkness for some indication of a ghostly presence. According to Henry, she should be feeling a chill and a distinct sense of unease. It was supposed to be impossible to miss.

"So why am I missing it?" she muttered, propping herself up on an elbow and reaching for the light.

The room was empty of everything but Henry's scent.

Out in the apartment, the phone rang.

"Who was that?"

Celluci very carefully set the flat, almost featureless, high-tech receiver back into its cradle. "Fitzroy," he said without turning.

"Well if he wants to know what I asked the ghost, he's S.O.L." Vicki dropped a shoulder against the living room wall and crossed her arms over her breasts. "Our spectral friend didn't show."

"It showed." Celluci drew in a deep breath and let it out slowly. Things had just gotten a lot more complicated. "It followed Fitzroy. Appeared to him this evening just like always."

"Shit. Now what?"

"He's coming back."

"Here?"

"Here."

Vicki straightened and her voice rose. "And what does he expect me to do?"

"He didn't say." Hands spread, Celluci finally turned to face her. She'd thrown on an oversized shirt but hadn't bothered doing up the buttons. Momentarily sidetracked, he forced himself past his immediate reaction and added gruffly, "The way I see it, we've got two choices. We go home, or we stay and you get another chance to prove your point."

Her eyes narrowed. "If you'll remember, it was Henry's point we proved. We can't be together without fighting."

Celluci sighed and propped his right thigh on the dining room table. "Vicki, *we* can't be together without fighting, but that doesn't seem to stop us. If you can't leave Fitzroy to take care of his own problem— a course of action which gets my vote, by the way— then the two of you are going to have to work something out."

"How do we *work out* a biological imperative?"

"You're the one who said you wouldn't be ruled by your nature."

After a moment, she stared down at the floor and growled, "I was wrong."

It had never been difficult for Michael Celluci to figure out what Vicki was thinking, and her metamorphosis hadn't changed that. For her to actually admit she was wrong without a three-hour argument and half a dozen pieces of irrefutable evidence could only mean that losing the fight to Fitzroy had upset her world view more than he'd realized. Time to put it right. "Fitzroy provoked that fight, Vicki. He had no intention of giving the two of you a chance to work it out."

Vicki's gaze snapped up off the pattern of pieced hardwood and locked onto his face, her eyes silvering. "You know this for a fact?"

"He admitted it before he left."

"And you're just telling me now!"

"Hey!" Celluci lifted both hands to chest height, a symbolic defense at best. "I'm not the bad guy here."

"No . . ." Teeth clenched, Vicki fought to free the

memory of the actual fight from the cloud of mixed emotions obscuring it.

"You insisted we could work together," he reminded her mockingly.

"We could if you'd stop this Prince of Darkness bullshit and back off!"

"Why that lousy son of a . . ." Profanity somehow seemed inadequate. Fingers curled into fists, she spun around on one bare heel and headed back toward the bedroom.

"Where are you going?"

"To get dressed!"

An innocuous statement on its own, but the way Vicki spat it out, it sounded very much like a threat. With the strong feeling he was going to need the caffeine, Celluci headed into the kitchen for another cup of coffee.

"Sorry I'm late. I almost got clipped by a Caddie on the way over, and . . ." Tony's voice trailed off as Celluci came into the entryway and he got a look at his face. "What's wrong?"

"Fitzroy's coming back. It seems the ghost is appearing only to him."

Tony stared down at his helmet. A hundred tiny reflections in beads of rain stared back at him. "Coming back here?" When the detective didn't answer right away, Tony looked up to meet a speculative gaze. "What?"

"You don't want him coming back here?"

"That's not what I said." He tossed the helmet down beside his roller blades and shrugged out of his damp jacket. "I mean, jeez, it's his condo, isn't it? What's Victory gonna do?"

"Victory's going hunting."

The two men turned toward the voice, their motion almost involuntary.

Tony, who'd been expecting a variation on Henry's Prince of Darkness attire, was surprised to see Vicky in jeans, sneakers, and bright, a not even remotely vampiric cotton jacket. Although she no longer wore glasses and she'd left her shoulderbag back in the bedroom, she looked no different than she had on a hundred summer nights in Toronto when he'd still been living on the street.

And then she looked very different.

And then she didn't again.

He blinked. Looking at her was like looking at one of those pictures that could be either a vase or two people. "Uh, Victory, your vampire's showing."

She looked startled, and then she laughed. With a subtle shift in emphasis, she fitted the civilized mask more firmly in place. "Better?"

"Yeah. But, uh, if Henry's coming, shouldn't you . . ." He glanced over at Celluci who was obviously going to be no help at all. ". . . should you be here?"

"Are you warning me against hunting in Henry's territory?"

He knew this mood. He'd seen Henry wear it a hundred nights. "Do I look stupid?"

"No." When she smiled at him, he barely resisted the urge to lift his chin and he released a thankful breath when she turned her attention to Celluci. "If Henry gets here before I get back, make my excuses, would you?

"Vicki." He placed his hand on her arm and Tony thought he saw the edges soften as she looked up at him. "Be careful."

"I'm always careful."

"Bullshit." But he let her go.

She paused at the door. "Trendy people still gather on Denman, Tony?" He'd barely begun to nod when she was gone.

Henry liked to hunt on Denman. Tony chewed on a corner of his lip and turned toward the detective. "I thought you were going to ask her not to go."

Celluci snorted. "Not likely. It's safer not to have her around when she's in that mood."

"Yeah, but . . ." He spread his hands, unsure of the words.

"I know what she is, Tony." Celluci's voice was surprisingly gentle. "I don't always like it, but I like the alternative even less." He cleared his throat, suddenly embarrassed by the spontaneous shared confidence. "Have you eaten?"

After Tony pointed out that Henry didn't like the apartment smelling of food, Celluci ordered a pizza.

"Give him something else to think about."

"Besides Vicki?"

"Besides Vicki."

Expecting to be uncomfortable, Tony was astonished to find himself relaxing. They were just two guys thrown together by mutual friends, age the biggest difference between them. They even argued over which toppings to order.

Halfway through a large double cheese, mushrooms, tomatoes, and pepperoni, Celluci sat back, wiped sauce off his chin, and said, "You want to tell me what's wrong?"

"Nothing's . . ." Tony let the protest hang half said. He could tell from the expression on the other man's face there was no point in finishing it. "You wouldn't understand."

"Tony, if it has to do with Henry, the odds are I'm the only person in the world who *would* understand."

"Yeah, I guess." He chewed and swallowed, unsure if he was trying to think of what to say or if he was avoiding the question entirely. He could feel Celluci waiting, not impatiently but like he really wanted to know. After a moment, he put down the half-eaten slice and scrubbed at the grease on his fingers. "This is just between you and me?"

"If that's what you want."

After a few minutes of expectant silence, he sighed. "When I first met Henry, I wasn't anything, you know? And I wouldn't be what I am now without him. I mean, he sort of made me go back and finish high school just because, well, he believed I could, and . . ." He poked at a congealing piece of cheese. "I guess that sounds pretty dumb."

"No." Celluci shook his head, remembering how he'd fallen into position by Henry Fitzroy's side on more than one occasion. "The little shit has a way of making you live up to his expectations."

"Yeah, that's it exactly. He just expects." Tony ripped his napkin into greasy squares before he continued. "Trouble is, sometimes he doesn't really see me in those expectations. I mean, he didn't choose for me to know about him, Vicki just kinda dumped me on him and he never really felt about me like he did about her." Realizing who he was speaking to, he colored. "Sorry."

"It's okay. I know how he felt." *But it's my life she's a part of, not his,* his tone added smugly. "It seems to me it's time for you to get out and find a life of your own."

"I guess." He lifted his head and met Celluci's eyes. "But how do you just leave someone like Henry?"

Vicki had the taxi drop her off in front of the Sylvia Hotel on English Bay. Her memory of the three nights with Henry in the vine-covered Victorian building, learning to manipulate the world she was no longer a part of, was one of the few memories she had of her "childhood" in Vancouver not drenched in blood. She stood for a few moments in front of the building, remembering how Henry had taught her to survive. Then she drew in a deep breath of night-scented air and walked the two blocks to Denman Street.

Bisecting the West End, running vaguely southwest to northeast, Denman was a lovely walking street—and that made it prime hunting territory.

The rain had stopped and well-lit sidewalk cafés, still glistening from the last shower, had filled. Vancouverites never let a little rain bother them—since it rained so frequently, there wasn't much point—and they were serious about their cafés. Scanning the crowds, Vicki noted certain similarities in the mix as the young and trendy rubbed elbows with the old and somehow still trendy, all dressed in what could only be called a sporty and health-conscious style—very unlike the Gothic punk so prevalent in trendy Toronto. In spite of the hour, everyone seemed to have an "I'm going roller blading/mountain biking/sea kayaking after I finish my cappuccino" look. In any other mood, Vicki might have found it amusing. Tonight, it pissed her off.

Denman, she mused, glaring a pair of young men in chinos out of her way, *might have been a mistake.* She wanted something with an edge, something to definitively establish her presence in Henry's territory. *There's never a motorcycle gang around when you need one.*

Then she saw him.

He was sitting inside one of the cafés, alone, all his attention focused on the notebook in front of him. A slender shadow amid the surrounding proto-jocks, he looked disturbingly familiar.

He looked remarkably like Henry.

A closer examination proved the resemblance purely superficial. The clothes were black, the skin pale, but the blond hair was too long, and the face more angular than Tudor-curved. Were he standing, he'd probably be significantly taller.

Still . . .

When he glanced up, Vicki met his gaze through the glass, held it for a moment, then vanished into the night. Safely hidden in the darkness between two buildings, she watched the front of the café and smiled. She knew the kind of man he was. The kind who, against all urgings of common sense, wanted to believe there was something more. The kind who wanted to believe in mystery.

Wanted to believe, but didn't quite.

The door opened, and he stood on the sidewalk. Vicki could hear his heart pounding, and when he closed his eyes she knew he was searching for the moment they'd shared, searching for the mystery. An older man, with a strong Slavic accent and his arm across the back of a well-dressed woman, asked him to move away from the door. Visibly returning to reality, the young man apologized and started along Denman, a slightly rueful smile twisting his mouth, one hand trailing in the planters that separated the sidewalk café from the sidewalk proper.

Vicki allowed the Hunger to rise.

She followed the song of his blood at a safe distance until he started up the broad steps of a four-story Victorian brownstone on Barclay Street. When he put his key in the lock, she moved out of the night, laid a hand on his shoulder, and turned him around. Somewhere, down in the depths of eyes almost as silver-gray as her own, he was expecting her.

He wanted to believe in mystery.

So she gave him a mystery to believe.

"Who do you think'll be back first?"

"Fitzroy." Celluci surfed a few more channels, wondering why someone with Fitzroy's money didn't buy a better TV—from the looks of it, he'd spent a fortune on the stereo system. "It's Monday night, won't be much traffic in from the mountains, so he'll make good time."

"He'll probably want to feed before he gets here, though. So that he's not overreacting to things."

"Things meaning Vicki? Well, my guess is she's taken that into account. He's going to expect her to be here when he arrives, so she's not going to be—not even if she has to hide across the street and wait for him to drive up." He flicked past three syndicated sitcoms, two of them from the seventies, an episode of classic *Trek* he'd seen a hundred times and the same football game on four channels. "Five hundred channels and four hundred and ninety-nine of them still show crap. What's this?"

Tony stuck his head out of the kitchen where he was cleaning up the debris from their meal. "Local talk show," he said after watching for a moment. "The woman is Patricia Chou. She's really intense. One of my night school teachers says she does kamikaze reporting and thinks she's trying for a big enough story to get her a network job. At least half of City Council is terrified of her, and I heard she was willing to go to jail once to protect a source. I don't know who the old guy is."

"The old guy," Celluci snarled, "probably has no more than ten years on me."

Tony prudently withdrew.

On screen, Patricia Chou frowned slightly and said, "So what you're saying, Mr. Swanson, is that the fears people have about organ donations are completely unfounded?"

"Fear," her guest declared, "is often based on lack on information."

It was a good response; Celluci tossed the remote onto the glass-topped coffee table—Fitzroy had a distinct fondness for breakable furniture—and settled back to watch.

Mr. Swanson settled back much the same way and looked into the camera with the ease of a man often interviewed. "Let's take those fears one at a time. People with influence or money do not have a better chance of getting a transplant. Computers suggest the best possible match for each available organ based on blood type, size, illness of patient, and time on the waiting list."

Patricia Chou leaned forward, a slender finger extended to emphasize her point. "But what about the recent media coverage of famous people getting transplants?"

"I think you'll find that media coverage is the point to that question, Ms. Chou. They're getting the coverage because they're famous, not because they've had a transplant. Hundreds of people have transplants and never make the news. I assure you, my wife would still be alive today if I could have bought her a transplant."

"Your wife, Rebecca, died of chronic kidney failure?"

"That's right." He had to swallow before he could

go on, and Celluci, who over the years had seen grief in every possible form, was willing to bet it was no act. "Three years on dialysis, three years waiting for a match, three years dying. And my wife wasn't alone; approximately one third of all patients awaiting transplants die. Which is why I'm an active supporter of the British-Columnbia Transplant Society."

"But in this time of cutbacks, surely the cost of transplants . . ."

"Cost?" His gaze swung around and locked on her face. "Ms. Chou, did you know that if all the patients waiting at the end of last year had been able to receive kidneys, health care savings would exceed one billion dollars?"

Ms. Chou did not know, nor, from a certain tightening around her eyes, was she pleased at being interrupted. "To return to the public's fears, Mr. Swanson, what about the possibility of organ-legging?" Her emphasis made the last word hang in the air for a moment or two after she finished speaking.

"That sort of thing is an impossibility, at least in any first world nation. You'd have to have doctors willing to work outside the law, expensive facilities, you'd have to contravene a computer system with massive safeguards—I'm not saying it couldn't be done, merely that costs would be so prohibitive there'd be no point."

Good answer, Celluci allowed. *Although slightly less than spontaneous.* Swanson had obviously been expecting a variation on the question.

"So from a purely marketing standpoint, there'd be no profit in it?"

"Exactly. You'd have to hire thugs to procure unwilling donors and I imagine that a reliable thug, provided you could find such a creature, doesn't come cheap."

She ignored his attempt to lighten the interview, "So the body found floating in the harbor, a body that had a kidney surgically removed, had nothing to do with organ-legging?"

That, Celluci realized, was where she'd been heading all along.

Mr. Swanson spread his hands, manicured nails gleaming in the studio lights. "There are a number of reasons you can have a kidney surgically removed, Ms. Chou. The human body only needs one."

"And you don't believe that someone needed one of his?"

"I believe that this kind of yellow journalism is why there's a critical shortage of donated organs and people like my wife are dying."

"But wouldn't someone be willing to pay . . ."

The screen returned to black, and Henry put the remote back on the coffee table.

Celluci, who hadn't even been aware he was in the room until he'd crossed directly into his line of sight, attempted to relax a number of muscles jerked into knots by Fitzroy's sudden appearance. "Did you have to do that?" he snarled.

"No, I didn't." The implication of Henry's tone suggested that he'd achieved exactly the effect he'd intended. "Where's Vicki?"

Glancing over Henry's shoulder and then disregarding Tony's silent warning from the kitchen, Celluci drawled, "She's gone hunting."

"Hunting." It was an emotionless repetition that nevertheless held a wealth of meaning.

"You knew it was going to happen when you asked her to come out here."

"Yes." With his fingers laced tightly together lest he lose control of his reaction and put his fist through the glass, Henry walked over to the window and stared down at the lights of Granville Island. "I knew it was going to happen."

"But that doesn't mean you have to like it."

"You needn't sound so superior, Detective."

"Superior? Me?"

In the kitchen, Tony winced. He wondered if surviving a number of years as a cop created a personal belief in invulnerability or if that belief was necessary before starting the job. Whichever it was, Detective Sergeant Michael Celluci seemed to be having one heck of a good time flirting with death.

"I told her that you deliberately provoked her attack." Not as relaxed as he appeared, Celluci watched the muscles across Henry's back tense and untense beneath the raw silk jacket. If it came to it, he knew he couldn't survive an all-out attack. Or even a half-strength attack for that matter—proven the last time he and Henry had tangled.

"If you're attempting to divert my attention from Vicki to you, Detective, the sacrifice is unnecessary. If we are to lay this specter, we have no choice but to work together. It seems I must allow the possibility that we can overcome our territorial natures."

"Big of you."

"God damn it, Vicki!" Celluci catapulted off his chair so fast he lost his balance and slammed down on his knees, denim-covered bone cracking against the polished hardwood floor. "Do you have to sneak up on people like that?" He heaved himself onto his feet. "First him, now you?"

Her hands on the back of the chair he'd so recently vacated, Vicki forced herself to smile down at him, forced herself to take her eyes off Henry Fitzroy. "Maybe you ought to cut back on the caffeine."

"Maybe you lot ought to whistle when you come into a room," he snarled.

You lot.

Her and Henry.

Impossible now to ignore the heated connection between them. He was standing by the window, his face expressionless, eyes shadowed. She couldn't tell what he was thinking, nor was she entirely certain she wanted to know. His heart beat slower than the mortals they fed from; hers matched it. His blood sang not an invitation but a warning; hers echoed it. His scent lifted the hair on the back of her neck.

"So . . ." If only to prove that she could, she kept the challenge out of her voice and, if the words weren't exactly neutral, at least the tone was purely human. "I hear you owe me an apology."

"Yes." He inclined his head. "But I've spent over four-and-a-half centuries believing vampires are incapable of sharing a territory, Vicki. Don't expect me to change my mind overnight."

Her tone grew distinctly sarcastic. "Apologies usually begin with 'I'm sorry.' "

"I'm sorry. You were right. I was wrong. I didn't give us a fair chance. I will this time."

"Because you have to."

He shrugged. "Granted."

"You try that Prince of Darkness bullshit on me again, Henry, and I'm out of here."

"So you've said in the past." All at once he smiled, and she saw not competition but one of two men she'd learned to love in spite of herself. "You haven't changed, you know, not beyond the obvious—you continue to be so definitely you. After I surrendered the day, I became an entirely different person."

Celluci, still standing between them, measuring gaze flicking constantly back and forth, snorted. "Yeah. Right. You were a royal bastard before, you were a royal bastard after—with all the baggage that carries. Since you were barely seventeen when it happened, I'd say if you changed, you grew up, and *that* change comes to everyone."

Henry opened his mouth and then closed it again, the protest dying behind his teeth. Even Vicki looked slightly stunned.

Pleased with the effect, Celluci moved out into the room until he formed the third point of the triangle and said, "Now that's settled, we have a few other problems to deal with. The first, where's Vicki spending the day? Not in your bed . . ."

"I assume you're implying, not in my bed with me. That isn't actually possible."

"You bet your ass it isn't."

Henry ignored him. "There's an empty condo across the hall with an identical layout to this one. It wouldn't take long to secure the small bedroom. The woman who owns it recently died. I called her companion on the way in . . ."

"You have a cellphone?"

"Try to keep up, Detective; these are the '90s. Anyway, Mrs. Munro is leaving to spend the next week with her son in Kamloops and has graciously allowed us the use of her late employer's condo."

"Nice of her."

"Isn't it? But I assure you my persuasions were, for the most part, monetary. While Mrs. Munro is likely to receive the lion's share of the estate, she's just lost her job and will have no income until after the will clears probate. I swung around and picked up the keys and I think it should suit our purposes." He drew a key chain out of his pocket and threw it to Vicki, who snatched it one-handed out of the air.

And threw it back. "It never occurred to you to ask me what I thought?"

"You can always spend the day locked in your van," he reminded her.

"The hell you can; it's already been ripped off once." It gave Celluci great pleasure to ignore Henry's startled exclamation. "Take the keys, Vicki. He asked you to come here, it only makes sense he finds you accommodation."

Reluctantly, Vicki held out her hand. "If you put it that way . . ."

"That's exactly how I put it." He waited until the keys had changed hands once again, then he continued. "My second point concerns territory and keeping the two of you from each other's throats. This is a big city. Why can't Vicki hunt an area you don't use? You seemed to have implied that was possible back when that other vampire moved into Toronto."

"Unfortunately, Detective, it isn't just the hunting, it's all contact. I have shared cities in the past, but there have been very clear boundaries drawn with neutral areas in between. Our paths never crossed."

Vicki broke in before Celluci could respond.

"Wouldn't work, Mike. If I'm going to find out who offed our restless spirit, the restrictions of the night will be more than enough. I don't know, can't know, where leads are going to take me until I'm there, and *very clear boundaries* will only get in the way."

"Uh, I've got an idea that might help."

Vicki spun around, then glared, not at Tony but at the other two men. "Why didn't you tell me he was there? Both of you were facing the kitchen!"

"Very careless, Vicki." Henry fell easily back into his role of teacher and guide because at least that role had parameters he understood. "You should have known he was there. Caught his scent. Heard his heartbeat."

"His scent permeates this apartment. And his heartbeat got lost in the sound of the dishwasher."

"The perils of the modern vampire," Celluci muttered.

Tony grinned as he stepped forward. "And that's my point. You guys are modern vampires. I mean this not sharing a territory stuff probably made sense back in the Middle Ages when villages were only like a couple hundred people and more than one vampire would be kind of noticeable, but this city has nearly three million people in it."

"He has a point," Vicki allowed. "There're probably as many people in this condominium complex as in a good-sized village of the 1500s."

"But it is my city . . ."

"Jeez, Henry, you've never even been to West Vancouver. There could be another vampire, six ghouls, and a family of aliens over there for all you know, and you already said cities can be divided. That has nothing to do with this."

"Look, it's an attitude thing." Tony stopped just outside the perimeter of the triangle. "You've said it yourself, Henry, times don't change you, so you have to change with them or be left behind. And when you get left far enough behind, well, the next thing you know, you're spreading your towel for that last suntan."

"Last suntan?" Vicki repeated with an incredulous look at Henry.

"I never said that."

"Maybe not those exact words," Tony admitted, "but that was what you meant." He grew suddenly solemn and fixed both Vicki and Henry with an intent, worried stare. "Change or die, guys."

After a long moment, Vicki shrugged. "Look, I'm not trying to take over your territory, and there's plenty of food here for both of us, so we can't logically be a threat to each other. There's no reason we can't put up with each other for the duration."

"Listen to your blood and tell me you believe that."

"I'm listening to my brain, Henry. You should try it some time."

He growled. She echoed it. They each took a step forward.

"HEY!" Celluci's voice didn't so much cut through the tension as smash it aside. "Get a grip! I expect this sort of thing from mongrel dogs but not from two supposedly sentient people." No longer able to blush, they both suddenly became interested in the toes of their shoes. "Times change. Change with them, or admit you can't and stop wasting my time—I've a hell of a lot less of it than you do."

Gaze still on the floor, Vicki murmured, "Tell you what, Henry. I promise to not go on a childish rampage through your territory if you promise to let go a little."

"It won't be easy."

"Nothing worthwhile ever is."

"Oh, spare me," Celluci muttered.

Henry stepped away from the window and Vicki backed up, carefully maintaining the distance between them. He paused for a moment, as though testing their relative positions. When neither of them seemed inclined to move closer, he said, a little wearily, "I've got the supplies you'll need to secure that window down in my locker. Why don't you two check out your accommodations while Tony and I go get them?"

Barely suppressing the urge to snarl as he went by, Vicki nodded, not trusting her voice. Celluci took one look at her face and pulled her carefully to his side. She jerked her arm free but remained close, using his scent to mask Henry's.

"There," she said when the door closed and they were alone, "that wasn't so bad. We've definitely made progress."

"So unclench your teeth."

A muscle jumped in her jaw. "Not yet."

When it seemed that time enough had passed to give them a clear path out the door and down the hall, they made their way to number 1409.

"Jesus H. Christ."

"On crutches," Vicki added.

The walls had been marbled. The windows wore four different types of swag. The furniture appeared to have been upholstered in raw silk. The overlapping carpets were Persian. Artwork, two dimensional and three, had been arranged for effect. Number 1409 looked like it had been decorated for the benefit of photographers from *Vancouver Life Magazine.*

"I didn't think people actually lived like this." Turning her back on the splendors of the living room, Vicki started down the hall. "Do you think the rest of the place is the same?"

A pair of concrete Chinese temple dogs guarded a huge basket of dried roses in one corner of the master bedroom. One end of the king-sized bed had been stacked with about fifty pillows in various shapes and shades. The silk moire duvet cover matched the wallpaper. The drapes, although the same fabric, were several shades darker.

"This room probably cost as much as my whole house," Celluci muttered.

"Certainly classier than the Holiday Inn," Vicki agreed, stepping back into the hall and opening the door to the smallest of the three bedrooms. "Oh, my God." She froze in the doorway. "I can't stay in this."

Celluci peered over her shoulder and started to laugh.

A huge doll, with a pink-and-white crocheted skirt, sat in the middle of the pink satin bedspread. The pink frilly bedskirt matched the pink frilly curtains which complemented the pink frills on the pale pink armchair tucked into a corner. The dresser and the trunk at the foot of the bed were antique white. The bed itself was the most ornate brass monstrosity either of them had ever seen, covered in curlicues and enameled flowers, with a giant heart in the center of both the head and footboard.

Laughing too hard to stand, Celluci collapsed against the wall clutching his stomach. "The thought," he began, looked from Vicki to the bed, and couldn't finish. "The thought . . ." A second attempt got no further than the first.

"What's the matter, chuckles? Can't handle the thought of a vampire in such feminine surroundings?"

"Vicki . . ." Wiping his streaming eyes with one hand, he waved the other into the room. ". . . I can't handle the thought of *you* in these surroundings. I hadn't even started thinking about the other."

Her lips twitched. "It does look like it's been decorated by Polly Pocket, doesn't it?"

A few moments later, Tony found them sitting shoulder-to-shoulder on the hall floor, wearing the expressions of people who've nearly laughed themselves sick. "No one answered when I knocked," he explained. "What's so funny?"

Vicki nodded toward the room and gasped, "A pink plastic crypt that fits in the palm of your hand."

"Yeah. Okay." He glanced inside, shrugged, and looked back down at the two of them. "I have no idea of what you're talking about, but the stuff to block the window's outside. Henry thought it would be best if he didn't come in. You know, keeping his scent out."

Braced against the wall, Vicki got to her feet, extended a hand down to Celluci, and stopped herself just before she lifted him effortlessly upright—displays of strength bothered him more than anything else. When she noticed Tony watching her and realized he understood what she'd done, she clenched her teeth in irritation. "This is not a case of a woman being less than she can to save the machismo of some man," she growled. "This is a person making a compromise for someone she cares about."

Tony backed up, both hands raised. "I didn't say anything."

"I could hear you thinking."

As she stomped by him, Tony glanced over at Celluci. "Has she always been that moody?"

Celluci ignored him. "What machismo?" he demanded following her down the hall. "What the hell are you talking about?"

Tony sighed, "Never mind." Trailing along behind, he waited for a break in the argument and announced, "Henry says that once you get the stuff inside and before you put it up, we should all meet in his apartment to discuss the case."

Resting two sheets of three-quarter-inch plywood against the wall, Celluci frowned. "Wouldn't finding neutral territory make more sense?"

"He says his place'll do since Vicki's already scented it."

"He what?"

"Hey! Victory!" Eyes wide, Tony backed up until he hit a sideboard and he stopped cold, one hand flung out to steady an antique candelabra rocked by the impact. "Chill. I'm just repeating what Henry said."

"He makes it sound as though I've been spraying the furniture."

Remembering his earlier conversation with Celluci, Tony didn't think it would be wise to add that Henry had also drawn in a deep breath, his expression had softened, and he'd murmured, *"God, how I miss her."* At the time, Tony had been tempted to remind him none too gently that Vicki was just down the hall and that if he missed her it was his own damned fault. That wasn't, however, a tone one took with Henry Fitzroy.

"While Vicki and I secure that room, I suggest you head over to the city morgue at Vancouver General and ID a corpse."

Henry looked down the length of his dining room table and raised a red-gold brow. "I beg your pardon?"

"If there's a ghost, odds are good that somewhere there's a body." Fully conscious that their precarious truce would need constant maintenance, Celluci buried his initial reaction to being patronized by a man who wrote romance novels and managed to keep his voice calm and his body language noncommittal. "The odds are better that a handless body, if found, is going to make the paper. So this afternoon, while you two were getting your beauty sleep, I went through your recycling." He picked up the folded newspaper and tossed it down to Henry. "A handless body got pulled out of the harbor right about when your ghost showed up."

"It isn't my ghost," Henry told him tersely.

Celluci shrugged. "Whatever. Body's still going to be at the morgue. Police haven't been able to ID it or that would be in a later edition."

"And if it is the right body?" He slid the paper back down the length of the table.

"We find out what the police know," Celluci began, "and then . . ." Cold fingers closed around his wrist like a vise.

"Mike. My case. Before you solve it, don't you think you ought to maybe talk things over with me?"

He half turned to face her. Fully aware of the danger, he didn't quite meet her eyes. "Vicki. Our case. I assumed we'd talk things over while Henry was at the morgue. Or would you rather I just bunked with Tony and went on vacation until you decide to go home?"

Eyes narrowed, she let go of his arm. Unwilling to look at either him or Henry, she swept her gaze around the room and suddenly laughed. "I think Tony's terrified you might actually make good on that threat."

"Not terrified," Tony protested as the other three turned to stare at him. "It's just I'm staying with friends and they haven't got room and it's not like . . ." His voice trailed off, and he directed a withering gaze at Vicki. "Thanks a lot."

"You can come home," Henry reminded him. "My initial plan seems to have been . . . discarded."

"Nah." The younger man shifted in his chair. "I already moved my stuff, and John and Gerry made room for me, so it'd be rude to just leave."

"Suit yourself." His brow furrowed thoughtfully, but just as he was about to speak, Celluci, who'd been watching Tony's face carefully, cut him off.

"Better see if you can get a copy of the autopsy report while you're at the hospital."

The red-gold brow rose again, but if Henry suspected the other man's timing, he let it go. If Tony wanted to keep secrets with Michael Celluci, that was none of his business. "Anything else?" he asked dryly as he stood.

"Yeah, write out a full description of your ghost—especially noting any differences between it and the body in morgue."

"And the other spirits? Those within the scream?"

"Can you describe them?"

Never fond of admitting inability, and less fond of it under these circumstances with these listeners, Henry shook his head. "No."

"Then let's just forget them for the moment and stick with the description you can give."

"You can put it in with the autopsy report," Vicki declared, standing as well. "Now, if you'll excuse us . . ." Her tone made it clear he could excuse them or not, it made little difference to her. "We're going to seal off my sanctuary while you put flesh to your ghost."

"Vicki."

She paused, one hand on the back of her chair.

"As I said before, it isn't easy putting aside a tenet I've held for over four hundred and fifty years. Even if I've never tested it, even if it's no longer true, the belief that vampires are incapable of physical contact is, if nothing else, a strong tradition."

Her hand moved up to Celluci's shoulder and gripped it reassuringly as it tensed. "I'm not exactly a traditional vampire, Henry."

He smiled, and it was the smile she remembered from before the change. "Then stop being such a deliberate pain in the ass."

Five

The city morgue was in the basement at Vancouver General Hospital. Henry supposed it worked on the same principle as the crypts under cathedrals—the deeper in the ground, the cooler the ambient temperature, the less chance of the rot seeping into the rest of the building.

Hospitals had never been one of Henry's favorite places. Not because of light levels kept painfully high for eyes adapted to darkness. Not even because of the omnipresent and unpleasant odor of antiseptic mixed thoroughly with disease.

It was the despair.

It hung in the halls like smoke; from the patients who knew they were dying, from the patients who feared they were dying. That modern medicine resulted in far more successes than failures made little difference.

Predators preyed on the weak. The defenseless. The despairing.

Even though he had already fed, the Hunger strained against Henry's control as he stepped over the threshold and into the building. His reaction wasn't about feeding; it was about killing, killing because he could, because they were all but asking him to. As the door closed behind him, he could feel civilization sloughing away, exposing the Hunter beneath.

He'd decided to gain access through Emergency, reasoning that he could hide his movements in the chaos that always seemed to exist in the ER of big city hospitals. As far as it went, the reasoning was sound, but the bloodscent hanging over the crowded waiting room came very close to loosing the Hunger. Acutely conscious of the weak and injured around him, their lives throbbing in an atmosphere reeking of despair, Henry stepped away from the door and moved deeper into the building.

No one tried to stop him.

Those who saw him quickly looked away.

Passing as swiftly as possible through the crowded emergency waiting room, he slipped unnoticed into the first stairwell he found. The air was clearer there, but he had no time to compose himself.

Folklore aside, vampires not only showed up in mirrors but in security cameras as well.

There are times, he thought, racing down the stairs at full speed, a dark flicker across a distant monitor, *when I hate this century.*

Two flights down, he opened a door marked, CITY MORGUE/PARKING LEVEL TWO and stepped gratefully into a dimly lit corridor. While he suspected that budget cuts were the reason for two out of three fluorescent banks to be off—there'd be no patients wandering about down here after all and, given the hour, few staff—it was hard not to appreciate the atmosphere created by the lack of light. The hall leading to the morgue *should* be barred with shadow.

Teeth bared but more comfortable than he'd been since leaving his car, Henry followed the trail of death to an unlocked door. Pulling on a pair of leather driving gloves, he passed silently through an outer office and into the actual morgue.

Here, he breathed easier still. In these rooms, the blood spilled was lifeless and the dead were past fear.

Only six of the refrigerated drawers were in use. Five were labeled with the occupant's name. The sixth held the body of the handless man pulled out of Vancouver Harbor.

His face had taken a beating—although it was un-

clear whether it had happened in the water or before—
but enough areas of definition remained for Henry to
recognize his ghost. Had he any doubts, the fuzzy blue
homemade tattoo of a dripping dagger on the left
forearm would have convinced him.

Although there were computer files as well, paper
copies of recent autopsy reports were stored in a huge
filing cabinet against one wall of the office. It only
took a moment to match the number on the drawer
with the number on the file folder and a moment more
to set the first page on the photocopier.

He heard the jangle of keys in the hall the instant
after he pushed print.

Kevin Lam tossed his car keys from hand to hand
as he hurried down the corridor. It had been one hell
of a shift and all he wanted to do was go home, eat
something that didn't taste like disinfectant, and see
if maybe there was a ball game on. He didn't actually
like baseball that much, but a ten-hour shift had left
him so brain dead he figured it had the only plot on
the tube he'd be able to understand.

*Once I'm in the car, I'm safe. They can't call me
back. I can go home.* Eyes locked on the entrance to
the parking garage at the end of the hall, he almost
missed the flash of light from the morgue office.

The supposedly deserted morgue office.

The frosted glass in the upper half of the door was
dark. From the hall outside, it seemed that no one
was working late.

"So who the hell is running the photocopier?" Kevin
glanced toward the parking garage and sighed. If he
called hospital security, he could be stuck here for
hours even if it turned out to be nothing. And if it
did turn out to be nothing, he'd be the butt of every
morgue joke in the hospital. "I'll just open the door
and turn on the light, see that it's nothing, and then
go home."

And if it is something? he asked himself as he
shoved his keys in his pocket and reached for the

door. He shook his head. *Yeah, right. Like someone's actually going to be standing in a dark morgue at midnight making photocopies.*

Henry had plenty of time to hide. He just didn't bother.

In the instant the orderly stood silhouetted in the open door, one hand reaching for the light switch, Henry grabbed the front of his uniform, dragged him into the room, and closed the door.

The Hunger roared in his ears, restraints rubbed raw by Vicki's presence, then further torn by his passage through the massed despair and bloodscent in the building above. Self-preservation barely held him in check as he shoved the young man down onto a desk.

It wasn't completely black in the room. LEDs gleamed on various pieces of equipment and an exit light glowed over the door. Kevin saw the pale oval of a face bend over him, felt himself fall into the bottomless depths of dark eyes, and choked back a scream when a cold voice told him to be silent.

Strong fingers gripped his wrist, the touch both chilling and burning, sensations racing up his arm with his pulse and causing his heart to pound. His breathing quickened. It might have been fear. It might have been something darker.

He didn't understand when the pale face withdrew and that same cold voice muttered, "And I accused her of acting like a child." When the face returned, when the voice told him to forget, he forgot gladly.

Tony had left just after Henry had. Vicki'd sent Celluci to bed at about two. All the lights were out except a small crescent moon lamp on a shelf in the entryway. With the curtains open, the city spilled into the living room, banishing anything approaching darkness for those who lived at night. Having carefully moved two days' worth of unopened mail to one side, Vicki sat at the mahogany desk staring down at a blank piece of paper and waiting for Henry.

He'd be back soon. He had to be if he wanted to

give her any chance to study the autopsy report and maybe come to a few conclusions before dawn.

If she thought about waiting for *Henry,* she was fine. When she started thinking about what Henry was, her thoughts were tinted red.

Vampire.

But he always had been—he wasn't the one who'd changed.

She fidgeted with the heavy fountain pen she'd found in one of the desk drawers, turning the smooth black weight over and over, the repetition vaguely soothing.

All right. I'm not what I was, but I'm still who I was. I accepted the limitations of the RP—okay, not gracefully, honesty forced her to admit, *but I accepted them. I didn't let it keep me from living my life exactly as I pleased. I am here to find a murderer, and I'm not going to let Henry Fitzroy change the way I operate. He's my friend, and we're going to act like friends if I have to rip him open and feed on his steaming entrails!*

The pen snapped between her fingers.

"Shit!"

Breathing heavily, Vicki barely kept herself from throwing the pieces aside and spraying a room full of very expensive upholstery in ink. Trembling with the effort, she set both halves of the pen gently in the middle of the desk then surged to her feet and viciously kicked the chair away.

While a small voice in the back of her head wondered where the hell this was coming from, she headed for the door, the Hunger rising. Eyes gleaming silver in the mirror wall of the entry, she reached for the doorknob and realized another heart beat in unison with hers.

Henry.

In the corridor. Almost at the door.

Vampire.

Then memory added Celluci's opinion.

Romance writer.

Vicki grabbed onto that and used it to bludgeon

her instinctive response back into the shadows. Her breathing slowed and the roaring in her ears dimmed to a gentle growl. Vampires did not share territories with other vampires, but there was nothing that said vampires could not share a territory with romance writers.

As Tony had said, it was an attitude thing.

And if there's one thing I excel at, it's attitude. Holding tightly to that thought, she opened the door and said, "What the hell took you so long?"

Henry recoiled a step at her proximity, eyes darkening, a snarl pulling his lips back off his teeth. "Don't push it, Vicki."

"Hey . . ." She spread her hands, the gesture serving a double function of emphasis and of readiness should she need; to go for his throat. "I just asked you a question, you're the one who's overreacting." Somehow it came out sounding like a challenge, which was not at all what she'd intended. It had been easier with the door between them; face to face, her visceral reaction to the threat he posed was harder to ignore. "Look, Henry, it was getting late. I was getting worried, okay?"

"Why worried?"

Because you're old and slowing down . . . Where the hell did that come from? Shaken, Vicki shoved the thought back into her subconscious. "Forget it. What did you find out?"

Forgetting was safer for them both than responding. He'd seen the threat surface, seen her push it away. Considering the short time she'd spent in the night, her control was nothing short of incredible. A faint hint of jealousy, that she should so easily push aside the demands of her nature, added itself to the emotional maelstrom below his barely achieved surface calm. "The ghost has a body. As requested, I made a copy of the autopsy report and added a full description."

"Thanks." Her fingers crumpled the yellow file folder and, stepping backward, she closed the door between

them once again. Acutely aware of the moment he
lingered, when she finally heard him walk away and
go into his own condo, she sagged back against the
carved cedar. "So much for the romance writer defense." Old instincts told her to follow and patch
things up. New instincts told her to follow and destroy him.

Leaning on the door, she breathed deeply until his
scent had been thoroughly mixed with the nonthreatening, expensive potpourri scent of the apartment.
"This is really starting to piss me off. Nothing runs
my life like this. Nothing!" Returning to the desk, she
slapped the creased file folder down on the polished
wood. "I am going to beat this . . ."

She trapped the tag behind her teeth. Under the
circumstances, adding "if it kills me" seemed a little
too much like tempting fate.

Down the hall, Henry stood staring out at the West
End, rubbing his throbbing temples. It could have
been much worse—he'd expected it to have been
much worse. Neither of them had actually attacked,
and their conversation, while short, had been essentially civil. It was beginning to look as though Vicki
had been right all along. Perhaps the old rules could
be changed.

After all, coyotes had been solitary hunters for centuries and *they* were learning to hunt in packs. One
corner of his mouth quirked up as he remembered a
recent news report of coyotes eating household pets
in North Vancouver.

"On second thought, perhaps that's not the most
flattering of comparisons," he murmured to the night.

Vicki's strength had surprised him, although he supposed it shouldn't—her strength came from who she
was, not what. After he worked past the jealousy, he
found a tenuous faith in that strength beginning to
push aside his expectations, beginning to allow him to
have faith in himself.

The desire to throw her out of his territory in bleeding chunks persisted, but, for the first time, he realized the feeling didn't necessarily have to be acted upon.

Suddenly hopeful, he headed for the shower to wash off the lingering stink of the hospital.

"Mike, wake up. We need to talk before sunrise." Only experience allowed her to translate his mumbled response as "I'm awake," but since his eyes remained closed and his breathing had barely changed, she chose not to believe it.

Rather than use borrowed bedding, he'd rolled his sleeping bag out in the center of the king-sized bed but hadn't bothered to zip it up. Kneeling by his side, Vicki reached through the gap and wrapped her fingers around the warmest part of his anatomy.

"Jesus H. Christ, Vicki! Your hands are freezing!"

She grinned, having jerked back too quickly for his wild swing to connect. "*Now* you're awake."

"No shit." Squinting past her, he managed to focus on the clock beside the bed. "4:03. That's just great. Whatever we need to talk about had better be fucking important."

"You actually heard me say we needed to talk?"

"I told you I was awake." He yawned and dragged in another pillow to prop up his head. "So what is it?"

"If it's *our* case, then *we* should discuss it."

"*You* couldn't have left *me* a note?"

"What, and let you sleep?" Picking up the file folder from the end of the bed, she crossed her legs and started to read. "Henry's ghost was a male Caucasian between twenty and twenty-five, a smoker who probably died of a beating he'd received sometime before he went into the water, who'd had a kidney surgically removed within the last month which was not, by the way, what killed him. After death, his hands, wrists, and about two inches of forearm were removed, probably with an ax. His body was later found in Vancouver Harbor." She frowned down at the photocopy of the autopsy pictures. "We can assume, since he's still lying unnamed in the morgue, the police scanned his picture into the system and didn't find a match. At this point, there're three things they should be doing."

Brows raised at her phrasing—he'd just bet the Vancouver police would love to hear what they *should* be doing—he indicated she should continue.

"They should be showing the photographs around at different hospitals, hoping someone can ID him from the kidney perspective."

"And I'm sure they've thought of that," Celluci muttered. "Can't be a lot of places around that take out kidneys."

"Depends on what you're calling *around*," Vicki reminded him. "This guy could've been anywhere in the world just hours before he came to Vancouver and got killed." Grinning, she smacked him on the chest with the file folder. "Fortunately, we know something the police don't. The body was naked when they pulled it out of the water, but according to Henry's description, his ghost is wearing a T-shirt advertising a local band. We can ignore everything outside this immediate area."

"Then shouldn't we tell the police this guy's local? In case you've forgotten, withholding evidence is a crime."

"Okay. Let's tell them." She mimed dialing a phone. "Hello? Violent crimes? You know that handless John Doe you've got in the morgue? Well, he's local. How do I know? His ghost is appearing to this vampire friend of mine, and he identified a T-shirt." Hanging up an imaginary receiver, she snorted. "I don't think so. Anyway, they should also be investigating this tattoo." She passed over a page of photocopied pictures.

He sighed, turned on a light, and studied the collection. "He's pretty beat up. Henry ID from the tattoo?"

"I didn't ask."

Since her tone suggested he not ask why, he merely handed back the page. "Looks like a street job. Not much to go after. And thing three?"

"They should be checking out the gang connection."

"The what?"

"Well, why do *you* think they took off his hands?"

Celluci shrugged. "Somewhere his prints are on file."

"Then so's his picture."

"Not looking like that it isn't." He fanned the photocopies. "The computer isn't going to spit out a match to a face like that and looking through mug shots takes so much time no one has that it becomes real *low* priority."

"*I* think they took off his hands because they wanted to use them."

"Dead man's prints?"

"It's a possibility. And organized crime ties into your organ-legging theory."

"Hey! It's not my theory," he protested. "I just repeated what I heard on that cable show."

"It adds up, Mike. Organized crime's always looking for new ways to make a buck. They provide bodies so that the rich can buy organs for transplant, then, in their own warped version of reduce, reuse, and recycle, they use the hands to print weapons for hits. It even explains why the body was found in the harbor. The Port Authority is fully unionized, and unions have always had ties to organized crime."

"What? When Jimmy Hoffa disappeared, he moved to Vancouver?" Celluci tossed the papers down on the bed and jerked both hands back through his hair. "You're really reaching, Vicki."

"All right, forget the unions. But I still say the simplest explanation is usually the right explanation."

"You think that's a simple explanation?" he asked, the incredulous tone only slightly exaggerated. "And in case you haven't noticed, there's only been one body. Not many bucks made there."

"There's only been one body *found*. Either they're just getting started and their disposal's still a bit sloppy, or this one got caught in the wrong current. Either way, no one's going to set up something so complicated for just one kidney."

"If the kidney has anything to do with the murder and isn't just a coincidence. You remember those, don't you Vicki?"

She ignored him. "Besides, we have to start somewhere, and God knows, we've got bugger all else to go on. I'll look into the gang aspect tomorrow night. Given the recent rise in Chinese immigrants, odds are good there's a triad presence at the very least."

"Unfortunately, I can't argue with that . . ."

Her mouth made a sarcastic moue. "Poor baby."

". . . but I think perhaps if all this is what the police *should* be doing, maybe we should leave it to the police. You know as well as I do, that the last thing the investigating officers are going to want is some out-of-town PI—and an out-of-town cop on vacation"—he added hurriedly when her eyes started to silver—"butting in where they don't belong and screwing up the case."

"Normally, I'd agree with you." She frowned at his expression of patent disbelief. "I would. Unfortunately, Henry's ghost seems pretty specific about Henry avenging him, so we have to find the murderer before the police do or Henry could be playing twenty questions with the dead for eternity."

"I'm willing to risk it," Celluci snorted, rather enjoying the possibility of Henry Fitzroy backed into a corner.

"I'm not."

And that was that.

"So why should a ghost care who avenges him?"

"How the hell should I know?"

"I won't allow Henry to play vampire vigilante."

"No one's asking you to."

"It's too early in the morning for that argument." He half-covered a yawn. "But we'll have it, I promise. Hell's going to freeze over before I let Henry take the law into his own hands."

"Again?" Vicki asked dryly.

"Just because he's done it before, doesn't make it right." Prodded by his conscience, Celluci shifted uncomfortably in place. The lines between justice and

the law had a tendency to blur around Henry
Fitzroy—he didn't like it, but so far he'd done absolutely nothing to stop it. *Where,* he wondered, *do I
draw the new line?*

Sighing deeply, he peered up at Vicki, wishing she'd
move into the circle of the light so he could see her
expression instead of just the pale oval of her face. "I
take it that I'm to run a few daylight errands for you?"

She nodded, one finger tracing lazy circles in his
chest hair. "I want you to ask that cable interviewer
why she thinks it's organ-legging. What's she basing
her theory on? Maybe she knows something, or has
heard something . . ."

"Or maybe she's making it up as she goes along."

"Maybe. And you're right . . ." She smacked him
as he recoiled in pretend shock. ". . . the missing kidney could be coincidence, but I'd still like to hear her
reasons for bringing it up."

"And if her reasons had more to do with ratings
than facts?"

"Then we still have the gang angle to work on."

The gleam in her eyes evoked another deep sigh.
"You're looking forward to doing some shit-
disturbing, aren't you?"

"Don't be ridiculous."

"You're still a lousy liar, Vicki." Reaching out, he
enclosed her hand in his. "Try to remember you're
immortal, not invulnerable."

Vicki leaned forward and covered his mouth with
hers. A few heated moments later, she pulled back
just enough for speech. "I'll be careful if you'll admit
my theory might be valid."

"You know me, I always keep an open mind."

She flicked his lips with her tongue. "If you weren't
such a good liar, I might even believe you."

The alarm went off at 5:00. Ronald Swanson reached
up to slap it off before he remembered it wasn't bothering anyone but him. Sinking back against his pillows,
he smoothed nonexistent wrinkles out of the far side

of the big bed and thought about the phone call he was about to make.

Basic groundwork had been laid for months. Details had been worked out by a trusted employee back east last night. This morning, he would close the deal.

It would probably be safer to distance himself from that as well as from the donors, but he couldn't. A personal touch, his thumb never leaving the pulse of the company, had made him an obscene amount of money, and successful habits were hard to break.

"If it ain't broke, don't fix it," he muttered, throwing back the single blanket and swinging his legs out of bed. His feet imprinting the plush carpet with each step, he strode into the en suite bathroom, habit closing the door behind him before he switched on the light.

In the dark, empty bedroom, the clock said 5:03.

"Tony? It's Mike Celluci. I didn't wake you up, did I?"

Tony blinked blearily at the clock on the bookshelf and dragged himself up against the back of the sofa bed. "Yeah. You did. It's only eight. What's up?"

"Only eight." The repetition arrived complete with an implied and weary, *kids.* "Aren't you working today?"

"Yeah, but not till ten." He yawned and scratched at the near stubble covering his head. "I got lots of time."

"Good. I need to know the channel of the cable show I was watching yesterday."

"Cable show?" Staring across the den at the multipane window partially hidden behind hanging plants, he got lost in an attempt to figure out if the ripples were in the glass or in his vision.

"It was on yesterday evening before Henry came home. Patricia Chou was interviewing a businessman named Swanson about kidneys."

"Oh, yeah." Beginning to wake up, he decided the ripples were in the glass. "So?"

Celluci's voice came slowly and deliberately over the phone line. "What channel was it?"

"The number?"

"No, the name, Tony."

Tony yawned again, suddenly remembering why he'd never liked Detective-Sergeant Celluci very much. "I think it's called The Community Network. Anything else? You like want me to make an appointment for you?"

"No, thanks; but keep your ears open today. If, as Vicki's current theory insists, there's a gang actually organ-legging . . ." His tone made it clear he considered that highly unlikely. ". . . there'll be a buzz of some kind on the street."

"Sure, but I'll be spending eight hours in a video store, and the only buzz I'm likely to hear today is while I'm rewinding weekend tapes returned by inconsiderate assholes who can't read the contracts they signed."

"You've got to get there and get home. And you've got to eat lunch. Vicki says you're the best, Tony. If there's a buzz out there, you'll hear it."

Cheeks hot, Tony mumbled an agreement.

"My apologies to your hosts if I woke them as well."

Dropping the receiver back on the cradle, Tony stretched and wished he could erase his personal tapes as easily as the ones at the store. In spite of how far he'd come, some reactions still seemed impossible to control. "I get a pat on the head and I'm just like a fucking stray dog." He sighed, drew in a lungful of air redolent with the aroma of freshly brewed hazelnut cream coffee, and decided he might as well get up since either Gerry or John was obviously in the kitchen. Pulling on a T-shirt to go with the boxer shorts he'd slept in, he realized he was going to enjoy having someone to share breakfast with.

Especially since he wasn't on the menu.

The Community Network was in the basement of a three-story, sloped-roof building on the corner of Tenth

Avenue and Yukon Street just in back of City Hall. Which made a certain amount of sense, Celluci figured as he cruised slowly along the block looking for parking, since most of their business seemed to be concerned with broadcasting city government.

"Might as well stay close to the source," he muttered, adding, "Lousy son of a bitch," through clenched teeth as a smaller and infinitely more maneuverable vehicle nipped in front of him, taking the only empty spot he'd seen. While not as kamikaze as drivers in Montreal, Vancouver drivers were anything but laid back. Although he hated to do it, he ended up leaving the van in a municipal lot and only cheered up when he remembered that Henry'd be paying the bill.

Nine steps down, more at half-ground than basement, The Community Network reception area had been painted a neutral cream and then covered in flyers, memos, messages, and posters of every description. The woman at the desk had four pencils shoved through her hair just above the elastic securing a strawberry-blonde ponytail and was taking notes with a fifth. It sounded as though she was dealing with a scheduling conflict, and her end of the phone conversation grew less polite and more emphatic as the call progressed. From what he could hear, Celluci had to admire the amount of control she managed to maintain.

"So, bottom line, what you're saying is that the councillor won't have time for an interview until the current session is over?" Her notes disappeared behind heavy black cross-hatching. "But after the session is over, we won't need to speak with the councillor about the zoning change because it'll be over, too. Well, yes, I'd appreciate it if you'd get back to me." The receiver went back into its cradle with a little more force than necessary. "You sanctimonious little kiss-ass."

Taking a deep breath, she looked up, smiled broadly at Celluci, and said, "I don't suppose you'd consider forgetting you heard that?"

He returned the smile with a deliberately charming one of his own. "Heard what?"

"Thank you. Now then, what can we do for *you?*"

"I'm here to speak to Patricia Chou." When her expression started to change, he continued quickly. "My name's Michael Celluci. I called earlier."

"That's right, she mentioned you." Standing, she held out her hand. "I'm Amanda Beman. Her producer."

She had a grip that reminded him of Vicki's— Vicki's before she gained the unwelcome ability to break bones. "Do producers usually work reception?"

"Are you kidding? With our budget, I also work the board and empty the wastebaskets. Come on." Pencils quivering, she jerked her head toward a door adorned with only two sheets of paper. Given the coverage on the surrounding walls, it was essentially bare. The upper piece read: *If there's no one at the desk, please ring the bell.* The sign underneath it declared, in pale green letters on a dark green background: BELL OUT OF ORDER. PLEASE KNOCK.

"We're a lot busier later in the day," Amanda explained as she led the way along an empty corridor. "Our morning programming's all educational tapes from UBC, so we operate with a bare minimum of staff until about noon." She shot him a wry glance. "And little more after that."

"Yet Ms. Chou was here first thing."

"She'll be here last thing, too. Our little Patricia would like to be Geraldo Rivera when she grows up."

"And you were here . . ."

"I am always here." Stopping in front of an unmarked steel door, she raised a hand and lowered her voice. "You must have been pretty persuasive to get Patricia to talk to you at this hour, and you look like you can handle yourself, but I couldn't live with my conscience if I didn't warn you about a couple of things. First, if she invites you to call her Patricia, that's exactly what she means. Patricia, never Pat. Second, nothing you tell her is off the record. If she can

find a use for it, she will. Third, if she can find a use
for you, she'll use you as well, and, given that you're
not exactly hard on the eyes, it might be smart to
present a moving target." She rapped on the door and
stepped aside, motioning for Celluci to enter. "Good
luck."

"I feel like I should be carrying a whip and chair,"
he muttered reaching for the door handle.

"A cyanide pill might be more practical," Amanda
told him cheerfully. "We need her. We don't need
you. Remember, keep moving."

As the door closed behind him, he heard her humming, "Ding Dong, the Witch is Dead," then he heard
nothing at all as the heavy steel cut off all sound from
the hall. *So I can assume no one will be able to hear
me if I scream.*

The room had originally been one large cinderblock
rectangle, but bookcases had been used to divide it
into two smaller work spaces, one considerably smaller
than the other and windowless besides. Betting on
what seemed like a sure thing, he walked into the
larger of the two.

The woman working at the computer terminal
didn't acknowledge his presence in any way although
she must have heard both her producer's knock and
his entrance. Celluci got the impression that it wasn't
a deliberate slight but rather that he simply wasn't as
important as her work in progress. Marginally *more*
insulting upon consideration. After a dozen years in
police work, however, insults meant little unless ac-
companied by violent punctuation.

Hands clasped behind his back, he looked around.

Bookcases made up not only the dividing wall but
covered two of the other three and rose to the lower
edge of the windows on the third. Their contents
seemed about equally divided between books, videos
and binders with a number of framed photographs
propped up in front.

Patricia Chou accepting something from Vancouver's Mayor. Patricia Chou being congratulated by the

current Premier of British Columbia. Patricia Chou with a serenely smiling man Celluci recognized as the right-to-lifer who'd put a high velocity, 7.62-mm rifle bullet into a fifty-seven-year-old obstetrician because he objected to the doctor performing legal abortions at city hospitals. Although Ms. Chou was still smiling in that particular photograph, her expression as she gazed at the handcuffed gunman seemed to suggest she'd just squashed something unpleasant she'd found under a rock and was happy to have done it.

Detective-Sergeant Celluci personally believed the world would be a significantly better place and his job one hell of a lot easier if the victims were given the kind of coverage criminals usually got and if criminals were ignored by the press, their names and pictures never appearing outside of rap sheets and court documents. He didn't approve of giving them time on talk shows no matter how local the market.

"You're Michael Celluci." When he turned, she tossed a silken fall of midnight hair back over her shoulder and continued before he had a chance to speak. "You wanted to talk to me about yesterday's show." Her tone suggested he not waste her time.

Studying her face, Celluci discovered what the cameras had camouflaged; she was young. Not long out of university. Not long enough for the sharp edges of ambition, intellect, and ego to have been dulled by the world.

A lot like Vicki when they first met.

Been there. Done that. Got the scars. "As I said on the phone, Ms. Chou, I have a friend who wants to know why you think the body found in Vancouver Harbor was an organ-legging victim."

"And as I said on the phone, I'd like to know why your friend wants to know why."

"My friend thinks much the same thing you do."

"Your friend is the only other person in the city who does. You don't."

Celluci shrugged, the gesture carefully neutral. "I try to keep an open mind."

"An open mind?" The repetition fell barely to one side of mockery. "Why doesn't your friend want to talk to me? Why send you?"

"She was busy."

"Busy," she repeated, her eyes narrowing. Leaning back in her chair, she stared at him for a long moment; then, one ebony brow lifted. "You're not with the local police department, are you?"

He matched her brow for brow, beginning to regret giving her his real name. "What makes you think I'm with any police department."

"First, your gaze is constantly going flick, flick, flick around the room. Second, in spite of styles, your cuffs are loose enough to áccess an ankle holster. Third, although it's less obvious in person, over the phone your voice mannerisms are pure law enforcement. Forth, you're not local or you would have identified yourself earlier." Her gaze grew fiercely speculative, almost sharklike. "You're federal, aren't you? This is bigger than I thought, isn't it? Maybe even international."

Her ambition burned so brightly he could almost feel the heat. If Tony's theory was correct, and Patricia Chou was looking for a story big enough to get her a network show, she seemed to believe—for reasons unclear to Celluci at the moment—that this was the story. Although who the hell she thought he was, he had no idea.

"If I tell you what *your friend* wants to know," she continued, leaning forward, eyes blazing, "I get exclusive rights to this story when it breaks."

Celluci sighed. "Ms. Chou, there might not be a story."

"Exclusive rights," she repeated with no room for negotiation.

He knew when to surrender—especially when it didn't make a damned bit of difference to him. In his opinion, there was as much chance of the John Doe in Vancouver Harbor having been killed by organleggers as there was of Henry Fitzroy winning the

Governor General's Award for fiction. "All right. The story's yours." Raising a cautioning hand, he added, "As soon as there is a story."

She nodded and sat back. "So you want to know why I think that missing kidney is the reason for the young man's murder. Simple, there're a lot of people who need them, giving an organ-legger a large database to chose their buyer from—a database that's fairly easily tracked given that every one of them is on dialysis."

"Wait a minute." An uplifted hand cut her off. "You said buyers."

"They're hardly going to give them away, Mr. Celluci. And, considering that it can lead to infections, stroke, heart attacks, and peritonitis, I think I can safely say dialysis sucks. I'm sure they could find people willing to pay big bucks to get off it. What's more, because kidney transplants have a 98% success rate, you can pretty much guarantee your product. Which is why they only took a kidney and not the heart and lungs and corneas and all the other things people so desperately need. The left kidney—the one missing from the body—is the one most often used for transplant purposes. Also, it's one of the easiest transplants to perform, giving you a larger database of doctors to choose from, and the more doctors you have, the better the odds you'll find one who can be corrupted."

"That's two completely different computer systems to access; it can't be that easy."

"These are the '90s, Mr. Celluci. Twelve-year-olds are hacking into international defense systems every day."

Unfortunately, he couldn't argue with that. "The newspaper reported that the surgery to remove the kidney was well on the way to being healed."

She picked up a pencil and bounced the eraser end against her desk. "Your point?"

"Why do you think they kept him alive for so long? Why not just take the kidney and let him die?"

"I expect that they kept him alive long enough to

be certain that the buyer's body didn't reject the kidney. If it did, well, with him still around, they'd have a spare and could try again."

"So why remove the hands?"

"Fingerprints." Her tone added a silent: *Don't play dumb with me.* "An identity makes it much easier for the police to gather the information that could lead to the person or persons responsible."

"And what does Mr. Swanson have to do with it?"

"Swanson was just the mouthpiece of the BC Transplant Society. I was trying to get someone in a perceived position of expertise to admit the possibility."

Ms. Chou apparently had an answer for everything, but that was by no means a complete answer. She reminded him more of Vicki every second. "And?"

She leaned a little forward, and her teeth showed between parted lips. "And I've decided I don't like him. When I was researching him for that interview, I discovered that not only is he filthy rich but he has absolutely no bad habits. He works very hard, he gives a lot of money away, and that's it."

"The rich aren't allowed to be nice, hardworking people?"

"Not these days. Now, I'm not saying he's a part of this organ-legging thing, but he certainly has, as you people would say, motive and opportunity." She raised one emphatic finger after another. "His wife died of kidney failure waiting for a transplant. He has more money than most governments, and with enough money you have the opportunity to do everything."

"He also seems to think this organ-legging thing isn't possible. His arguments made a great deal of sense."

She sat back and waved a dismissive hand. "They would, wouldn't they? Did you know he funded a private clinic where people in the last stages of renal failure can wait for a kidney?"

Celluci spent a moment hoping she'd never decide she disliked *him.* "No, I didn't. I take it the police found your theories less than helpful?"

Her lips curled into a sneer. "The police as much as accused me of sensationalizing an urban myth for the sake of personal gain."

How could they possibly have come up with that idea? Celluci asked himself dryly. "You've a lot of conjecture, Ms. Chou, but no facts."

"And what does your friend have?"

He half smiled, acknowledging the hit. "More conjecture. But she also says that since we have bugger-all else, we have to start somewhere. Thanks for your time." Holding out his hand, he added, "The moment we get a fact, I'll let you know."

Her hand disappeared in his and yet gave the impression that she was fully in charge of the gesture. Standing, she was a great deal shorter than her personality suggested. When she smiled, she showed enough teeth to remind him that many of the people he'd run into over the last couple of years weren't exactly human. "See that you do."

It was pleasantly enough said, but a threat for all of that. *Dick me around, and you'll be the story. It won't be fun.*

Under other circumstances, he might have reacted differently, but short women made him vaguely uncomfortable, so he merely showed himself out—counting on his fingers in the corridor to make sure he'd gotten them all back.

A few moments later, he was sitting in the van going over what he had.

A handless body short one surgically removed kidney had been found in Vancouver Harbor.

Patricia Chou's information on why the kidney could have gone to an illegal transplant was entirely plausible even if her dislike of Ronald Swanson was not.

Organized crime did have a history of using dead men's prints, which would explain the missing hands. And Vicki was right about organized crime always looking for a new way to make a buck. Some sort of criminal body shop made more sense than a well-respected, socially conscious businessman selling used organs like they were high-priced radios ripped out of parked cars.

According to Patricia Chou, there *was* a market out there for kidneys.

Resting his forehead against the top curve of the steering wheel, Celluci closed his eyes. *Great, now they've got me beginning to believe it. . . .*

Six

"Keep your ears open . . ."

Tony stuffed another cartridge in the rewinder with more emphasis than was absolutely necessary. So far he'd overheard a totally unbelievable excuse about a destroyed tape, a conversation that could be used to script a bad made-for-TV movie, and three long-winded reviews from a retired office machinery sales-man who expressed opinions on his weekend rentals every Monday. Not exactly the buzz on the street.

"Vicki says you're the best . . ."

"Yeah, right," he muttered, staring out the window. While he wasn't stupid enough to wish himself back into cold and hunger and fear, he couldn't help feeling cut off from the one thing he did well.

On the other side of Robeson, two teenagers leaned against a bank building soaking up the sun. One was thin and black. The other, thin and white. Skin color their only visible difference. They both wore filthy army pants, old scuffed Doc Martens, and sleeveless black T-shirts—one faced with a red peace symbol, the other with an ivory skull. Steel rings glinted in both noses above moving mouths.

Eyes narrowed in irritation—lipreading was *not* as easy as it looked on TV—Tony started to ad-lib the words he couldn't hear. "You know about that gang selling organs? Yeah, man, like I'm droppin' off a kid-ney tomorrow."

"What the hell are you talkin' about, Foster?"

Tony jumped and whirled to face his boss, who'd returned, unnoticed, from the store room. Squelching the lingering instinctive street response to growl, *"None of your business,"* he muttered. "Nothing."

The older man shook his head and handed him a pile of boxes to reshelve. "I've said it before, and I'll say it again: you're a weird one. Get back to work."

"Vicki says you're the best . . ."

It wasn't so much that he was letting Vicki down, more that he'd lost a part of himself.

Scooping up the boxes, he came around the end of the counter just as one of the teenagers across the street held out his hand to the other. It was such an unusual gesture that it caught his attention and he stopped for a moment to watch. They shook hands formally, uncomfortably, then moved apart. As one of them turned to face the store, the ivory skull smiled.

Tony rubbed at his eyes with his free hand and looked again. It was a T-shirt, old and faded and nothing more.

Of course the skull was smiling, you idiot. Skulls always smile. Tony Foster, you have been hanging around with vampires too long. But a line of sweat dribbled icy cold down the center of his back, and the hand that set the video boxes on the shelves was shaking.

"You got my money?"

The driver's smile was so nonthreatening it was almost inane. "It's in the bag."

The bag had been printed with a cheap rip-off of the Vancouver Grizzlies logo. There were at least a million of them around the city. After a brief struggle with a zipper that seemed intent on snagging, it opened to show several packets of worn tens and twenties.

"All right!" Considering how many dreams it held, the bag weighed next to nothing as it lifted off the floor. "Hey? What the fuck are you grinning about?"

The driver's smile broadened as he guided the dark

sedan onto the Lion's Gate Bridge heading for North Vancouver. "I'm just happy when someone gets off the streets."

Thin arms tightened around the bag. "Yeah, like you're a real fucking Good Samaritan." He scowled at the dashboard. "Hey, weren't you in a gray car before?"

"You don't think I'm using my own car for this, do you?" The tone was mocking, superior.

"No. Guess not."

They drove in silence along the North Shore, the only sound the quiet hum of the air-conditioner fan. When the car turned off Mt. Seymour Parkway onto Mt. Seymour Road, the teenager in the passenger seat shifted nervously. "Shouldn't I be, like, blindfolded or something?"

"Why?"

"So I can't, you know, tell anyone about this."

"Tell who?" the driver asked quietly.

"No one, man. Fuck . . ." Contrary to romantic belief, those who lived on the street actually learned very little about life. The one and only lesson the survivors learned was how to survive. If they failed to learn it, then by definition they were just another sad statistic. The boy in the car figured himself for a survivor. He knew a threat when he heard one. There was suddenly more to the gorilla behind the wheel than those big, friendly doggy eyes.

Palms leaving damp prints on the cheap nylon bag, he stared unfocused through the tinted windshield and built a pleasant fantasy of beating the driver's smug, self-satisfied face in. His eyes widened a little as they passed a security gate and turned onto a private road. They widened further as the clinic came into view.

"This don't look like no hospital."

"That's right." A sign by the edge of the drive read STAFF ONLY. "Our clients don't like to think they're in a hospital, and they pay big bucks to maintain the illusion they aren't."

"Fuck, what kind of clients you got?"

The driver smiled. "Rich ones."

Rich ones. His right hand patted the rectangular bulges stretching the side of the bag. Rich ones like him.

Standard police procedure maintained that a personal visit elicited more information than a phone call. Not only were facial expressions harder to fake, but the minutiae of surrounding environmental clues were often invaluable. As Mike Celluci pushed open the door leading to the offices of the British Columbia Transplant Society, he recognized that no aspect of this "case" resembled standard police procedure, but when it came right down to it, he didn't have anything else to do.

"Can I help you?" The woman behind the reception desk at the BC Transplant Society fixed him with the steely-eyed, no-nonsense gaze of the professional volunteer. Celluci felt as though he were being assessed for potential usefulness and could almost hear her thinking: *How nice, muscle. I'm sure we have something around that needs moving.*

"Is Ronald Swanson in?"

Her eyes narrowed. "Is this about that dreadful woman?"

"If you mean the cable interview . . . ?"

"Look, you're the fourteenth person who's asked about it since I came in—although the other thirteen were satisfied with a phone call." Two spots of color blazed through the powder on her cheeks. "I'll tell you the same thing I told them; there is absolutely no truth to anything Patricia Chou said, and she should be prosecuted for spreading such a horrible, horrible story. Donated organs go to the most needy person on the list. They are not ever sold to the highest bidder. Ever."

Somewhat taken aback, Celluci spread his hands and arranged his features into his best information-eliciting expression. "Not within the system, no, but if someone were to circumvent . . ."

"That doesn't happen."

"But it could."

"I believe Mr. Swanson made it perfectly clear that such a horrific concept is impossible."

"No, ma'am. He merely said it would be difficult and expensive. Which is why I wanted to speak with him." He'd been half tempted to wander into one of the rougher sections of the city and see if he could find some gang action, but upon reflection decided he'd rather live a little longer. While he had no doubt he'd survive the gangs, Vicki'd kill him for taking the risk.

Her nostrils pinched shut, the receptionist laid both hands on the desk and leaned forward. "We are extremely fortunate that a man of Mr. Swanson's wealth and social standing is willing to do so much work for the society, but given the demands on his time, he does not spend his days here. If you want to speak with him, you'll have to call his office. You'll find Swanson Realty in the Yellow Pages."

It was as efficient a dismissal as if she'd hung up on him. Thanking her for her time, Celluci turned and left the office.

I pity the fifteenth caller, he thought as he waited for the elevator.

Swanson Realty actually was in the book, and from the size of the accompanying ad, Ronald Swanson was indeed doing very well for himself. Unfortunately, there was no way a company that size would put through a call to the owner unless the caller identified himself as a homicide detective. Too bad he was just a guy on vacation.

Frowning, Celluci let the phone book fall back into its plastic case and left the booth. For the first time, he had a good idea of how Vicki'd felt when her deteriorating eyesight pushed her off the force. He didn't much like the feeling.

Fortunately, it wasn't important he speak to Ronald Swanson. He'd mostly wanted the meeting for his own peace of mind. Since the man had obviously given some thought to the impossibility of setting up an organ-legging operation, Celluci'd hoped he could get him to expand on his reasoning.

Patricia Chou had almost convinced him Vicki was right about the organ-legging, and that meant—Ms. Chou's personal vendetta aside—Swanson was as much a suspect as the faceless crime lords of Vancouver.

But one body, one kidney, wasn't going to generate much in the way of profit.

So, somewhere, there had to be more bodies.

Or there were going to be more bodies.

He didn't much like either option.

The room was small with a single window up near the ceiling. The bottom four feet of the walls were a soft pink and so was the blanket on the bed. He guessed it was supposed to be soothing, but it made him think of Pepto Bismol and he didn't much like it.

He didn't much like the pajamas either, but the driver had made it perfectly clear he was expected to shower, then put them on.

At least the son of a bitch hadn't stayed to watch.

He locked the bathroom door behind him before even unlacing his boots and got in and out of the shower as fast as he could, unable to cope with an extended vulnerability. Unfortunately, the pajamas left him feeling little safer.

At least they don't have a hole in the front for my dick to fall out of.

Bag of money clutched tight against his side, he tried the exit. Locked. But he'd expected that. They wouldn't want him roaming around bothering their rich patients.

When the handle began to turn under his fingers, he hurriedly released it and backed toward the bed, heart pounding. He relaxed only slightly when the familiar form of the doctor entered the room pushing a stainless steel cart.

"Good afternoon, Doug. Are you comfortable?"

" 'S okay. What's that for?" He eyed the equipment laid out on the top shelf suspiciously.

"Donor-specific blood transfusions enhance graft survival. So . . ." She ripped open a cotton swab with brutal efficiency. ". . . I'm going to need to take some blood."

Later, when it was over and he was lying in bed feeling weak and dizzy, his fingers plucked at the bag searching for reassurance. *It wouldn't be so bad,* he thought, refusing to acknowledge the fear that closed his throat and lay cold and clammy against his skin, *if I could only see out the window. . . .*

Jerked out of sleep, Celluci scrambled across the king-sized bed toward the ringing phone. The clock beside it said 7:04 P.M. Forty minutes to sunset. He'd lain down at three for a half-hour nap but was obviously more tired than he thought. The dainty, ladylike receiver almost disappeared in his hand, but eventually he got the right end to his ear. A quick glance at the call display showed him a familiar number. "What've you got for me, Dave?"

On the other end of the line, his partner, Detective-Sergeant Dave Graham, sighed deeply. "I'm fine, Mike. How are you? I got the names and addresses you wanted."

"Thanks. How come you're calling from home?"

"Maybe I was on my way out of the office when you called. Maybe pulling these things off the system took a little time and I wanted to spend what was left of the evening with my family. Maybe I thought you didn't want the whole office wondering why you were suddenly interested in Vancouver gangs and real estate salesmen. You choose."

Celluci grinned. "What were those options again?"

"Fuck you, too, buddy. Got a pencil handy?"

"Hang on." He hit the hold button and headed into the kitchen, where he'd seen a pad and a jar of pens beside an extremely expensive replica of an old-fashioned wall phone. "Okay. Go ahead."

"You'll notice I'm not asking why you want these things."

"And I appreciate that, Dave."

"I mean, I'm willing to believe that you're just making some exciting vacation plans and are not being drawn into one of Vicki's weirdo, made-for-Fox-TV investigations."

"Thanks, Dave."

"Yeah, well, I'm gullible that way. Try not to get yourself killed."

The first half of the list, from the firmly entrenched to the up-and-coming, was longer than he'd thought it would be. There was nothing about Ronald Swanson at all. The man didn't have so much as an outstanding parking ticket.

Henry woke angry, but that was to be expected as Vicki's scent—the scent of an intruder, a competing predator—still clung to the bedroom. He'd been lying with his upper lip half lifted in a snarl, and it took him a moment to peel the flesh off air-dried teeth.

"I bet Brad Pitt never has this problem," he muttered, reaching for the light.

The handless ghost waited impatiently at the end of the bed. The body in the morgue had been less disturbing—it was only dead. This spirit had moved beyond death, and shadows clung to it. *Eldritch shadows,* Henry found himself thinking and shook his head to dislodge the thought. *Oh, that's just what I need—now I'm channeling adjectives from H.P. Lovecraft.*

The ghost began to lift its mutilated arms, but before it could open its mouth to scream, Henry snarled, "That was you at the morgue, wasn't it?"

Arms still uplifted, its expression bordered on petulance as it disappeared.

Alone again, Henry swung his legs out of bed; then, as they touched the carpet, he paused. The lingering scent of a second vampire had been acknowledged if not dealt with. The ghost had been banished for one more sunset. And yet, an uneasiness remained. There was something more.

Or more precisely, something less.

Tony.

Although he could hear the throbbing heartbeat of the surrounding city, no bloodsong called from within the limits of his sanctuary. With so many other things there, Tony's absence stood out in sharp relief.

Henry stared at his reflection and realized it felt surprisingly good to be alone.

"What're you looking so excited about?"

"Me? Nothing." With the denial the gleam of anticipation in Vicki's eyes switched off.

Celluci frowned. The things she thought she had to hide from him were never good—in fact, most of the time they were *very* not good. He watched her carefully as she crossed the living room, pulled out a slat-backed chair, and straddled it but could see nothing that might give him any explanations. "That chair's a Stickley," he grunted as she tipped it forward on two legs and reached across the table for his notes. "Try not to break it."

"Chill, Michael. I don't know why you think you can't trust me with expensive furniture. What've you got?"

He pushed a sheet of paper toward her groping fingers. "The reasons Ms. Chou thinks the missing kidney is our motive."

Vicki scanned the familiar handwriting. "She's pretty convincing."

"I didn't know you needed convincing." Before she could answer, he handed her another page. "The reasons Mr. Ronald Swanson thinks it's impractical."

"You spoke to him?"

"No. It's what I remembered from the cable program."

"If Swanson works for the transplant programs, it's in his best interest to squash this kind of speculation, so his is not exactly an unbiased opinion."

"It's in Ms. Chou's best interest to promote scandal. Not exactly an unbiased opinion either."

"But it's the only possible motive we've got and so should be investigated."

"What about a simple gangland killing, take the hands to use later?"

"And leave the kidney out of it?" She flashed him a serene and totally false smile as she picked up a pencil and a blank piece of paper. "We have what; a dead body missing both hands and a kidney. We have where; thanks to Henry's ghost's wardrobe which indicates he's local. We have why . . ."

"We have a potential why," Celluci broke in.

"Fine. A potential why; missing kidney equals organs for profit. So . . ." Flicking the pencil into the air, she watched it rise toward the ceiling, then caught it as it tumbled down. "Next on the list, who. Our only clue is the missing hands, missing hands often mean gangs who are always looking for new profit and who can certainly find and finance crooked hackers, crooked doctors, and loyal thugs." The gleam of anticipation had returned. "I think that takes care of your Mr. Swanson's objections."

"And what about Mr. Swanson himself?"

"Why is Mr. Swanson chopping off the hands?"

"I hate it when you answer a question with a question," Celluci growled.

"I know. There're two reasons I can think of for the killer to remove the hands. One, the prints are on record, and dumping the hands will hide the identity—a belief which shows an appalling lack of knowledge of modern police forensics. If that body had a record, he'd have been identified by now. Or, two, the prints aren't on record and are useful because of that. Which brings us back to the gangs. We can have this sucker solved by morning."

"How?"

"I find out who's running the top gangs in this fair city." Her teeth showed, too long and too white. "And I ask them a few questions. The boss men always know what the other gangs are up to—that's how they stay the boss."

Celluci had a sudden vision of a great deal of blood spilled over very expensive suits. "How are you going to find out who the top men are?"

"I'll ask a few *questions* farther down the ladder."

There were certain aspects of Vicki's new nature he found so difficult to understand that he didn't ever bother making the attempt. This wasn't one of them. "You're looking forward to this, aren't you?"

"And why shouldn't I be?" Her tone was as much defensive as challenging. "You have no idea of how hard it is to always hold back. To be less than you're capable of being!"

"What? Less violent?" He leaned toward her, forearms flat on the table, biceps straining against the fabric of his golf shirt. "I hate to burst your bubble, Vicki, but we've all got to live with that. It's the price we pay for civilization."

"Give it up, Celluci." She leaned forward as well. "You can stop being so god-damned holier than fucking thou! You can't possibly feel sorry for the type of lowlife I'm going to be . . ." As his eyes narrowed, she paused for a heartbeat. ". . . dealing with. What's that?" She stared suspiciously at the list he held out to her.

"It's an easier way. I had Dave pull the names and addresses of the people you want off the computer."

"Oh." The paper drooped between thumb and forefinger.

If he'd been willing to risk pandering to her desire for mayhem, he'd have reminded her that she still had to get to those people through what would no doubt be tight security. As he neither wanted to remind her of her potential for violence nor himself of her potential danger, he said neutrally. "There're a lot of names for one night. Why don't you split them with Henry?"

"Henry?" Her eyes silvered. "No. No Henry. This is *my* hunt! Mine!"

"As much as I hate to say this, he's not totally incompetent. He's even done this kind of stuff for you before."

"Before," Vicki reminded him, the last syllable more growl than spoken word.

Celluci stared at her for a few seconds then sat back, shaking his head. "So he was right."

"About what?"

"About your childish inability to work with him." In spite of her sometimes tenuous control of what she'd become, Celluci'd always believed that Vicki would never hurt him. He'd wondered occasionally, as he prodded at the limits of her new nature, if he deliberately put that belief to the test. He wondered it now as she slowly stood. She seemed taller than he knew she was. The hair on his arms lifted, and he felt his chin begin to rise, an instinctive surrender bypassing his conscious control. He forced it back down.

Eyes blazing, Vicki stepped forward, closed her hands around the chair she had been sitting in, and ripped it into kindling, one handful of wood at a time. A moment later, breathing heavily—not from the destruction but from the effort of regaining control—she snarled, "See what you made me do!"

"I made you do?" His heart beat so loudly even he could hear it. Considering how well attuned she was to that sort of sound, he was a little surprised she could hear his voice over it. "I don't think so."

"No." Her eyes were almost gray again. The silver remaining could have been a trick of the light. "I guess not." She reached across the table and brushed the curl of hair back off his face. "But you've got no right accusing me of living dangerously."

"No. I guess not." Capturing her hand, he laid his lips against the cool skin of her inner wrist, a mirror image of a position they'd held a hundred times. "Now what?"

"Now, I'm going to call Henry."

"Call?"

"Yeah. On the telephone." She pulled free of his grip and patted him lightly on both cheeks. "You're not the only one who can think of an easier way to get through this, sweet knees."

He frowned as she walked away. "Sweet knees?"

". . . suppose one of them turns out to be the man we're looking for?" Henry asked as he folded the list and slipped it into his pocket. He'd tried to sound neither sarcastic nor superior and had been, all things considered, remarkably successful at both. But then, they'd always been able to manage over the phone.

"What? You mean suppose one of your . . . subjects says: Yeah, I'm the guy. I've been selling organs all up and down the West Coast. Usually we dump 'em at sea, but that body in the harbor must have got caught in the tides?"

With an effort, he kept his smile from showing in his voice—Vicki had sounded so incredibly indignant at the mere possibility he might discover the information before she did. "Yes. Suppose one of my . . . subjects says that. If you've given me half the list, the odds are fifty-fifty."

"You don't need to tell me the odds, Henry. I may be a childish vampire . . ."

He heard Celluci protest in the background and was quite happy to have missed the earlier argument.

". . . but I have been doing this living thing a lot longer than you did, and I've certainly been an investigator one hell of a lot longer."

"I hadn't intended to suggest you hadn't."

"Oh, no, you just intended to suggest you didn't need me here at all."

Frowning slightly, he went back over the conversation and tried to determine how she'd arrived at that particular conclusion. "Vicki, I may be *able* to strong-arm crime lords, but it would never have occurred to me to do it."

"Oh."

"If I'm going to get rid of my nonblithe spirit, I do need you here."

"Oh." He heard her sigh. "I can't decide whether you're being mature or patronizing."

"Which would you prefer?"

"You know, that's a very Celluci question. I don't want you guys hanging around together any more." But he could hear the sound of her smile, so it was all right.

"I fully understand."

She snorted, a purely human sound. "You couldn't possibly. Whoever gets back first leaves a message on the other's machine."

"You don't think we should meet?" He had an unexpected memory of the pulse that beat at the base of her throat, her skin the soft, sun-kissed tan it would never be again, and missed her reply in the sudden surge of loneliness. "I'm sorry, I . . . ."

Her voice was as gentle as he'd heard it since the change. "I'm sorry, too, Henry."

"Everything all worked out?"

Her hand still resting on the phone, Vicki turned to face Celluci and shrugged. "I gave Henry every other name. He knows what we need to find out. Like you said, he's not totally incompetent."

Celluci's brows drew in at the hint of melancholy in her voice. "And the phone thing went okay?"

"No reason why it shouldn't, is there? Across the country, across the hall, it's basically the same thing."

You miss him, don't you? But that was one question he wasn't stupid enough to ask. She didn't miss Fitzroy—the undead royal bastard was still around— she missed what they'd had, and he didn't want to remind her of that because she could never, ever have it again, and while he reveled in the certainty, he had no intention of coming across as an insensitive prick.

"Need to feed?" he asked instead.

Melancholy gone, she grinned and her eyes frosted. "No, thanks, I'm dining out."

"Yeah. Right." Actually, he found the thought of her gorging on the blood of Vancouver's crime lords less problematic than her gentler meals. Those were the nights he didn't want to think about. Standing suddenly, he joined her on the way to the door. "Hang on and I'll go with you as far as the lobby. Tony's working till nine. I think I'll head over to the video store and see if he wants to join me for a bite." When both her brows rose, he sighed. "You know, eating never used to come with this many double entendres."

She'd half turned to answer him as he closed the door. By the time they became aware they weren't alone in the hall, it was too late to do anything that wouldn't seem like a retreat.

"Henry."

"Vicki."

Oh, shit. Still, they're sounding practically conversational, so maybe this won't be a complete disaster. They both wore black jeans and black T-shirts. Vicki wore sneakers and a black cotton sweater. He knew it was cotton; he'd bought it for her. Fitzroy wore desert boots and a black linen blazer. He knew it was linen; he had one just like it, which he was going to get rid of the moment he got home. Celluci'd never noticed before how much alike they looked.

It wasn't the clothes. Thousands of vampire wanna-bes all over the world dressed with more undead style than these two.

It wasn't their coloring. Although both were fair, Fitzroy's hair had more red in it and Vicki was a definite ash blonde. It said so on the box.

It was just, merely, simply, purely the way they were. They shared a *belle morte*—a deadly beauty. Celluci wasn't sure why the words came to him first in Italian; he was family-fluent only, and it wasn't a language he'd ever thought in, but somehow English—plain old workaday English—didn't seem sufficient.

And not only a deadly beauty; they also shared a complete and utter certainty in themselves and their place in the world.

Certainty, Vicki had never been short of, but her sheer, bloody-minded belief that she was as right as anyone had been refined during the moment she locked eyes with Henry Fitzroy, refined and sharpened to a razor's edge. Fitzroy, of course, had always had it. It was one of the things Celluci'd always hated. Always responded to.

His heart began to beat in time to the power that throbbed between them. That surrounded them. That surrounded him. In that hallway, at that instant, watching the two of them watch each other, he understood the declaration: *I am.*

And that is quite enough of that*!* Italian description arriving out the blue he could cope with, but blasphemy was something else again! *Forgive me, Father, for I have sinned; it's been two years since my last confession, but that's only because I've been sleeping with a vampire. Yeah. Right.*

As a musical chime shattered the silence, he lifted his right foot, put it down, and almost miraculously followed the movement with his left—walking directly through their line of sight. "I hate to break up a Kodak moment, kids, but the elevator's here."

For a heartbeat the power gained a new focus. He could feel it flaying his back, simultaneously hot and cold, and he had a brief vision of Vicki's pale fingers shredding that chair. A little amazed he was still able to move, he stepped over the threshold into the elevator and turned around. As expected, they were both staring at him. Vicki's mouth twisted up in a half smile; her sense of the ridiculous overwhelming the melodrama. Fitzroy had on his Prince of Darkness face. Celluci squared his shoulders, resisting the pull. No one survived a relationship with Vicki Nelson—alive or undead—without an equally strong sense of self and he was not going to bend the knee to Henry Fucking Fitzroy. "You coming, Vicki?"

When she nodded and stepped toward the elevator, he stepped back to give her room.

She paused, just inside, and her smile sharpened. "Coming, Henry?"

Even Celluci could hear the challenge. Hell, a deaf man in the next building could've heard the challenge. "Vicki . . ."

One pale hand rose. A prince indicating there was no need for the masses to get involved. "I don't think so. No."

"Why not? Afraid of losing your vaunted control? Too old to cope?"

"Vicki!" He might as well have saved his breath. The words were thrown back with all the finesse of a school-yard taunt and were just as impossible to ignore.

His back against the wall, with Vicki between him and the exit, Celluci watched Henry advance toward the elevator. He wanted to grab her and shake her and demand to know what the hell she thought she was doing. Except he knew. *Trust Vicki to drive her point home with a god-damned sledgehammer. I should've taken the fucking stairs. . . .*

When the doors closed, the fabric of Henry's blazer whispered against it. "Parking level one, please."

Head tilted slightly down, silvered eyes locked with shadow, Vicki pressed the button without looking at the panel.

It wasn't the elevator that lurched into motion, Celluci realized; it was his heart.

They shifted position simultaneously, too fast for a mere mortal to see them move. One moment they stood facing each other—Henry's back against the doors—the next Vicki stood to Celluci's left and Henry to his right. They continued to face each other but had gained what might be a survivable distance between them. A low, warning growl—felt, not heard—vibrated through the enclosed space and lifted every hair on Celluci's body—not a pleasant sensation. Realizing how little it would take to tip the balance into bloody chaos, he resisted the urge to scratch. *Now if we can just make it to the lobby without anyone else getting . . .*

The elevator stopped on the seventh floor.

The doors opened.

Both vampires whirled to face the intrusion.

Celluci didn't know exactly what the couple waiting

at the seventh floor saw nor did he want to. Faces blanched of color and the spreading stain on the front of an expensive pair of silk pants gave his imagination information enough. Teeth clenched, he jerked forward and jabbed a finger at the panel.

The closing doors cut off a rising, mindless wail. All at once, he was no longer worried about either of his companions losing control. He lost it himself.

"That's it!" he snarled as he turned. "I've had it up to here . . ." The edge of his hand chopped at the air over his head. ". . . with the two of you. You can both stuff that creature-of-the-night shit back where it belongs! Did you see what you did to those two kids? Did you! Did either of you even notice they got in the way of your petty little power struggle?"

"Petty?" Vicki began, but he cut her off.

"Yeah. Petty. No one fucking cares which one of you's top ghoul *except* the two of you! And that'd be fine except there's a whole goddamned world around you and neither of you seems to give a fuck who gets hit with the shrapnel!"

"*You're* still alive. . . ."

He whirled toward Henry. "Well, whoop de fucking do!" Too furious to consider the consequences, he dared the dark gaze to do its worst.

Henry's lips drew off his teeth.

Vicki moved to deny him.

Celluci threw out both arms. Muscles strained as he held them apart, one hand on each chest, the utter audacity of the attempt allowing him to succeed for one heartbeat. Two. Three. Teeth clenched, he refused to give in. His vision started to blur.

Impossibly held, memory rose to overwhelm Hunger.

The three of them had just laid Vicki's mother to rest for a second time. The two men were physically wounded and emotionally flayed—but Vicki had been dying. Henry had done what he could, but he hadn't been strong enough to finish; he needed more blood.

Michael Celluci had offered his, even though he believed that it meant he'd lose everything.

In over four hundred and fifty years of living as an observer in humanity's midst, it had been the most amazing thing Henry Fitzroy had ever seen.

Until now.

Detective-Sergeant Michael Celluci was very large and very strong; but it wasn't his physical strength that stopped the Hunger. It was the attitude that dared to announce, "I will not allow this!" even knowing he didn't stand, as he himself might say, a snowflake's chance in hell of being listened to.

Once again, Henry was shown the quality of the man, and he was ashamed that he had to be reminded.

Eyes still locked with Henry's, Vicki remembered what he remembered and felt what he felt. For the first time in his presence she was forced to think about someone else. Tearing her gaze away, staring in horror at the pulse throbbing among the corded muscle of Mike's neck, she replaced Henry's shame with her own.

Celluci felt their surrender and allowed his arms to drop. He didn't have much choice. Without the pressure against them, he couldn't hold them up. The air still held a certain frisson, but strangely it didn't seem to be coming from either Vicki or Henry.

"I think we've forgotten," said a quiet voice he almost didn't recognize, "that with great power comes great responsibility."

"I think I forgot what mattered." No mistaking Vicki's voice, but it had a ragged edge he didn't often hear.

"Same thing." To his surprise, Henry, just Henry, a man Celluci suddenly remembered he'd come to respect and even like, held out a pale hand. "My apologies, Detective. I wish I could promise that it won't happen again, but I can't. I can promise that I'll do better in the future."

His grip was cool, like Vicki's.

Then he was gone.

"Where . . . ?"

"Parking level one. The van's on level two. I assume one of us is going to be using it?"

He blinked to clear the sweat from his eyes, and allowed her to slip her shoulder under his arm, taking most of his weight. "You can have it. I'll never find parking."

"I'll drop you off."

"Fine." The parking level had the damp, un-air-conditioned coolness that came from being deep underground. Celluci found himself thinking of graves. "Vicki. What did I just do?"

"You leaped a tall building in a single bound."

"I don't mean the physical . . ."

She sighed. It wasn't something she did much any more; she'd lost the habit when she'd lost the need to breathe on a mortal scale. "You reminded us to be more, instead of less."

He stopped and looked down at her. "Try again."

"You told us to stop acting like idiots."

"Yeah, I know, but you don't usually listen."

"This time . . ." She paused, then reached up and pushed the curl of hair back off his face.

Henry listened.

Wrapping her arms around him, she laid her cheek against his chest and found what comfort she could in the steady beat of his life. "I love you, Mike."

"Hey, I believe you." His chin resting on the top of her head, he wondered just what it was she hadn't said.

Seven

By parking across an access alley, Vicki managed to find curb space only two blocks from the video store where Tony worked.

Celluci opened the passenger door, then closed it again. "Will you do something for me?"

"Anything."

His snort was an eloquent testimony to his disbelief. "Just try to be careful. Don't expect anything as civilized as the *Godfather* . . ."

"Not even the bit where Sonny gets offed or the brother-in-law gets strangled? Or where they dump Fredo in the lake?" Her brow furrowed dramatically. "And didn't they kill the Pope in part three?"

"Vicki . . ."

"Michael," she mimicked. "Look, I was a cop. I helped bag the bodies. I *know* these aren't the good guys."

"Yeah, well, organized crime has changed over the last few years." He twisted in the seat until he faced her. "Most of the old school has been buried, one way or another, and the new lot's a group of vicious young punks who kill because they can. There used to be rules of a sort. The rules are gone." Once, he might have thought he gripped her arm too tightly. Now, he didn't think he could hold her tightly enough. "Power is an end with these new guys, not just a means."

She smiled, her teeth gleaming unnaturally white in

the light from the passing traffic. "Power won't be a problem."

"Maybe. Just keep two things in mind, will you? You're there to ask a few questions, not to clean up the streets." He didn't like the way her brows lifted, but he ignored them because he didn't have a lot of choice. As little as he liked it, he had to trust her judgment. "And don't forget the difference between immortal and invulnerable." He leaned forward and kissed her, then got out of the van before he could give in to the urge to ask her just what exactly she was going to do.

"I won't take any stupid risks, Mike." The pale oval of her face seemed farther away than distance alone could account for. "At the risk of sounding like some whacked-out action hero, I'll be back."

At least she hadn't told him not to worry. "Sunrise is at 4:16."

"What the . . . ?"

"What the what, Bynowski?"

"I don't know." Brow furrowed, Frank Bynowski leaned closer to the monitor that showed a long shot of the front approach. "Something flickered . . ."

The front door alarm went off.

Two pairs of eyes locked on the screen linked to the camera over the front door. Instead of a solid barrier between the house and the world, the steel reinforced door swung lazily back and forth on its hinges.

Gary Haiden turned a flat, accusing stare on his companion. "The boss told you to lock up!"

'I did!"

He jerked his head at the image. "That says different." His tone suggested the lapse would be reported, that Bynowski would suffer for it, and that he, Haiden, wouldn't much mind.

"Yeah? Take a closer look, shit-for-brains."

Both halves of the lock had been twisted into impossible angles.

The monitor showing the front hall—the only view of the inside of the house—flickered, but neither man noticed. They'd kicked in too many doors to miss the significance of the broken lock.

"Shit, shit, shit, fuck!" Bynowski reached for the intercom button. A leather-covered hand closed over his finger before it had quite covered the distance. He grunted as the bone snapped, too astounded to scream. When he looked up and fell into silvered eyes, he wished he'd taken the time because screaming might've helped. A backhanded blow he never saw coming flung him out of his chair to crash against the far wall and slide down a trickle of his own blood to the floor.

Haiden whirled around to watch the arc of the other man's flight and used the motion to propel himself to his feet. Instinct took over while reason protested, and his gun had cleared the holster by the time he was standing. His eyes saw a tall woman, dressed all in black. His brain did its best to convince him that this was the last thing he was going to see if he didn't leave immediately. Haiden ignored it. He hadn't gotten off the streets by giving in to fear, and he wasn't going to start now.

Her pale gaze flicked down to his gun, then back to his face. "No," she said softly.

A lot of people had said no to him throughout the years. Some had begged. Some had shrieked. Some had repeated it, over and over, in stunned disbelief. In all its varying forms, the word had held fear, but it had never been a warning. So although it was definitely a warning this time, he didn't recognize it.

He'd been a predator all his life; this was his first time as prey. He still had a lot to learn.

A heartbeat later, he gibbered in terror while fingertips pressed white half-moons into his throat. Bones had been broken in both his hands, but the pain got lost behind the gleaming white smile he couldn't seem to take his eyes off of.

"Is the boss at home?" the smile said.

Up until this point, Gary Haiden had been positive he'd give his life to protect Sebastien Carl, that he'd look death in the face and say, *"Fuck you."* Instead, he found himself saying, "Him and his wife are upstairs, in the big bedroom at the back, dressing for dinner." He hoped it was enough.

Mr. Carl was alone in the bedroom pulling on a pair of black silk socks. A blow-dryer running in the en suite suggested the location of his wife.

Although Vicki knew she'd never seen him before, there was something familiar about Sebastien Carl. She was across the room with one hand clamped around his throat before she realized what it was. He had an awareness of his own power that was almost vampiric in intensity. *All this is mine,* it declared. *You are nothing unless I choose to make use of you.*

She almost killed him before she brought the sudden surge of rage under control. "I am nothing like you," she snarled, ignoring the hands that clawed at her wrist. "I only want to ask you a few questions." A silk-covered heel caught her just below the knee. "Stop it."

Smarter than Haiden, he stopped. He glared at her through narrowed eyes, fingers wrapped around her wrist, chest rising and falling in short, shallow breaths, all the remains of his windpipe would allow. *Death is my weapon,* his expression said. *Not yours.*

She let more of the Hunger rise, barely stopping it from breaking free. "Organ-legging. Are you doing it?"

"No." His answer was little more than a breath rasped out in denial. For all he might deny Death in the silvered eyes that held his, he couldn't lie to them. Nor could he look away.

"Do you know who is?"

"No."

With her free hand, she pulled one of the copies Henry'd made of the photos in the autopsy report out of her back pocket, shook out the folds, and held it up. "Have you ever seen this guy before?"

"No." *Go on,* his gaze dared. *Do your worst.*

Frustrated, she threw him to the bed. He bounced, rolled across the quilted red satin bedspread, and came up firing the .22-caliber pistol that had been laid out beside his clothes. By the time he'd squeezed the trigger the second time, he was dead.

Switching off the blow-dryer, Jenna Carl threw sun-streaked hair back off her face and frowned. "Sebastien?" she asked stepping out of the bathroom. "Did you just . . . oh, shit."

No stranger to her husband's business, the body on the floor didn't surprise her much. It surprised her only a little more when it turned out to be her husband. It surprised her a great deal when she discovered he was not, as she'd supposed from his face, lying on his back. Someone . . .

Or something, a whimpering little voice in the back of her head insisted as she bit back a scream.

. . . had turned his head completely around.

Leaping over the corpse, she crawled up the bed and fumbled open the safe built into the padded headboard. Everything was there. Breathing heavily, she clutched at the packets of bills and tried to think. She could still get out of this. All she had to do was get Sebastien's body to the foot of the stairs—thank God she'd squelched his plan to build a bungalow. A terrible accident. His lawyers would know what to do, who to pay. A quick funeral, and she'd take the money and . . .

"I'd never get away." If the cops didn't hound her to death, her husband's business associates would as they ripped his empire to bloody shreds. "Well, screw them."

Twenty minutes later, the safe emptied, her Porsche roared out of the garage and disappeared down Marine Drive.

Haiden and Bynowski stared empty-eyed at the monitors.

The part of Vancouver known as Kitsilano had become overtly yuppie as the tag end of the baby boomers—stockbrokers, system developers, securities analysts, crime lords—in the prime of their earning years had settled down with a mortgage and kids. For all of that, it was a nice neighborhood and not a place Henry'd expected to be Hunting in tonight.

Gabriel and Lori Constantine were having a barbecue. Standing motionless in the shadows, Henry sniffed the breeze and firmly squelched the desire to sneeze at the lingering scent of seared squid. As host, Gabriel Constantine would be among the six lives by the house.

Two cars, each containing a pair of gunmen, and two men who were definitely not a couple walking along the beach, convinced him that he'd best take an oblique approach. A few moments later, he stepped up onto the neighbor's composter, over the fence and into a pool of deep shadow cast by a clump of lilac, lip curled at the smell of dying blossoms.

Their yard could have been any of the yards he'd crossed. The house was only superficially different from the rest on the street. The gathering could have been happening anywhere up and down the block.

Except for the people involved.

Henry suspected the Constantines seldom entertained their immediate neighbors. After all, predators have only one reason to associate with prey.

Four large men wearing jackets over golf shirts patrolled the yard. Henry waited until one reached the edge of the shadows and came forward just enough to interrupt the constant sweeping movement of the enforcer's gaze. In the instant before awareness dawned, Henry grabbed onto the simple pattern of his thoughts and twisted them into new shapes. "Tell Mr. Constantine there's something he should see over by the fence. Tell him it isn't dangerous, but you thought he should take a look."

Most people caught in the Hunt responded like a rabbit caught in headlights—conscious thought completely overwhelmed by their imminent and incontestable death. Those susceptible to more overt control were few and far between, but primed to follow orders and only follow orders, the enforcer nodded, turned, and made his way toward the pool. It wouldn't last long. But then, it didn't have to.

Henry, who could hear the heartbeat of the child sleeping in an upstairs bedroom, had no difficulty hearing the conversations at the other end of the yard. Private schools and music lessons and how hard it was to find a reliable housekeeper and imported cars versus domestic and how certain people never realized that expenses were going up all wrapped around each other like tangled yarn. It was all very innocent; a casual eavesdropper would never know how the bills were paid. Finally, he heard the thread that concerned his meeting with Gabriel Constantine.

Frowning, waving off a question from one of his guests, Constantine suggested that the enforcer should lead the way. There was something out there, he'd read that off the other man's face, but he had confidence in both his security and in the normality of the neighborhood.

What could hurt you here? Henry asked himself as they approached. *Here, surrounded by satellite dishes, gas barbecues, and lawns all maintained by Mr. Weedman. What could touch you in the midst of all of that?* He smiled as the two men reached the lilac. It had been, after all, a rhetorical question.

Unaware that his enforcer's mind had less in it than usual, Constantine put him on guard and threw a skeptical glance into the shadows. To his horror, the shadows threw it back.

"If you move, I'll kill you."

All the death he'd ever dealt returned to greet him.

Had their night sight been good enough, his guests
might have seen his shoulders stiffen and a spreading
patch of sweat darken his T-shirt. Because he faced
away from them, they couldn't see the expression of
horror that drained the blood from his face.

A few *gentle* questions, voiced too low for listening
ears, determined he knew nothing of selling organs
for profit nor of the identity of the ghost. But he did
know a great many other unpleasant things.

In spite of certain incidents that had occurred during
the year Vicki had been his mortal lover, Henry had
never considered himself a vampire Batman, a comic
book hero out hunting down evil in the night. Although
willing to destroy any that put itself in his way, much as
he would a cockroach that did the same thing, he had
no desire to spend immortality searching evil out and
destroying it. There was just too damned much of it.

For the sake of the sleeping child, Henry let this
cockroach live, merely suggesting that, in return, it go
into another line of work.

"That was good food." Celluci stepped to one side
of the restaurant door and was almost run over by a
trio of young women. Two of them spun off to either
side, the third looked him over, grinned, and hurried
to catch up to her friends—now giggling around the
corner on Robeson Street. Definitely not working
girls—over the years he'd booked enough hookers to
recognize them in any situation—they didn't look old
enough to be out so late.

"Feeling your age?"

Startled, he stared down at his companion. "Did I
say that out loud?"

Tony shook his head. "No. You sighed."

"Yeah, well, it's something old people do." He took
a deep breath to clear the atmosphere of the restaurant from his lungs. "At least I still have all my teeth.
And I do enjoy a good meal."

"I figured if you come to the Coast, you should eat
seafood. At least once."

"Yeah? I suppose Fitzroy has sailors on Friday."

Pale eyes wide, Tony stared up at the detective. "Man, you've changed. You're not as . . . uh . . ." During the pause, he received only a polite, questioning expression. "Well, as uptight as you used to be."

"A lot of things have changed in the last few years."

"Yeah? Like what?"

"Vicki."

"Ah. She changes, and you change because you love her?"

"Something like that." Celluci sighed again and peered down Thurlow Street toward the distant waters of English Bay. "How far are we from your place? Fitzroy's place, that is, not where you're staying now."

Tony shrugged again, allowing just whose place it was, to pass. "It's a bit of a walk."

"Doable?"

"Sure. Straight down Thurlow to Davie, along Davie to Seymour and home. I go that way on my blades." He looked down at his feet and shook his head. "Tonight it'll take a while longer. You'd better not be in a hurry."

Somewhere to the south, a siren wailed.

Celluci's mouth set into a thin line. "I'm in no hurry." Stepping away from the restaurant, he tried with little success to block out the distant sounds of the night. "I'm not very good at sitting around and waiting."

The man who answered to the second name on Vicki's list had left town for a few days.

"*. . . I don't know any more than that. I don't! Please!*"

The third had been working late. She caught him just leaving the office.

There was only one enforcer between them. Then there were only the persistent fumes of a pungent aftershave. Then . . .

His other three boys found him a few moments

later, crouched behind a dumpster in the alley next to the office. He stood slowly as they approached, visibly pulling himself together.

"Boss? What happened?"

"The night," he said, then paused to swallow fear. Lines of sweat that had nothing to do with the cool breeze blowing in off the street glistened down both sides of his face. "I was taken by the night."

The most senior of the three shot a startled glance at his companions but switched from Chinese to English if that was how the boss wanted it. "Are you okay?"

"Where's Fang?" Narrowed eyes searched behind three sets of shoulders, shying away from the shadows. "He was supposed to protect me."

"He, uh, disappeared. Right when you did."

Fingers curled into fists to hide their trembling, but the lingering terror honed a razor's edge on the voice. "Then where the fuck were you!?"

The steering wheel creaked a protest. Vicki glanced down at it, frowned, and forced her fingers to relax their grip. It was getting harder and harder not to feed, not to drink in the terror with the blood.

Once you acquire the taste, Henry had warned her, *the desire for it will lead you to excess after excess. Be very, very careful.*

"Yeah. Right. *'Once you turn toward the dark side, forever will it dominate your destiny.'* Stuff a sock in it, Obi Wan." Grimacing, she gunned the engine, raced a yellow light, and whipped the van around the corner, the two wheels still in contact with the pavement loudly objecting.

Frustration sizzled along every nerve. It was like having sex for hours with no orgasm in sight. "Celluci'd better be well rested when I get back; he's going to need his strength."

Yuen-Zong Chen, known to his associates as Harry, waited in the corridor while one of his boys vetted the

men's room—not so much from fear of assassination
as that he intensely disliked pissing in front of an audience. He stepped aside as two of the club's less distin-
guished patrons were escorted out.

"All clear, Mr. Chen." As the crime boss entered,
the enforcer nodded to a companion at the end of the
hall and took up a position outside the door, one foot
in its handmade size eight shoe keeping the beat that
throbbed throughout the club.

Inside, Harry Chen relieved himself, sighed deeply
in contentment, and crossed the room to the row of
stainless steel sinks. He shook his head in unfeigned
distaste at the residue of white powder. Only weak
fools destroyed themselves with drugs. Weak fools
who had helped to make him rich, perhaps, but that
made them no less weak, no less foolish.

He passed his hands under the taps and, as the
warm water poured over them, glanced up at his reflection in the mirror. "There's never enough fucking
light when . . ." The rest of the sentence caught in his
throat. Death looked over his shoulder.

Behind him, Henry smiled, showing teeth. "Harry
Chen, I presume?"

He stiffened, recognizing it was not a question and
that the pale-haired man knew exactly whose life he
held. Dripping hands held out from his sides, he
turned.

"If you call for help, you'll be dead before the first
word reaches air," Henry told him as he opened his
mouth.

"I'm dead anyway." But he wasn't dead yet, so he
kept his voice low, ignoring the quaver because he
couldn't prevent it, hope warring with fear. "Who sent
you? Was it Ngyn, that Vietnamese prick? No," he
answered his own question. "Ngyn wouldn't use a
fuc . . ." Suddenly realizing that some racial slurs
might not be wise under the circumstances, Chen
began again. "Nygn wouldn't use you. Look, you're a
professional, right? So am I. Whoever sent you, I can
pay you more. Lots more. Cash. Drugs. Girls. What-

ever the fuck you want, man. I can get it for you."
Finding courage in the silence, he raised his eyes. The
small, nonshrieking part of his mind decided it was
very glad he'd just relieved himself. "You're . . .
not . . . possible."

The protest emerged one word to each short, shallow breath. Even Henry had to strain to hear it.
"Aren't I?" he asked quietly, impressed by the
strength of will in spite of his contempt for the man.
"Then you're in no danger, are you?"

"Just . . . do it, you . . . son of a bitch."

"Not until you answer a few questions."

He swallowed and fought the urge to lift his chin.
"Fuck . . . you."

Henry growled low in his throat.

A few minutes later, as another song began, the
enforcer in front of the door pushed it open a crack.
"You okay, Mr. Chen? Mr. Chen?"

There wasn't a mark on the body. No way to show
how he died.

Harry Chen had known nothing. Henry threw the
leather driving gloves down on the seat beside him,
slammed the BMW into gear, and jerked it out into
traffic. He needed to feed, needed to let the Hunger
free to wash away the memory of men he'd questioned
with blood. He'd barely been able to stop himself from
feeding on Harry Chen.

But to feed on such a man would mean he fed on
all the lives that man had destroyed, and that he would
not do.

But he needed to feed.

Bars were closing. After hours clubs, tucked into
lofts and behind stage entrances, were opening. There
was a lot more traffic on the streets than Celluci had
expected.

"It's 'cause people live in the West End, they don't
just drink and shop here." Tony waved a hand to in-
clude the apartment towers that rose to block the stars

amidst the five- and six-story brownstones tucked along both sides of the street. "It's not like Toronto, it's all mixed. Last fall, some American guys came up from Seattle to see how we make it work so well."

Celluci smiled at the pronoun, then jerked around as a crash of falling cans, a soft thud, and assorted profanity spilled out of the alley they'd just passed.

"Relax." Tony grabbed his arm. "It's just dumpster divers."

"It's just *what*?" Celluci asked, allowing himself to be pulled to a stop.

"Street people who go through dumpsters looking for stuff they can sell. Some of 'em got hooks, some just dive right in." He shoved his hands into the front pocket of his jeans and kicked at a bit of broken sidewalk. Although his face was in shadow, Celluci got the impression he was embarrassed by his comparative affluence. "Lotta homeless people here. Well, it makes sense, doesn't it? I mean, it beats freezing your ass to death back East." *You wanna make something of it?* his tone added.

But Celluci, who'd bagged the bodies of those who froze to death every winter huddled at the base of million-dollar office towers, exposed skin stuck to the steel grates of the subway air vents, said only, "Good point."

They walked in silence for a few minutes.

"I got a new life here," Tony announced suddenly. "I got a job, I got school, I got a chance; and I wouldn't have if it wasn't for Henry."

"And you feel like you owe him for that?"

"Well, don't I?"

"Has Henry suggested you owe him anything?" Celluci knew damned well he hadn't. Henry Fitzroy might be an arrogant, undead *romance writer,* but he wasn't the type to put a lien on a man's soul.

"He doesn't have to. I feel it." One hand slapped a dramatic punctuation against his chest. "Here."

"All right, what about the things you've done for him?"

Tony snorted. "What things?"

"The things that have to be done in daylight. The people who have to be dealt with. The arrangements that have to be made during office hours." He glanced down to find Tony's pale blue eyes locked on his face. "Leaving aside certain other aspects of the relationship . . ." His right thumb rubbed the tiny scar on his left wrist. ". . . I think you'll find things haven't been all that unequal."

"He trusts me with his life." It almost sounded like a question.

"You trusted him with yours."

Overhead, a streetlight buzzed, the recent hit of a popular grunge band throbbed through a dark but open window, and both men jumped back as a convertible Ford Mustang roared down Granville Street toward the bridge.

"What does sixty k mean to you, asshole!" Tony yelled, leaping out onto the street and flipping the car the finger as bright yellow molded bumpers disappeared into the night. "Idiots in fast cars think the bridge is a goddamned highway," he muttered as they crossed to the other side. "Probably wouldn't slow down if they fucking ran over you."

"Feel better?"

Uncertain whether the older man referred to his outburst or the conversation preceding it, Tony shrugged and discovered he did, indeed, feel better. "Yeah." After they'd walked another block, he added, "Thanks."

When she opened the warehouse door, the blood-scent spilled out into the night. Vicki swallowed hard and fought for control. While an incredulous voice in the back of her head demanded to know just what she thought she was doing, she stepped over the threshold and moved silently along the dark corridor created by two racks of floor-to-ceiling shelves stacked with industrial tile.

At the first cross corridor, she found a body. He'd

been shot four times in the back at skin-touch range—
the choice of professionals as it soaked up the muzzle
blast and decreased the chance of being heard.

She could hear movement up ahead and the quiet
drone of voices beyond that. It sounded very much as
though the voices were being surrounded. The rising
Hunger made it hard to think, hard to plan. She
should leave. This hunt did not concern her.

Scrubbing one hand over her face, trying to block
the distraction of the spilled blood, she stood and
glanced up into the steel rafters. No one appeared to
have taken the high road. Smiling, she reached for the
crossbrace on the closest rack and began to climb.

"No. The bottom line is if weapons move out of
this city, I move them. Me. Not me and you." The
older of the two men sitting at the table leaned forward, scowling. "You're what, twenty-six? Twenty-
seven? You've come far, David Eng, and you think
you're hot shit, but you're not hot enough yet to take
me out and you know it."

The other man nodded, but the motion was more
acknowledgment of a point made rather than agreement with it. "Street wars are bad for business, Mr.
Dyshino."

"Fuckin' A, they are. Which is why you and me are
going to work this out if we have to fucking sit here
until dawn."

The table sat in the middle of the open area where
the forklifts were usually stored. One section of the
overhead lights had been turned on, but they didn't
quite manage to illuminate the oil-stained floor. The
shadows of the six men standing blended into the surrounding shadow.

"You don't have to take this," one of the six announced belligerently from behind David's left shoulder.

"Let's hear Mr. Dyshino's suggestion of compromise."

Adan Dyshino rolled his eyes. "We aren't going to
'compromise,' you fool. You're going to stop."

A manicured hand rose to cut off the protest from his enraged second. "Admittedly, arms dealing is a very small part of what I do, but I do not wish to stop doing it. We appear to have reached an impasse once again."

From her seat in the rafters, Vicki watched Eng's men take up positions just outside the open area. Grinning ferally, she enjoyed the view. If the vermin wanted to slaughter each other, that was fine by her.

The unexpectedly close whisper of metal against metal drew her gaze to the top of the nearest rack. A prone gunman, his sights sweeping the perimeter of the light, lay half hidden behind a crate of "parquet style" vinyl tiles. Carefully searching the shadows, she spotted another three.

This could get interesting. . . .

David Eng had the advantage in numbers, but Dyshino's men held the high ground.

Brought up short by Vicki's scent, Henry wondered what the hell was going on. Growling low in his throat, he pushed open the warehouse door. The air inside smelled of sweat and fear and anticipation.

"We haven't reached anything, you immigrant punk!" Dyshino surged to his feet. "This isn't Hong Kong, this is Canada, and I say . . ."

A 9-mm round from a burst of machine gun fire caught him in the right shoulder and spun him around. The rest of the burst killed the man behind him. He hit the floor and rolled under the table as all hell broke loose.

Crouched beside the man who'd been shot in the back, Henry flinched away from the sudden roar of gunfire. By the time answering shots had been fired, he was on his feet and racing toward the sound. *Vicki . . .*

*   *   *

Vicki watched in amazement as Henry exploded out into the light, face and hair a pale blur above the moving shadow of his body. The gunman on the nearest rack muttered something that sounded like "Police!" as she realized he had Henry in his sights.

He got the shot off just as she knocked him into the air. Henry's howl of pain drowned out the ripe melon sound of the gunman's head making contact with the concrete floor, nine meters down.

The scent of Henry's blood rose to obliterate the singed sulfur smell of the gunpowder, the hot metal smell of the spent casings, and the warm, meaty smell of the men below. Henry's blood. The blood that had made her.

The Hunger ripped aside all controls.

Time slowed as Henry stared from the red stain across the fingers of his right glove to the hole in his left arm. It didn't seem to hurt. *I'm in shock,* he thought. When he lifted his head, he saw a cold-eyed young man swing a submachine gun around until it pointed in his direction—each movement deliberate and distinct. Feeling as though he were moving underwater, Henry reached out, grabbed the muzzle, and smashed the weapon into the gunman's face.

As the body fell, the wound throbbed once, sending a ripple of pain racing through Henry's body, and time took up its normal pace again.

He felt, rather than heard, Vicki's scream of rage, and he didn't have strength enough to stop himself from responding.

Clutching his shoulder, Dyshino stared out from under the table in horror as another of his men hit the floor. This one was dead before impact.

Shots ricocheted off the metal rafters.

Head buzzing from the adrenaline, one of Eng's people leaned around a forklift and, grinning widely, sprayed bullets in the general direction of Dyshino's bodyguard. Some of the guys thought he was crazy, but he loved this kind of stuff—the noise, the chaos, the way death was so completely impersonal. It was like being inside a video game. What fun in quiet stalking and a single shot?

All at once his grin twisted into a grimace of pain as an unbreakable grip locked onto his shoulder and yanked him up into the cab of the machine.

He screamed.

His finger tightened on the trigger.

He sent Death on an impersonal visit to two of his companions.

Both sides realized they had a common enemy at about the same time.

Unfortunately, by then it was too late.

The last sniper scrambled down off the racks, desperately trying to outrun his own death. He slipped, managed to stop his fall, and hit the floor running. One step, two . . .

Vicki reached out a hand and grabbed the back of his head, slamming him to his knees and exposing his throat in one motion.

This was not the slaughter David Eng had planned. Crouched behind a roll of no-wax vinyl flooring, he grabbed his second's shoulder and waved his Ingram toward the distant doors. "Let's get the fuck out of here!"

The other man nodded, and they began to make their way down the corridor, back to back, each guarding the other's retreat. They were almost at the door when a pale face appeared out of the darkness.

"I don't think so," Henry snarled. His hand around the barrel of the Ingram, he pushed it toward the floor. When the magazine had emptied in a spray of concrete chips, he yanked it out of Eng's hands and hurled it away.

Howling with fear, the second started back the way they'd come and ran into Vicki's outstretched arm.

A few moments later, she dropped the body and wiped her mouth on the sleeve of her sweater. When she saw Henry watching her, Eng lying lifeless at his feet, she smiled, eyes glittering silver. "There're a few left."

He half turned toward the interior of the warehouse, then shook his head. "No. Not worth the risk."

"They've seen us . . ."

"They saw something, but not us. They don't want to see us when we Hunt; it reminds them of why children are afraid of the dark."

"Then what's the risk?" She stepped toward him, drawing in deep breaths of the rich, meaty, blood-scented air. Another step and her palm lay flat against his chest. "They can't stand against us." Leaning forward, she licked a bit of blood from the corner of his mouth. Not since the earliest days after the change when the world had been a kaleidoscope of new sensations had she felt so alive.

He caught her tongue between his teeth, carefully so as not to break the skin.

Her arms went around him. His good hand tangled in her hair.

She moaned against his mouth and pushed David Eng's body out of their way with the side of her foot.

It was over very quickly.

The darkness began to lift from Henry's eyes as he held out a hand to help Vicki to her feet. "We'd better get out of here before someone reports the gunfire."

"But . . ."

He could see the deaths not dealt glittering in her eyes. "No." When she took a step back toward the light, he caught her arm. "Vicki. Listen to me. We have to leave before the police arrive."

This was the voice that had guided her through the year of chaos that followed the change. The silver faded. Reluctantly, she allowed him to guide her out of the warehouse.

An ocean breeze tattered the bloodscent that shrouded them.

Vicki snarled softly at Henry's touch, but when he released her, she stood where she was, staring at his face.

"What?"

"Just remembering." Her tone clearly stated she wouldn't identify the memory. "It's almost dawn. Wait for me in the parking garage, and we'll ride up together. I think we should talk." Then she was gone.

Peeling off gloves that were already beginning to stiffen, Henry shook his head. "She thinks we should talk," he said to the night. Once, before Vicki, he'd thought that nothing remained to astonish him. He'd been wrong.

Those still alive inside the warehouse, two of Eng's men and Adan Dyshino, gathered together in the light and waited, without knowing exactly why, for the dawn.

She was waiting for him at his parking spot, showing no outward signs of either the slaughter or the aftermath.

"Handi-wipes and hairbrush," she explained when Henry raised a red-gold brow at her clean face and slicked-back hair. "And I think I've discovered why we wear black."

They stayed a careful ten feet apart on the way to the elevator. Once inside, in opposite corners, Henry studied her carefully. "Are you all right?"

"I think I have a bruise on my butt." She rubbed it and snorted. "Next time, you're on the bottom."

"Next time." From the moment they'd met, Vicki Nelson had delighted in overturning his world, but this, this he hadn't expected. "There shouldn't have been a this time. It went against everything . . ."

"What? In the manual? Give it a rest, Henry. One . . ." She raised a finger. ". . . sex is a well documented response to violence, and two . . ." A second finger lifted. ". . . obviously the blood scent was overwhelming, so maybe if we wear nose plugs, we can get along, and three . . ." Her eyes began to glitter again. ". . . it was so glorious finally being able to let go."

"You enjoyed it?" When she started to grin, he raised his hand. "No. I mean the letting go."

"Yeah, I did. And what's the harm in that? These were bad men, Henry. Leaving aside what they've done previously, tonight they were planning on killing each other."

"Suppose there aren't any bad men around the next time you want to experience that feeling?"

"I wouldn't . . ."

"Are you sure?"

The silver faded. "I could've controlled myself if you hadn't been shot." Had she still been able, she'd have blushed as she suddenly realized what she'd just said. "Uh, speaking of, are you okay?"

"The bullet merely grazed me." He'd tucked his left hand in his waistband to support the injured arm. Now he poked a finger through the hole in his jacket. "By sunset tomorrow you won't be able to find the wound."

"Why on earth did you run out into the open like that?"

He shrugged and winced. "When I heard the gunfire, I thought you were in trouble."

Vicki snorted. "Christ. You're as bad as Celluci. I can take care of myself."

"I know, but you haven't lived in the night for very long."

"Henry, I hate to break this to you, but it was the guy with the centuries of experience who jumped into the middle of a gang war."

They stepped out onto the fourteenth floor and increased the distance between them to the width of the hall.

"So what happened tonight?"

"We'd both fed," Henry said thoughtfully but without much conviction.

Vicki shook her head. "I think it's more than that. I think that once we let go of control, we let go of all the baggage that comes with it. It seems that as long as we're focused on wholesale destruction, we get along fine."

"Then perhaps that's why we're solitary hunters. If what happened tonight is what happens when our kind join forces, we'd soon wipe out our food supply."

Key in hand, she paused outside the door to the borrowed condo. "What happens tomorrow night?"

"With you and me? I don't know." He smiled, and stroked the curve of her cheek into the air because they stood too far apart to touch. "But I have no doubt it will be an *experience* finding out."

Celluci was sound asleep. Vicki stood just inside the master bedroom and watched him. Watched the rise and fall of his chest. Traced the curve of the arm he'd flung over his head. Listened to his heartbeat.

He shifted position and a curl of hair fell down onto his face.

She stepped forward, hand outstretched to brush it back but stopped as the movement pulled the saturated cuff of her sweater across her wrist, drawing a dark smear on the pale skin.

All at once she didn't want Mike to see her like this.

Her clothes, all her clothes including her sneakers, went into the washing machine—cold wash, cold rinse, more soap than necessary.

Then she stepped into the shower and watched the water run red down the drain.

Eight

"4:09." Celluci shifted his barely focused gaze from the clock to Vicki. "Cutting it a little close, aren't you?"

She'd stayed in the shower longer than she'd intended, stayed until the approaching dawn drove her out from under the pounding water. And then, wrapped in borrowed towels, she'd hesitated by the side of the bed, unwilling to wake him, afraid that he'd see . . . See what? The blood had swirled around her feet and down the drain. Nothing else showed. At least, she didn't think it showed.

"Vicki?" When her head jerked up, he sighed and propped himself against the headboard, the gray suede soft and yielding against his back. Her diet may have changed, but her mannerisms hadn't, and right now she intended to hide something from him. "What's the matter?"

"Nothing."

Frowning slightly at her tone, he reached out and folded his hand around hers. To his surprise, it was almost warm. "Are you all right?"

"If you mean, have I been injured, I'm fine." No one had touched her. Except for Henry. "We haven't got much time . . ." The sun waited just beyond the crest of the mountains. ". . . so I'll cut right to the chase. If someone's harvesting organs, it isn't organized crime. The people Henry and I spoke to knew

147

nothing about it. They weren't doing it, and they hadn't heard rumors of anyone else doing it."

"You sure they were telling the truth?"

Slowly lifting her head, she stared directly at him. "I'm sure."

She was sitting just beyond the limited light of the reading lamp that stood on the bedside table. A pair of silver sparks appeared within the shadowed oval of her face then disappeared again before Celluci felt their pull.

"Okay. You're sure." He didn't know what the limitations were on this whole Prince-of-Darkness thing—though he suspected it wasn't as all-powerful as both Vicki and Henry wanted him to believe—but Vicki'd interviewed enough perps over the years that he had to trust her ability to know when one was lying. "Lets just hope you didn't give them any ideas," he added dryly.

"Not about organ-legging."

Her voice lifted the hair on the back of his neck and made asking what ideas she *had* given them unnecessary. "If organized crime isn't involved, then we lose our best support for selling organs as a motive. Henry's ghost could've been killed for any number of reasons."

"Granted. But as he's still missing a kidney, let's follow this hypothesis for a while. Maybe your Patricia Chou's right about Ronald Swanson."

"She's not my anything, and Swanson has a completely spotless life as far as the law is concerned."

"So, he has to start somewhere."

"Killing people for their kidneys seems a little far up the ladder to me." She shrugged noncommittally, but it was clear she wasn't going to let it go. Cops got that way occasionally, clinging to a theory based on nothing better than a hunch, often in the face of opposition. When it turned out they were right, they were said to have intuitive abilities beyond the norm. When it turned out they were wrong, as was more often the case, they were said to be pigheaded, self-absorbed, and unwilling to do the grunt work needed to break the case. That Vicki had been right more often than she was wrong made her no less pigheaded. "Now what?"

"I think we should stop working on who and take a look at where." Impossible now to ignore the sun. Her shoulders hunched up as though expecting a blow from behind. "Mike, I've got to go."

He lifted a hand to touch his cheek where a strand of wet hair had brushed against him. That, the lingering pressure of her mouth, and the faint taste of toothpaste, were all that remained to show she'd ever been in the room. The clock read 4:15. Sixty seconds to sunrise.

Lying on her back in the pink bedroom, a hastily folded towel under her head to keep the pillow dry, Vicki wondered why she felt no guilt at all for the . . . for the . . . She frowned, realizing she had no clear idea of how many men she'd actually killed in the warehouse. The number had been washed away in blood.

It didn't matter. Because they didn't matter. Not to her. Not their lives. Not their deaths.

But Henry . . .

"So the violence is fine, but the sex is a problem." She sighed and swiped at a drop of water dribbling from temple to ear. "Well, doesn't that just sum up the ni . . ."

4:16.
Sunrise.
Celluci stretched out an arm and switched off the lamp. He'd be glad when midsummer arrived and the nights started getting longer. Not that more time would make Vicki more forthcoming, but it would give him more opportunity to get the truth out of her.

"Good morning, Dr. Mui. You're here early."
She glanced at her watch. "It is almost 6:45. Not

exactly early. Did that blood work come back from the lab?"

The night nurse passed over a manila envelope. "Everyone had a quiet night."

"I didn't ask." Envelope tucked under one arm, the doctor stepped into the lounge and let the door to the nurse's office swing shut behind her.

Bitch. But none of the sentiment showed through her smile just in case Dr. Mui glanced back through the open blinds on the windows that were the top half of the office walls—the clinic's attempt to simultaneously create both a feeling of security in its patients and to prevent the place from looking too much like a hospital. In a time of drastic health care cutbacks, the job paid too well to jeopardize. For what they were paying her, faking friendly with the dragon lady was the least of what she'd be willing to do.

Averting her gaze from the ferns and Laura Ashley prints that adorned the lounge, Dr. Mui crossed to the closer of the two consultation offices, pulling the lab work out of the envelope as she walked. By the time she reached the desk, she was distinctly unhappy.

"Stupid, stupid boy. How could he be such a stupid boy?"

She sank into the chair and let the paper fall to the desktop. This changed everything.

The phone rang just as he was pouring the tea. Although he drank coffee at the office, he drank tea at the house because Rebecca had always preferred tea to coffee—except when they were traveling in the States. "Where," she'd remarked, "they started out making it in Boston Harbor with cold salt water and hadn't ever quite gotten the hang of doing it differently."

He pulled the receiver out of its base, tucked it under his ear, and barked a terse "Hello" while he went to the refrigerator for milk.

"It's Dr. Mui. We have a problem with the donor. The blood test I had run last night shows him as HIV positive."

"I thought he was clean?"

"He was. I expect that when he heard the good news, he went out and celebrated."

"This is going to be very awkward." He took the milk from the fridge and quickly closed the door. It would only cost a few pennies to leave it open, but he hadn't made a fortune by giving money to BC Hydro. "The recipient and his father will be getting on a plane in less than two hours."

"It would be a lot more awkward if we infect him."

They both considered the consequences for a moment.

"All right." He took a swallow of the tea and then set the cup down on the table beside the bowl of fresh flowers Rebecca had always insisted on having in the kitchen. "I'll call. As long as he's not actually on the plane, I can get through to his father's cell phone. And the donor?"

"We don't want him to talk . . ."

"No. Of course not. All right, no difference between him and the others, then. Just get him out of the clinic as soon as possible."

When the doctor had hung up and the milk had been returned to the fridge, he pressed the power button and dialed the buyer's number from memory. The conversation was, as he had anticipated, very awkward. However, in order to make a sizable fortune in real estate—even in the fast-selling Vancouver market—it was necessary to be a damned good salesman. Although he hadn't personally sold a property for some time, the old skills were still sharp, and it certainly didn't hurt that he was still the son's best chance.

By the time he returned to his tea, it was cold. He drank it anyway. Rebecca had never minded cold tea and had often shared it with the cat. The cat had died for no apparent reason three months after Rebecca. The vet had shrugged and implied it might have been due to a broken heart.

He envied the cat; its mourning had ended.

"And in city news, violence connected with organized crime hit a new high last night with death tolls up into double digits."

Fork full of scrambled eggs halfway to his mouth, Celluci stared at the radio.

"Eleven men, including crime boss David Eng, were found dead in a Richmond floor-covering warehouse when employees of the warehouse arrived for work this morning. Some had been shot, but some appeared to have been savaged by an animal. As a number of the men are known to belong to the organization run by Adan Dyshino, police are assuming that negotiations of some sort erupted into violence. They are not yet certain that the death of Sebastien Carl in East Vancouver is connected and are now attempting to find his wife. Anyone with information about these or other crimes is invited to contact Crime Stoppers or your local police."

"Yeah. Right." He snorted and continued eating. No one ever came forward with information about gang violence; the thing about organized crime was that it was *organized*. Witnesses were efficiently dealt with.

So Vicki was safe.

And then it hit him. Eleven men. Maybe twelve. Maybe more; unreported, made to look like accidents or like natural causes.

All at once, he wasn't hungry. He stared down at the eggs, searching for answers in the pattern the salsa made against the yellow. Eleven men. Maybe twelve. All members of a criminal organization and, the odds were good, probably all killers. All men the world was a lot better off without.

But still . . .

The law had to apply to everyone, or it applied to

no one. Whoever killed these men, no matter how much removing them might have improved things, had broken the law. Probably several laws. If it was Vicki . . .

"You're jumping to conclusions," he snarled, shoving his chair away from the table. "Henry was out there, too. It wasn't necessarily Vicki."

If it was Henry, did that make it any better?

It didn't *have* to be either of them. "Two gangs together in an enclosed space, that sort of stuff happens. Probably had dogs with them." Opening and closing the kitchen cupboards, trying not to slam them lest he smash the etched glass set into the doors, he found three complete sets of dishes but no garbage bags. Vague memories of a laundry room sent him down the hall. It was behind the second door he opened and had obviously been used that morning.

The washing machine was a European model. It loaded from the front like some of the big commercial machines and was supposed to use half the water. They were still incredibly expensive in North America and Celluci, who'd had to listen to one of his aunts extolling their virtues, wondered what happened in five years when the seal went and they flooded the laundry room. Vicki's clothes—jeans, shirt, sweater, underwear, sock, high tops; everything she'd worn the night before—were lying in a damp heap, cradled in the bottom curve.

Eleven men. Maybe twelve.

Maybe mud. Maybe a hundred other things.

He put the clothes in the dryer, grabbed a garbage bag from the utility closet in the corner and was on his way back to the kitchen when he heard a quiet tap at the apartment door.

The woman standing in the hall looked as if she were about to cry. "I'm sorry," she declared, waving one hand in the general direction of the open door as she dug in her purse for a tissue with the other. "It's just coming here has brought it all back."

"Mrs. Munro?" Celluci hazarded.

Mrs. Munro blew her nose and nodded. "That's

right. I'm sorry to be such a watering pot, but it just sort of hit me looking in the door like this, that Miss Evans is really gone."

Celluci knew he should move out of the way. That there wasn't any good reason now for her not to come in. *I've got a vampire asleep in here, so could you come back after sunset* just didn't cut it.

"I've just come by for a few things I forgot to take with me the night Miss Evans passed on." She looked up at him expectantly. "I won't take long, my daughter's waiting in the car."

There didn't seem to be anything else he could do so he stepped aside.

"So you're a friend of Mr. Fitzroy's." Sighing deeply, she walked purposefully through the entrance hall, her gaze darting from side to side like she was afraid to let it rest for long on any one object. "Miss Evans thought the world of Mr. Fitzroy. He flirted with her, you know, and that made her feel young. I don't mind letting friends of his stay here. And you're a police detective, aren't you? Just like on television. Are you and your lady friend having a nice visit to Vancouver?"

Wondering exactly what Henry had told her, Celluci said they were and then, as she headed straight for the pink bedroom, lengthened his stride to get ahead of her, hurriedly adding in a voice calculated to disarm middle-aged women, "Uh, Mrs. Munro, we have a bit of a problem."

She paused, her hand actually cupping the doorknob, and frowned slightly. "A problem, Detective?"

"My, uh, lady friend is asleep in there."

"Still?" Her watch had large black numbers on a plain white face. "It's almost ten. She isn't sick, is she?"

"No, she's not sick." And then, because there was nothing like the truth for that ring of sincerity: "She has an eating disorder."

"Oh, dear."

"And she had a bad night." He met her gaze and smiled hopefully down at her, an expression that had caused innumerable witnesses to suddenly remember a wealth of detail. "I was hoping she could get a couple more hours' sleep."

"Well . . ."

"If you leave a list, we could have Henry bring anything you need to your daughter's this evening."

"No, no, there's no need to disturb Mr. Fitzroy. He's already been more than generous, and, well . . ." Her pupils dilated as she remembered the unexpected visit. ". . . he asked me not to come by while you're here."

Celluci's heart started beating again when she let her hand drop and turned from the door. *My persuasions were, for the most part, monetary,* he heard Henry say. For the most part.

"I didn't need anything important. I wouldn't have even come by except that we were in the neighborhood and my daughter-in-law can be most persuasive."

More than you have any idea. If her daughter-in-law had been able to overwhelm one of Fitzroy's requests, even momentarily, formidable would not be too strong a word to use when describing her. There were other words, but Vicki'd pretty much forced him to stop using them. "We're very grateful that you're allowing us the use of your home."

Her face grew still as she glanced around the living room. "Yes. I suppose it is my home now. Miss Evans left it to me, you know."

"No, I didn't know."

"Yes, but I expect I'll sell it." She picked up a small brass sculpture, stared at it as though she'd never seen it before, and slowly put it down again. "This is all too grand for me. I like things a little cozier."

Cozy was not a word Celluci would've used to describe the pink bedroom. In fact the only word that came to mind was overwhelming. He trailed silently behind her as she crossed back to the apartment door.

"I'm sorry to have bothered you, Detective. If you could ask Mr. Fitzroy to call me at my son's when you leave."

"If we're an inconvenience, Mrs. Munro . . ."

"No, not at all." She smiled at him reassuringly, then stopped, forehead creasing in sudden puzzlement. "I'd have thought you'd be using the master bedroom."

"Actually, I'm using the master bedroom."

"Oh, of course." Her tone suggested this explained everything. "You're a friend of Mr. Fitzroy's!"

By the time Celluci realized what that meant, Mrs. Munro was gone—which was just as well because his reaction was succinct and profane.

Breakfast had been pretty good for hospital food. There hadn't been enough of it, but at least it hadn't come out of a dumpster. Sitting cross-legged on the bed, he smoked a cigarette and wished they'd bring him back his clothes. Or just his boots. He'd had to panhandle tourists for almost a week last summer to get them, and if he didn't get them back, the shit was going to hit the fan, big time. Sure he had enough money now to buy anything he wanted, but that wasn't the point. Those boots were his.

He ground the butt into a pitted metal ashtray and lit another. It was kind of weird they let him keep his cigs but since they weren't using his lungs he guessed it didn't matter.

When the door opened, he blew a cloud of smoke toward it, just to show he didn't care; that he wasn't freaked by what he'd agreed to do.

Her lips pressed into a thin line, Dr. Mui stopped short of entering the thin, gray fog and stared at him with distaste. "It's time for your shot."

He couldn't help it, he giggled. It was too much like something out of a bad horror movie. "Eet's time for your shot," he repeated in a thick, German accent. "And then you steal my brain and stick it in some robot, right?"

"No." The single syllable left no room for a differing opinion.

"Fuck, man, chill. It was a joke." Shaking his head, he went to pinch out the cigarette, but the doctor raised her hand.

"You may finish."

"Thanks, I'm sure." But he couldn't, not with her watching. He took two long drags and pinched the end, tucking the still warm butt back into the pack for later. "Okay." His chin lifted and he gave her his best *I don't give a fuck about anything* glare. "Do it."

"Lie down."

He snorted but did as he was told, muttering, "Man, I hope you've got a better bedside manner with the paying customers."

Her fingers were cool against his skin as she pushed up the sleeve of his pajama top, and he watched the ceiling as she swabbed his elbow with alcohol.

"Hey? You gonna take more blood?"

"No."

Something in her voice dropped his gaze from the ceiling to her face, but her eyes were locked on the liquid rising in the syringe. When she was satisfied, she pulled it from the small brown bottle cradled in her left hand, put the bottle back in her lab coat pocket, and looked down at him.

The hair lifted off the back of his neck. All at once, he didn't want that shot.

"I've changed my mind."

"You weren't given that choice."

"Tough shit." As he spoke, he shot out of the bed and as far away from her as he could get and still be in the room; his back was pressed hard against the outside wall, fists held waist-high.

Dr. Mui looked pointedly at the gym bag tucked up behind the pillow. "You took the money," she reminded him. "Do I take it back?"

"No!" He stepped forward, stopped, and stared at the gym bag. Money enough to get out. He didn't know where to, but he was intimately familiar with where from and he never wanted to go back. After a moment, he said "No" again, more quietly. What the hell was he afraid of anyway? They weren't going to do anything to him. They needed him healthy. The floor was cold under his bare feet as he walked back to the bed. He shivered and slid under the covers.

"Is this it?" he asked, refusing to flinch as the needle pierced his skin.

"Yes." With one efficient motion, she depressed the plunger. "This is it."

She left the room while the sedative did its work.

"We don't want a repeat of what happened the last time," she said to the orderly waiting in the hall, her tone intimating that what she did or did not want was all he should be concerned with. His expression suggested he agreed. "I don't care how he dies, but he is to be properly disposed of. Do you understand?"

"Yes, Doctor."

"Good." She stepped away from the door. "Go ahead."

He moved forward like a dog let off his leash.

Suppressing the urge to remain in the apartment in case Mrs. Munro returned while he was gone, Celluci locked up and headed for the elevator. The sooner they solved this thing, the sooner they could go home and get on with their lives.

Their theory about those responsible for Henry's ghost had been off base. Unfortunately, now that they knew organized crime wasn't involved, that left only a couple million potential suspects. Maybe a few less if the gangs were growing as fast as the media reported.

Of course, it also left Ronald Swanson. Multimillionaire philanthropist, bereaved husband, and all around nice guy.

The elevator arrived almost instantly.

Vicki insisted they continue to assume organ-legging. Since the police hadn't yet identified the corpse, it seemed obvious he hadn't lost that kidney through conventional surgery. Since they knew he'd

lost it locally, organ-legging was beginning to make
more sense. And the motive for removing the organ?
That was the only easy answer. Profit.

So maybe we should look for a Ferengi, he snorted
as he pushed the button for the parking garage.

The ghost's garage band T-shirt said he'd lived, and
died, in the immediate area. Since he hadn't yet been
identified, he was obviously someone who wouldn't be
missed. Unfortunately, the immediate area offered a
wide choice of potential donors. As Tony'd pointed
out, a West Coast winter beat freezing to death in
Toronto or Edmonton.

Since the transplant centers weren't involved, a private clinic had to be—those willing to buy organs
would, no doubt, draw the line at having body parts
hacked out in someone's basement. There were a page
and a half of clinics listed in the Vancouver Yellow
Pages, but sixteen of them could be immediately disre-
garded as he very much doubted there was a holistic
way to remove a kidney. The Vancouver Vein Clinic
had been intriguing but not as much as a quarter-page
ad promising live blood cell analysis. An accompanying photo showed a smiling woman with long dark
hair, obviously someone very happy with her blood.
He couldn't decide whether he should mention it to
Vicki or leave well enough alone.

A balding man in a golf shirt and white pants got
on at the third floor. Celluci nodded, noted the Rolex
and the expensive aftershave, then assumed elevator
position—his gaze locked on nothing about halfway
up the doors.

The list of buyers with the right combination of
need, cash, and willingness to keep their mouths shut
would necessarily be finite. It would, therefore, be in-
efficient to pick up a random drifter and hope for a
match. They'd need some kind of medical information.

Stepping out into the parking garage, he walked
toward the imposing bulk of the van, listening to the
echoes as he tossed his keys from hand to hand.

There was a street clinic in East Vancouver that

seemed to serve a less-than-upscale neighborhood and offered, according to their ad, HIV testing.

It was a place to start.

He closed the van door and adjusted the mirror, trying not to think of a load of wet laundry and how well the dark seats would hide stains.

Had he stopped to think about it, he would've taken a taxi. The clinic was on the corner of East Hastings and Main, tucked between the faux historical Gastown and the bustling stores of Chinatown in one of the oldest parts of the city. The streets were narrow, the traffic chaotic, and parking spaces at a premium.

Reaching Pender at Carrall Street, Celluci glowered at the ONE WAY/NO ENTRY that blocked his progress. Habit noted the license plate numbers of the two cars ahead of him which turned left after the light went from yellow to red; then he sat, drumming his fingers on the steering wheel, waiting for a break in the steady stream of pedestrians that would allow him to make his right. While he waited, he watched the people heading toward the Chinese Cultural Center and hoped that the trio of middle-aged women, draped with cameras and loudly calling everything, including the bilingual street signs, cute, were American tourists.

When the light changed, he moved out into the intersection only to be blocked by pedestrians crossing Pender. Halfway through the green, he took advantage of a group of teenagers agile enough to get out of the way and finally got around the corner. As traffic inched past a delivery truck, not exactly double-parked, he sucked in an appreciative lungful of warm air. Fresh fish, ginger, garlic, and car exhaust; familiar and comforting. Before her change, Vicki had lived on the edge of Toronto's Chinatown and this air, trapped between the buildings out of reach of all but the most persistent ocean breezes, evoked memories of a less complicated life.

By the time he reached Columbia Street, one short block away, he'd had enough nostalgia. When a parking spot miraculously appeared, he cranked the van into it, rolled up the windows, locked the doors, checked to see that the man lying against the base of the Shing Li'ung Trading Company was breathing, and still managed to beat the car that had been behind him to the corner.

The East Hastings Clinic wasn't quite a block away, but even such a short distance was enough to leave the prosperity of Chinatown behind.

The dimensions of the windows—now filled with wire-reinforced glass—suggested that the building had once held a storefront. Standing on the sidewalk, Celluci peered inside and swept his gaze over three elderly Asian men sitting on the ubiquitous orange vinyl chairs and the profiles of a scowling teenager arguing with a harried-looking woman behind a waist-high counter. While he watched, the woman pointed at an empty chair, gave the teenager an unmistakable command to sit, and disappeared into the back.

Still scowling, the boy stared after her for a moment then, shoving aside a cardboard rack of government pamphlets, snatched up a small package from behind the counter and raced for the door.

Celluci grabbed him before he cleared the threshold.

"Fuck off, man! Let me go!"

"I don't think so." Maneuvering his struggling captive back into the clinic, he kept himself between the teenager and the door.

"This is assault, asshole! Let go of me before I call a cop!"

"Would you like to see my shield?" Celluci asked quietly, releasing his grip on the thin shirt.

The boy jerked away, whirled around to stand back against the counter, and looked up. Quite a way up. "Oh, fuck," he sighed philosophically when he realized it hadn't been a rhetorical question.

"What is going on out here?"

Celluci opened his mouth to answer and left it open as he stared down at the most beautiful woman he'd ever seen.

"You're wastin' your time, man." Grinning broadly, the boy turned and held out his hand. Balanced on the palm was a rectangular box of condoms. "I decided not to wait for the safe sex lecture, Doc. This guy nabbed me on the way out."

The doctor lifted onyx eyes to Celluci's face. "And you are?" she asked.

"Um, Celluci." He shook his head and managed to regain control of his brain. "Detective-Sergeant Michael Celluci, Metropolitan Toronto Police."

The teenager glared at him in disbelief. "Toronto? Get fucking real, man."

"Aren't you a little out of your jurisdiction, Detective?" Blue-black highlights danced across a silk curtain of ebony hair as she tilted her head.

His explanation of how he'd noticed the boy reach behind the counter left out the fact that the clinic had been his destination. When he finished, the doctor switched her gaze to the boy. "You steal from this clinic, and you steal from your friends."

"Hey! You were gonna give them to me!"

"Not the whole box." She opened it, removed six plastic squares, and handed them over. "Now sit. The rules say these come with a lecture and you're hearing it before you leave."

Hands shoved into the pockets of baggy jeans, he sat.

The doctor put the box back behind the counter and glanced back up at Celluci, her lashes throwing fringed shadows against the porcelain curve of her cheek. "You've done me a favor, Detective. Is there anything I can do for you?"

"Join me for lunch?" His eyes widened as he realized it was his voice he heard issuing the invitation. The doctor looked to be more than a full foot shorter than he was. He'd always found short women intimidating. His grandmother barely topped five feet. *Lunch? What was I thinking?*

One of the old men muttered something in Chinese. The other two snickered.

The perfect curve of the doctor's chin rose to a defiant angle. "Why not?"

The Jade Garden Palace was a dim sum restaurant that had not been "discovered" by tourists. Those who stumbled onto the rundown, residential side street by accident, if not discouraged by the green insul-brick siding, took one look at the tile missing from the floor just inside the door and the scratched formica table-tops and usually decided to try some place a little less colorful. Although the doctor and the detective arrived at what should have been the height of the lunch rush, the only other patrons were an old man in terry cloth slippers and a harried mother with two children under three. The baby was gumming a steamed dumpling. So was the old man.

"I usually have three wartips, deep-fried tofu with shrimp, and a spring roll," the doctor said as she sat down.

"Sounds good." Celluci exchanged his chair for one with four functional legs and lowered himself gingerly onto the mottled gray seat. The place smelled significantly better than it looked. "But double it for me."

"They have a couple of brands of Chinese beer, if you're interested."

"I don't drink."

"Isn't that unusual for a police officer? I'd always heard you were a hard drinking bunch."

"Some of us are." The waiter set down a stainless-steel pot of green tea. "Some of us have other ways to take the edge off."

He watched, mesmerized as her brows lifted, like the wings of a slender, black bird. "And your way, Detective?"

"I fight with a friend."

She blinked. "I beg your pardon?"

"I have screaming fights with a friend."

"Who screams back?"

He grinned, beginning to relax. "Oh, yeah. It's very cathartic." Removing the paper sleeve from his chopsticks, he broke them apart. "It just occurred to me, you haven't told me your name."

Her cheeks darkened. "Oh. I'm so sorry. Eve Seto."

"No need to be embarrassed. After all, you only came to lunch with me because the old men in the clinic said you wouldn't."

"Was it that obvious?"

Celluci waited until the waiter set down the plate of spring rolls and a shallow dish of black bean sauce, then he shrugged. "I'm the only male in my generation and I have a ninety-three-year-old grandmother. Trust me. I know the power of age."

Dr. Seto stared at him for a moment, then she covered her mouth with her hand and laughed.

Spring roll halfway to the sauce, Celluci suddenly found it difficult to breathe. It wasn't a sexual response, exactly; it was more that her beauty elicited one hundred percent of his attention, leaving no room for such mundane concerns as inhaling and exhaling. After a moment, he forced himself to dunk, chew, and swallow, finding a certain equilibrium in the familiar food.

As far as gathering information went, lunch was a total disaster. Dr. Seto seemed both surprised and relieved by the distinctly light tone of the conversation.

Walking back to the clinic, out of inanities to discuss, Celluci turned gratefully as the doctor shaded her eyes with one hand, gestured across the street with the other, and murmured, "I wonder what's going on over there?"

Over there, at the Chinese Cultural Center, a bright yellow cable van had pulled up onto the broad walkway and was in the process of disgorging piles of electrical equipment.

"It's like watching clowns get out of that little car at the circus," Celluci said as another stack of indistinguishable black boxes was balanced precariously on top of the pile. Dropping his armload of cables, a tall thin man with a ponytail straightened the stack at the last possible instant and began a spirited argument with someone still in the van—an argument that got cut off before it really began when Patricia Chou stormed out of the building.

Seconds later, cables were once again being laid and equipment continued to be unloaded. Dr. Seto looked intrigued. "I wonder what she said."

"You know Ms. Chou?" Something in her voice suggested she did.

The doctor nodded. "She did a story on my clinic, two, maybe three, months ago. Overall, a favorable story but a little like being operated on without anesthetic." Her tone grew speculative as they moved away from the Center. "I'm surprised you know her, though. Didn't you tell me you've only been in Vancouver for a couple of days?"

"I don't exactly know her. I did see her interview with Ronald Swanson . . ."

"Would that be the Ronald Swanson who's in real estate?"

All at once, Celluci remembered why he'd gone to the clinic in the first place. Why he'd invited Dr. Seto out for lunch. "That's the one. Do you know him?"

"He's not a friend, if that's what you mean, but we've met. His company donated the computers we use in the clinic, and there're a number of volunteer organizations around the city that depend on his generosity. He works tirelessly for the transplant society."

"So I gathered from the interview." Then, before she could change the subject, he added, "I find the whole thing amazing—that you could take an organ out of one person, sew it into another, and save a life."

"It's not quite that easy, I'm afraid." She pressed the walk button and they waited while the light changed. Then they waited a moment longer as a mid-seventies orange truck ran the yellow.

"Is it something you've done?" Celluci prodded, stepping off the curb.

"Detective, think about it. If I were a transplant surgeon, would I be practicing street-front medicine?"

"No. I suppose not."

"You can be certain of it."

"I'd heard that kidney transplants weren't that difficult."

"For transplants. Afterward, they carry the same risk of rejection or infection as any other transplant, and infection kills." She half turned to look up at him from under a fall of silken hair. "Do you know what the greatest advancement in medicine was in the nineteenth century?"

"Convincing doctors to wash their hands." He couldn't help preening a little at her sudden smile. "Hey, I'm not as stupid as I look."

Vicki would have taken advantage of a line like that. Dr. Seto looked so aghast that he might possibly think she believed he was, Celluci found himself apologizing and going out of his way to be charming for the rest of the walk.

Back at the clinic, the doctor readily agreed to conduct a quick tour. "As long as it's very quick." The same three old men, at least Celluci thought they were the same three, watched their every move.

Unless there was a hidden operating theater in the basement, kidneys were not being transplanted on the premises. However, many of the clinic's patients were the sort of people who could disappear without questions being raised. A number of them had.

"They just never come back." Dr. Seto sighed as she slipped back into her lab coat. "It gets discouraging."

"Do you have any idea where they might have gone?"

"Back East, maybe. Hopefully, home." Her eyes focused on faces he couldn't see. "Unfortunately, I'm afraid that too many of them have ended up as police statistics of one kind or another."

When he pulled out the creased photocopy of the autopsy photo, she shook her head. "No. Not one of mine."

Celluci'd seen liars just as sincere and almost as beautiful, but he believed her.

A clearly stoned woman staggered in, doubled over in pain, and howling for a doctor. Celluci murmured a good-bye he doubted anyone heard, and left. Walking back to the car, he fought a rising melancholy. He and Vicki used to go for dim sum about once a month. They were often the only two Caucasians in the second-floor restaurant and they both towered over the rest of the clientele. The elderly women serving the food would occasionally walk right on by, shaking their heads and muttering, "You don't want."

It was something they'd never be able to do again.

A twenty-dollar parking ticket didn't help his mood. Traffic didn't ease until he was almost at the library.

Back when he'd been in uniform, an old staff sergeant at 14 Division had been fond of saying, "You get someone talked about three times during an investigation, and you go for a conviction 'cause that's the son of a bitch that did the crime."

Ronald Swanson's name had come up twice now.

A little digging unearthed the name of the clinic Patricia Chou had mentioned, ". . . *a private clinic where people in the last stages of renal failure can wait for a kidney.* . . ." According to old issues of the weekly newspaper, *Business in Vancouver,* Ronald Swanson had been responsible for its development, was on the board of directors, and contributed a large portion of its financial support.

Project Hope wasn't listed among the clinics in the phone book, but that was hardly surprising as it probably took a doctor's recommendation to get in.

Rubbing his eyes, Celluci left the microfiche carrel, dug out his phone card, and called the clinic from the library lobby. Without identifying himself, he asked if they had a transplant surgeon on staff. Coolly professional, the duty nurse admitted they did. Celluci thanked her and hung up.

Motive. Swanson's wife had died of kidney failure

waiting for a transplant. Swanson could want revenge against the system that failed him. Or maybe her death had pointed out a market waiting to be exploited.

Means. Swanson had access to facilities and the finances to buy any talent he wanted.

Opportunity. Suppose Dr. Seto didn't know she was supplying the donors? Swanson's company had donated her computers. Could he access them again for the information he needed? According to Patricia Chou, skilled hackers were a dime a dozen, and past experience proved that one in twelve law-abiding citizens could be bought.

"With enough money you have the opportunity to do anything."

A hard point to argue with, but he had nothing that could be called evidence by any stretch of the imagination. Nothing he could give to the police that would justify an arrest and keep Henry Fitzroy from taking the law into his own hands.

But the link, however circumstantial, between Ronald Swanson and Henry's ghost was strong enough to make a quick trip out to Project Hope worthwhile.

As he got back into the van, Celluci wondered where the transplant society's computers had come from. In Toronto, where his badge meant something, he'd have grounds enough to make inquiries. Were Vicki and Henry not involved, he'd check out the bar where Vancouver's finest hung out and find out just where their investigation was heading.

Except, of course, that I wouldn't be involved had that undead royal bastard of a romance-writing vampire, Henry Fitzroy, not gotten Vicki involved.

"You didn't need to come along," the little voice in his head reminded him.

"Yeah. Right." He snorted as he pulled out into traffic. "Like she'd be accomplishing anything on her own." He deliberately chose not to think about what she may or may not have accomplished between sunset and sunrise the night before.

Unfortunately, he wasn't in Toronto, vampires were

involved, and he couldn't think of a plausible reason why anyone should tell him anything.

Project Hope occupied a fairly large parcel of land on the eastern edge of North Vancouver. Celluci parked the van on the side of Mt. Seymour Road, spread out a map over the steering wheel, and cultivated a confused expression in case those passing by wondered what he was doing. From where he sat, some five hundred feet beyond the long driveway on a slight rise, he could see a one-story building designed so deliberately to look noninstitutional it couldn't look anything but, a half-filled parking lot, a dumpster, and a number of empty benches scattered about pleasantly landscaped grounds. The orientation of the building allowed him to see one side and part of the back. The distance from the road meant that he could see bugger all in the way of details.

Sighing, he pulled a set of folding, miniature binoculars out of the glove compartment. In one of her more whimsical moments, Vicki had ordered a pair of them from a magazine ad that insisted they were exactly like those used by the KGB. Celluci questioned the KGB connection, but he had to admit—although not to Vicki—that, for their size, they weren't bad.

A closer inspection told him only that the windows all had venetian blinds and that Dailow Waste Removal emptied the dumpster twice a week.

"So how long do I sit here?" he asked his reflection in the rearview mirror. Stakeouts away from masking crowds were always a pain in the butt, and the lost tourist routine wouldn't be plausible for long. "Maybe I should go in and ask for directions. See if they could lend me a hand . . . Hello."

A large man in pale jeans and a red T-shirt crossed the parking lot and got into one of the trendy sport/ utility hybrids that every second person on the Coast seemed to drive. He had to have come from inside. Through the binoculars, Celluci watched him back the truck toward the clinic. When it stopped, the angle of the building blocked everything but a bit of the front right bumper.

"Why do you back up to a building? Because you're loading something into the trunk." Squinting didn't help. The clinic remained in the way. "And what are you loading? That's the question, isn't it?"

It could be anything.

The odds of it being a body with only one kidney were astronomical.

"But life's a crap shoot, and sometimes you get lucky." He tracked the truck as it moved down the drive, tossed the binoculars onto the passenger seat, and put the van into gear. Still apparently studying the map, he let the man in the red T-shirt drive by, then pulled out to follow a safe distance behind. Their route led directly into Mt. Seymour Provincial Park.

When his quarry turned onto a logging road, Celluci went on by. Even he couldn't be expected to blend into traffic when there was no traffic to blend into. An illegal U-turn later, he parked as far over on the shoulder as seemed safe, hoping the bushes would hide the van should the car suddenly reemerge.

It wasn't exactly sudden. An hour and ten minutes later, the truck nosed back out onto Mt. Seymour and headed toward the city.

"All right, wherever he went, it's no more than thirty-five minutes in."

Fourteen minutes in, Celluci began to realize that, for all they were so close to a major metropolitan area, there was a whole lot of nothing out here. He didn't do well with nothing. Concrete and glass he understood, but trees were a mystery to him.

Sixteen minutes in, another logging road angled into the first. There were definite tire tracks in the ruts, obviously laid since the last rain. He flipped a mental coin and went up the new road; the tracks had to be recent, the last rain had fallen over lunch, the skies opening, emptying, and clearing between ordering the food and eating it.

Eight minutes in, he stopped at what seemed to be an abandoned logging camp.

"Jesus H. Christ, you could bury an army in this mess." Bodies buried in the wilderness were usually found because the area had been disturbed. This particular area couldn't get more disturbed—the men who'd hacked their living space out of this piece of forest had not been gentle. Tire tracks, old and new, crisscrossed the artificial clearing, and the boot marks told him nothing. "Great. Where's the ident crew when you need them—I want some plaster molds of those treads, and I want this whole place dusted for prints."

He snorted and shook his head. He could dig up every patch of fresh dirt he found, or he could . . .

"You lookin' for me?"

Grinning broadly, Celluci turned. "I'm looking for anyone who can get me unlost." The man in the red shirt was a little bigger than he was. That didn't happen often. *And doesn't it just figure that it's happening now.* He had the familiar proportions of men who spent their time in prison lifting weights—an impressively muscular upper body on regular guy type legs. Big brown eyes seemed out of place in the midst of his belligerent expression although the nine millimeter semiautomatic pistol he held, almost engulfed by one huge fist, matched perfectly. Still hoping he could talk his way out of whatever he'd gotten into, Celluci stared in astonishment. "Hey! What's with the gun?"

"You were parked watching the clinic. You followed me here. You tell me."

"I don't know what you're talking about. I'm just a guy from Ontario who got lost looking for the park lodge."

"Toss me your wallet."

"Oh. Oh, I see. I'm in the middle of fucking nowhere and I'm being mugged." Celluci jerked his wallet out of his back pocket and threw it on the ground at the other man's feet. The leather folder holding his police ID was still in his pocket. He had a chance. "You want the keys to the van, too? It gets lousy gas mileage, so be my guest."

"Shut up." Mild eyes never leaving Celluci's face, the gunman squatted and scooped up the billfold. He flipped through the compartments, peered at all the credit cards, never quite distracted enough for Celluci to make a move.

Then he stopped and shoved one finger deep into an inner recess and hooked out a photograph. His lips rearranged themselves into a triumphant sneer, and something glittered deep in the puppy-dog eyes. "This your granny standing next to you, Officer Celluci?"

Nine

Even before the day had fully released him, Henry could feel the cold tracing frosted patterns on his skin in a macabre parody of a lover's caress. Opening his eyes, he almost thought he could see the icy currents drifting in the air like winter fog.

It knew he was awake. He could feel it waiting.

Brows drawn down in annoyance, he turned on the lamp, and sat up.

It wasn't waiting. They were.

The second ghost was a little younger; late teens rather than early twenties. A metal ring glinted in one nostril. The ivory skull printed on the sleeveless black T-shirt grinned at Henry as though it appreciated the irony of a death's head worn by the dead. As far as Henry could tell, he was anatomically correct—this second specter had retained his hands.

"Blessed Jesu . . ." At the last instant, he realized he shouldn't have spoken aloud, but by then it was too late.

No audible sound emerged from either mouth stretched open far beyond the boundaries skin and bone would have allowed. As they howled, the soul heard the torment the ears could not.

Henry's heart began to race until it beat at nearly mortal speed, but a sudden anger provided a barrier against the waves of despair. How dared they make him responsible for the lives around him! How dared they buy his help with blackmail! How dared they . . .

A strangled moan from outside his sanctuary broke through where the spirits couldn't. It dragged him off the bed and across the room. *Tony* . . . Henry fumbled with the bolts, amazed to find his hands shaking, more affected by the shrieking dead than he was willing to admit. He spun around to face them, but they were gone; only the effect of their cry remained.

Ripping the last lock right out of the wood, he yanked open the door.

"Tony!"

Curled into a fetal position in the center of the hall, Tony slammed his forehead over and over into his knees and whimpered, the shrill noise pulsing to the rhythm of the action. Dropping down beside him, Henry wrapped both hands around the younger man's head and forced him to be still. "Tony, it's over. Listen to me, it's over." Gently, but inarguably, he turned Tony's head until he could look down into the wildly staring eyes. He didn't realize how frightened he'd been of what he might see until relief turned his muscles to jelly and he sagged back on bare heels. Insanity would have been no surprise, had, in fact, been almost expected. "You're all right. I have you."

"H . . . Henry?"

"Yes. It's me." Sliding an arm under shaking shoulders, Henry pulled him up against his chest.

"It was darker . . ."

He laid a cheek against sweat-damp hair. "I know."

Tony sighed and pushed against Henry's body—as though to test its strength as a shield—then he wet his lips and leaned back just far enough to meet the worried gaze. "Henry?"

"Yes?"

"What the hell did you ask it?"

"I was wondering that myself."

Henry managed to stop the snarl but only because he felt Tony's reaction when he tensed. "Not it," he said, lifting his head, his expression warning Vicki to come no closer. "Them."

"Your Greek chorus of backup screamers?" When

he shook his head and the implications sank in, she smashed her fist through the drywall. "Fucking, goddamned shit!"

Tony winced at the impact.

Henry tightened his grip. "That's not helping," he growled.

"I know. I'm sorry." She drew in a deep breath and visibly fought for calm. "You okay, Tony?"

He swallowed and shrugged, still within the circle of Henry's arms. "I've been better."

The wail of distant sirens drawing closer cut off Vicki's reply. Tony closed his eyes and added, "Could be worse."

When the sirens stopped and the sounds of the emergency teams were lost in the building's sound-proofing, Henry cradled Tony against one shoulder and met Vicki's gaze. "Was Celluci affected?"

"No. Fortunately, he's not back yet."

"Back from where?"

"How the hell should I know? You can ask him yourself when he shows."

"With him or without him, we have to talk."

She nodded and turned away.

"Vicki!"

A step forward became a pivot.

"Where are you going?"

"To get dressed." One hand held closed a ruffled pink robe, at least two sizes too small and obviously borrowed from the wardrobe Mrs. Munro had left behind. The other, knuckles white with plaster dust, she waved in his general direction. "An idea you might also consider."

Which was when he remembered he was naked. "We'll join you in about half an hour."

"I thought it was safer if we only used your place."

"We're not the only people involved." He watched her expression soften as she worked through his reasoning. Glancing down at Tony, who'd need to put some distance between himself and the terror, she nodded, and left.

Tony waited until he heard the door close before he began to free himself from Henry's embrace. "Henry, I can't . . ."

It took a moment for understanding. "I didn't expect you to," he said gently, wondering if he'd ever given Tony cause to assume his needs could be so inconsiderate.

"But you said . . . you told Victory half an hour."

"I know." He stood and all but lifted the other man to his feet. "I thought you might want to shower."

Tony glanced down at the darker stain on the front of his bicycle shorts, suddenly aware of what it meant. His cheeks flushed. "Oh, man . . . You think Victory noticed?"

It would serve no purpose to remind him that Vicki had a predator's sense of smell, so Henry lied.

"He's still not back?"

Vicki snorted as she led the way into the apartment. "You know he isn't. And the sun's well and truly down; he has to know I'm awake."

"He's probably following a lead."

"I *know* that, Henry."

Henry stopped at one end of the couch, allowing her to put the length of the living room between them. The events of the previous night aside, distance was still their best defense. "Are you concerned?"

"No. I'm annoyed. The bastard didn't even leave a fucking note." Behind her back, Henry and Tony exchanged a speaking glance. Vicki turned in time to catch the end of it. "What?"

"Your use of profanity always increases when you're worried," Henry reminded her.

Vicki flipped him the finger. "Increase this."

"Vicki . . ."

"I'm sorry." She turned and rested her forehead against the window, her right hand crushing a fistful of antique satin drapes. "Your ghosts have got me jumpy, that's all. There's no reason he has to be here at sunset. He's almost forty years old, for chrisakes; it's not like he can't take care of himself."

"I should imagine that he's very good at taking care of himself."

"I wasn't *asking* for reassurance," she snarled.

Tony opened his mouth, but Henry raised a cautionary hand, and he closed it again.

A heartbeat later, Vicki sighed. "All right. Yes, I was." Releasing the drapes, she glanced around for her notes, found them on the end table by Henry's knees, stepped forward, and stopped.

Henry's gaze dropped to the spiral-bound notebook, then rose to lock with Vicki's.

She shifted her weight onto the balls of her feet, ready for whatever he chose to do but unwilling to make the first move. The unexpected conclusion to last night's carnage had reminded her of what she'd arrived in Vancouver believing. If they were willing to try, they could get along. *All right, if we're willing to kill a dozen people we can get along,* she amended silently at memory's prod.

Without looking down again, Henry bent, picked up the notebook, and held it out.

The hair lifted off the back of Tony's neck and continued lifting until it felt as though every hair on his head stood on end. *Jeez, you could play "Dueling Banjos" on the tension between them.* He fought the completely irrational urge to reach out and pluck at the air as he waited and wondered what, if anything, he should do. He knew what he wanted to do; he wanted to turn on another lamp. *They* never considered that the people around them found shadows frightening.

Slowly, each step stiff-legged and graceless, Vicki crossed the room. Her fingers closed around the book. *Cue the ominous music.* Too emotionally abraded to cope, Tony closed his eyes.

"Tony? Are you okay."

He opened his eyes. Vicki was sitting in an overstuffed chair by the window, notebook on her knee. Henry'd propped one thigh on the arm of the couch. He looked from one to the other and back again. More than ever, they reminded him of cats; smug, self-righteous, and wearing identical, guarded expressions.

"We both fed heavily last night," Henry said when Tony turned a questioning glance toward him. "It seems to be helping."

"Feeding makes you less territorial?" That didn't sound right. They'd both fed the first night; it hadn't helped.

"*Heavy* feeding," Vicki reiterated, without looking up.

Tony had the uncomfortable feeling that, had she been able, she would have been blushing. While curious about what could possibly embarrass Victory Nelson, Tony decided not to press the point. The eleven bodies found in the Richmond warehouse had been front-page news, the press dwelling lovingly on the gory details, and if either Vicki or Henry were responsible, he didn't want to know. Some days, he could barely contain the knowledge that vampires existed—the fewer details he had to lock away with that knowledge, the better.

"I don't even know why I'm here," he sighed, rubbing his hand over his hair and dropping onto a stool.

"You're a part of this, Tony."

"Am I?" He wiped his hands on his jeans and stared down at the damp imprints of his palms. "Yeah, I guess I am."

Henry stood and took a step forward. Tony'd showered and changed and insisted he was fine, that the ghosts' shriek had done no actual damage, but obviously he wasn't and it had.

"So what's the story on the new spook?" Vicki demanded before he could speak.

Amazed that she could be so insensitive to what Tony was going through, Henry turned to glare at her. She met his gaze and shook her head. His brows dipped down over the bridge of his nose. How dare she. *Stay out of this. Tony is mine, not yours.* The words were in his mouth, ready to be spoken aloud when he looked in Tony's direction and realized it was no longer true.

Worst of all, it came as no great surprise.

Four-hundred-and-fifty-odd years of living masked among mortals allowed him to hide his reaction. "The second specter," he said slowly, answering her question because there wasn't really anything else he could say, not there, not then, "is a younger man, with hands. He looks like a street kid, pierced nose, lace-up boots . . ."

"A grinning skull on a sleeveless black T-shirt." A reprise of the scream threaded through the cadences of Tony's voice.

"You know him?" Eyes gleaming, Vicki leaned forward. Henry growled low in his throat and she whirled around, her own teeth bared. "What is your problem? If Tony knows him, it'll break the case."

"If Tony knows him, he's just lost a friend."

"And we're in a position to make sure he doesn't lose any more friends!"

"I didn't know him, and he wasn't a friend! All right?" Elbows on his knees, Tony buried his face in his hands. "I just saw him on the street. That's all. I didn't know him."

"It's not exactly a unique look." Keeping part of his attention on Vicki, Henry crossed the room and dropped to one knee by Tony's side. So things were changing—had changed—between them; they hadn't changed enough to keep him from offering comfort. "Maybe it wasn't him."

"It was."

"You're sure?"

He was as sure of it as he'd ever been of anything in his life. He wouldn't have been at all surprised had Henry said the skull joined in the screaming. "Yeah, I'm sure. He was saying good-bye to one of his buddies across from the store. They shook hands—that's why I remember. There's not a lot of hands get shook when you're living on the street." He found himself strangely reluctant to tell them about the way the skull had grinned at him. They'd seen stranger things—*Hell, they* were *stranger things*—and the odds were good they'd believe him, but it'd been just too weird and he'd had enough weird for one night.

"Do you think you could find his buddy?" Vicki asked before Henry could speak again.

"I don't know." He lifted his head. "I guess I'd recognize him if I saw him. You think he knows where it . . . where the dead guy went?"

"I think it's worth a shot."

"If it causes you pain," Henry began, gripping Tony's shoulder, "you don't . . ."

"I do." Shifting position on the stool, he looked into Henry's eyes. "I have to do *something.* I can't just sit around and wait for it to go away."

Vicki felt the fabric of the couch begin to tear under her fingers and hurriedly forced her hand to relax. Henry on his knees had always affected her strongly. *Maybe this is why we Hunt alone,* she thought, as he stood and lightly touched Tony's cheek. *Together there's a constant reminder that the intoxicating intimacy shared before the change is forever after denied you.* Every *other vampire becomes your ex.* "I hate to interrupt," she snarled, looked a little surprised at her tone, and attempted to modulate it, "but the night is short, and we've got a lot to do."

"Do we?" Henry let his hand fall back to his side.

"There're almost three million people in this city, Henry. And Tony doesn't have your advantages."

"I'm going with him."

"Is that smart?"

"He shouldn't be alone."

"Hey! I'm not alone now." Exhaling forcefully, Tony got to his feet and glared at both of them. "And I really hate that arrogant I-know-best-because-I'm-an-undying-creature-of-the-night crap. You can both just fucking chill! I'm going back to my room to change into a look that's more street smart. If you," he jabbed a finger toward Henry, "want to come with me to find the ghost's bud, fine. I can use your help. If not . . ."

"We were just concerned about you, Tony."

He sighed and rolled his eyes. "Fine. Thank you. Did I say you weren't?" Shoulders hunched, hands shoved into the front pockets of his jeans, and still muttering, he left the condo.

An awkward silence followed the closing of the door.

"Well," Vicki murmured after a long moment, "as one of my old sociology professors used to say, change is constant."

"Except for us. We don't change."

"That's bullshit, Henry, and melodramatic bullshit at that. You change, you adapt, or you die."

Or you die. Territorial imperatives broke through the surface civility they'd managed to maintain. Henry's eyes darkened and his voice grew cold. "Are you threatening me?"

Vicki could feel herself responding to his challenge. She didn't want to, she wanted to hold onto the tenuous truce that slaughter and sex had evoked; not only because it meant she'd been right all along and vampires could coexist, but because this was Henry, and she wanted him—them—back. *I don't give up easily,* she warned the world at large. *We are going to get along if I have to kill him!* Holding his gaze, she slammed an instinctive reaction back under conscious control. "No," she said when she thought she could trust her voice. "I'm not threatening you."

The phone rang.

"That'll be Celluci checking in. If you'll excuse me." The pencil she still held in her right hand snapped, but she managed to break eye contact and turn to answer the phone. It'd been a close thing, and if Henry pushed, he could go right through the flimsy barriers that barely restrained her desire to attack, but this time, at least, she wasn't giving in to biology. She'd never surrendered to it during the day and she'd be damned if she let it rule now the sun had set. It was, as they said, time to take back the night. The receiver creaked in her grip but the plastic held. "What!"

Henry forced himself to turn and walk away, reminding himself with every step that he was not leaving to *another* the territory he'd claimed as his. To his surprise, it was easier than it had been other nights. Like most things in life, even in an immortal life, it seemed practice made a difference. By the time his heels rang against the Mexican slate in the entrance hall, reason had gained the upper hand. *This is Vicki,* he pointed out to his reflection in the gilt-edged mirror. *She doesn't want your territory.*

His reflection answered with a wry smile. *This is Vicki,* pretty much covered the situation. She'd been unique as a mortal—nothing she did now should surprise him. During the short time they'd had together, he'd done things he'd never have considered doing on his own. *Perhaps there's no need to throw the baby out with the bathwater.* It wasn't St. Paul on the road to Damascus, but it was an epiphany nevertheless. *Perhaps,* he repeated thoughtfully to himself.

"That wasn't Celluci. It was someone who didn't know Ms. Evans had died."

Henry walked back to the archway that separated the living room from the entrance hall. In the interest of mutual nonaggression, he went no farther. "You're worried about him."

"No shit, Sherlock." Both hands splayed against the glass, she stood staring down at the city, not for that moment a predator looking down on prey.

"Why?"

"I don't know. I just . . ." She shrugged self-consciously.

"Have a hunch?" Henry offered, wishing he could cross the room and stand by her side.

"Yeah. A hunch. Doesn't seem very vampiric, does it?"

"It is if *you* have one."

Vicki turned to glare at him, one hand rising toward

the glasses she no longer wore in a not-quite-forgotten gesture. "Are you making fun of me?"

"No. I'm not." Although he could see how it might sound as if he was. "Vicki, no one ever told you how to be human, you were human just by being. Don't let anyone tell you how to be what you are now."

"Not even you?"

"Not even me, not anymore. I taught you what you needed to know in the year after the change. The rest is . . ." It was his turn to shrug.

"Ego?"

His eyes narrowed, and his chin rose. "Tradition. But just because we've always responded in such a way, doesn't mean we have to."

Had the window not been right behind her, she'd have stepped back in simulated shock. As it was, she raised both hands to shoulder height and exclaimed, "Good lord, Henry, you're evolving!"

"Don't push it."

The words came shaded with a dark warning that would've brought an answering snarl had Vicki's sense of fair play not acknowledged it was no more than she deserved. *Ah, hell, that was worth one snarl.*

Leaning back against the glass, she hooked her thumbs in her belt loops, the most nonaggressive posture she could manage. They still had the length of the living room between them, would probably always need a physical distance between them—except on those rare, intoxicating occasions of mass slaughter and mindless, blood-soaked sex—but now it looked as if other distances might not be insurmountable. "You'd better get going, Tony'll be waiting."

Tony. Mutual awareness of a dissolving relationship hung in the air. Henry brushed it aside. "What about Michael?"

"I don't know. I guess I'll wait here for him to call; or something."

"That's not the way it was supposed to be, is it? You waiting here, me out investigating."

"Well, I can't do everything myself."

Red-gold brows lifted. "Seems like I'm not the only one evolving." The small fringed cushion very nearly smacked him square in the face. "You have my cell phone number? Remember conversations can be picked up on short wave," he cautioned when she pulled his card from her pocket and waved it at him.

Vicki snorted, shoving the card away. "Do I look like a member of the royal family?"

The bastard son of Henry VIII threw the cushion at her head and was out of the condo by the time she caught it.

Although Vicki would have denied it had anyone brought it up, she was glad that he was gone. Within a certain proximity, the complicated stresses linking them dominated her thoughts, and right now that made her feel disloyal to Celluci.

You know how you wanted Henry and me to stop ripping at each other? Well, we went on a completely unpremeditated rampage together, killed I don't know how many people, and ended up screwing almost on top of a corpse. It seems to have helped. She snorted. *I don't think so.*

His absence chewed at her, and she couldn't remain still. She had no reason to believe he might be in trouble but, equally, no reason to disbelieve. Finding herself in the master bedroom, she sank down onto the edge of the bed and gathered up his sleeping bag, wrapping herself in his scent.

Would I be as concerned, she wondered, *without the guilt? Never mind. Stupid question.*

Returning to the living room, she sank back into the chair by the window and picked up her notebook. It had always helped to write things down—that hadn't changed, although she missed the balance of a coffee cup in her left hand. Scanning her scribbled description of the second ghost, she turned to a fresh page and glanced around for her pencil. Both pieces were over by the window.

"Oh, damn."

She could see the end of a pencil sticking out of the

Yellow Pages on the phone table. About to pull it free, she paused and opened the book instead. It wasn't her bookmark, so it had to be Mike's.

Her finger traced up and down the columns of private clinics. Vancouver either had one of the healthiest populations in the country or a thriving colony of hypochondriacs. Apparently Celluci'd done as she'd suggested and gone looking for the facility where the kidney had been removed. The East Hastings Clinic at East Hastings and Main had been circled and "start here" had been scribbled beside it in the margin.

Figuring he hauled ass out of bed by ten or eleven at the absolute latest; if he went there first thing, there's no way he's still there. She glanced down at her watch. It was past nine P.M. *Michael Celluci has been a cop for fourteen years, he can take care of himself. He probably met someone at one of these places and joined them for dinner.*

"Oh, shit." Tossing the pieces of the pencil aside, she called herself several kinds of an idiot. *He has to eat, Vicki. Just because you and Henry . . . well, it doesn't mean he has.*

But he hadn't been there when she woke and he hadn't called in and he knew she'd want to know what, if anything, he'd found.

The East Hastings Clinic at East Hastings and Main.

She'd told Henry she'd wait until Mike called. Or something.

It looked like something had come up.

If nothing else, she had a place to start.

"Where to now?" Henry slowed the BMW to give a cyclist room to maneuver around a line of parked cars. They'd started their search for the ghost's companion at the video store and had searched a widening circle without any luck. None of the locals had seen anyone matching his description.

"The Eastside Youth Center. If he's not there, someone'll probably know him."

"That's east of Gastown, isn't it?"

Tony's gaze remained aimed out the window of the car. "Yeah. So?"

"It's just that it's a bit of a distance away. If you saw him here, in this neighborhood . . ."

"The Center's a safe place, Henry. A guy'll go farther than that to find one."

"Tony."

Although he wasn't using his Prince of Darkness voice, something in the way Henry said his name drew Tony's head around.

"You're still safe with me."

"I know." For a change, looking away would've been the easier course—the hazel eyes held no touch of darkness, nothing that compelled him to continue. Tony swallowed and found the strength to say, "Maybe too safe." For a heartbeat, he thought he was being mocked, then he realized Henry's answering smile held as much sadness as humor.

"I assume you're speaking of life in general and not our immediate circumstances?"

"What circumstances? You mean you driving without watching the road!" His voice rose on the last word as he grabbed the dashboard and watched the world narrow to a corridor of moving metal. "Christ, Henry, that was a truck! That was two trucks!"

Henry deftly inserted the car back into the curb lane. "I know."

"Look, man, if you didn't want to talk about it, you shouldn't have brought it up."

Had he done it on purpose? Henry didn't think so; he'd seen a break in traffic and used it. Hadn't he? Whether he'd intended the result or not, the moment for shared confidences had passed.

Like any other city of its size, Vancouver had its share of rundown neighborhoods. The area east of Gastown, an area widely quoted in reports on crime and poverty, was one of the darkest. Theoretically, social assistance paid most of the bills, but the reality was considerably less benign.

The dividing line between the haves and have-nots

was astonishingly abrupt. Leaving the lights and tourist attractions of Gastown on one side of the intersection, Henry began to drive past boarded-up and abandoned stone buildings—once the main Vancouver branches of the seven chartered banks—standing shoulder to shoulder with shabby hotels and rooming houses. Back in the forties and the fifties, this was the bustling center of town, but the core had moved west and left only the architecture behind.

As they drove down Cordova, where the hotels and equally shabby bars seemed to be the only thriving businesses, Tony glanced over at Henry and frowned at the vampire's expression. "Why are you looking worried? There's nothing here you can't handle."

"Actually," Henry admitted dryly, "I'm a little concerned about parking the car."

Tony snorted. "It's a BMW. I'd be a lot concerned."

An unshaven man in a pajama top, dress pants, and rubber flip-flops stepped off the curb, ignored the squeal of tires, and wandered aimlessly across the street.

Watching the pedestrians a little more closely, Henry put his foot back on the gas. "Another six inches and I'd have hit him."

"He probably wouldn't have noticed."

As they approached the Youth Center, the sidewalks became more crowded. A group of First Nation teens, backs against the wire-covered window of a convenience store under siege, watched them pull to the curb, heads turning in unison.

"Don't lock it," Henry advised as Tony reached in to depress the mechanism.

"Are you crazy?"

"No, I'd just prefer not to have the windows shattered. If anyone opens the door, I'll be back here before they take the car anywhere."

The Youth Center was next to the Cordova Arms.

"People are actually living here?" Henry muttered as he glanced over the front of the building.

"Hey, this is an expensive city," Tony replied, fighting to keep his shoulders from hunching forward in the old wary posture. "Where else can a person on welfare afford to live?"

Over the centuries, Henry had certainly seen worse. From a historical perspective, the area was neither particularly violent nor destitute. Problem was, this wasn't the fifteenth century. He'd never hunted this neighborhood and never would—unlike most four-legged predators, he preferred not to feed on the injured or the sick.

Stepping over the legs of a sleeping drunk, they picked up the pace as the pungent smell of old urine and fresh vomit wafted by on a warm breeze.

Compared to the streets, the Center itself was painfully clean. The plywood-and-plastic decor might indicate a lack of funds but not a lack of commitment.

Tony froze just inside the door.

"Are you all right?" Henry asked softly, moving up close behind him and laying a hand on each shoulder.

"Yeah. No. It's just, well, memories . . ." He jerked forward, out of Henry's grip, trying not to resent the knowledge that he couldn't have broken free had Henry not allowed it. "Come on. Let's find whoever's in charge."

"Him." Henry nodded toward a tall man with graying hair tied back off a pocked face.

"How can you tell?"

"Power recognizes power."

"Oh, that's fucking profound," Tony complained, following Henry through the crowd. He could feel the hair lifting off the back of his neck, and he had to fight the feeling that the last couple of years had been a lie, that this was where he belonged, that he couldn't break free.

Henry turned and caught Tony's gaze before he could look away. "You're out," he said. "You've gone too far to go back."

"What're you talking about?"

"I could smell your fear."

"What?" Tony jerked his head to either side. "In

this lot?" When Henry nodded, Tony sighed. "Jeez, I guess I'm changing my shirt when I get home." They held their positions for a heartbeat, then Tony shrugged. "Look, thanks, okay?"

He didn't say what for. Henry didn't ask.

Except that he was cleaner than most of the people in the room, both physically and chemically, Joe Tait, the director of the Center, could've been one of the many drinking free coffee and hoping for an hour or two without fear. He had an edge that could only have been acquired on the street, a look that said, *I'm not one of them* where *they* were the people who talked about how something had to be done and did nothing.

"Yeah, I might know them." Tait had listened quietly to the description of the two young men Tony'd seen talking across from the video store, and now he studied first Tony then Henry through narrowed eyes. "Why're you looking for them? Are they in trouble?"

"One of them. We think the other can help."

"Do what?"

"We're hoping he can tell us where his companion went."

Tait folded muscular arms over a broad chest. "What kind of trouble's he in?"

"Deadly trouble," Henry said, allowing the Hunger to rise. They didn't have time to stand around all night playing twenty questions with a man whose suspicions, however justified under other circumstances, kept throwing up barricades. "I need their names and where I can find them."

"Kenny and Doug." He gave them up grudgingly. "And I don't know."

"Which one's which?"

"Which one's missing?"

"The white kid."

"Doug. But I still don't know where you can find Kenny." His lip curled as he indicated the room at large. "Feel free to ask around, but don't expect much. These guys have no reason to trust anyone."

Henry nodded and replaced the masks, releasing the other man. "Thank you."

As he moved out into the room, Tait closed thick fingers—not noticeably weighed down by heavy silver rings—around Tony's arm. "Just a minute, kid."

The words brought Henry back, eyes narrowed under lowered brows, but Tony waved him away. Whatever was going on, he wasn't in any danger.

Tait released his hold and propped one thigh on a plywood table. Together they waited until Henry began speaking to a table of teenaged girls. "You okay?"

"Me?"

"Yeah. You. That guy you're with, I know his type. We call them predators down here." He raised a calloused hand as Tony opened his mouth to protest. "I'm not saying that he's not good to you, but he's obviously the one with the power."

"It's okay." Tony fought a near hysterical desire to laugh. It had been a long night, and it wasn't even half over. "Really. He's not that kind of a predator."

"You're sure?"

His right thumb rubbed the tiny scar on his left wrist. "I'm sure."

No one in the Center knew any more than Tait had told them although Henry was certain three of the people they spoke to were lying.

"Half of them might know them to see them," Tony explained as they left, "but not know names or anything else. You stick with your own crowd when you're on the street, and you don't even open up to them. It's safer that way. Now what do we do?"

"I could wait for the liars to leave, ask them a few private questions."

"Yeah. Or you could ask those guys standing by the car . . ."

There were three of them. Tony heard Joe Tait's voice say, *"We call them predators down here."* Had he not seen the real thing, he would have been afraid. As it was, they were merely cheap copies, dangerous but by no means as terrifying as they thought they were—at least not in comparison. "I've got a vampire by my side," he murmured, "and I'm not afraid to use him."

Henry smiled and lifted a speculative brow. "Shall we see what they want?"

"I should think that's obvious," Tony sighed, falling into step.

The largest of the three heaved his butt off the BMW's hood and hooked his thumbs in the waistband of his jeans, rippling the complex pattern of blue tattoos that covered both bare arms. "We hear you bin askin' some questions."

"Did you?"

Oh, that's bright, Tony sighed silently, recognizing Henry's dealing-with-idiots voice. *Provoke them. Like they need the encouragement.*

The three exchanged triumphant glances, then the largest spoke again. "We might have some answers."

"Really?"

"The two you're lookin' for. Names are Kenny and Doug. They work for me. You want them, you go through me."

"Work for you?"

"Yeah. For me." The leer made his meaning plain.

Hands clenched, Tony conquered the urge to step behind Henry, to use him as a shield. *I am* not *that kid anymore.*

Henry's voice picked up an edge. He could smell the resurgence of Tony's fear and knew the source. It made it difficult to maintain any kind of civility—even the distant, arrogant civility he'd been using. "Do you know where they are?"

"Sure. We can take you to them. For a price."

"We pay when we see them."

Tattoos rippled again as he shrugged. "Suit yourself."

Tony's attempt to match Henry's nonchalance as the five of them walked toward an alley was hindered by his certain knowledge of what was about to happen.

A dumpster, just barely narrower than the alley, made it effectively a dead end.

Mouth dry, Tony tucked himself into a corner.

Henry touched him lightly on the shoulder and turned around. "Unless they're in the dumpst . . ." He caught the fist driving toward his face and tightened his grip. Bones crushed.

The tattooed man stared in astonishment at the screaming body rolling in the filth at his feet. "You fucking shit!" He flicked free a knife and flung himself forward.

His remaining companion did the same.

Henry dropped the masks. After the slaughter in the warehouse, he had no need to feed, but he loosed the Hunger anyway, driving it forward with rage fueled by Tony's fear. These men fed off the youth of the children they exploited. They were the filthiest kind of parasite, and they were about to get off far too lightly for what they did. They were only going to die.

A moment later, he squatted by the first man, the man whose fist he'd crushed, and grabbed his jaw, forcing him to meet his gaze. The screaming faded to a whimper. "Your friends are dead," Henry told him softly. "And so are you."

The rank stench in the alley grew ranker as the injured man's bowels let go.

"Where is Kenny?"

"Samson's got a room he uses, down the street. Doug . . . Doug's gone."

"Gone where?"

"Don't know. Somebody gave him money. Lots of money. Thousands." The words spilled out in a panicked rush, as though they could buy redemption. "Kenny says that's all Doug told him. This ain't the first time. Talk says there's a guy who'll buy you off the street. Give you another chance. Talk says you gotta be special."

"Do the police know this?"

"Who the fuck talks to the police?"

Henry had to acknowledge that, considering the source, it was a valid point. "Is that all you know?"

"Yeah. That's all." He couldn't move his head, so he rocked his body back and forth, tears spilling down both filthy cheeks. "I don't want . . . I don't want to die!"

Henry's hand moved from jaw to throat.

"Henry." Tony stumbled over a sprawled body, grateful for the lack of light, and gently touched the rigid line of Henry's shoulder, adapting the comfort Henry had offered him a long moment before. "Don't. Please."

"If you're sure."

"I am."

Leaning forward until the darkness swallowed the other man's will, Henry said softly, "Do not remember us, but remember what happened here tonight. Remember why it happened. Find another line of work." He straightened his legs, fitting the masks back in place. "Are you all right?"

"Me? I wasn't in the fight." Brushing past, Tony hurried for the gray rectangle of light at the end of the alley, unable to be anything but glad the pimp was dead and not liking himself very much for that feeling. "Come on, before they strip the car."

Careful not to touch the pitted metal, Henry heaved both bodies into the dumpster. Aware of the dichotomy in Tony's voice, Henry kept his own carefully neutral. "Hopefully, the scavengers are waiting to see if these three return to claim the prize. I got the impression they weren't nice people."

"No shit."

The immediate neighborhood seemed eerily deserted as they emerged onto the street. "What they don't see they don't have to lie to the cops about," Tony explained as they ran for the car.

The BMW was fine, although a stray cat had sprayed both curbside tires.

"Do you think anyone's made a note of the license plate?" Henry asked, starting the engine and all but popping the clutch as he pulled out of the parking space.

"Yeah. Sure. They all carry around pocketbook computers to jot their observations down in. Get real, Henry, most of these people can't focus on the car let alone the license plate." He mimed breaking an egg. "You know, 'this is your brain on drugs'?" When Henry didn't answer, he sighed deeply and closed his eyes. "Looking at the bright side, Doug's not just the second guy to disappear, but you've only got two of the ghosts."

"Why would anyone sell themselves to a stranger without knowing what they're selling themselves for?"

"They'll *do* a stranger for twenty bucks. For a thousand, who's going to ask questions?" Wiping his palms on his jeans, Tony opened his eyes. "Where to now?"

Pulling up at an intersection, Henry shrugged. "I don't . . ." His head swiveled toward the open window.

"What?"

"That scent . . ."

"You mean stink."

"No. I mean Vicki."

The clinic was closed, the waiting room dark and empty, but Vicki could sense a life in the building. A line of light, barely visible around the perimeter of an inner door, suggested someone was working late in the back. A fairly sophisticated alarm system convinced her not to attempt a frontal assault.

"There's got to be another entrance," she muttered, "if only to keep the fire marshal happy."

Keeping to the shadows, she turned down Columbia and then into the alley that bisected the block. Two people were sleeping in the first dumpster she passed. An old woman was fishing a meal out of the second. She dropped down off her perch as Vicki approached, clutching a greasy box of beef fried rice in one hand and length of pipe in the other.

"Damn kids! Leave me alone!"

She wasn't drunk or on drugs—Vicki could've smelled

either, even over the combined stink of the alley and its occupants—so she was probably one of the thousands of psychiatric patients cutbacks had put on the street.

"I'm tellin' ya, get away!"

Vicki caught the pipe, a little surprised by the force of the blow, and stuffed two tens under the old woman's fingers. White-middle-class guilt money, Celluci'd call it. Maybe. It did nothing to solve the problem, but it beat doing nothing. Marginally.

The old woman sniffed at the money, then thrust it back toward Vicki. "I ain't goin' with ya," she said. "Not even if you bring the big guy."

"The big guy?"

"The one what usually offers the money. Big guy. Real big. Got cow eyes like shit wouldn't melt in his mouth, makes ya wanna trust him, but he's mean underneath. I know." Her brain made a right turn, and the money disappeared under at least three layers of clothing. "Watch out for that big guy, you." All of a sudden, she squatted at the base of the wall, tucked the pipe under one arm, and began to eat. "Damn kids," she added.

Vicki moved on.

The clinic had a parking space, a tight squeeze even for the tiny import that filled it, and a back door made of industrial steel. Blinking back tears in the glare from the security light, Vicki noted the pattern of dents. Boot marks mostly although someone had unsuccessfully taken a crowbar to the area by the lock. A small sign read, *When the light is on, ring the bell.* Vicki assumed that the Chinese characters below it said much the same thing.

Why not. She heard the bell ringing inside the building, sensed the life drawing closer.

"Yes? Can I help you?"

It was a woman's voice and not a very old woman at that. Vicki directed a neutral stare at the intercom grille. "My name is Vicki Nelson. I'm a private investigator and I'm looking for Michael Celluci."

"Michael Celluci?" The surprise in her voice didn't seem directed at the name itself but rather at hearing it again.

"Yes. I have reason to believe he came to see you today. He's my partner, and I have a feeling he's in trouble."

"Just a minute, please."

Okay, Vicki, if this woman's a part of the kidney scam, you've just leaped into the frying pan. That was bright.

The door creaked open.

But at least I've gotten inside.

Bolts slammed back into place behind her and a figure in a loose smock appeared silhouetted in the light at the end of the short hall.

"I'm Dr. Seto. I run this clinic. Please, come into the office."

By the time Vicki rounded the corner, her eyes had adjusted to the light. "Oh, my God . . ."

Dr. Seto frowned, lifted her hand off the back of an old wooden desk chair and pushed a silken strand of ebony hair back behind one ear. "I beg your pardon?"

Unaware she'd spoken aloud until the doctor had reacted, Vicki mumbled an apology, thankful she could no longer blush. *If you're one of the bad guys, Celluci's in big trouble. The stupid ox is a pushover for short, beautiful women.* "You, uh, weren't what I was expecting."

The doctor sighed, nostrils pinched together, used to and irritated by the reaction her looks evoked. "Detective-Sergeant Celluci didn't mention he was working with a private investigator. Perhaps you should show me some identification."

"You should've checked it before you let me in," Vicki pointed out, reaching into a side pocket on her shoulderbag.

"I would have if you'd been a . . ."

"Man?" Vicki finished, handing over the folded plastic case.

"Yes." Obviously annoyed with herself, Dr. Seto

glanced at the ID and passed it back. *Now we're even,* her expression said as clearly as if she'd said it out loud. *Let's get on with it.* "I assume the detective is missing?" When Vicki nodded, she leaned against the edge of the desk and folded her arms. "He was here this morning, about 11:30. He grabbed one of my street kids who was trying to walk off with a box of condoms. We had lunch together. I showed him around the clinic. I got busy and he left."

You had lunch together? "You don't know where he went?"

"No."

You had lunch together! "Are you sure?"

"I didn't actually see him leave. I had patients come in."

Okay, so they had lunch together. Big deal. The man has to eat. Vicki stared at a poster of an ulcerated stomach, knowing that if she looked at the doctor she'd rip the answers from her by force. "You don't happen to remember what you and the detective discussed over lunch, do you?"

"Nothing much. Mostly we made small talk."

Small talk? Celluci had never managed to keep small talk from becoming an interrogation in his life. Or for as long as she'd known him, which was all of his life that mattered.

"You know, comparing Toronto and Vancouver." The extended silence had made the doctor nervous. "He never said that he was working on a case; I assumed he was on vacation."

"Technically, he is. He's just helping me out."

"You've known him for a long time?"

Whatever else had gone on between them, the tone of that question made it clear that Dr. Seto was not responsible for Celluci's disappearance. If she was going to knock him out and toss him in the cellar, it wouldn't be because she wanted his kidneys. Vicki turned around—she couldn't help herself—caught and held the doctor's gaze. "Yes. A very long time."

Dr. Seto blinked, swayed, and put a hand on the desk to steady herself. For a moment, she'd felt as though she were falling into silvered darkness, buffeted about by waves of raw energy barely under control. *I've got to get more sleep.* "I'm afraid I can't help you find him," she murmured, straightening. "I just don't know where he went after he left the clinic."

Logically, he'd have gone to the other clinics—but which ones in which order? The trail was hours cold. Vicki shoved aside a numbing sense of futility and rummaged in the depths of her purse for one of Henry's cards. "Thanks for your time. If you remember anything else, could you call the cell phone number?"

"There really isn't anything else to remember, Ms. Nelson."

"*If,* Doctor."

"Very well. If."

"I thought Victory was waiting back at the condo for Celluci to call."

"Maybe he called."

Tony snorted. "Maybe she got tired of waiting."

"I wouldn't doubt it." Head cocked toward the window, Henry sifted through the lingering scents of the Eastside and the equally pungent although infinitely more pleasurable scents of Chinatown, trying not to react to the certain knowledge that another stalked his territory. "It's strongest here." Teeth clenched, he eased the car over the curb.

Tony stared past him at the dark windows of the East Hastings Clinic. "You think she went there?"

"I think that's her at the corner."

Even squinting, Tony could make out only a vague shape. "Hey, why're you getting out of the car?"

Henry smiled darkly. "Maneuvering room."

Although she'd known that the only way Celluci would still be at the East Hastings Clinic was as a prisoner, Vicki found herself infuriated by his absence. A prisoner she could've freed! "When I catch up to him, he'd better be in manacles, or I'm going to stuff the nearest pay phone up his . . ."

She whirled to face the breeze, hands out from her sides, weight forward on the balls of her feet.

"Did he call?"

"No."

Henry nodded slowly. It was, after all, the answer he'd expected. "You got tired of waiting."

"I found notes he'd left that indicated he might be here, at this clinic."

"And was he?"

"No." She spat the word out onto the street between them, her anger switching from Celluci to Henry, just because he was there. In another moment, she'd be diving for his throat; she could feel herself tensing, preparing for the attack.

He braced himself, control made easier because the one who maintained control would win. "That isn't helping, Vicki."

"You think I don't know that?" she snarled. "And you have no idea how much it pisses me off that I can't get angry with you without attempting to kill you." A raised hand cut off his reply. She stood motionless, forcing the memory of how it had been after the slaughter to re-evoke calm. To her surprise, it worked. Mostly. "So," she stepped forward, heading for the car, "any luck finding Tony's witness?"

"In a manner of speaking." Henry fell into step beside her, a prudent arm's length away. "The ghost's name was Doug. We had a little chat with his pimp."

"Who you killed." It wasn't a question; she could hear death in his voice. The part of her that still remembered the person she'd been wondered where such casual justice had been all the years she'd tried to get that kind of scum off the streets. *He was sitting in his condo writing romance novels. Never mind. Sorry I asked.* "Did he tell you anything?"

"Only that someone's paying lots of money for special people."

"Special as in the same blood type as the buyer of the kidney?"

"Perhaps. But how would they find out?"

Vicki waited until a truck roared past, then nodded toward the clinic. "Access records."

"What? Through Hackers for Hire?"

"If you can buy a kidney, Henry, you can certainly afford to buy someone with that kind of rudimentary hacking ability." She told him about her conversation with the old woman in the alley. "Sounds like they've bought some muscle with mean cow eyes."

"Bull."

"Bull?" Her tone advised a quick explanation.

"It was a joke, Vicki. A man would have *bull* eyes."

"I think I liked it better when we were trying to kill each other. What now?"

Henry stopped by the car, his hand on the driver's door. "We go back to the apartment and see if Celluci's returned."

"He hasn't." Ducking her head, she nodded a greeting at Tony. "If he got back and none of us were around, he'd call on the cell phone."

Which rang.

"Speak of the devil," Henry murmured, reaching in through the open window.

Tony mouthed a silent warning as he handed over the shrilly chirping piece of plastic. *If it's Celluci, be polite.*

Brows raised in an exaggerated, *Who me?* Henry flipped open the mouthpiece. "Fitzroy."

"This is Dr. Eve Seto, from the East Hastings Clinic. I was speaking with a Ms. Nelson a few moments ago; she gave me this number, and . . ."

"Just a minute, Doctor." Smiling, he offered the phone to Vicki. "It's for you." His smile faded when he discovered it was almost impossible to let go, to hand over to *another* a possession of his. Snarling, he shoved it back into the car. "Tony, give her the phone."

Resisting the urge to crush something scented so strongly by another predator under her heel, Vicki raised it to her face. "Hello?"

"Ms. Nelson?"

"I ran into Mr. Fitzroy by accident, Doctor," Vicki answered the unspoken question. "He was driving by as I came out onto East Hastings."

"Oh." Her tone suggested it was an accident she didn't quite believe in. "It's just that I remembered something that happened after lunch. It was a minor thing but I thought you might want to know."

"After lunch?"

The two men exchanged speculative glances.

"What's she got against lunch?" Tony whispered.

Henry shrugged. He could hear six separate heartbeats pounding up out of the basement apartment across from the clinic, but electronics interfered with eavesdropping.

"Yes. On our way back to the clinic, we saw Patricia Chou outside the Cultural Center and . . ."

"The cable television reporter."

"That's right. The detective mentioned that he'd seen her interview with Ronald Swanson and . . ."

"Ronald Swanson, the real estate guy?"

"He's more than just real estate, Ms. Nelson." Her tone was sharp, possibly in defense of Ronald Swanson, more probably in response to the interruptions. "He's donated money to a thousand causes all over the city. He donated our computer system here at the clinic and was pretty much one hundred percent responsible for Project Hope."

"Which is?"

"It's a hospice on the edge of North Vancouver where transplant patients wait for kidneys to become available. It's sort of a shrine to his dead wife. A lovely place, quiet, tranquil."

"Dead wife?"

"Yes, she died of renal failure before they found a donor for her."

Vicki blinked, a little overwhelmed. "Did you tell this to Celluci?"

"No, but we did discuss kidney transplants although only in light of me actually performing them."

"Do you perform transplants, Doctor?"

"This is a street-front clinic, Ms. Nelson, what do you think?" She continued before Vicki could tell her. "Funny thing, though, the detective asked me that as well. I may be completely out of line here, but does your investigation have to do with the handless body they found in the harbor, the one missing the kidney?"

"I'm not at liberty to discuss that."

"Very well. But I'm telling you now, if you're investigating Ronald Swanson, you're dead wrong. The man is continually giving his money away. Around this area, he's practically considered a saint."

"Not many saints make millions in real estate," Vicki noted dryly.

"I have no intention of arguing with you about this, Ms. Nelson. I only thought that if you were looking for Detective Celluci, you might want to speak with the people at Project Hope."

"If I recall correctly, Doctor, you said earlier that you didn't tell him about the clinic."

"He's a detective, Ms. Nelson." Her tone suggested he was the *only* detective involved. "In this city, Mr. Swanson and kidney transplants together will lead you right to Project Hope."

Teeth showing, Vicki thanked the doctor for calling, hung up, and filled the others in on the conversation. "So who's going with me to take a look at Project Hope?"

Henry shook his head. "It's too much of a coincidence, all the pieces falling so neatly into place. I think you're jumping to conclusions."

"Really, *I* think I'm formulating a hypothesis." Her eyes silvered briefly. "Which I intend to test by going out to Project Hope and finding out just how long these people are actually waiting for those kidneys. And if I recognize anything in the fridge, I'm going to tear the place apart."

"Go out to Project Hope? All of us?" Tony's gaze flicked from Henry to Vicki and back to Henry again. "In one car? Is that safe?"

"Good question," Henry allowed. "Vicki?"

"We'll be fine, she snapped impatiently. "As long as we keep our minds on finding Mike, and there's the possibility of mayhem at the end of the trip."

"Oh." Tony closed his eyes for a moment and took a deep breath. Speaking as much to himself as to the night, he murmured, "I don't actually think I'm up to mayhem." Another deep breath, and he got out of the car, turning to stare across the roof at Henry. "I'll, uh, go back to the condo, and if he checks in, I'll call you."

They stayed that way for a long moment. "If you're sure," Henry said at last.

"Yeah. I'm sure." He swallowed heavily and shifted his weight back and forth, from one foot to the other. "I'm sorry, Victory. I just can't."

She drew in a deep breath and let it out slowly. When she spoke, her voice was as gentle as Henry'd heard it since the change. "I understand. And there's no reason you should risk your safety because we can't act like civilized people." Rounding the car between one heartbeat and the next, she cupped Tony's face in her hands. "Will you be okay if we leave you here? Should we take you home first?"

He lightly touched the backs of her wrists and her hands fell away. "You have to get to Detective Celluci."

"I won't trade you for him."

His eyes filled with tears as he realized she meant it. Acknowledging only that he was more tired than he thought, he scrubbed them away. "I'll be okay. I can get a cab by one of the restaurants in Chinatown."

"Do you have enough money?"

"Goddamn it, Henry!" Ears burning, he backed to the far edge of the sidewalk. "Would you guys just get going!"

They left the windows open and kept their faces in the breeze. It was enough. But only just.

"Do you think he's there?" Henry asked as they sped around an erratic, albeit fast-moving, old caddie and headed for the bridge.

"I know he *went* there. I know how he thinks. There aren't any coincidences in police work; once Ronald Swanson turned into a recurring character in this little drama, Mike'd check him out. He'd find out about Project Hope, and then he'd check it out."

"Do you think he's in trouble?"

When she considered the possibility, she felt as though someone were stroking her exposed skin with a wire brush.

"I'm certain of it."

Ten

"There's nowhere to hide the car."

"Don't hide it. Pull into the parking lot, and park."

"It's after one," Henry pointed out as he passed the sign for Project Hope, turned between the gateposts, and started up the long drive. "While normally I wouldn't consider arguing with your expertise in skulking about, don't you think we'll be noticed? There'll be a night nurse on at the very least."

"So?"

"So, you're going to walk in and ask her if they've got Detective Celluci strapped to a bed in one of the rooms?"

"Why not?" Her voice had very little of the police officer, the private investigator, or the mortal left in it. Henry fought to suppress his reaction as she continued. "It's not like I'm going to be lied to. Besides, if he's in there, I'll know."

"And if he isn't?"

The ivory gleam of teeth made her smile a threat. "I go looking for a big guy with cow eyes and ask *him* a few questions."

Beyond the edges of her control, edges sharply enough defined to draw blood, Henry could hear the surging violence surging back and forth. She sounded close to letting go. Hardly surprising given the proximity they'd been in since leaving the clinic—the tension between them sat like a third presence in the car. He could feel his own barriers weakening and trying to convince himself that this was a continuation of the year they spent in a parent/child, teacher/student relationship helped not at all. If the anticipated mayhem didn't materialize inside Project Hope, they'd be at each other's throats before he got the keys back into the ignition.

Vicki leaped from the car the instant it stopped moving and sucked in a lungful of air untainted by *another's* breathing. If it came to it, she decided, dragging her bag up onto her shoulder, she'd walk back to the condo before she let Henry drive her anywhere, ever again. He slowed for yellow lights. He didn't pass when he could. He took corners too slowly. It had been the most frustrating fifty minutes she'd ever spent. Only iron control had kept her from dragging him out from behind the wheel and taking over herself. *I have* got *to get my driver's license again.* Lips pressed into a thin line, she strode toward the building. "Remember, Vicki, not being noticed is infinitely better than having to correct a dangerous impression."

"Christ, Henry. You sound like an old *Kung Fu* episode."

He locked the car and hurried to catch up. "I'm speaking from experience. . ."

"I know, I know, over four hundred and fifty years. No wonder you drive like an old woman," she added under her breath as she yanked open the clinic's cedar slab door.

Half a dozen battling scents almost knocked her back outside—a bouquet of roses in a large glass vase, a chemical air freshener designed to mimic the ocean breezes kept out by hermetically sealed windows, and over, under, and through it all, the eau d' disinfectant worn by every medical establishment in the world.

She could sense perhaps a dozen lives, the delineations between them removed by sleep—natural or drug-induced, Vicki hadn't the experience to tell the difference. Somewhere in the mix, she thought she felt the unmistakable flavor of Celluci's life. *But why can't*

I tell for sure? She'd been so certain she'd know if he was in the clinic that this sudden ambivalence was unsettling. *Do I just think he's here because I want him to be here so badly? Would I have known for certain before last night's horizontal dance down memory lane with Henry?* A heartbeat later, she found an answer she could live with. *Christ, Vicki, don't be such a goddamned idiot.*

The lingering despair—despair with very little hope in it, she noted, in spite of the name of the clinic—made it difficult to get a clear fix on anyone's life. Since that also included Henry's life, she supposed she just had to take the bad with the good.

The only nonsleeper glared a question at them from behind the glass walls of the nurse's station.

"I was right," Henry murmured. "We've been noticed."

"Good," Vicki declared a little too emphatically. Unable to blush, she winced. Ever since she could remember, women in nurses' uniforms had made her feel inadequate. Maybe because they seemed so competent. Maybe it was all that white. She had no idea. Feeling less like an all-powerful creature of the night and more like she was somewhere she shouldn't be, she skirted the lounge and stepped into the dimly lit office.

"Yes? Can I help you?" While civil enough, the nurse's tone clearly indicated that the only help she intended to give them involved showing them the exit.

"I'm looking for a friend."

"This is a private treatment center, not the local emergency ward. You won't find your friend here."

"He would have been admitted this afternoon."

"There was no one admitted this afternoon."

"Would you like me to do this?" Henry asked quietly, not entirely able to keep the amusement from his voice. He'd seen Vicki face demons, werewolves, mummies, and a multitude of murderous mortals with more elan.

She growled a wordless reply, caught the night nurse's

gaze, and held it, overcoming old programming for pride's sake. "Are you alone here?"

Dilated pupils reflecting a faint silver gleam below an annoyed frown, the other woman shook her head. "There's an orderly."

"Where is he?"

"Asleep on a cot in the staff room."

"Why is he here?"

"He stays sometimes, in case there's trouble."

"Trouble with what?" Vicki rested her hands on the desk and leaned forward. "Trouble with the *donors* of purchased body parts?"

The night nurse stood, still held in the silvered depths of Vicki's eyes, and mirrored her movement. She was almost as tall. "I don't know what the hell you're talking about."

This was not the usual response. Somewhat taken aback, Vicki allowed a little more of the Hunter off the leash, dropped a little more of her mortal camouflage. "You've never noticed anything strange going on? Patients who don't quite match their records? Locked doors?"

Breathing heavily, the nurse shook her head. "Whatever you are, you don't scare me. You want to know what scares me? Having two teenage kids and a husband who's been out of work for six months and losing this job, that scares me. I'm not telling you anything."

"If you're dead," Vicki snarled, patience exhausted, "you *won't* be working."

"You might be death for some people, I can see . . ." Fear finally showed, trapping her voice in her throat. She swallowed hard and continued. ". . . see that, but whatever you are, you aren't death for me."

"She's right," Henry said softly, impressed by a strength of will that refused to be blinded by terror. "She knows you won't kill her without reason. She's called your bluff."

Reaction split equally between irritation and embarrassment, Vicki held her position at the desk. "This does not make me weak," she warned him, fingers curling into fists.

Amused, but careful not to let it show, he moved a little closer. "I meant it as a compliment to her, not an insult to you. Perhaps you'd best let me . . ."

"No!" This mortal was hers. Whether or not Henry could convince her to speak was irrelevant. Eyes narrowed, Vicki muttered, "Must be a damned good job."

"It is . . . mostly."

Mostly. Vicki smiled. "If I had a job with good money in these times, I guess I'd be willing to ignore things that don't quite fit, too."

"Hey, I take care of the patients, and I do what I do very well." She straighted and folded her arms across the broad shelf of her breasts. "What goes on in the back is none of my business."

"Of course it isn't. Forget you ever saw us."

Lips pressed into a thin, disapproving line. "You got that right."

"Mike's in here."

A sign on the door said ELECTRICAL ROOM.

"Are you sure?"

Vicki ignored him, rummaging in the depths of her shoulderbag for her lock picks.

"I can feel a number of lives, Vicki; up, down, all around us. Most of them are drugged, all of them have been blended by their condition into one amorphous mass. How can you be sure one of those lives belongs to Michael Celluci?"

She dropped to her knees and inserted her two heaviest picks. "I'm a lot closer to his life than you are."

"And you want to find him very badly. I shouldn't be the one reminding you of this, but we don't know for certain he came out here. We don't know what the nurse thinks goes on in the back."

"And we won't find out unless we take a look."
The door opened onto another short hall. One door
led to the electrical room.

The other led to a room like most other hospital
rooms except for the cinder block walls and the small,
high window. Vicki stood in the doorway, staring at
the body on the bed, feeling curiously light-headed as
all the pieces of her world clicked back into place.

His face was bruised. Blood had dried in the corner
of his mouth. The skin had split across the knuckles
of his right hand. His heart beat to a rhythm not quite
the rhythm she knew. He smelled of drugs and there
were leather restraints holding him to the bed.

She wanted to rip him free, gather him into her
arms, and carry him to safety, but they were in no
immediate danger so, for his sake, she'd find out what
they'd done to him first. Slowly, deliberately, she
crossed to the bed and unbuckled the restrains. Later,
she'd give in to the violence. Later, someone would
pay.

"Mike?"

A quick inspection, hands stroking patterns on flesh
as familiar as her own, determined nothing obvious
had been removed.

"Mike, come on. Snap out of it."

His pulse was strong. She traced the line of his jaw,
her finger rasping against dark stubble.

Henry watched from the doorway, knowing he'd
been forgotten, marveling at how much it hurt. Territorial imperatives, attacks, counterattacks, edged civility, barely maintained control, all disappeared under
memories of loving her. At the moment he hated Michael Celluci more than he'd ever hated anyone in
his life.

But the moment passed.

Celluci would never have the ultimate intimacy that
he and Vicki had shared—her life recreated in his
arms, her blood to him, his blood to her. Everything
after that . . .

He smiled, unable to stop himself. Everything after was a breaking of traditions he'd held unbreakable, a slaughter-induced passion, a blood-soaked truce, and something that had a chance of becoming a reclaimed friendship in spite of the odds.

He couldn't hate Celluci when he'd gotten back more of Vicki than should have been possible.

"It smells like a sedative. Try and wake him."

Vicki jerked toward the door, moving to put herself between the threat and the body on the bed. It took her a moment to realize it was Henry who'd spoken and a moment after that to remember, in this instant at least, he was no threat. "A sedative? How can you tell?"

"Experience."

"I really don't want to know how you got that experience, Henry." She turned back to Celluci, tugged off one running shoe, grabbed the softer flesh in the arch of his foot between thumb and forefinger, and pinched.

His leg twitched.

"What are you doing?"

"It's an acupressure technique. I'm working a pressure point in his foot that'll help him shake off the drugs."

"How . . . ?"

"I don't know how!" she snapped. "An old staff sergeant showed it to me. We used to use it on barbituate ODs; if it didn't work, they were probably dead. Come on, Mike. Shake it off." She pinched him again.

This time he grunted and tried to yank his foot away. By the time his eyes fluttered open, Vicki had both hands clasped around his face. He blinked blearily up at her, then the lids began to sink and the irises to roll up.

"Michael Francis Celluci, don't you dare close your eyes while I'm talking to you."

"Christ, Vicki . . . you sound like . . . my grandmother."

"Do I?" His lips were dry, so she moistened them with her tongue, licking the blood from the corner of his mouth.

"That wasn't . . . a challenge," he pointed out when she pulled away. His gaze flicked past her. "Where am . . . oh, shit."

"I wanted to make sure there were no broken bones before we moved you."

"Considerate." Then he frowned. "We?" He turned his head until he could see Henry, still in the doorway. "What is this . . . truce?"

The two men locked eyes for an instant, then Henry said softly, "The van disappeared with you. Someone had to drive."

"You could've let her borrow . . . your car."

"I don't think so. The last time she borrowed my car, she got broadsided by a truck."

"Yeah . . . but the werewolf was . . . driving."

"Enough with the male bonding. It's a truce. Okay?" Vicki gently pulled Mike's jaw around until he faced her again. "And since the nice people who cut out kidneys are sure to come back, are you all right? Can we move you?"

"No."

"No? No, what?"

"No, you can't move me."

"What's wrong? What have they done?" Her voice promised an eye for an eye at the very least.

"So far, only kidnapping." His thoughts were clearing, but his body remained weak. He tried to sit up and didn't have the energy to protest when Vicki lifted him, tucked a pillow between his shoulders and the wall, and lowered him gently back down again. "You've got to leave me here." He struggled to find the words that would convince Vicki to do as he said—never an easy proposition even at full mental strength. "You take me out of here and we're never going to find out what's going on."

"Hey, we *know* what's going on."

"We don't know squat except that some people

overreact when they're followed by people who turn out to be the police." He kept his explanation of exactly what had happened short and to the point— things got out of control only momentarily when Vicki realized he had no idea of where her van was. "Look, can we worry about the van later, when we've got a little more time?"

Vicki's eyes narrowed. "We'd have plenty of time if you'd stop being such a pigheaded . . ."

"Think of it as going undercover."

She smiled tightly. "Think of it as going under the knife."

"Vicki, these might not be the people selling body parts, it might be something as simple as selling drugs. All we've got is kidnapping and unlawful confinement."

"And grand theft auto." Lightly touching her fingertips to the bruise on his cheek, she added, "And assault."

"I think he could claim self-defense."

"Mike, you came out here originally for the same reason we did; Ronald Swanson's name cropped up one too many times to be coincidence. First we find out he's behind a private clinic that specializes in kidney transplant patients and then we find you strapped to a bed. That's enough for me."

He closed his hand around her wrist as her eyes silvered. "Stop reacting and start thinking. Suppose you break into Swanson's house and force a full confession, what then? You've got nothing that'll stand up in court. If we want to find out what's actually going on, there has to be an investigation."

"What am I doing? Wandering aimlessly through the night?"

Eleven dead in a Richmond warehouse; but wandering aimlessly was a lot easier to deal with. "Yeah, mostly. Picking this mess apart is going to take resources we don't have."

"If I get a full confession, I have resources enough to deal with Ronald Swanson."

"No."

There was such finality in that single word that the silver fled from Vicki's eyes. "What do you mean, no?"

"If Swanson dies, if you kill him, it's more than I can ignore."

She pulled her hand free and rubbed the band of warmth where his fingers had been. More than he could ignore. Those were the sort of words that came right before good-bye. "But . . ."

"No buts, Vicki." He gripped her shoulder, shaking her, willing her to listen. "This is where I draw my line in the sand."

One heartbeat. Two.

"I'm not really happy about ultimatums, Mike."

"And I'm not really happy about premeditated murder."

Put like that, without either the masking rhetoric or the heat of the Hunt, neither was she. She supposed. One corner of her mouth twisted up in a wry smile as she reached out and pushed the overlong lock of hair up off his face. "I guess every relationship means compromises." A little surprised by the relief that softened his expression—What had he expected?—she laid her hand flat against his chest, reassured in turn by the steady beat of his heart. "Now that's settled, what *do* you want me to do?"

"I want you to leave me here . . ."

"Forget it."

"Goddamn it, Vicki, would you just listen for a minute? The only way we'll find out what's happening is if we don't spook them. Leave me like you found me . . ." He paused. "Okay, there's no need to drug me again, but other than that . . ." When she didn't smile, he sighed and continued. "Go home, and call the police. Tell them you'd parked to check out a road map when you saw a big guy in a red T-shirt carry a body in the back door. They'll come out and they'll find . . ."

"Nothing. This is a hidden room. The night nurse

doesn't even know for sure that it's here; how the hell are the police going to find you?"

"All right, fine. Tell them you were visiting a sick friend, were getting back into your car, saw the guy in the red T-shirt with the body, stuck your head in the back door and saw this room. You took off before he could spot you and after dithering for a couple of hours decided to call the cops."

"Can I ask you a question?"

His eyes narrowed at her tone. "What?"

"You're a cop, try thinking like one. Would you believe a cock-and-bull story like that?"

"It doesn't matter if they believe it, as long as they check it out."

"I think I can come up with a story they'll believe."

Celluci snorted as Vicki turned to glare at Henry. "That's right, you're a romance writer."

"Stay out of this, Henry."

"Let's start by remembering that you're working for me, and that I think the detective has made a very good point. If we let them know we're on to them, they'll vanish."

"So you're all in favor of leaving Mike in danger?" Vicki pushed the words out through clenched teeth, shifting position slightly to better defend the man in the bed.

Celluci sighed. "Vicki, calm down. Whatever they're going to do to me, *nothing's* going to happen until morning."

"How do you know?"

"How do you think? I overheard the bad guys talking in the hall right before they drugged me."

"The bad guys?"

"Big guy who brought me in . . ."

"Cow eyes?"

"I wouldn't know. The closest I've ever been to a cow is in a burger. He was talking to a woman, but I never saw her. I'm pretty sure she was the one using the needle, but he covered my face with a pillow before she came into the room. They don't matter now."

Trying to find a position where his head wasn't pounding, he shifted against the pillow. "All you have to do
is make sure the police get here before morning and
I'll take them to where I got jumped and let them
leap to the same conclusion I did."

"Which is?"

"That you could bury an army out in those woods."
His voice gentled. "I promise nothing will happen in
the time it'll take the police to get here. All you have
to do is spin them enough of a story that they have
to find me. I'll do the rest."

"Why don't we take you to the police and you can
spin them the story?"

"How did I get out of the restraints?"

She threw up her hands. "Do I have to think of
everything?"

"But you're not thinking." He caught her gaze and
held it, unafraid of what he'd find. "We have to set
this up so that we, I, can answer the questions they're
going to ask. You and Fitzroy *can't* become involved."

Statements, court dates—no chance at all that the
system would only want them after sunset. Vicki
turned to look at Henry and saw the two men were
in complete agreement. Worst of all, she had to admit
to herself it made sense. To herself. Not to them.
"You've been drugged all evening. You're in no condition to make plans."

"My body is tapioca and my head is pounding, but
my cognitive processes are unimpaired."

"Sure. And you usually talk like that." Sighing, she
began to flick the hair on Celluci's arm in the wrong
direction. "I still don't like it."

"Stop that." His hand covered hers. "Vicki, it's
going to take you what, an hour to get back to the
condo? It's June. Sunrise is at 4:14. You haven't time
to do anything tonight, so, please, let the police handle it."

"The ghosts want Henry to avenge their deaths."

"Then let Henry make the call. It's the only way
everyone involved will get what's coming to them."

Her lips curled back off her teeth. "If they hurt you, Mike . . ."

"You can hurt them back." He wouldn't have said it except that he was certain he wouldn't be hurt—her answering smile was everything he was afraid it would be. "This is the only way to cover all the bases, Vicki. I'm not asking you to be happy about it, I'm saying that it's the way it's got to be. Now redo the restraints and get out of here, and it'll all be over in a couple of hours."

"If Swanson dies, if you kill him, it's more than I can ignore . . . This is where I'm drawing my line in the sand."

The words hung in the air between them.

If she carried Celluci out of the clinic, he'd never forgive her and that was a certainty. If she left him, and Henry sent the police in immediately, what could go wrong?

In spite of the lingering scent of another woman—and for Celluci's sake she hoped it was the woman with the needle—her smile took on a different flavor as she buckled down his wrists. "You know, this has possibilities." When a gentle caress up the inside of his bare arm raised goose bumps, she took the waistband of his jeans in her teeth and tugged.

"Vicki!"

"Michael . . ."

"Fitzroy, would you please get her out of here."

She shot him a warning glance. Henry raised a speculative brow. "As tasty as he looks, perhaps now is not the time."

Celluci grunted as Vicki vaulted the bed, hand still on his thigh. "Touch him and I'll rip you into pieces so small you'll be able to . . ." Then she stopped, straightened, and frowned. "You did that on purpose."

"Yes." In spite of their progress, it took remarkably little to evoke a territorial response. He looked past her to Celluci struggling against the restraints and allowed that that particular response could have been evoked almost as easily before she changed. "Don't worry, Detective. I have no desire to feed at this time. Say good-bye, Vicki, and let's go."

Muttering under her breath, Vicki turned back to the bed and Michael Celluci. She bent to kiss him and paused just above his lips where she could taste his breath. "I'm not sure I can just walk out and leave you here."

"Bullshit. You can do anything."

"Don't patronize me, Celluci."

"Then stop being such a tragedy queen. I'll be fine until the police arrive." His mouth moved under hers. "Now go."

"We should go out the front. The back door's probably hooked to an alarm."

"I don't see anything." Vicki quickly ran a finger around the door edge. "And I don't feel a wire. Look, the car's right outside in the parking lot. Let's just do what Mike said and go." She pressed down on the bar and pushed. The ambient noise of the clinic remained unchanged. "See, no alarm. These are sick people in here, probably don't want to terrify them with loud noises. Come on, old man, I'll race you to the car."

As Henry had observed, it took very little to evoke a territorial response. Once she started running, he had to chase after her. Moving too fast for mortal eyes to follow, they reached the car before the door slammed.

He was awake instantly, on his feet the instant after, unsure of what he'd heard but sure he'd heard something. If he'd learned anything in prison, he'd learned to sleep lightly. The muffled sound of car doors closing brought him to the window of the staff room where, tucked to one side, invisible from the parking lot, he watched a BMW reverse and pull away. The two people in it seemed to be fighting. He didn't recognize either silhouette.

Probably kids looking for a quiet spot to mess around

in. He yawned, thought about going back to sleep, thought about what the doc would say if anything went wrong, and decided it wouldn't hurt to look in on their uninvited guest.

The access door to the electrical room was unlocked. He knew he'd locked it.

Crepe-soled shoes silent against the tile, he entered the hidden room, half expecting an empty bed. The big cop was still tied down and out cold. He flicked on the light, hand raised to shield his eyes from the sudden fluorescent glare. The body on the bed didn't so much as twitch. A closer inspection seemed to indicate that nothing had changed.

But something had.

Hadn't there been a hunk of hair in the cop's face? No way he could brush it back tied down like he was.

He tested the restraints with his finger. The left wrist was in the fourth hole, the right in the third. He usually did them up equally but, even half stunned, the cop had been fighting him and maybe . . .

The cop shifted slightly, muttering a little. That was good. The sedative should be wearing off and a more natural sleep taking over. They used sedatives a lot in the prison hospital as it was easier than actually treating the patients and in his practiced opinion, the cop's chest now rose and fell in an unsedated rhythm.

He frowned. Just over the left hip, there was a dark half circle on the pale blue denim. It looked moist, like . . .

He touched it. It was almost dry but it looked like someone had been chewing on the cop's jeans. He closed his thumb and forefinger over the spot and tugged.

"I don't wanna know what was going on in here," he said. The skin on the back of his neck prickled as he felt the weight of the cop's stare. When he turned his head, narrowed eyes were glaring up at him. "You got kinky friends, cop. Wanna tell me why they left you?"

"I don't know what you're talking about."

"Sure you don't."

Unable to avoid it, Celluci rolled with the back-handed slap. "Fuck you," he growled.

"Maybe." The closest phone was in the staff room. "We'll see what the doc has to say."

"Where are we going?" Vicki spat the question through gritted teeth. Henry was driving again because he'd refused to give her the keys, had put on his Prince-of-Man face and said "No" in a tone that suggested arguing would be a waste of time. She'd gotten back in the car for Celluci's sake and had continually regretted it. In a minute, Henry was going to regret it, too. "The condo is that way."

"There's a coffee shop on the corner up here, and we need to talk to a police officer."

"Christ, Henry, this is Vancouver, there's a coffee shop on every corner." She reached for the wheel.

When Henry maintained his grip, the resulting tussle was short; Vicki having spent thirty-two years mortal had no illusions about surviving the results of a moving car gone out of control. Besides, the seat belts got in the way of her attack.

"Unlike most, this coffee shop has parking," Henry told her when she was back in the passenger seat, glaring out the window. "Somewhere for them to put the cruiser."

And there was, in fact, a cruiser in the parking lot.

"Go ahead, reinforce stereotypes," Vicki muttered as Henry parked the car and turned off the engine. "Now what?"

"Now I go and have a word with the two constables, interrupting their break with a story of a body glimpsed from the side of the highway."

She got out of the car when he did, grateful for the chance to untangle her personal space from his. "I can't believe you're actually going along with this. Hell, I can't believe I'm actually going along with this. We left him back there, Henry." With the car a barrier between them, she allowed a little of the anger to slip from her grip—although who exactly she was angry with, she couldn't say. "We walked out on him. Left him helpless and alone."

"It's a minimal risk, Vicki, and a risk he's willing to take in order to finish this once and for all. The police will be there within the hour. What could possibly go wrong?"

"Famous last words." The night smelled of car exhaust and heated metal, less strongly here on the Coast than in Toronto but still too many people crammed into too small a space. Vicki turned back toward the clinic and tried not to think how things that could go wrong usually did. "I left him there because he asked me to," she said softly, silvered gaze locked on Henry once again. "I'm doing it for Mike, but you've never cared what he thinks of you."

Haven't I? Michael Celluci is an honorable man and the opinions of honorable men are sometimes all we have to define ourselves by. But there was little point in sparking another territorial dispute over Celluci's affections even though her previous reaction had more amused than infuriated him. "I'm no vigilante, Vicki, no matter how it may have seemed in the past. If I can be responsible for a solution within the parameters of the law, then everyone should be happy."

"A solution within the parameters of the law?" she repeated. Shaking her head, she folded her arms on the roof of the car and rested her chin on their pillow. "Go ahead. And make it good."

Henry had no doubt he could spin a story that the police would believe, add enough detail that they not only had to check it out but also found everything they needed to. There was, however, no need to tax his imagination. When it came right down to it, it wasn't what he said but how he said it that mattered.

"Excuse me, Officers, may I have a word?"

Resisting the completely inexplicable urge to come to attention, the police constable in the driver's seat put down his coffee and snapped out an efficient, "Yes, sir."

When the constable in the passenger seat, wondering what the hell was going on with her partner, leaned past him for a better look, she found herself reacting much the same way.

The bastard son of Henry VIII, Duke of Richmond and Somerset, inclined his head in recognition of their deference. "I have some information you might find worthy of investigation." His father would have approved of the tone.

Tony woke up as Henry came into the condo, sat up on the couch, and rubbed his eyes. "Did you find him?"

"Yes."

"That must've made Victory happy."

"Not exactly."

"Oh, man. Henry, you didn't kill her before you got to the clinic?"

"I don't know what you're talking about."

"And don't try that more-princely-than-thou crap on me either. I'm not in the mood. If you didn't kill Vicki before you got to the clinic and if you found Celluci, why isn't she happy?"

"Because we left him there."

"You what?"

"It was his idea. He thought if we rescued him, it would alert the people behind this whole organ-legging thing that we're on to them. He told us to inform the police and let them handle it while the evidence is still out in plain view."

"Yeah, but unless he's missing a kidney, how are they going to connect him with the body in the harbor?"

"Celluci seems to think he knows where the bodies are buried."

"And Victory just let him stay?"

"Not exactly. He had to appeal to her better nature."

Tony snorted. "I didn't know she had one where he was concerned. Did you tell the police?"

"I did, and with luck that'll be enough to satisfy my visitors." Henry glanced down at his watch. "Why aren't you in bed? Don't you have to work to-morrow?"

"I wanted to know if Celluci was safe before I went back to Gerry's and John's." He scrambled to his feet, folded the blanket haphazardly, and stood staring at the floor.

Henry sighed, wondering when exactly things had gotten so awkward between them. "Tony, it's late. The sun will be up in a few short moments. Why don't you stay here in your own room?"

"I don't . . ."

"I know."

Tony's head came up, drawn by the understanding in Henry's voice.

"When this is over, as it easily could be by tomor-row evening, we have to talk, but for right now there's no reason for you to leave."

"I guess not." He glanced over at the clock on the VCR, and his eyes widened. "Henry, sunrise is in less than five minutes."

"I'm aware of that." Starting down the hall, Henry motioned Tony into step beside him. "Can you keep an eye on the news tomorrow—maybe tape the morn-ing broadcast before you go? I'm sure Detective Cel-luci will keep Vicki and me out of range when it hits the fan, but I'd feel better if I knew for certain."

"No sweat. I'll set it up to tape the news at noon and the six o'clock report, too."

"That won't interfere with it taping *Batman*, will it?"

Tony grinned. It was the nonvampire, nonprince parts of Henry that had kept them together for so long. "Chill. You'll get your cartoon." They were at the door, Henry's hand was on the knob, and in an-other moment he'd lock himself away until sunset. Tony suddenly wanted to prolong that moment. "You, uh, got a question for the ghosts? One that'll cover both of them?"

"Vicki suggests I ask if they were killed by the same person."

"You figure she knows what she's talking about?"

"It is why I asked her to come here, but, hopefully, it won't be a problem. Hopefully, they'll be resting in peace by sunset." He opened the door, reached out, and stroked Tony's cheek with two fingers. All he could think of to say was "good-bye," but he didn't want to say that yet, so he said nothing at all.

"I can't stand it. This bedroom exudes pink even in full dark." Vicki punched the pillow into another shape and threw herself back down, fully aware that the bedroom had nothing to do with her mood and equally aware that she had nothing else to take it out on.

The ride back to the condo had been easier than the ride to Project Hope. The more time she and Henry spent together, the more they forced the truce to endure, the easier it got. But she still wanted to kill something.

Not Henry.

Mike.

"It was a mistake leaving him there. I know it. I just know it. After all these years," she asked the night as it fled, "why have I suddenly decided to start listening to . . ."

Eleven

"What is going on here?"

The question cut through the argument at the nurse's station, leaving silence in its wake. The two police constables and the night nurse turned toward the voice, three very different faces wearing identical expressions of relief that said as clearly as if they spoke aloud, *Thank God, here's someone who knows what to do.*

The night nurse took a step forward. "Dr. Mui, these two police officers want to have a look around. Apparently someone reported seeing a body carried in through the back door late this afternoon."

"Really." Dr. Mui slowly swept a peremptory gaze from the nurse over to the police. "As there was no one admitted to the hospice this afternoon, I'm afraid your informant was mistaken."

"This body wasn't on a stretcher, it was allegedly flung over the shoulder of a large man in a red Tshirt. I doubt that's the way your patients usually arrive, Doctor . . . ?"

"Mui." Ebony brows rose into a finely drawn arc. "And you are?"

"Police Constable Potter, ma'am." She nodded at her partner. "This is Police Constable Kessin. Do you usually come in at this hour, Doctor? It's barely five; a little early to start your day."

"I am often in at odd hours." *Not that it's any of your business,* her tone added. "You can ask Nurse

Damone if you don't believe me. As it happens, I have a patient who has just moved to status four—he'll be dead within the week unless a match is found. I came in to check on him. You have both signed organ donor cards, I assume?"

She so pointedly awaited an answer, it would have been impossible not to give her one.

After a ragged duet of "Yes, ma'am," Dr. Mui nodded. "Good. As you'll be dead, you'll certainly have no use for otherwise healthy organs. Hundreds of people die every year for no other reason than the lack of those signatures. Now then, about this, as you say, alleged body. If you intend to search the premises, I assume you have a warrant?"

PC Potter blinked, taken slightly aback by the lecture and the sudden change of subject. "Warrant, Doctor?"

"Warrant, Constable."

Fighting the feeling that she was back in Catholic School—it helped only a little that none of the nuns had been Asian—Potter cleared her throat and glanced down at her occurrence book for support. "We had hoped we could have a look around without having to get a warrant."

"Had you. I see."

"We can get one if we need one." PC Kessin wished he'd kept his mouth shut as the doctor's level gaze moved over to him. He couldn't help the sudden suspicion she was measuring him and finding him wanting. *We'll take none of his organs. He's an idiot.*

"Of course you can." Her inflection suggested the exact opposite but before either constable could decide to be insulted, she continued. "Fortunately, since I've arrived, that won't be necessary." When it appeared that PC Potter was about to speak, she added with some exasperation, "We have a dozen very sick people in this building, Officers. I'm sure you didn't expect Nurse Damone to allow you to wander about on your own or to leave her station and accompany you. Since I'm here, that's no longer a problem. What would you like to see first?"

Just in from the back door, the hall jogs to the left. You'll find a door marked electrical room. Behind it is a short corridor. Off that corridor is a hospital room . . ."

"I think we can start at the back door, Doctor."

"Fine. Nurse . . ."

Hope rose in the breasts of both constables that Nurse Damone would be going with them while the doctor watched her station.

". . . I won't be long."

Hope crashed and burned.

"There's no alarm on this door?"

"As I mentioned before, Constable Potter, we have a dozen very sick people in this building. Should anyone need to exit the building, an unnecessary alarm could easily cause enough excitement to kill one or two of them."

"They're that sick?"

"They come here when their only options remaining are death or transplant—yes, they're that sick."

PC Kessin frowned at the heavy steel door. "But suppose someone came in from outside the building?"

"This door doesn't open from the outside."

"There are always people who can get a door open, Doctor."

Dr. Mui smiled tightly. "And what good would an alarm do against those kinds of people?"

"Do you always keep the door to the electrical room locked?"

"Two points, Constable." Dr. Mui pulled out her keys and slid one into the lock. "First of all, this is not the door to the electrical room. It leads to a short access hall. Secondly, no, we don't always keep it locked."

"Then why is it locked now?"

"I don't know."

*   *   *

"The room you're searching for looks like any other hospital room except that the walls are painted cinder blocks and there's a high, inaccessible window. There'll be a man on the bed . . ."

PC Potter stopped just over the threshold and had to be pushed gently ahead by her partner. For some strange reason, she felt as though she were stepping up out of a deep, dark well. It must have been the lights—the room was all hard, high-gloss surfaces with nothing to soften the intensity.

Blinking and grumbling in the sudden glare, the large man on the bed sat up and rubbed at his eyes.

"A hidden room, a man who is obviously not a patient; do you have an explanation for this, Dr. Mui?"

"This room was originally supposed to be the laundry, but we found it much more cost effective to send the laundry out. Since the plumbing was already installed, it took little effort to turn it into a temporary residence room. As for the man on the bed . . ." Her tone changed from weary lecture to distinct pique. ". . . his name is Richard Sullivan, he's one of our orderlies, and he is not supposed to be in here—which explains why that last door was locked."

"Orderly," Kessin repeated. "That explains the uniform." He took half a step back as the doctor shot him another less than complimentary look.

Sullivan, standing now, stared down at the mattress and muttered an inaudible protest.

"Again, Richard. Louder."

"The cot's uncomfortable."

"Are you the orderly the nurse told us was asleep in the staff room?" Potter asked, wondering why it felt as though she'd changed channels in mid-program.

"Obviously not. He's the orderly who was *supposed* to be asleep in the staff room." Dr. Mui indicated the door with a sharp jerk of her head. "Go to my office, Richard. I'll speak with you later."

"Just a minute, Mr. Sullivan." As he turned toward

her, Potter saw that he had the longest eyelashes she'd ever seen on a man—long and thick and fringing deep brown eyes so mild they completely mitigated any threat his size might suggest. Her cheeks warmed as she realized he was waiting patiently for her to speak.

". . . ask him how he came to be in that room."

Except they already knew that.

"Do you, uh, own a red T-shirt?"

He nodded.

"Did you wear it to work today?"

He nodded again. "I never wear my uniform to work, it gets sweaty. I bring a clean uniform in a bag."

"A bag."

Huge hands sketched a rectangle in the air. "Like a garment bag."

"A garment bag." Potter looked at her partner and saw he was leaping to the same conclusion. From the highway it was entirely possible that a man in a red T-shirt carrying a garment bag could look like a man in a red T-shirt carrying a body. Especially when there was no body.

"Once you've found the room, and the man, and found out what he's doing there, I have every faith in your ability to deal with the situation."

She frowned. What situation?

"Hope we didn't get that guy in too much trouble." PC Kessin turned back onto Mt. Seymour Road heading toward North Vancouver. "That doctor wasn't someone I'd want to cross. Man, I hate that 'I'm the next best thing to God Almighty' most doctors put on. Make you wait forty-five minutes in their waiting rooms like you've got no life of your own, but just hear them howl if we're more than three seconds getting to a call." Scratching at his mustache, he shot a glance into the passenger seat. "What's bugging you?"

Potter, who'd been silent since radioing in the false alarm, shrugged. "I was just thinking: we never actually saw that garment bag."

*   *   *

". . . and you're followed to the disposal site by a police officer from a city half the country away. Tonight, two visitors drop in, leave their captured friend where they find him, and send the local police out to have a look around on no better pretense than they supposedly saw you carry a body in here this afternoon while they were passing." Dr. Mui steepled her fingers and peered over them at Sullivan. "Now, what does that say to you?"

He sighed. She never asked him a question she didn't already know the answer to. "That we're busted?"

"No. Detective Celluci's friends don't want to become involved with the police."

"Not very good friends, leaving him tied to a bed."

"They expected the police to find him, and then we would have been, as you so crudely put it, busted."

"You told me to lie down on the bed . . ."

"To cover the obvious fact that someone had been lying there. And I told you to put him in the back of your vehicle," she added caustically, "because we didn't have time to put him anywhere else."

He *knew* that. "So what now? Do I bring him back in?"

"No. His friends, whoever or whatever they are . . ." She frowned, hating ambiguity. ". . . found him here once, and if they find him again, they won't leave him. You'll have to take him to one of the guest cottages." Reaching into her drawer, she pulled out a single key on a leather fob and tossed it across the office. "Use the one farthest from the house."

Sullivan deftly caught the key and shoved it in his pocket. "Mr. Swanson won't like it."

"I'll deal with Mr. Swanson."

The soft brown eyes looked no less mild as he suggested, "I could kill him."

"The detective? Don't be ridiculous, Richard. He has two perfectly healthy, very large kidneys—a perfect match for one of Mr. Swanson's buyers that I'd considered to be unmatchable given his size and that our usual sources tend toward the undernourished. Alive, he can do some good."

"Should I stay with him?"

"Yes, you'd better. Be sure you park your car where it can't be seen from the house. I'll go over and explain things to Mr. Swanson in a couple of hours, as soon as I've finished here."

Pushing upward through layer after layer of sticky cotton batting, fighting to keep it away from his face, forcing himself to keep moving toward a distant light, Celluci managed to get his eyes open just long enough to catch a brief glimpse of trees and cedar siding before darkness descended again. Vaguely aware of movement, he remembered he'd been captured, knew he should struggle but couldn't seem to make his body obey.

A mattress compacted underneath him, releasing a faint scent of honeysuckle as he flopped back against a pile of pillows.

Obviously, he was no longer in the hospital.

As rough hands secured him to the bed, he reviewed his options and realized he didn't have any. Reluctantly surrendering to the sedatives, he felt almost sorry for the people who'd moved him.

Man, Vicki's going to be pissed.

"Dr. Mui, this is a surprise." His expression polite but not exactly welcoming, Ronald Swanson stepped back from the door to allow the doctor to enter his front hall.

"I realize this is certainly an unexpected visit," Dr. Mui acknowledged, stepping by him, "but what I have to tell you needed to be said in person. Since your neighbors are aware of your connection to Project Hope, they should assume the obvious."

"Very likely, although my neighbors are far enough away I doubt they even noticed you arrive." His attention caught by the white convertible gleaming in the early morning light, he added, "New car?" as he closed the door.

"I bought it last week."

"Can you afford such an expensive car right now, Doctor? I'd have thought the condominium you bought recently had taken all your available resources."

"You assured me a condo in Yaletown was a secure investment, Mr. Swanson." She followed him to the kitchen. "And as for the car, I've heard you say you get what you pay for. German engineering is built to last. Besides, you pay me very well."

"And I get what I pay for." He smiled a little nervously and waved a hand toward the table. "I'm just finishing breakfast. Would you care to join me?" He hadn't had an informal visitor since before Rebecca had died, and he couldn't remember her ever entertaining in the kitchen. Still, abandoning his breakfast now would mean wasting a perfectly good bagel and there was no sense in that.

"Thank you, no."

"Do you mind if I continue?"

"Not at all." She took the offered seat and waited for him to circle the table and sit facing her. 'We have another match."

His eyes narrowed, and he carefully set the bagel back on his plate. "Already? That's two in little more than a week. Three in two months. Don't you think we're likely to start attracting attention? The more regularly something happens the more likely people are to notice it."

"True. However, given the size of the organ, this particular match was too good to pass up. The donor is about six feet four, two hundred and sixty pounds. Late thirties and in perfect health for our purposes." Which was really all her patron either wanted or needed to know. Dr. Mui waited patiently for Swanson to make the connection.

As he did, he sat back and stared at her. "You said we'd never find a donor that big."

"I was wrong."

"Still . . ." He shook his head. "Three in two months. I'm concerned about the frequency. If we're caught, we won't be doing anyone any good." His mouth twisted. "Especially ourselves."

Dr. Mui leaned forward, fingertips touching. "This donor came to us under rather unusual circumstances. However," she amended as he raised a hand in protest, "I'll merely point out that if we don't take advantage of this opportunity now, we won't have a chance later. I've taken the liberty of changing certain parts of the routine so we won't attract the attention you're worried about."

"It would be a shame to miss the sale . . ."

She waited while he chewed and thought, secure in his reputation of *never* missing a sale.

"All right," he said at last. "What have you done?"

This could be the difficult part. "I had Mr. Sullivan escort him to one of your guest houses. He doesn't know where he is, and he's not at the clinic attracting attention."

Swanson's mug hit the table hard enough to slop tea over the edge. "And you were worried about the neighbor seeing *you*?"

"He arrived just after dawn, I doubt anyone saw him. And if they did—you often have guests." As soon as possible after the transplant, the buyers left their careful seclusion at the clinic and recovered under close supervision in one of Ronald Swanson's guest cottages—equally secluded and much less likely to be accidentally discovered. Who, after all, would wonder at a wealthy man having wealthy friends? "I can only stress that this may be our one chance for this particular match."

"But here . . ."

"I can do all the preliminaries here. He won't have to be moved until the last possible moment." She watched Swanson openly as he stood and walked to a window that looked out over the property, the closest of the two guest houses clearly visible through the trees. "It is, of course, your decision."

"And if I tell you to get rid of him, I take it it will cost me as much as if I tell you to go ahead."

He didn't seem to expect an answer, so she waited silently.

"Well," he sighed at last, pausing to drink a mouthful of tepid tea. "As I've said before, it's a waste of money if you hire a specialist and then don't listen to them. You're the doctor, and if you believe this is our best possible chance for this match . . ."

"I do."

"Then go ahead. I'll call our buyer." All at once, he jabbed finger at her. "You're sure he's healthy?"

"I'm positive."

"Good. Because after that last fiasco, a satisfied customer can only be good for business."

". . . midmorning showers are expected to clear by noon and the greater Vancouver region will enjoy a beautiful afternoon with temperatures reaching a high of twenty-seven degrees. The department of Parks and Recreation reports . . ."

Tony hit the mute button and frowned. Television had become an immediate news source—the camera crews occasionally arrived at crime scenes before the police. Even if they were keeping the whole black market kidney thing under wraps during their investigation, there should've been something about a Metropolitan Toronto Police Officer beaten up and strapped to a bed in a North Vancouver clinic.

Henry had said the police were going to the clinic, so the police had gone to the clinic. That much was inevitable.

"Okay, so the rest of the country hates Toronto— they still wouldn't have just left him there, would they?"

He put the sound back on for the baseball scores,

set the VCR to record the news at noon and at six, and turned off the TV, unable to shake the feeling that something had gone terribly wrong.

"You're overreacting," he told himself as he stuffed a clean shirt in his backpack. "So it didn't make the early news; so what? It was probably too early." He picked up his roller blades, then he sighed and put them down again. Scribbling, *I'll be at Gerry's* and the phone number on a piece of paper, he stuck it to the fridge with a Gandydancer magnet.

Henry'd thought it would all be over by sunset, that there'd be no uneasy spirits waiting at the foot of his bed. Tony didn't plan on being around when Doug and his handless friend arrived to prove him wrong.

"Is he awake?"

"Yeah. He had a piss and a glass of water. We going to feed him?"

"Of course we're going to feed him. Go and see if there's any food in the kitchenette."

"I'm not cooking for him," Sullivan grumbled.

Dr. Mui paused on her way to the bedroom and half turned, the black bag she carried bumping against her legs. "I beg your pardon?"

The big man shuffled; in place for a moment, defiantly meeting her gaze, then his eyes dropped, he mumbled inaudibly, and headed toward the fridge.

"Make enough for yourself as well, you'll be staying here as long as he is."

He leaned back over the counter, looking worried. "What about the clinic?"

"Harry and Tom can manage without you for a few days." She waited pointedly for him to continue doing as he'd been told, then went into the bedroom. "I know you're awake, Detective. Open your eyes."

Celluci'd heard that voice before, back in the clinic. This was the woman the orderly had been talking to in the hall, the woman who'd sedated him. Although he hadn't mentioned it to Vicki—it'd been hard enough to convince her to leave him as it was—he thought that the lack of emotion in the quiet voice, the cold, clinical discussion of his fate, had made her sound the way he'd always assumed vampires should sound—as though people were cattle. She sounded a lot more like a member of the bloodsucking undead than Vicki ever had.

Except that the sun was up and this woman was still walking around and he had to admit, she certainly didn't look as dangerous as she sounded. Watching her cross to the bed, he suddenly remembered a line from the first Addams Family movie, *"I'm a homicidal maniac, we look just like everyone else."* All thing considered, it wasn't very comforting.

"So." He was pleased to hear he sounded a lot less shaky than he felt. "What are you planning?"

"So," Dr. Mui mimicked his tone, mocking him. "How much do you know?" When trying to decide whether or not Richard had panicked unnecessarily when he'd brought the detective in, she'd had him try beating the answer to that question out of his captive—without success. In the end, she'd concluded it was better to be safe than sorry. After all, he had been following Richard's vehicle, so he had to know something.

"Obviously, what I do or don't know doesn't matter any more, or you wouldn't be in here."

"Very astute, Detective." Because the guest cottages were used by recovering buyers, the ruffles, and comforters, and pillows covered a hospital bed. Sullivan had installed the standard restraints. "I had a lab run a blood sample last night, and although your cholesterol level is slightly elevated, you're a very healthy man."

"Under other circumstances, that might be good news." Twisting his neck at a painful angle, he managed to keep her in sight while she lifted equipment out of her case. The clear plastic bags with the hose attached looked very familiar. When she set them on the edge of the table, one end swung free. Blood bags. "Jesus H. Christ . . ."

Dr. Mui glanced down at him and shook her head.

"You needn't look at me like I'm some kind of vampire, Detective. Your blood will be put to very good use."

To very good use? All at once, it became clear that hiding just how much he knew would give him no advantage at all. "Pretransplant transfusions to help the new body accept the kidney?"

"Precisely." But she volunteered nothing further, merely continued making her preparations.

Celluci'd given blood before, on numerous occasions, but this time he couldn't take his eyes off the needle. It looked about six inches long and as big around as a drinking straw. He jumped when she swabbed the inside of his elbow with alcohol and tried to jerk his arm away from the length of rubber hose.

"This doesn't have to hurt," she told him, needle poised for entry, "but it can. If you move, it may take two or three attempts to find the vein."

"Two or three?" He watched the point descend. "Put like that, I think I'll stay still."

"Very wise."

His blood surged up into the hose and disappeared over the edge of the bed. *Oh, yeah, Vicki's going to be really pissed now.* It was a comforting thought. He let his head fall back onto the pillow. "What am I to call you?"

"If you must call me something, Doctor will do."

"Can I assume you're not going to spill your guts about your motives, your methods, and the reasons you don't believe you'll be caught."

"You can."

From watching her work, he'd thought it was a fairly safe assumption. There didn't seem to be much else to say, so he kept quiet. In Celluci's experience, few people could handle silence. After a very short time they'd start to talk just to fill it with noise. He'd gotten a number of confessions that way.

He didn't get one today. Finally, unable to stand it any longer, he said, "You'd have gotten away with it if they hadn't found that body in the harbor."

"The body found in the harbor has not been identified. The police will find no record of his operation in
any of the local hospitals, so they'll assume he came
from out of town." Moving with a speed that said
she'd done this many times before, she deftly exchanged an empty bag for a full one. "The removal
of his hands, added to the recent gang-related carnage,
will direct the search even farther from the truth. As
the entire incident becomes more and more complicated, and no one steps forward to advocate for the
deceased, budget cuts should kill the investigation
entirely."

"The *police* investigation," Celluci pointed out
meaningfully.

"Your investigation has ended," Dr. Mui reminded
him. "Your friends don't wish to become involved
with the police, and the officers they sent to find
you . . ." She spread her hands. ". . . did not. Your
friends will not find you here."

*You have no idea how resourceful my friends can
be.* But he didn't say it aloud as he had no desire to
put the good doctor on her guard. She seemed like
the type who'd hang garlic over the door, just in case.

"Besides . . ." A drop of blood glistened on the end
of the needle as she pulled it from his arm. ". . . you
won't be here long." A cotton ball and a bandage
later, she was on her way to the door.

"Doctor?"

Her expression, as she turned, clearly said she was
not happy about being questioned.

Celluci grinned, figuring a little charm couldn't hurt.
"I was just wondering. Will I ever play the piano
again."

Dr. Mui's lips pressed into a thin line. "No," she
said and left.

A few moments later, as he was testing the restraints yet again, the door opened. Tensed muscles
relaxed slightly as he saw it was nothing more dangerous than the big man carrying a bowl.

"Doc says I've got to feed you."

"And you are?"

"Sullivan. That's all you've got to know."

It didn't take long for Celluci to realize why Sullivan was smiling. The instant oatmeal had been micro-waved hot enough to burn the inside of his mouth and the big hand clamping his jaw shut kept him from taking in any cooling air until he swallowed. When he coughed orange juice out his nose, the mild eyes glittered. Vicki'd called them cow eyes, but they looked more like puppy eyes to him. Unfortunately, the puppy appeared to be rabid.

The cloth that scrubbed his face hard enough to lift skin, squeezed soap into his mouth.

"Christ, where did you learn your bedside manner?"

"Kingston Penitentiary."

"You worked in the infirmary at Kingston Pen?"

Sullivan nodded.

"Why?" Celluci spat out soap. "Because you've got a deep abiding need to nurture?"

The smile, constant throughout the torment, broadened. "Because I like to hurt people, and there's not much sick people can do to stop me."

Hard to argue with, Celluci admitted, grunting in pain as Sullivan heaved himself onto his feet helped by a fist grinding knuckles deep into thigh muscles.

He slept most of the morning, waking once to have a bottle of water poured down his throat.

"You need to replace your fluids," Sullivan told him as he choked.

Lunch was a repeat of breakfast as far as Sullivan getting his jollies was concerned only it involved soup and a shackled trip to the toilet. Celluci knew the escape attempt was doomed before he tried it, but he had to try.

"Do that again," Sullivan growled as he slammed the detective's head into the wall, "and I'll break your legs."

He was still searching for a witty response when his head reimpacted with the wallpaper.

* * *

"On Thursday afternoons, Ronald Swanson always visits the hospice he created as a tribute to his dead wife." Followed by the cameraman, Patrica Chou took several quick steps across the parking lot and shoved her microphone in the face of the man climbing out of the late model Chevy. "Mr. Swanson, a few words, please."

He looked down at the microphone then up at the camera and finally at Patricia Chou. "A few words about what?" he asked.

"The work that's being done here. The dire necessity for people to sign their organ donor cards so that places like this don't need to exist." She smiled, looking remarkably sharklike. "Or perhaps you'd like to use the time explaining rewarded gifting—a disingenuous oxymoron if I've ever heard one. Do you actually believe that camouflaging the payment changes the underlying reality that organs would be provided for remuneration?"

"I have nothing to say to you."

"Nothing? Everyone has something to say, Mr. Swanson."

Irritation began to replace the confusion. "If you want to speak with me again, make an appointment with my secretary." He pushed past her, shoulders hunched, striding toward the building.

The cameraman danced back out of the way with practiced ease, never losing his focus. "Do we follow?" he asked.

"No need." She switched off her mike and indicated he should stop taping. "I accomplished what I came here to do."

"Which is?"

"Rattling Mr. Swanson's cage. Keeping him off balance. Nervous people make mistakes."

"You really don't like him, do you?"

"It's not a matter of like or dislike, it's all about getting a story. And believe me, there's a story under all that upstanding businessman philanthropic crap."

"Maybe he's Batman."

"Just get in the car, Brent, or we're going to miss the library budget hearing." *The library budget hearing,* she repeated to herself as she peeled rubber out of the parking lot. *Ooh, that's cutting edge journalism, that is.* She wanted Swanson so bad she could taste it. *I wonder what's happened to that detective. . . .*

"I just ran into Patrica Chou in the parking lot." His tone suggesting he'd have preferred to run over Patrica Chou in the parking lot, Swanson closed the door to Dr. Mui's office. "Something has to be done about that young woman."

"Ignore her." Dr. Mui stood and smoothed the wrinkles from her spotless white lab coat. "She's only trying to goad you into creating news."

"Why me? This city's crawling with television crews and movie productions. Why doesn't she go bother an actor?" He swept his palm back over the damp dome of his head. "You don't think she knows anything, do you?"

The doctor studied him dispassionately. The exchange with the reporter had clearly unsettled him. "Knows what?" she asked as though there were, indeed, nothing to know.

"If she's watching my house and she saw you this morning . . ."

"She'd assume, like anyone else, my visit concerned the clinic."

"But . . ."

"She's making you paranoid."

Swanson visibly pulled himself together. "I beg your pardon, Dr. Mui. Something about that woman invariably causes me to overreact."

"Apparently, she has that effect on most people," the doctor allowed. "Do we have a buyer?"

"We do. He'll be here tomorrow afternoon."

"Good. I'll set up the transfusions as soon as he arrives, and if all goes well, we'll perform the surgery the day after." She brushed past him and opened the door. "Shall we?"

"Before we go around, have there been any changes I should know about since last week?" he asked as he followed her into the hall.

"Mathew Singh died this morning."

"Mathew Singh," Swanson repeated. The mix of grief and anger in his voice contrasted sharply with the clinical detachment in the doctor's. "He was only thirty-seven years old."

"He had been on dialysis for some time. He went to status four two days ago."

"It's criminal. Absolutely criminal." As it always did, anger began to overwhelm the grief. "We're talking about an uncomplicated operation with broad parameters for a match, and still people die. What is wrong with our legislators that they can't see presumed consent upon brain death is only the moral option. I mean, look at France—they've had presumed consent since 1976 and their society hasn't crumbled. Well, except for that Jerry Lewis thing, and you can hardly blame that on transplants."

As Swanson continued his familiar diatribe, Dr. Mui worked out a timetable for the next forty-eight hours. Attention to detail had brought them this far undetected, and although the odds of their unwilling donor causing any trouble were slim, he was a detail that had to be carefully considered. Live transplants had a ninety-seven percent initial success rate over ninety-two percent for cadavers, and, since the very rich could not only afford the best immunosuppressant drugs but tended to be paranoid about post-op infections, all of their buyers had, thus far, beaten the odds. Perhaps in this particular instance she should forgo that five percent. . . .

Celluci jerked awake out of a dream that involved a great deal of blood and not much else he could remember. He lay quietly for a moment, listening to the pounding of his heart, feeling the sweat pool beneath the restraints, a little surprised that he'd slept at all. From the change in the pattern of shadow on the opposite wall, he figured it had to be close to four, maybe five in the afternoon. Sunset was at 7:48. By nine at the absolute latest, Vicki would be riding to the rescue.

She'd tear the clinic, and anything that got in her way, apart looking for him. *Almost a pity Sullivan won't be there,* he thought, amusing himself for a moment or two with a vision of Vicki and Sullivan face to face.

If the clinic came up empty, Vicki'd go after Swanson. If Swanson was involved, the calvary would arrive before midnight, and at this point, he'd worry about bringing the police in after his butt was safe and sound. But if Swanson wasn't involved—and there was still no sure indication that he was—Vicki'd have no quick way of finding him.

And she'd only have until dawn.

He had an unpleasant feeling that dawn would be the deadline in more than one respect. The bandage over the puncture in the crease of his elbow itched, suggesting he not wait around to be rescued. If they were taking his blood, what else would they take? Could surgery be far behind? And after surgery . . .

"Oh, Christ, that's just what I need—an eternity haunting Henry-fucking-Fitzroy."

Twelve

They were still there. Henry knew it before he opened his eyes. As the day's weight lifted off him, the certainty of their presence settled down to replace it. One of two things had to have happened; either the people who'd grabbed Celluci had evaded arrest, or there were other people involved the police investigation hadn't yet uncovered.

There is, of course, the third possibility. He lay silently listening to the lives around him, senses skimming past the absence of life that waited at the end of his bed. Perhaps due process wasn't good enough. *They want a vengeance more visceral and less . . .* Unfortunately, the only word he could think of to finish the thought, was legal. *Which leaves Detective Celluci, up until now the most involved, no part of the end result.*

But he'd known from the beginning if it came to that evisceral vengeance, it would be in spite of Detective Celluci. For honor's sake, he'd attempted to stay within the parameters of the law; it hadn't worked.

And what about Vicki?

Even before the change she'd been willing to acknowledge that law and justice were not necessarily the same thing. While she couldn't strike the final blow, not without crossing the line Celluci had drawn in the sand, Henry doubted that she'd try and stop his hand. His lips drew off his teeth in an involuntary snarl at the thought.

Finally, because he could put it off no longer, he opened his eyes.

They stood where they had for the past six nights. Doug. The companion he'd acquired in death. And wrapped in shadows too dark for even Henry to pierce, the unseen chorus; an added emphasis from the damned.

Henry sighed. "You guys still here?"

An inferior question at best and not the one he'd intended to ask. Although the spirits clearly didn't like it, it was enough.

Celluci was not in the condo.

Vicki was as certain of that as she was of anything. Teeth bared, she glared around the darkness as though she might scare up an answer or two. Celluci knew when sunset was. If he could be here, he would. Since he wasn't, he couldn't.

And that meant someone, somewhere, was going to pay.

As she yanked on her clothes, muttering threats, a saner voice in the back of her head suggested that perhaps he'd merely been held up by the police, the long arm of the law being festooned as it was in red tape.

Fourteen hours of red tape? she asked it scornfully, rummaging around in the bottom of her duffel bag for a pair of clean socks. *Not even in Canada.*

And if he's just stayed late talking shop? the little voice inquired.

Then I know who's going to pay, don't I? She had a sudden vision of pinning Celluci to the bed by his ears and grinned ferally.

But she didn't for a moment believe there was such a simple explanation for Celluci's truancy. *Something* had gone wrong.

"I'm not saying that something *hasn't* gone wrong," Henry snarled. "I'm saying that charging blindly out to the rescue isn't the answer."

"Then what do you suggest?" She stormed past him, into the condo, aware of his response to the anger she'd thrown at him when he opened the door but ignoring it. His reaction to her, hers to him, territorial imperatives—they were all unimportant under the circumstances. "Shall we wait around until his body shows up floating in the fucking harbor?"

Henry managed not to slam the door behind her, but only just and his success probably had more to do with the mechanism of the door than self-control. "I'm saying two things, Vicki. One, I'm not giving you my car keys and two, before *we* go anywhere, shouldn't *we* get a little more information?"

"We?" Vicki repeated leaning over the back of the couch, her fingers imprinting the green leather right next to where her fingers had gone through the green leather on that first night in Vancouver. "You had your chance to get more information at sunset, and you blew it. *I* am the investigator. *You* are the romance writer. You called me for help. And I won't hurt your stupid car."

"You're not getting my stupid car, and you were willing enough to use my services in the past."

"That was before I had *services* of my own."

"With me, Vicki. Or not at all."

She jerked erect, eyes silvering. "Are you threatening me?"

"I want to help you!" he spat through gritted teeth.

Vicki stared at him in some surprise, her eyes slowly losing their silver. "Why?"

"Because we're friends." His teeth remained locked together, making the pronouncement sound less than friendly, but his hands weren't around her throat and he figured that had to count for something. "Isn't that what you kept saying? That we're friends, and there's no reason for that to change just because you've acquired a new lifestyle? Aren't those your exact words? This may come as a surprise to you, but I consider Michael Celluci a friend as well—at the very least, a comrade in arms." His lip curled. "And I do not desert my people."

As territorial imperatives went, there were things Vicki was willing to share and things she was not. By the time Henry realized his mistake and remembered that Celluci was firmly entrenched on the side of not-willing-to-share, Vicki's fingers had closed around his shoulders. Over four-and-a-half centuries of experience had no chance against the intensity of her rage. A fraction of a heartbeat later, he hit the floor, her thumbs hooked to rip the arteries on both sides of his neck, her teeth bared, and her eyes blazing silver shards of pain into his.

"Michael Celluci is mine."

There was no possibility of compromise in the words and only one possible answer, for he could not let her get away with intimidation. He was older. This was *his* territory.

"Trust me, Vicki, he's not my type."

If a soft answer had the potential to turn away wrath, a smart-ass response saved the situation from melodrama.

Vicki blinked, loosened her grip on Henry's throat, and sat back. "I could have killed you," she growled, her tone shading from anger to embarrassment.

"No." With her hands resting on either side of his neck, he decided not to shake his head. The emphasis might end up entirely misplaced. "I think we're past that, you and I."

"Ha! So I was right. I was right, and *you* were wrong."

He couldn't stop the smile. She was, after all, barely three years old in the night and this was one of those times it showed. "Yes, you were right." When she stood, creating a careful distance between them, Henry rose as well. "Celluci has always been yours, Vicki," he told her softly when they were eye-to-eye again. "If you doubt that, you do him a disservice."

Had she still been mortal, she would have reddened.

As it was, she backed away until her calves hit the couch. "Yeah, well, that you consider him to be one of yours will no doubt thrill him all to bits." Since she was at the couch, she sat. "So let's have a look at those news programs Tony taped. Maybe we'll get a better idea of what's going on."

Emotional self-discovery had never been one of Vicki's strong points, Henry reminded himself as he picked up the remote. The prospect of eternity had cracked the protective shell she'd worn most of her life, but there were pieces remaining that still needed to be levered free. *Celluci's problem,* he acknowledged thankfully and turned on the television.

A Metropolitan Toronto Police officer had not been found tied to a bed in a North Vancouver clinic.

No one had been arrested for selling kidney transplants.

Red-gold brows meeting over his nose, Henry stopped the tape. "I don't understand," he said, more to himself than to Vicki. "I sent the police out to Project Hope."

Vicki's first impulse was to suggest that age had robbed him of persuasion, but June nights were too short for her to provoke another fight merely for the sake of pissing him off. "Then they didn't find him."

"He wasn't exactly well-hidden."

"Then he wasn't there."

"If he's been moved . . ." Henry let the sentence trail off. Vancouver was a very large city. He shuddered at the sudden vision of Michael Celluci spending an eternity haunting the end of his bed.

"I'll find him."

"How?"

She stood, the motion fluid and predatory. "First, we make a few discreet inquiries and find out what actually happened last night at the clinic after we left. Then . . ." Her eyes glittered. ". . . we play it by ear. Or whatever other body parts we have to tear off to get an answer."

*   *   *

Typical, Celluci thought, craning his head to see the IV line that had been inserted into the back of his hand. *Good doctors, evil doctors—none of them ever bother to mention what the hell they're doing to you. Like you haven't any right to know what they're fucking around with.* "Excuse me, but it's still *my* body."

"Yes, it is."

Startled, he swiveled his head around to stare up at the impassive face of the doctor. Then he realized he'd spoken that last thought out loud. Although earlier attempts indicated he wouldn't accomplish much, he supposed it wouldn't hurt to try and continue the conversation. "Then would you mind telling me just what is it you're doing?"

"Replacing fluids." She packed the bag of blood away in the small cooler.

"You know there's a limit to how much of that stuff you can take out."

Dr. Mui snapped the cooler closed and turned to go. "I know."

"So there's a lab involved in this, too, eh?"

One hand on the door, she paused and gave him much the same look he could remember receiving from his third-grade teacher—who, if he remembered correctly, had never liked him much. "Don't be ridiculous, Detective. The labs do the work they're sent. There's no need to involve them in the details."

Okay, no evil labs. While that bit of good news had no bearing on his present circumstance, it was encouraging in a larger sense. "What about during the operation? You're going to need an assistant— because as good as you may be you don't have three hands—and with two people under, you'll need an anesthesiologist as well."

"What makes you think there'll be two people under, Detective? Packed in sterile ice, a kidney can safely last almost forty-eight hours after removal."

"Two separate operations would increase the risk of detection." He kept his voice level, disinterested, as though he were not going to be intimately involved

in those operations. "My guess is you do them both
at once. Sequentially if not simultaneously."

Dr. Mui inclined her head, acknowledging his theory. "Very perceptive of you, Detective. Your point?"

"I was just wondering how you keep those other
people from talking."

"Why?"

Shrugging as deeply as the restraints allowed, he
gave her his best *let's charm the truth out of this witness* smile. "I haven't much else to do."

"True enough." The corners of her mouth might
have curved upward a fraction, but Celluci couldn't
be certain. "The other people involved know only
what they must to perform their specific function, so
even if they did talk, there'd be a limited amount they
could say. However, as they are obviously breaking
the law themselves, the odds of them talking fall
within a reasonable risk. And you'd be amazed at how
little it takes to convince some people to break the
law."

Celluci snorted. "No, I wouldn't. But murder . . ."

"Who said anything about murder? They only know
what they need to. Now, try to get some sleep. You're
going to have a busy day tomorrow."

Tomorrow. The word lingered in the room long
after the doctor had left.

"Check the IV in about an hour and give him a
bowl of broth."

"Ball game'll be on in an hour," Sullivan protested,
looking sulky.

Somewhat surprised at the way she'd opened up to
the detective, Dr. Mui ignored him. Her world had
been built from certainties, and if she hadn't believed
that Sullivan would obey her implicitly, she'd have left
him where she found him.

Lips pulled back off her teeth, her fingers closed
around the carved handle with enough force to crack

the wood, Vicki yanked open the door and stepped into the clinic.

Michael Celluci's life no longer added its familiar beat to the muted roar.

"Shit god-fucking-damn!"

"Very expressive." Entering on her heels, Henry managed to slide by without actually making physical contact. Keeping her under careful surveillance in case her anger should widen its focus, he added, "And given that the detective has apparently left the building, what exactly does it mean?"

Vicki jerked her head toward the nurse's station. "It means it's a different shift and there's a different nurse on. She's not going to know squat."

"Not that the last one was particularly helpful," Henry observed quietly to himself, allowing a prudent distance before he followed Vicki across the lounge. With her attention so fixated on rescuing Celluci, the ride to the clinic had involved nothing worse than an extended snarling match—unpleasant but survivable and no worse than he'd seen Celluci live through on a daily basis. He wasn't sure whether this meant their relationship had progressed or deteriorated, but if she'd growled "old woman" at him one more time, he'd have been sorely tempted to have defined it by tossing her into traffic.

Unaware that death stood behind her, the nurse turned from the drug cabinet and found herself falling into the dark light of silver eyes. The brown glass bottle she held slipped from suddenly nerveless fingers.

Henry caught it before it hit the floor. "We were here later last night," he said as he straightened. "I can feel healthy lives mixed in with the sick. I doubt all the visitors have left yet. Do what you have to do quickly and don't attract any attention." It was the voice he'd used while teaching her to Hunt; with any luck she'd listen to it. Setting the bottle carefully on the edge of the desk, he moved to stand in the doorway.

Awareness narrowed to the life she held and the life she searched for, Vicki heard Henry's voice as part of the clinic's ambient noise, a noise all but drowned out by the cry of the Hunt ringing within her head. "Last night," she said with quiet menace, "there was a man being held in the hidden room. Where is he now?"

Confusion battled fear. "What hidden room?"

"The room at the back of the building."

"You mean the old laundry? There was no one in there."

The menace grew. "He was there."

Caught between what she knew to be true and the truth she saw in the silver eyes, the nurse whimpered low in her throat.

"He was there!" Vicki repeated. The Hunger rose. Her fingers closed around a white-clad shoulder and soft flesh compacted under her grip. "Where is he now?"

"I don't know." Tears trickled down cheeks blanched of color, and the words barely made it past trembling lips.

"Tell me!"

"I don't . . ." A strangled sob broke the protest in half. ". . . want to die."

The staccato pounding of the nurse's heart, the panicked racing of her blood, made it difficult to think. The Hunger, barely held in check, urged Vicki to take the fear and make it hers. To rend. To tear. To feed. She took a half step forward, head slightly back, nostrils flared to drink in the warm, meaty scent of life seasoned with terror. After the exhilarating experience in the warehouse, it would be so easy to let go.

"Do what you have to do quickly . . ."

Yes.

"Those of our kind who learn to control the Hunger have eternity before them. Those the Hunger controls are quickly hunted down and put to death."

Henry's words again, but a deeper memory, an older lesson.

Nothing controls me.

If "Victory" Nelson lived by any maxim, that was it.

She released the nurse so quickly the woman swayed and would have fallen had she not taken another, less threatening hold. "You have not seen us and you will not see us while we are here."

"I will not see you," the nurse repeated almost prayerfully. "I will not see you." This time when Vicki let her go, she staggered sideways and collapsed into a chair. A heartbeat later, she was alone in the room, certain she'd always been alone, staring at the brown glass bottle in her hand and wondering if it was possible to dream, to have a nightmare, while awake.

"I almost killed her." The Hunger raged against its restraints and Vicki determinedly ignored the almost painful feeling that she'd left something important unfinished.

"I know."

"Then why didn't you try to stop me?"

"I didn't need to, did I?" Henry glanced over her shoulder as she flipped through the communication book she'd taken from the nurse's station. They were standing in the hall next to the operating room, safely far enough away from everyone else in the building. "I had to trust what I'd taught you, or there wasn't much point in teaching it."

She twisted around far enough to see his face, "You ought to lay off the reruns of *Kung Fu,* Henry. You're sounding like a pompous ass—and I'm telling you this for your own good because we're friends." Before he could respond, before he'd figured out *what* to respond, she added, "Maybe you should've trusted your teaching all along."

"All along?"

Her lip curled. "All along—from the moment I arrived in Vancouver."

"If you remember, I taught you we couldn't share a territory."

"Which just proves what you know," she announced

triumphantly and turned her attention back to the communication book. "Ah. Here it is." She tapped an entry with one finger. "5:09 A.M., two cops show up, so does a Dr. Mui—apparently one of her patients was dying—she shows the cops around, they leave. They must've moved him before the cops arrived. Son of a bitch."

"I don't see how . . ."

"Does it matter? Come on." She tossed the book into the operating room—let them wonder—and started down the hall. "I doubt there's a forwarding address, but they might've left something in that room we can use."

Nothing, except the lingering scent of three men and a woman.

Vicki stood by the empty bed, forcing herself to recognize other lives but Mike Celluci's. "Dr. Mui."

Henry frowned, recognizing Death beneath the recent patina of life. "What about her?"

"She's in on it. This . . ." Vicki waved a hand in the air, scooping it toward her nose. "This is the woman who gave Celluci that shot."

"Are you sure?"

"Trust me. I make it a point to remember the other women he smells like."

I suspect I owe the detective an apology, Henry mused as he stepped back out of Vicki's way. *He was definitely better acquainted with territorial imperatives than I assumed.* "Now where?"

"Dr. Mui's office."

". . . and he's safe at second! Can you believe that speed. From anyone else in this game that would've been a single!"

His attention on the television in the other room, Sullivan crumpled the empty saline bag and shoved the IV stand aside. It hung, suspended for an instant at forty-five degrees and then crashed to the floor, the noise all but drowning out the enthusiasm of the sportscaster.

Kicking the stainless steel pieces out of his way,

Sullivan stomped out of the room and cranked up the volume until the sound began to distort.

"What are you looking so happy about," he snarled as he returned to the bed. "You an Oakland fan?"

"Not likely." Unaware that he'd been looking anything but pained—the needle had been roughly yanked from the back of his hand and the bandage applied with bruising pressure—Celluci winced as the crowd at the Kingdome responded to a double play and the television speakers squealed.

"Then what?" Sullivan's eyes narrowed as a second of silence led into a commercial, the sales pitch almost deafening in comparison. Grumbling under his breath, he went back to the TV and turned the volume down. "You thought someone'd notice that, didn't you? Maybe complain about the noise." Callused fingers closed on the end of Celluci's nose and twisted. Cartilage cracked. "Don't ever think I'm stupid."

Blinking away involuntary tears, Celluci snorted, "Hadn't occurred to me." If truth be told, nothing much had occurred to him for most of the evening. It might've been the blood loss, it might've been the residual effect of the sedatives but coherent thought took more effort than he seemed capable of.

"So why're you smilin', shit for brains?"

Except that he had to make the effort and he only had one source of information. If nothing else, he needed to find out more about his jailer. Celluci jerked his head toward the bowl of broth on the bedside table. "The doctor says you've got to feed me."

Deceptively gentle eyes narrowed. "Yeah, so?"

"You're either going to have to turn up the TV and risk attracting attention, or miss the game. Either way, I win."

"Maybe I just won't feed you."

"And make the doctor angry?"

That was clearly not going to happen. The bowl all but dwarfed in the curve of a huge hand, Sullivan grinned unpleasantly. "Open your mouth or I'll open it for you."

Confronted with violent death day after day, police officers coped by either ignoring the inevitability of their own death or by thinking about it so constantly it lost its mystery and became a part of life, like breathing. Choking on broth, Celluci realized he'd never considered drowning in consomme as a serious possibility.

He was still coughing and gasping for breath when Sullivan left the room, snarling, "You can piss later," as he slammed the door.

Struggling to keep from vomiting—if he didn't choke on it and die, he'd have to lie in it, and the second option thrilled him as little as the first—he gradually regained control of his body. Panting, each breath a little deeper than the last, he swallowed hard to discourage one last spasm of gagging.

When it was all over, he lay limp and exhausted, feeling like he'd just gone ten rounds with Mike Tyson. But he had a better idea of Sullivan's temperament.

And he had a plan.

Of sorts.

"Find anything?"

"Vicki, I'm a writer. I turn on my computer, I play a few games of solitaire, I answer my E-mail, and I write. Anything more complicated, I don't worry about." Frowning at the screen, Henry tapped his nails gently against the edge of the keyboard. "This is more complicated."

Vicki glanced up from an aggressive search of the filing cabinet and peered across the room at the monitor. "Looks like point and click to me," she growled.

"The whole thing's encrypted. I can't access anything without Dr. Mui's password."

"I don't see why the paranoid bitch can't keep a Rolodex like everyone else," Vicki snarled, slamming shut one drawer and opening another. All she wanted were a couple of addresses, preferably one marked *this is where we're keeping Michael Celluci,* but failing that she'd settle for *this is where the people in charge live and you can rip the location of Michael Celluci out of them.*

With Vicki's anger beating against him in heated waves, Henry decided it would be safest not to respond—besides, she had a point, a Rolodex would've been much simpler. *I can't believe we're doing this.* But it wasn't breaking into Dr. Mui's office that he was having difficulty with.

As much as he shared Vicki's concern over the detective's safety, he found himself continually distracted by the circumstances. They were working together. Not, certainly, as they had before the change, but co-operating in close contact nevertheless. It was such an amazing experience that he desperately wanted to tell someone about it. Unfortunately, only two people could fully appreciate the ramifications—Vicki wasn't interested, and there wasn't much satisfaction in talking to himself.

"There's nothing in this thing but patients' records. You getting anywhere?"

He dragged his attention back to the task at hand. "Dr. Mui has a modem—could she get into those other systems from here?"

"Back in Toronto, I could make six phone calls and get half a dozen people who could do it in their sleep. So the short answer is yes, but that doesn't help us . . . Ha!" Straightening, Vicki lifted a file folder out of the bottom drawer. "At least the government's still supporting the pulp and paper industry. According to the BC Department of Motor Vehicles, the good doctor just bought a new car. Must be nice." Her voice trailed off as she flipped through the legal documents. A few moments later, she shook her head and glanced up at Henry. "Did you know you two are neighbors?"

She jerked toward him as he snatched the file from her hands but kept herself from snatching it back.

"No, she's in the other tower, phase two. It just went on the market this spring, and it's pricey." Although it twisted muscles into knots, he managed to stop himself from grabbing Vicki's arm as she started toward the door. This wasn't the time to test the limits of their new boundaries. "Where are you going?"

"We know where Dr. Mui is. Dr. Mui knows where Celluci is." There were now three points of light in the office, the monitor and Vicki's eyes. "He might even be in that condo. We might've spent the day a hundred feet from him."

"I doubt it. The selling point for these units is the security system. They've got *full* video coverage. It would be far too dangerous for her to take him there."

Her fingers dimpled the back of the chair. Metal creaked. "She's still going to know where he is!"

"She's probably with him." He didn't need to say why. Glancing back down at the paperwork, Henry frowned. "She bought the unit from Swanson Realty."

"Swanson? His name just keeps coming up," Vicki snarled. "On that cable show, regarding transplants, donated computers to street clinics, here . . ."

They got the idea at the same time, but Vicki made it to the keyboard first.

His name did, indeed, keep coming up, and it got them into Dr. Mui's system.

"What are you looking for?"

"Swanson's home address." It came out sounding like a threat. "He's not going to be at the scene; he's no doctor, there's no need. The puppet master stays in the background pulling the strings." The need to rescue Celluci fought with curiosity as she raced deeper into the files; this would be her only chance to gather information, and she couldn't just walk away from it.

Dr. Mui had extensive E-mail archives, neatly categorized and most of them going to financial institutions.

"Swiss bank accounts," Henry hazarded.

"Among other things not quite so old-fashioned. The doctor appears to be sending a great deal of money into off-shore tax shelters."

"Doctors make a great deal of money."

"Yeah, well this is considerably more than you can explain by extra-billing even in BC—and there's still the car and the condo. I'd say we can safely assume Swanson's bought her and that she didn't go cheap. He must be charging a fucking fortune for those kidneys in order to make a profit on it."

"What price life?" Henry asked her quietly.

Vicki turned and met his gaze. After a heartbeat, after the slow, languorous beat of an immortal heart within a body that would never see the day again, she nodded. "Good point."

For a moment, Henry thought they might be able to touch, without blood, without passion, in friendship. The moment passed, but the feeling lingered. "Let's not forget that Swanson can reinvest the money he offers to his donors."

"Another good point." Lips pressed into a thin, white line, Vicki shut down the system. "Now we know where he is, let's go. . . ."

They heard the life approaching the office in the same instant. Leather soles slapped against tile, coming closer, cutting off their escape.

"What about heaving the desk through the window?"

Henry shook his head. "It'd attract too much attention. They'd see us leave and trace the plates, so we'd do it only if we wanted to abandon the car, and we don't."

The office door opened into the hall. Vicki moved to the right and waved Henry to the left.

Sensitive eyes turned away from the fluorescent glare streaming in from the hall, Vicki grabbed the hand that reached in for the light switch and yanked the stranger into the room.

Henry closed the door.

Dr. Wallace believed there was very little he hadn't seen. He'd joined the Navy at seventeen, gone to Korea, came home in one piece unlike so many others, gone to university on his military benefits, spent time in Africa with the flying doctors, and finally settled into a comfortable family practice in North Vancouver. He'd seen death arrive without warning, and he'd seen death settle in for a long, intimate final journey, but he'd never seen it wear the face that bent over him in Dr. Mui's office.

The diffuse illumination from the parking lot defined only shadow features around a pair of silvered eyes. Cold silver, like polished metal or moonlight, and they drew him in to depths much darker than logic insisted they should have been.

He'd always hoped he'd face death calmly when it finally came for him, but now he realized that given any encouragement at all, he'd do whatever he had to to stay alive.

"What do you know about Ronald Swanson?"

Not what he'd expected. Too mundane, too human.

"Did you hear me?"

No mistaking the danger. "He's rich, very rich, but he's willing to spend money on causes he considers worthy." Maintaining a clinical detachment, a lecturing tone, helped keep the panic from ripping free. "After his wife died of kidney failure, he began supporting transplant programs. He buys them advertising, pays for educational programs—many doctors haven't a clue of how to deal with the whole donor issue. Swanson paid for this hospice."

"That's it?"

Impossible not to tell more even if there was nothing more to tell. "I don't actually know him. Dr. Mui . . ."

"What about Dr. Mui?"

Wallace had a sudden vision of companions thrown to the wolves to lighten the sleigh in a wild race to safety. "Swanson handpicked her to run this place. Before that she was a transplant surgeon, a good one, too, but there was an allegation of carelessness. It turned out to be completely unfounded. Hardly anyone even heard about it outside the hospital."

"Would Swanson have heard?"

"I don't know, but it happened around the same time his wife died." Had his heartbeat always been that loud? That fast? It shouldn't be that fast. A dribble of sweat rolled into one eye and burned. "It might have been why he offered her this job."

"An unjust accusation turned her against the medical establishment."

"I wouldn't go so far as to say that." He was babbling now; he knew it, but he couldn't stop. "Dr. Mui told me, that is, we spoke after one of my patients came here—that's why I'm here tonight, to check on a patient—that she wanted to work more with people and less with hospital administrators and their legal bully boys. Hello?"

The eyes were gone, the darkness lifted, and he was sitting alone in an empty office, talking to himself. It was over. Best not think too long or too hard on what *it* had been. He was alive. He wiped damp palms on his thighs, stood, and walked quickly to the light switch by the door.

The room was full of shadows. The shadows, in turn, were full. He suspected they'd never be empty again.

"You handled that very well."

"Don't patronize me, Henry."

"I wasn't." He shifted the BMW into reverse and backed carefully out of the parking spot. The last thing he wanted was to attract attention, license plates could be traced. "You gave him nothing to remember but fear. I was impressed."

"Impressed?"

"Try to remember that you're still very young to this life. You show a remarkable aptitude."

Vicki snorted. "*Now* you're patronizing me."

"I was trying to compliment you."

"Do vampires do that? Compliment other vampires? It's not against the rules?"

Henry turned the car onto Mt. Seymour and sped up, swinging almost immediately into the passing lane and around two trucks in a maneuver a mortal would not have been able to complete. "I know you fight with Michael Celluci to relieve tension," he growled through clenched teeth. "I understand that. But I'm not him, and if you pick a fight with me, you'll find the results are regrettably different—surely it's become apparent that neither of us will be able to stop a disagreement from escalating beyond mere words."

"*I* can control *myself.*"

"Vicki!"

"Sorry." She strained against the limit of the seat belt, one hand on the dash, the other clenching and unclenching in her lap, her eyes locked on the road between the twin blurs of streetlights. "Jesus H. Christ, Henry, can't you go any faster?"

He had a sudden memory of the guilty relief he'd felt when she'd finally returned to Toronto after her year of learning to live a new and alien life. When she left this time, he strongly suspected there'd be no guilt mixed in with the relief.

That is, if they found Michael Celluci alive.

Thirteen

"Fucking Oakland."

Through half-closed eyes, Celluci watched Sullivan walk toward the bed. *This is it. Now or never.* He'd lined up a few more clichés that seemed appropriate but had no time to voice them before the big man grabbed his shoulder and shook him, hard. He let his head whip back and forth on the pillow, hoping it looked like he didn't have strength enough to fight the motion. As far as acting went, it wasn't much of a stretch. His head felt as though it were connected to his body by a not very thick elastic band.

"I'm gonna unbuckle you, so don't give me any shit 'cause I'm not in the mood. Damn Mariners finished three fucking runs behind and I had fifty fucking bucks ridin' on the game."

Celluci grunted as a thumb ground between the muscles of his left forearm and into the bone.

"Felt that, did you? Good."

The leather strap fell away. He flung his arm up off the bed and tried to close his fingers around Sullivan's throat.

A vicious backhand snapped his head back. His mouth filled with blood from lips caught between knuckles and teeth. *Well, you* wanted *him angry,* he reminded himself, trying to swallow without choking. *All part of the pl* . . . A sudden, agonizing pain in his left wrist cut off the rest of the thought and brought involuntary tears.

"Weren't you listening when I said I wasn't in the mood for this kind of crap?"

The pain painted red starbursts on the inside of Celluci's eyes. He didn't think the wrist was broken, but at the moment, that belief gave him very little actual comfort. *Only the left. I won't need the left. Christ, couldn't I have come up with a plan that hurt a little less?* If it had only meant the loss of a kidney, he'd have been tempted to just lie there and let it happen. Preventing loss of life however—his life—had to be worth a bit of discomfort.

As the last restraint fell away, he tried to lunge off the bed. This time, he rocked back with the blow so that Sullivan's hand impacted against his cheek with slightly less force than previously. Slightly. *What was that plan again. Let him beat you senseless, then escape in the confusion?* With any luck, the pounding in his temple was his pulse, not pieces breaking off the inside of his skull. *Oh, good plan.*

The room spun as Sullivan dragged him up onto his feet, muttering, "I should just leave you there to piss yourself."

Breathing heavily, the dizziness as much from the earlier blood loss as from the double contact with Sullivan's fist, Celluci managed to twist his split lip into a close approximation of a sneer. "You'd have . . . to clean it up, but maybe . . . you'd like that."

Sullivan blinked mild eyes and smiled. The smile held all the petty cruelty the eyes did not. "Yeah? Well, I'm gonna enjoy this."

The first punch drove all the air out of Celluci's lungs. He'd have fallen had Sullivan not maintained a grip on his shirt. Seams cut into his armpits as the fabric stretched to its limit and beyond. He took a wild swing while he tried to get his feet back under him but had no success at either.

He didn't feel the second punch connect, only the result. One minute he was more-or-less standing, the next, he was flat on his face on the floor. Which was where he wanted to be. Unfortunately, he'd intended to be just a bit more functional.

"You know what I keep forgetting?"

The words seemed to come from a very long way away.

"That you're a cop."

Oh, shit.

The sudden flurry of kicks that followed pounded out a rhythm along hip and thigh. They hurt, but nowhere near as much as they would've had Sullivan not been in sneakers or had he been able to reach more delicate targets. Or, for that matter, had the doctor not wanted his kidneys intact. Exaggerating the effect, Celluci tried to rise and fell, only partially faking as he'd forgotten that his left wrist was essentially unusable. Whimpering—and ignoring how good it felt to let some of it out—he squirmed frantically forward on his belly until his shoulder slammed into one leg of the dresser hard enough to rock the heavy furniture.

"Bet that hurt." Sullivan was breathing as heavily, but not from exertion.

Lying with his right arm stretched out under the dresser, Celluci walked his fingers over the floor. Just when he thought he'd made an unsurvivable mistake, they closed around metal. He didn't have strength to spare for a smile.

"I got the other guys when the doctor was done, but since you're not gonna survive the operation, I'm glad we had this time together." Sullivan bent over and grabbed the waistband of Celluci's jeans, jerking the heavy cotton up into the air. "Now, get back on your fucking feet."

Celluci went limp, neither hindering nor helping, conserving his strength. He kept his right arm stretched out, out of sight for as long as possible. The moment his hand cleared the edge of the dresser, he spent all his hoarded strength on one blow, swinging up and around and slamming the length of stainless steel pipe from the fallen IV tower between Sullivan's legs.

The mild eyes widened. Mouth opening and closing like a fish out of water, Sullivan sank slowly to his knees, both hands clutching his crotch.

Hauling himself to his feet on the edge of the bed, Celluci half turned, intending to smash the pipe against the back of Sullivan's head. To his astonishment, the big man got a hand up and intercepted the blow. The pipe spun off across the room.

All things being equal, the two men were about evenly matched but, as it was—as they were—Celluci didn't stand a chance without a weapon, and he knew it.

Injured arm cradled tightly against his chest, he staggered out of the bedroom and through the room beyond. As he fought with the outside door, he could hear Sullivan getting to his feet, yelling a mixture of profanity and threat.

Then he managed to lift the latch, and he staggered out into the night.

"Son of a bitch! He's not there."

Screened from the view of curious neighbors by double rows of cypress, Henry turned off his headlights and sped down the winding drive toward the low rectangle of Swanson's house nestled within its cocoon of security lights. "He could be in bed. We won't know until we're out of the car."

"He's not there," Vicki repeated, her voice rising in frustration. She didn't know why she was so certain, but the blank stare of the dark windows said empty—not asleep, not sitting with the lights off; not home. The instant Henry stopped the car, she leaped out onto the concrete, senses extended. "I told you we should have gone to Dr. Mui," she snarled after a moment.

"We agreed that the doctor is probably with . . ." Half out of the car, Henry paused, head lifted to catch the breeze. "Vicki! Do you . . ." He didn't bother finishing because she was already racing toward the back of the house.

* * *

The way Celluci saw it, he had two choices; he could try to outrun Sullivan on unfamiliar paths, hoping to reach a road and witnesses if not safety, or he could dive into the semi-wild growth the paths cut through and hope to lose him in the underbrush. Ten feet from the cottage, swaying like a sailor with every step, he realized he had no hope in hell of outrunning anyone, not even a man with his balls in a sling. Teeth clenched against the protests of his abused body, he pushed into the darkness.

The trees blocked the little moonlight that flittered through the cloud cover—he couldn't see as far as his feet, and higher obstacles like trees and bushes were patterns of shadows on shadow. *Big mistake. I'm no woodsman.* But it was too late to turn back.

A crashing in the shrubbery behind him flung him forward. Since he had to believe Sullivan could see no more than he could, he had to hope that the sound of his escape was drowned out by the sound of pursuit. It was pretty much the only hope he had.

He stumbled over something that poked sharp edges through his sock and into his ankle, caught himself before he fell, and realized that he was moving across a forty-five-degree slope. *Up or down?* Since he had no idea of where he was and no idea of where he was going, down seemed as good a choice as any. *Fuck it. Might as well have gravity work for me.*

A branch end slapped him in the face, hard enough to raise a welt. Thorns he couldn't see snagged his jeans and dragged bleeding scratches across bare arms. The slope got steeper. He began to pick up speed.

He flung out his left arm to block a sudden shadow and nearly cried out when his wrist slammed into the unforgiving trunk of a tree. The pain brought back the dizziness. Shadows whirled. He missed his footing, and the night tilted sideways.

Rocks and trees slammed into him as he passed, hard enough to hurt, never hard enough to stop him. He crashed through some kind of bush—it had no thorns, that was all he either knew or cared about—

picked up speed across an open clearing, and slammed into a concrete retaining wall on the far side.

The world went away for a while . . .

"You better not have damaged anything, asshole!"

. . . and came back in a rush.

Celluci drew in a deep breath—moderately relieved to find it didn't hurt as much as he thought it should—and, as the moon broke through the cloud cover, tried to focus on the man squatting beside him. In spite of the poor visibility, Sullivan's bovine features looked scared. "Doctor won't be pleased . . . if I'm not good . . . as a donor. Bet you got kidneys . . . she could use."

"Shut up. Just shut the fuck up."

The open-handed blow rocked Celluci's head back, but everything hurt so much he felt the motion more than the actual pain.

"All right. You're goin' back to the fucking cottage and I'm going to tie you down so tightly you're gonna need my permission to fucking breathe."

"You're going to have to . . . carry me."

"I'll fucking drag you if I have to."

"Better not damage . . . the merchandise." As he finished speaking, he threw himself at Sullivan's feet, trying to knock the big man off balance. With them both on the ground and a little luck . . .

Beefy fingers grabbed the front of his shirt and heaved his torso up off the ground. He saw the fist raised, a club-shaped shadow against the sky, then Sullivan disappeared, and he dropped flat on his back again.

"Are you all right?"

"Fitzroy?" Swallowing a mouthful of blood, Celluci propped himself up on his good arm, Henry's hand steadying him as he swayed.

Vicki had Sullivan on his knees in the middle of the small clearing, one hand dimpling the scalp under the short hair, dragging his head back so far the corded muscles of his throat cast lines of shadow. Her eyes were pale points of light in a face of terrible, inhuman beauty that Celluci almost didn't recognize.

"Vicki?" When she turned her burning gaze on him, he knew what she was about to do, and although the night was warm, he was suddenly very, very cold. "Vicki, no. Don't kill him."

"Why not?" Her voice had changed to match her face; seductive, irresistible, deadly.

There was no need, not even for emphasis, to shout his reply. She could hear his heart beating, his blood moving under his skin; he only hoped she could understand. "Because I'm asking you not to. Let him go."

Vicki straightened, the quiet plea reaching her in a way anger or fear would not have been able. She released her captive, ignoring him as he collapsed sobbing to the ground, and took a step toward Celluci. "Let him go," she repeated, her voice becoming more human with every word. "Are you out of your mind? He is mine!"

"Why?"

"Why? For what he did to you."

"Wouldn't that make him mine?"

Confusion replaced some of the terrifying beauty. "Vicki, please. Don't do this."

"This is where I draw my line in the sand. . . ."

The scent of terror drew her back around to face her prey. Without her hand to hold him, he whimpered when her eyes met his and flung himself backward toward the edge of the clearing.

The Hunger sang the song of the Hunt, of the blood.

It was all she could hear.

She tensed to spring, and it was over.

Henry let Sullivan fall to the ground, head lolling on a broken neck. Calmly, as though he hadn't just killed a man, he met Vicki's gaze across the clearing.

When he nodded, she turned to face Celluci, the Hunger fading now that the terror had stopped and the blood was cooling. She should have felt rage at the theft of her prey by another, but all she felt was grateful. She'd stood on the edge of a precipice and had just barely escaped plunging over. Her fingers curled into fists to stop their sudden trembling.

"Is he dead?"

"Yes."

Celluci looked from Henry to Vicki and realized he'd received exactly what he'd asked for. Vicki had not done it, Henry had. But he'd seen Henry kill before in a barn outside London, Ontario. He'd known for a long time what Henry was. Vampire. Nightwalker. Immortal death. Henry. Not Vicki. He closed his eyes. The lids had barely fallen when a familiar arm went around his shoulders and a familiar voice brushed warm breath against his ear.

"Are you all right?"

He shrugged, as well as he was able all things considered. "I've been better."

"Do you need a doctor?"

From somewhere, he found half a smile. "No."

"Then let's get you out of here. Henry's car is at the front of the house." She hesitated, ready to slide the other arm beneath his legs. "May I?"

"Just don't make a habit of it." Her lips pressed briefly against his face, then she carefully lifted him into her arms. He kept his eyes closed. Sometimes, love needed a little help being blind.

Swanson sighed as he turned onto Nisga's Drive, thankful to be almost home. The black-tie fund-raiser for the Transplant Society had been a depressing affair, most conversations either beginning or ending with the recent death of Lisa Evans and how much both she and her open checkbook would be missed.

He almost failed to note the one significant detail of the car pulling out onto the road, realizing only at the last moment that it pulled out of *his* driveway. There seemed to be three people in it although he only got a good look at the driver as it sped past. "Dangerous," he told himself, although he didn't

know why, and he wondered if perhaps his house had
been robbed while he was away. Shaking his head as
he turned in between the cypress, he told himself not
to be ridiculous. Thieves seldom drove BMWs.

Still, in a neighborhood where Bentlys were the car
of choice, it wasn't that farfetched a theory.

The house seemed undisturbed. He parked outside
the garage and sat studying it in the brilliant quartz
halogen glare of the security lights. He didn't want
any surprises. He didn't like surprises. After a careful
inspection, he left the car where it was and walked
over to the front door.

The security system hadn't been tampered with, but
that meant only that they might have used another
entrance. There were four—*No, five,* he amended remembering the French doors Rebecca had insisted on
having in the dining room. He hadn't used them since
she'd died.

Lights switched off and on automatically as he in-
spected the first floor. The lights had been Rebecca's
idea as well and only her memory kept him from dis-
mantling them. They always made him feel as though
he were being followed around by ghosts.

Upstairs, Rebecca's jewel case lay where she'd left
it on that last day. Swanson knew the order of the
contents the way he knew the order of his desk, and
they hadn't been touched.

Not thieves, then.

Who?

He turned to face the window that looked out over
the lawns, the gardens, and, ultimately, the two guest
cottages tucked a discreet distance down the wooded
slope. Although their locations had been chosen so
that they were as private as possible, there seemed to
be rather a lot of illumination filtering up through the
trees surrounding the farther building.

Dr. Mui had a donor in one of the cottages.

Perhaps the three in the car were colleagues of hers.

His fingers closed around the curtain edge, crushing
the fabric. He hadn't wanted the donor here. Dr. Mui

had no business turning Rebecca's home into an extension of the clinic; she'd had enough of hospitals and clinics during that last horrible year before she died. Whether it had been a good business decision or not, he should never have agreed to the use of the cottage. It was one thing to allow the buyer to convalesce in peace and quiet for a few days and quite another thing to open his home to the sort of people who provided the merchandise.

"I'm going down there to find out exactly what is going on. If the doctor thinks it a good idea I maintain my distance from the donors, then she shouldn't have left one on my doorstep."

As he turned from the window, he caught sight of his reflection in the mirror and wondered if maybe he shouldn't take a moment to change his clothes before he went to the cottage. Twitching a jacket sleeve down over a heavy gold cufflink, he decided not to bother. "If anyone complains," he told his reflection, "I'll explain that I'm making a formal investigation."

Had Rebecca still been alive, she'd have laughed and maybe thrown something at him. He'd loved making her laugh. But Rebecca was dead. His shoulders slumped and after caressing the cameo he'd had made for her in Florence, he left the bedroom.

At the back door, it suddenly occurred to him that the car could be connected with Patricia Chou. The reporter had accosted him as he arrived at the fundraiser, demanding to know how a room full of rich people sitting down to an expensive meal was going to help anyone but the caterers. So far, she'd been careful to confront him only on public property, but he had no doubt she'd consider a trespassing charge a small price to pay to get a story. She was becoming a distinct irritant, and sometime soon he'd have to do something about her.

He checked the perimeters of the security lights for a camera crew and only when he was certain he was unobserved did he step out the door.

As he drew closer to the lit cottage, he began to feel more and more uneasy. When he rounded a corner and saw the open door, he knew something was wrong. "Every light in the place is on," he muttered, stepping over the threshold. "Don't these people realize hydro costs money?"

The cottage was empty. Both the donor and the orderly that Dr. Mui had promised to leave in attendance were gone. Swanson frowned down at the restraints on the bed and tried to work out what had happened. Perhaps the people in the BMW were the donor's colleagues, not Dr. Mui's. Perhaps this donor hadn't come off the street but was one of the young turks who'd crashed and burned in the recent recession and now needed money from any source to maintain his lifestyle.

It explained why Dr. Mui had felt he couldn't be kept at the clinic.

Perhaps at the last moment he'd changed his mind and his friends had come for him.

But where was the orderly?

And more importantly, what was he supposed to tell the client coming into Vancouver on the 2:17 from Dallas?

Lips pressed into a thin, angry line, Swanson started back to the house after having carefully turned off all the lights and closed and locked the door. He'd missed the mess in the rhododendrons on the way down to the cottage, but a broken branch nearly tripped him up on the way back and brought it to his attention.

Although wisps of cloud blew continually over the moon, there was light enough to see that a large animal had gone crashing through his expensive underbrush. There'd been a recurring problem in the neighborhood with mountain lions eating household pets, but Swanson had always assumed the big cats were less obtrusive travelers. In his experience, only people caused that kind of destruction to private property.

Had the orderly not been missing, he'd have gone back to the house to call the police. As it was, he stepped off the path.

It wasn't a difficult trail to follow, even in the dark. Small plants had been crushed, large ones bent or broken. Then the moon went down.

Picking his way carefully down the slope and into the clearing above the retaining wall, Swanson swore softly to himself as his dress shoes slid on the damp grass and he went down on one knee. He put his hand on what he thought was a fallen log and felt cloth.

The moon came out.

"Oh, my God. Oh, my God. Oh, my God."

"So, now what do we do?"

Celluci sucked air through his teeth as he lowered himself down onto the bed. He'd walked up from the car to the elevator and the elevator to the condo under his own power. Mostly. "Now we figure out a way to bring in the police without involving the two of you."

"We tried that," Vicki snarled, reaching behind her for the first aid kit that Henry carried, "and it didn't work."

"So we try it again. There's a body in Ronald Swanson's backyard . . ." *Which we are not going to discuss,* his tone added. ". . . we might as well make use of it."

She began to wrap the elastic bandage around his wrist, the gentle rhythm of the motion a direct contrast to the brittle anger in her voice. "Swanson's rich and respected. The police find a body in his backyard, and they're not going to immediately connect it with him, especially when he wasn't home and no doubt has a rich and respected alibi. And second, it's not just Swanson that we want, and there's nothing to connect Sullivan's body to Dr. Mui except that he worked at the clinic. Which Swanson pays for. I'll bet long odds that the two of them could come up with an acceptable reason for that son of a bitch to be spending a few days in the cottage."

"Then perhaps I should go talk to Dr. Mui."

Celluci opened bloodshot eyes and stared past Vicki at Henry. "Talk to her?"

Henry nodded. "She has a condo in the next building."

"So you said in the car."

"So I should go see if she's home. We can make a decision when we have more information."

"You're only going to talk to her?" When Henry nodded again, Celluci exhaled noisily and added, "So why not tell her to go to the police and confess all?"

"You go on," Vicki announced quickly before Henry could answer. "I'll explain to Mike why that wouldn't work." It had been easy to deal with his presence when all her attention was on Celluci, but now the skin between her shoulder blades kept protesting *another* standing behind her. They needed to give frayed emotions a little more distance if they didn't want to return to the old animosity.

Henry read the subtext off her face, noted how she kept in physical contact with Celluci at all times, and left the room without comment. It made no sense for him to envy their intimacy, especially not in light of what had happened in the warehouse. It made no sense and was dangerous besides. He kept telling himself that as he walked away.

Celluci waited until he heard the outside door close, then he caught Vicki's hand in his—trying to prevent her from pouring rubbing alcohol into the scratches on his arms. "All right. Explain."

"It's simple, really." Twisting free of his grip, she swabbed the worst abrasions clean, ignoring his complaints. "We can't force anyone to act contrary to their own survival."

"Pull the other one, Vicki. People expose their throats to you."

"Most of them enjoy it."

Eleven dead in a Richmond warehouse. "Some don't."

She heard the memory of death in his voice and

sighed. "If Henry told Dr. Mui to turn herself in, she'd walk out of her apartment, maybe even make it to the car, but then, unless she had no strength of will at all—and considering what she's been doing in her spare time, strength of will doesn't seem to be something she lacks—then she'd suddenly ask herself just what the hell she was doing. Henry'd have to stay with her all the way and that would kind of defeat the purpose; wouldn't it?"

"But as long as he's with her, she'll talk? He can control her?"

"Probably." She remembered the crime boss who'd gone for his gun even though she hadn't released him. Of course, Henry'd been doing that sort of thing a lot longer.

Henry'd forgotten the full video security until halfway across the visitor's parking lot. Speed had kept his image from registering as he'd entered the building and raced up the stairs, but he was going to have to stop out in front of Dr. Mui's door, and he could figure out no way to prevent himself from being taped. As he left the stairwell on the eleventh floor, he could only hope she'd answer quickly. This was one of those times when he wished that Stoker had been right about certain laws of physics not applying to his kind. An ability to become mist would come in handy tonight.

He spared barely a thought for the couple in the hall until he noticed they were leaving the condo next to Dr. Mui's. Dressed all in black, they were laughing and talking nervously—although they had no idea of why they were nervous—their door half open. Henry slipped through before they pulled it closed.

Once inside, he stopped to catch his breath. The speed his kind used to escape detection was not meant to cover long distances. He'd need to feed soon.

Although there were video hookups inside the actual condominium units, they only activated if the electronic locks were forced. He should have no trouble leaving, but since he considered his presence here a solution, albeit an impulsive one, to the problem of standing in the hall, he had no intention of leaving too soon.

Electronics aside, the layout of the units seemed identical to the mirror-image layout in his building next door. He moved silently down the hall, wondering where on earth the owners had found the four-foot gargoyle in the entry.

Sifting through the stack of mail balanced incongruously on the stone guardian's head, he discovered that Carole and Ron Pettit had a number of *esoteric* interests. Amused, he set the correspondence back on its perch and murmuring, "They'll be sorry they missed me," went on into the master bedroom. The red silk sheets and truly astounding variety of candles perched on every available surface came as no surprise. Black, he discovered pushing through two neat rows of clothing in the walk-in closet, came in more shades than he'd previously imagined.

Resting his forehead on the wall adjoining Dr. Mui's condo, he could feel a life in the next room.

Sleeping.

Not having bothered to read the contractor's specifications provided when he bought his own unit, he had no idea how the walls were made but even if he could get through them, he couldn't do it without waking not only the doctor but the tenants above and below.

Then he smiled. While not in the habit of climbing headfirst down castle walls, he should have little trouble going from balcony to balcony, even with the doctor's solarium in the way. They couldn't possibly have video coverage on the balconies; too many people in Vancouver preferred to avoid tan lines.

As he turned away, he heard a phone ring next door.

The sleeping heartbeat quickened. Henry leaned back against the closet wall.

She hated being woken up in the middle of the night. Shift work was one of the reasons she'd left the hospital. A minor reason, granted, but a reason. Still, old training died hard, and she came instantly awake. "Dr. Mui."

"I found your orderly dead on my property. The cottage is empty."

Switching on the bedside lamp, she stared at the clock. Three A.M.

"Did you hear me, Doctor?"

She pulled the phone a little away from her ear before he deafened her. "I heard you, Mr. Swanson. What about the donor?"

"There was no one else here! Just a dead body!"

"Please, calm down. Hysteria will do no one any good." *How* could *that idiot have gotten killed?* she wondered. *He's going to ruin everything!* "Have you called the police?"

"The police? No, I, uh . . ." He took a deep breath, clearly audible, and his voice steadied a little. "I found *it* and came back to the cottage and called you."

Then the situation wasn't an irretrievable disaster. She began to pull coherent thought out past her immediate reaction. Either the detective had greater reserves than had appeared or the friends who'd left him at the clinic had managed the impossible and tracked him down. It didn't really matter which. Sullivan was dead, the detective was gone. But the detective's friends were proven unwilling to go to the police and so, apparently, was the detective, or the police would be at the scene already.

"Dr. Mui? Are you still there?"

Rolling her eyes, she wondered where he thought she might have gone. "I suggest, Mr. Swanson, that we cut our losses."

"You suggest we what?" He was beginning to sound as though he were reaching the end of his resources. That was good; a man with no resources was much easier to manipulate. "But the police . . ."

"If you'd intended to call the police, you'd have already called them. As you called me, I suggest you take my advice. Go back to the body and bury it."

"And what?"

"Bury it. Sullivan had neither family nor friends. If he disappears, no one will notice but the staff at the clinic and I can handle them."

"I can't just bury him!"

"Neither can you bring him back to life. Since he's dead and we don't want the police or the public discovering what we've been doing, I suggest you find a shovel."

"I can't bury him here! Not here."

She counted to three before replying. "Then put him in your car and take him out into the mountains. People disappear in the mountains all the time."

"Where in the mountains?" He was almost whimpering on the other end of the line. "You've got to come here. You've got to help me."

"Mr. Swanson, Richard Sullivan was over six feet tall. I'm barely five foot two. I don't see how I can be much help."

"But I can't . . ."

"Then call the police."

There was a long pause. "I can't."

Dr. Mui leaned back against her pillows. She'd known that, or she'd never have suggested it. "Then listen carefully and I'll give you what help I can." The more dependent Ronald Swanson was on her, the better. "There's an old logging road just inside Mt. Seymour Park . . ."

They'd moved out into the living room. With only one exit from the bedroom and Henry standing in it, Vicki had begun to grow agitated.

"So what you're saying is, Ronald Swanson is about to go bury Richard Sullivan out where Mike thinks the *rest* of the bodies are buried."

Henry nodded. "That's what I'm saying."

"Then let's go." Vicki began to stand, but Celluci pulled her back down beside him on the couch. "What?" she demanded, turning to glare at him.

"Look at the time," he said wearily.

"Mike, we've got over an hour."

"To do what?"

She stared at him for a long moment, then threw herself back against the sofa cushions. "I know, don't tell me, you want Henry to go find a patrol car and make up another story."

"No. With the amount of rain they have around here, it'd take a damned good forensics team to get all the evidence they need out of that clearing. I want this whole thing blown wide open with no chance of putting the genie back in the bottle."

"You want?" Vicki exchanged a *listen-to-him* glance with Henry; the haunting had begun as his problem and her case, but they'd both lost control. Any other time, Vicki would've stomped all over that, but with Mike safely back beside her, just exactly who was in charge didn't seem to matter—although honesty forced her to admit that was unlikely to be a permanent state of mind. "And how do you intend to accomplish what you want?"

Wincing as abused muscles protested the movement, Celluci reached into his back pocket and pulled out his wallet. Out of the wallet, he pulled a business card. "I'm going to wake up Patricia Chou. After all, I promised her the story."

"And what makes you think she's going to believe you when you tell her to climb a mountain at three in the morning in search of tabloid enlightenment?"

He shrugged and regretted it. "She really wants Swanson."

"Yeah? And how much of a part in her story is she going to expect you to play?"

"None."

"None?" Vicki repeated, lip curling. "Yeah. Right."

"Apparently, she's been willing to risk jail in the past to protect a source."

Vicki snarled softly but passed him the phone. "Well, you'd better hope she's *apparently* willing to risk it this time, too."

* * *

His hands white-knuckled around the steering wheel, Swanson turned onto the logging road. In spite of the hour, there'd been lights behind him all along Mt. Seymour Drive and he'd very nearly panicked as they followed him into the park. If they followed him again . . .

But they didn't.

He was watching the mirror so closely, he almost lost control of the car in the deep ruts. Trying to ignore the sound of the rear shocks compacting under a bouncing weight, he fought the expensive sedan back onto the road.

There was a sport utility vehicle parked behind the cottage, but it had to be Sullivan's, and he couldn't bring himself to drive it. He was upset enough without the added stress of driving a dead man's car as well as the dead man. He wished he had more of the doctor's detachment. His thoughts revolved around and around in a chaotic whirlwind, replaying over and over the finding of Sullivan's body, the phone call, the feel of the corpse as he lifted it up into the trunk. He knew he wasn't thinking clearly, but that was as far as awareness extended.

The road ended in a clear cut just as Dr. Mui had described. He drove the car as close as he could to the rotting stump of a Douglas fir and turned off both the engine and the headlights. The surrounding darkness looked like one of the upper circles of hell.

Dr. Mui had said it had to be done in the dark. Headlights in the woods at night would attract unwelcome attention. *And what would be welcome attention?* he wondered.

After a moment, he dried his palms on his trousers, got out of the car, and opened the trunk.

Sullivan stared up at him over one broad shoulder, the bouncing having twisted his head around at an impossible angle. His eyes bulged like the eyes of an animal in a slaughterhouse.

Unable to look away, Swanson stepped back and swallowed bile. *What am I doing here? Am I out of my mind? I should've called the police.* He passed a trembling hand over a damp forehead. *No. If I called the police, everything would come out. I'd be ruined. I'd go to jail. Dr. Mui's right. I bury the body, and no one has to know anything.* Over the course of a long career, he'd never hesitated to do what had to be done, and he wasn't about to start now.

Teeth clenched, he pulled the body out of the trunk. He tried to ignore the way it hit the ground, tried not to think of it as something that had once been alive. He dragged it about twenty feet, went back for the shovel, then began to dig.

"This is nuts. This is absolutely fucking nuts."

"Watch your language, Brent. And shut up, he'll hear you."

"Who?"

Patricia Chou grabbed her cameraman's arm and steadied him as he stumbled over a rut, the weight of the camera and light together throwing him off balance. "Ronald Swanson, that's who."

"You don't know he was in that car we were following."

"I do."

"Based on a phone call at three in the morning?"

"That's right."

"That's it?"

"That and finely honed instincts for a story. Now, *shut up!*"

They moved as quietly as possible as they approached the clearing. Eyes having grown accustomed to the dark during the walk up the logging road, neither had any trouble separating the parked car from the surrounding shadows.

Head cocked at the rhythmic sounds from up ahead, the reporter raised a hand and, breathing a little heavily, Brent obediently stopped.

Digging? she mouthed silently.

He shrugged and lifted the camera up onto his shoulder.

She guided him around the car and pointed him toward the man-shaped shadow. *This is it!* she told herself as she stepped forward and gave the signal.

Ronald Swanson, already knee-deep in the soft earth, stared up at her like an animal caught on the road—disaster bearing down and unable to get out of the way. The body stretched out on the ground beside him, the unmistakably dead body, was more than she could have hoped for. Her own eyes squinted nearly shut from the brilliant beam of light from the top of Brent's camera, Patricia Chou thumbed her microphone on and thrust it forward. "Anything to say to our viewers, Mr. Swanson?"

His mouth opened, closed, then opened again, but no sound came out. His eyes widened, pupils contracted to invisibility. He dropped the shovel, clutched at his chest, and collapsed forward onto his face in the dirt, just missing the corpse.

"Mr. Swanson?" The microphone still on, she knelt beside him and reached under his ear for a pulse. He was alive, but it didn't feel good. Scowling, she reached into her belt pouch for her cell phone. "That goddamned son of a bitch has had a heart attack or something before I got a quote."

"Do I keep shooting?" Brent's voice came out of the darkness on the other side of the light.

"No. Save the batteries." Grinning triumphantly, she called 911. "We'll likely get some good stuff when the police arrive."

Fourteen

Tony snatched up the phone on the first ring. "Henry?"

"You were waiting?"

"Yeah, well, I set my alarm for half an hour before sunrise, so if you called, I could answer right away." He yawned and sat up against the pillow. "Did you find Celluci?"

"Detective Celluci is back, safe and sound under Vicki's protection, and she's insisted he spend the day in bed recovering."

"Recovering from what?"

"Loss of blood for the most part."

"Say what?"

"Apparently he made a few involuntary donations." Tony winced. "Man, I bet Victory's pissed."

"No bet. What's more, we have Swanson."

"All right! So, no more ghosts?"

"God willing. Uh, Tony . . ."

The embarrassment in Henry's voice gave Tony a pretty good idea of what was coming. For all that the bastard son of Henry VIII had embraced the twentieth century, there were some things he just couldn't get the hang of.

". . . I was wondering if you might drop by and set the VCR to record the day's news broadcasts."

"I've shown you how to do it a hundred times."

"I know."

Biting back another yawn, Tony wished he'd thought

to provide himself with a thermos of coffee. "Jeez, Henry, what're you going to do when I'm gone?" Gone. That last word seemed to echo in the silence that followed. Gone. This wasn't how he'd meant to say it. *Oh, man, it's just too damned early in the morning for my brain to be working.* He closed his eyes. "Henry?"

"Shall I fight to keep you?" The words held the seductive danger of dark water although it almost seemed like he asked the question of himself.

"Henry, don't . . ." Don't what? Tony didn't know so he let the protest trail off.

"When you are gone," Henry said after a moment, the voice neither Prince of Men nor Prince of Darkness, but just Henry, alone, "I will miss you. And I will insist, as Vicki does, that distance is no reason for friendship to end. If she and I can find a way to be together, you and I can find a way to be apart."

Groping beside the sofa bed for something to wipe his nose on, Tony managed a shaky laugh. "Hey, didn't I always say our Victory was one smart vampire?"

"You said she was one scary vampire."

"Same thing. I'll, uh, see you again before I go."

"Yes."

He shivered at the promise in the word.

Stopped at the edge of her building's drive, waiting for traffic to clear, Dr. Mui was astounded by a rapping on her window.

Patricia Chou pressed the contact microphone against the glass. "Dr. Mui, Ronald Swanson was found this morning with the corpse of Richard Sullivan, an orderly who worked with you at Project Hope." Not even German engineering could keep her voice from penetrating. "Would you like to make a statement?"

Shaking her head in disbelief, Dr. Mui lowered the window a scant inch and, avoiding eye contact with the lens pushed over the reporter's shoulder, snapped, "You are a sick young woman!" She rather hoped she ran over a few toes as she drove away.

There were more reporters waiting at the end of the clinic drive, but she turned in without slowing and passed without incident. Few reporters had Patricia Chou's disregard for personal safety.

Inside the clinic, a pair of plainclothes police officers waited by the nurse's station.

"What is this about?" she demanded, striding across the lounge. Later, she'd feel the effects of a sustained adrenaline buzz, but right now, she felt remarkably calm. It was all a matter of maintaining control.

The detectives introduced themselves and suggested they move into her office.

She stared at them for a moment, frowning, then said, "Don't tell me that parasite actually knew what she was talking about?"

The younger man looked at his partner, then at the doctor. "Parasite?"

"Patricia Chou tried to shove her way into my car this morning with the preposterous story of Ronald Swanson being found with the body of Richard Sullivan, an orderly at this clinic."

"Patricia Chou," sighed the first detective.

"Why am I not surprised," sighed the second.

Having seen their colleagues on the receiving end of a Patricia Chou interview, they thawed considerably and were almost solicitous when Dr. Mui suggested, in a distracted sort of way, that perhaps they'd all better go to her office so that the rest of the staff could get some work done.

"Doctor, when was the last time you spoke to Ronald Swanson?"

"Just after three this morning," she replied promptly, aware that the call could easily be traced.

"Do you remember what he said?"

"I have no idea of what he said. He woke me out of a deep sleep, babbled hysterically at length, and hung up before I could figure out what he was talking about."

"You're sure of the time?"

"Detective, when someone wakes me in the middle of the night, I look at my clock. Don't you?"

They both admitted that they did.

She had no idea why Richard Sullivan would be staying in Ronald Swanson's guest cottage although when the restraints were mentioned, she raised a speculative brow.

"Didn't you work with Richard Sullivan in Stony Mountain Federal Penitentiary?" the older detective asked, his tone making it clear that he already knew the answer.

"That's correct; he was an inmate orderly in the prison hospital. I got him this job when he was released, and I see to it that he makes his parole appointments. Other than that," she added with distaste, "I am not responsible for his life."

"May we ask why you requested that the board hire him, Doctor?"

"Orderlies are required to perform a number of unpleasant tasks. Mr. Sullivan did them without complaining and that, gentlemen, was worth giving him a second chance." She frowned, catching the younger officer's gaze and holding it. "It occurs to me that you haven't told me what he died of."

"Uh, no ma'am." The phrase basilisk stare came suddenly to mind. "We're, uh, not at liberty to divulge that information, ma'am." He shot a hopeful glance at his partner. "I think we have everything we need?"

Before the detectives left, they suggested she talk to the gathered reporters if she ever wanted them out of the driveway. Although she didn't believe it would do any good, the doctor prepared a brief statement and read it. To her surprise, they asked a few questions then packed up cameras and microphones and returned to the city. Apparently, she wasn't big enough news.

Yet.

Having never left the clinic early during her time in charge, she remained in the building until 4:15, moving out and about, concentrating on the patients in case she was under surveillance. Finally, after buttressing her position as much as possible, she packed a few files into her briefcase and went out to her car.

Eventually, even if Ronald Swanson never regained consciousness, the police would pay her a return visit. She'd left as little evidence in her wake as she could but wasn't arrogant enough to assume that they'd never find it. A less-confident woman might have headed straight for the airport. Dr. Mui, who had no intention of leaving any of her investments behind, drove straight home and spent the evening making plans.

Henry had no need to open his eyes to know that this sunset was no different than the half dozen before it. The dead still stood at the end of his bed, waiting for justice.

"Do you know that Ronald Swanson has been stopped?"

Apparently, they did.

Apparently, it didn't matter.

Which brought them back to that visceral vengeance.

"Multimillionaire real estate tycoon Ronald Swanson, remains in a coma in Lion's Gate Hospital. The police are withholding the identity—and cause of death—of the body found with him pending notification of next of kin. So far, police appear baffled by the circumstances surrounding the case although Detective Post assures us the investigation is proceeding."

The detective, an attractive man in his mid-thirties, played to the camera like a professional. "Unfortunately, we have very few hard facts at this moment. Ronald Swanson was found early this morning just past the boundary of Mt. Seymour Park in the company of a corpse and a shovel. Upon being discovered, Mr. Swanson had what doctors are describing as a massive coronary. Everything else, I'm afraid, is speculation." He smiled reassuringly at the news audience. "We will, of course, learn more when Mr. Swanson regains consciousness and we can ask him a few questions."

Henry fast forwarded through the rest of the CBC News at Noon; when the News at Six came on, he slowed the tape to normal speed.

"In our top story today, multimillionaire philanthropist, Ronald Swanson, remains in a coma in Lion's Gate Hospital. Early this morning . . ."

If the police had discovered anything new between noon and six, they weren't telling the media.

"Why the hell don't they just dig up the rest of the goddamned clearing?" Celluci growled, shifting uncomfortably on the sofa. Furniture designed for little old ladies always felt too small for his butt. He supposed he should be thankful that Fitzroy'd brought the tape over, but he couldn't muster the energy.

Vicki reached over and tucked his left arm back into the sling. "No reason why they should dig it up. As far as the police know, they have an isolated incident. A moment of violence. A lover's quarrel that got out of hand. They haven't even pressed charges yet." She frowned, and looked absently toward the images flickering by on the television. "If Swanson in a coma in police custody isn't enough for Henry's ghosts, I wonder how much more they want."

"Not how much," Celluci declared suddenly, jerking toward the TV. "Who. Fitzroy! Wind it back and play that bit with the woman talking."

". . . am, of course, dismayed by what has happened. Richard Sullivan was a hardworking member of our staff who'd managed to rebuild his life after an unfortunate past."

"Prison," Celluci explained shortly. "And that's her. That's the doctor who . . ."

"Took your blood." The statement had edges that

flayed. "Dr. Mui. Now we know for sure." Vicki stood. And stopped. Slowly, very slowly, she turned her head and looked down at Michael Celluci.

He reached out and took her hand. "I want her, too," he said grimly. "But not like that. You can't kill her."

Vicki shuddered, once, the movement traveling through her body like a wave. "You're getting awfully goddamned pushy lately," she muttered when it was over. Then, still holding his hand like an anchor, she sat back down.

"I'm impressed by your control."

"Don't fucking patronize me, Henry." Her chin rose, but she managed to hold onto her anger even though every instinct told her to throw something at him and then throw him out the window. "Now, what do we do?"

"I'm an idiot!"

Eyes silvering just enough to keep Henry from commenting, Vicki patted Celluci's denim-clad knee with her free hand. "Don't be so hard on yourself," she suggested, "and tell me what you're talking about."

"Ronald Swanson was not the man responsible for those deaths. That's why Henry's ghosts are still around."

"Maybe he didn't do the actual killing, but he provided the resources."

Celluci shook his head. "He provided the resources to buy kidneys from the poor and sell them to the rich—but the poor can function fine with only one kidney. This sort of thing goes on in a number of third world countries."

"Your point?"

"Dr. Mui, already making good money doing the illegal transplants, saw a way to make a little more. The donor doesn't survive, and she pockets the purchase price. Simple."

"Yeah, but . . ."

"If she didn't have to hide the deaths from Swanson, why wait until they healed? And we know she

waited because of the body they found in the harbor."
He glanced from Vicki to Henry and answered his
own question. "She had to keep the donors around
until close to the time they'd normally be discharged
or Swanson would be suspicious."

"So he didn't know she was killing them?"

"She told me herself that she believed in only letting people know what they needed to to do their
jobs. Uh, Vicki? I can't feel my fingers anymore."
When she released his hand, he started to work the
blood back into the whitened fingertips. "Swanson's
job was to provide the money and the buyers."

"All right . . ." It wasn't agreement. It wasn't even
conceding he had a point. ". . . what about the missing
hands on the first ghost?"

"Sullivan disposed of the bodies—he found out this
guy had no record, and he thought of a way to make
an extra buck. He probably made plenty of gang contacts in prison."

Vicki shook her head. "Completely circumstantial."

"And completely unimportant. The loss of the
hands distracted us at the beginning, sending us out
after the gangs, and I don't want that to happen
again." Henry moved to stand by the windows. He
always thought better looking out at the city. His
city—in spite of the unfamiliar pattern of lights below.
His condo overlooked False Creek, Lisa Evans' overlooked the parking lot between the buildings. "I believe Mike's right about Dr. Mui being in charge. Last
night, Swanson went to pieces when he found that
body."

"Well, sure," Vicki snorted, even less willing to cut
Henry any slack, "he was afraid that the operation,
so to speak, had been discovered."

"I don't think so." He could feel Vicki bristling behind him, so he continued studying the traffic on Pacific Boulevard. "The first thing Dr. Mui asked
Swanson was, did he call the police. If Swanson knew
about the other deaths, that's not something he'd even
consider, and the doctor would know it. When she

found out he hadn't called anyone but her, she began planning the cover-up."

"Dr. Mui had both opportunity and motive," Celluci pointed out. "Ronald Swanson dropped the opportunity in her lap, and she got greedy."

"Thin," Vicki muttered, "very thin. You were being kept in one of Swanson's guest houses, remember?"

"That doesn't mean he knew why I was there. She could have told him anything."

"Most importantly," Henry finished, "nothing that happened last night has had any effect on the ghosts. Not Sullivan's death, not Swanson's heart attack."

Dr. Mui had taken Celluci's blood. Vicki was willing to condemn her on that alone. Nodding, as though she'd just been convinced, she sat back and said dryly, "So all evidence suggests the doctor's not just the hired gun, she's an opportunistic, murdering, hypocritical, amoral bitch. And if I can't kill her, what are we supposed to do about her? Call the police from a pay phone with an anonymous tip." She lowered her voice dramatically, "You don't know me, but you should check into Dr. Mui's finances. Make her explain where the money comes from."

"She'll probably have an explanation. That woman's got ba . . ." Celluci paused as Vicki pinned him with a silver gaze. ". . . ovaries of steel. She's got an answer for everything."

"Well, she's also got a small fortune tucked away in secure countries, and my guess is she's going to run. If she hasn't already."

"I don't think so." Head cocked, Henry stared across a patch of thin grass delineating the boundaries between his building and Dr. Mui's. "A cable van just pulled up next door, and I believe that's Patricia Chou getting out."

"How the hell can you see who it is from up here?" Celluci scoffed. Then he remembered. Henry, like Vicki, had very good night sight. "Never mind. Stupid question. If it's Patricia Chou, then the police probably chased her away from Swanson's sickbed. She's probably been hovering over him like a vulture all day."

Vicki stared at Celluci in exaggerated surprise. "I thought she was a friend of yours."

"Ignoring for the moment that I've only met the woman once, since when have I ignored the faults of my friends?"

Vicki made a mental note of the pointed emphasis. He'd pay for it after he healed. "So if Ms. Chou is there, then Dr. Mui is there—so, as I said, what now?"

Henry turned from the windows, his eyes dark. "We use Ms. Chou to make certain the doctor is in her apartment tomorrow at sunset and we let the only witnesses we have confront the accused. Isn't that what the law would require, Detective?"

Celluci felt himself caught by darkness and jerked free; it had been too easy over the last few days to forget the law. "No, actually, it's the other way around. The accused have the right to confront their accuser."

"All right." Henry nodded. "That, too."

"Look, Fitzroy, you can't just . . ."

"Why not? Is there a law against allowing the dead a voice?"

"You know damned well there isn't. It's just . . ."

"You can't confront her with the ghosts, Henry." Vicki cut him off, her tone suggesting this would be the final word. "If the radius of their . . . uh, effect was big enough, they'd have confronted her already. You'd have to get closer, and you can't."

"Yes, I can."

"They appear at sunset. That means you'd have to get closer at *sunrise*."

"I know."

This would be my territory, then. She did more than suppress the thought, she obliterated it. "Forget it. It'd be too dangerous."

"And what of the danger of never getting rid of

these ghosts, of having to ask the right question evening after evening, knowing that if I make a mistake,
innocents will die?"

"Then we bring her to the ghosts."

"And how do we . . ." He'd been about to say "get
rid of her body afterward" when a glance at Celluci's
face changed his mind. ". . . bring in the police?"
When Vicki couldn't answer, he said, "My plan will
put Patricia Chou on the spot and so far she's certainly
been . . ." A number of descriptions were considered
and discarded. ". . . effective."

Celluci grunted in agreement. Using the ghosts to
spook the doctor into the arms of the media, using
the media once again to inform the police—that he
could deal with.

"It also puts you on the spot, Henry. How do you
plan on surviving this plan of yours?"

Her concern was genuine; she might have been
speaking of any friend, any mortal friend. As a mea-
sure of how far they'd come in so short a time, it was
nothing short of miraculous.

"Don't get all choked up on me, Henry. Answer
the fucking question."

He shook his head, a little bemused by the speed
of the evolution. "I'll, uh, be spending the day with
the doctor's neighbors, Carole and Ron Pettit."

"Friends of yours?"

"Not yet." Ignoring Celluci's interrogative glower,
he picked up the phone and tapped in the number
he'd noted during his earlier visit.

As Henry seemed unwilling to explain, Celluci
leaned over and muttered, "What's he doing?" into
Vicki's ear.

"Do you remember the way Dracula got Lucy to
leave the house?"

"He stood outside in the garden and called?"

"Well, that's what Henry's doing."

"Dracula didn't use a phone."

"Times change."

"Hello, Carole. Carole, I need you to do something

for me. I need you to unlock your door, Carole. That's right, Carole, you know who I am."

The room seemed suddenly very warm. Celluci tugged at his jeans. When Vicki leaned over and flicked an earlobe with her tongue, he jerked away from the invitation. "Don't," he said hoarsely. "Not here, not now."

"Unlock your door, Carole, and be ready for company. It doesn't matter that you're not alone. That's right, Carole, unlock your door. I'll be there in a moment, Carole. Wait for me."

"That's it?" Celluci demanded as Henry returned the receiver to the cradle.

Henry shrugged, remembering the gargoyle. "Some people need less calling than others."

Wishing he'd worn looser pants, Celluci snarled something noncommittal and set about convincing himself there'd been no response.

They walked Henry down to the lobby and watched him cross to the other building.

"I take it he's going to suggest Carole and company leave the condo?"

"If it were me, I'd suggest they leave by sunrise and not come back for about twenty-four hours."

"It's a long time until sunrise, Vicki. What's he going to do in the meantime?"

She turned and stared at him.

His ears reddened. "Never mind. You'd better speak with Ms. Chou by yourself."

"Why?"

"Because you can make her forget the conversation, forget about you. I can't."

"Well, thank you so much for letting me have my case back." Patting him lightly on the cheek, she started toward the cable van. She had every intention of doing exactly what Celluci had suggested. *She'll forget about the conversation. And she'll forget about* you.

*   *   *

"Just make sure that she's in her condo at sunset."

Even lost in the silvered depths of Vicki's eyes, Patricia Chou had the will to protest. "And how am I supposed to do that?"

"From what I've heard, most of the city would stay home rather than face you."

"Well, she never goes in to the clinic on Fridays . . ."

"How do you know that?"

"I know almost everything and intend to find out the rest. It's why most of the city hates me." She smiled.

Vicki'd seen that smile before—had seen it three nights ago, reflected in the eyes of Bynowski and Haiden just before they died. Patricia Chou enjoyed her work. *And Henry was worried about sharing a territory with* me.

Henry sped down the hall and past the woman standing in her doorway, obviously waiting for him.

Once safe inside, he caught his breath and softly called her name.

She turned. Past forty and not fighting it, she'd tried to match herself to her pseudo-Gothic decor but was far too sun-kissed and healthy-looking to succeed.

"Come inside, Carole, and close the door."

The Hunger rose in response to the hunger on her face.

Eventually, she'll get bored and go away. Or some new scandal will arise in some other part of the city and she'll go away. Dr. Mui stood in her solarium and scowled down at the top of the cable van just visible in the parking lot below, the yellow rectangle standing out with irritating clarity against the gray pavement. *Or someone will drop a heavy object on her head and she'll GO AWAY.*

Patricia Chou had drastically altered her plans for the day.

By late morning she'd done everything she could

from her computer in the condo. Although her phone lines were as secure as her hacker-for-hire could make them, she'd known there was no such thing as a completely secure line—the computers at the Eastside Clinic and the drop-in center were theoretically secure, but that same hacker had accessed them both with apparent ease. In order for her to leave the country, wealth intact, and leave no trail, there were a number of matters that required a personal touch.

She should have been able to accomplish everything necessary in a couple of hours, but from the moment she'd left the parking lot, the reflection of the cable van had filled her rearview mirror. The reporter herself had followed, as it were, off road—never breaking any laws, never making too big a nuisance of herself, never going away.

Only two of the three errands had been done. The third, she had no intention of fulfilling in front of a witness and had returned home, Patricia Chou still on her heels.

Her station won't let her sit there forever. When she's called in, I'll make my move. Almost everything has been prepared, and there's no reason to panic. You are in no danger of discovery if you remain calm. Her nails scraped against the glass as her fingers curled into fists. She could just barely make out one slender, denim-clad leg thrust out of the van's interior. *Oh, for a truck to go by and take that off at the knee. . . .*

All afternoon she'd watched as Patricia Chou had traded on local recognition and interviewed almost everyone coming or going from the building.

It had been a very long afternoon.

"Patricia, please," Brent pleaded, digging his knuckles into bloodshot eyes. "Let's go. We're not going to get anything else today, and I'm wiped."

"Just a little while longer."

The cameraman sighed, collapsed back against a bag of equipment. "You've been saying that for the last hour."

"This time I mean it." She twisted out the door until she could see the red and gold streaking the bottom of the clouds. "Just wait until sunset."

"Why? What's going to happen at sunset?"

Between one heartbeat and the next, a silver shadow flickered in her eyes. "I have no idea . . ."

"Then why . . . ?"

". . . but I've been promised a story."

7:43. Celluci looked up from his watch and squinted out the window. The setting sun had turned the other building a brilliant white-gold. Whatever was going to happen, wasn't going to happen for another five minutes. He still had time to stop it.

His right thumb rubbed the scabbed puncture in the hollow of his left elbow.

Four minutes.

Still time.

Three minutes.

It wasn't because she was responsible for, at the very least, the deaths of the two young men whose spirits haunted Henry. It wasn't because of what she'd done to him personally.

She'd used their hope when hope was all those people had.

Two minutes.

The law could deal with murder, but if Henry's ghosts didn't have the right to deal with the death of hope, who did?

He saw the flaw in the plan at 7:47. By then, it was too late.

Henry'd spent the day wrapped in a theatrical blackout curtain, lying on the floor of the walk-in closet. Although wide open to suggestion, the Pettits had not been easy to get rid of. Having found him, they wanted to stay with him. He'd barely had time to gain his sanctuary and twist the door handle into an unusable chunk of metal when sunrise claimed him.

7:48. Sunset.

They were there. He could feel their presence more strongly than he'd ever felt it before. The air around him was uniformly cold, and when he drew in his first breath, it seemed to move reluctantly into his lungs, coating the inside of his mouth and throat with a frigid film.

Wormwood and gall. He swallowed reluctantly.

His hand rested on the switch of small desk lamp he'd brought into the closet with him. Too bright an illumination would be of no more use than the darkness; the overhead light would blind him and wash the spirits out to near invisibility.

When he turned the switch, he could see the two ghosts who'd haunted him from the beginning pressed up tight against his feet. All around them—all around him—were others. He couldn't count their numbers, they kept shifting in and out of focus—here a young woman with the corner of her upper lip pierced, there tormented eyes peering out from under a fringe of hair. Faces. Bodies. The invisible chorus made manifest.

Fear.

It rose off them like smoke, filling the space too thickly for even Henry to endure.

Dr. Mui turned from the window and peered into the shadows of her apartment. One hand rose, an involuntary warding against the sudden feeling she wasn't alone.

"I should turn on a light."

Her voice traveled no farther than the edge of her mouth, unable to make an impression on the silence.

One step back. Two.

Her shoulders pressed against the glass.

Henry found himself pressed back into the corner without remembering how he'd gotten there. The closet had filled with the amorphous shapes of the dead, only the original two maintaining form. And they seemed to be waiting.

Waiting.

For what?

He just wanted them to go away. He had his mouth open to demand that they leave him alone when he remembered. It wasn't him they wanted.

"Who's there?"

They were coming closer, whoever they were.

"There's a safe in the bottom left-hand drawer of my desk. Just take the money and leave me alone." The last word slipped from her control and rose almost to a wail before it faded.

The doctor's feet continued to push against the Mexican tile on the floor. The window creaked behind her.

He could feel her life. She wasn't in the next room, but it didn't matter. Her heart beat so loudly he could have heard it from the other building had his own heart not been pounding nearly loud enough to drown it out.

I am Henry Fitzroy, once Duke of Richmond and of Somerset, Earl of Nottingham and Knight of the Garter. My father was a king and I am become Death. I do not cower before the dead.

The Hunger rose to meet the fear and gained him ground enough to rise to his feet. Dark eyes narrowed. "Well," he demanded, "are you going to let her get away with it?"

There could, of course, be only one answer.

Dr. Mui had dealt out life and death with brutal efficiency, protected from pangs of conscience and wandering regrets by armor built of diamond-hard self-interest. The accusation in the donors' eyes when they realized their escape from poverty and the streets was not the escape they'd dreamed of making had never touched her.

It had nothing to do with her.

Until now. When it had everything to do with her.

                    *   *   *

The dead howled denial; a howl torn from those who'd first seen a fragile hope betrayed and then had lost the only thing they had remaining to them, their lives, taken without even the excuse of passion.

The doctor flung her head back against the glass, over and over. The glass held, but crimson rosettes appeared with each impact.

Despair closed her eyes, closed her mouth, her nose, choked off air from her lungs, closed over her like a layer of wet earth. Suffocating. Burying.

She fell forward on her hands and knees, gasping and retching, the damp ends of her hair drawing bloody lines against her face.

"I. Will not. End. Like. This." Armor so arrogantly forged could not be breached so easily. "I am," she breathed. "I live. And you are dead."

Triumphant, she lifted her head and saw the shadows move. Saw the last two boys, the one they hadn't used, the one before dumped unceremoniously in the harbor, the others, all the others . . .

They looked down at her.

And they were dead.

Their mouths were open. They screamed denial. Despair. Vengeance.

Forcing her to recognize the death she'd given them.

The body hit the roof of the cable van with a wet crunch. One leg flopped limply over the side, swung back and forth, and was still.

Ten feet away in the parking lot, miraculously unharmed by falling glass, Patricia Chou clutched at her cameraman's arm with a white-knuckled grip. "Did you get it?" she panted, ignoring a throat ripped raw by the force of her initial reaction. Professional or not, she was, she felt, entitled to that one scream of shock and horror. Later, she'd wonder if she'd been trying to drown out the cry of the falling woman, preferring to remember the sound of her own voice rather than the frenzied denial that had grown louder as gravity won, but for now she had more pressing concerns. "Did you get it?"

Brent nodded, still peering through the eyepiece with the detachment of cameramen from Northern Ireland to Lebanon. "I thought the windows on those new buildings were shatterproof."

"Shatterproof can be broken."

"Yeah? Then what did she break it with?"

There had been glass and, with the glass, the body—alive as it fell, but inevitably a body for all of that.

Reporter and cameraman stood in silence for a moment, then, handing Brent her cell phone and suggesting he call the police, Patricia Chou hurried toward the van, making mental lists of what to do and who to call and how to best use the rapidly disappearing light. "Now this," she said, as she reached inside for her microphone, ducking under the dangling foot that would provide a suitably ghoulish backdrop, "is a story."

"We all knew that was going to happen," Celluci said, hands pressed flat against the glass. "We all knew."

Vicki pulled him away from the window and turned him around. "No, we didn't," she said softly.

"Yes, we did. We knew the ghosts killed. They've killed before."

"She jumped through an unbreakable window, Mike. They didn't push her."

"We knew," he repeated, shaking his head. "We knew."

Vicki caught his face between her hands and tipped his gaze down to meet hers. It flared silver. "No, we didn't," she said.

When the police came to take their statements—along with the statements of everyone in a unit overlooking the accident—they got a pleasant surprise.

"Michael Celluci? That name sounds really familiar." The young constable frowned. "Did you report your van stolen, Detective?"

"Not his van, mine." Vicki leaned forward, silently willing Celluci to be quiet. It was too easy for him to forget that the police weren't necessarily on their side. "He said he misplaced it. That he knew where he'd left it, he'd just ended up on the other side of town and hadn't gotten around to going back for it yet."

"There's no point in him going back for it now, because it isn't there. Couple of uniforms found it just as it was about to be stripped. Nuts were loose, but nothing was missing. But the only ID they could find was *Michael Celluci* scribbled on a crumpled piece of paper in the glove compartment. They've probably run the plates by now, but they wouldn't be able to find you, Ms. uh," he checked his notes, "Nelson."

"*Probably* run the plates by now?" Vicki repeated, brows raised in a sardonic arch.

He blushed and was unable to stop himself from responding like some kind of rookie idiot instead of a three-year veteran of the Vancouver Police Department. "Well, there's been a whole lot of gang violence lately, and things have been pretty busy, and the system crashed two days ago, and we just got it up and running this morning."

"But my van's okay?"

"Yes, uh, as far as I know, yes."

"Good."

When she smiled at him, he was suddenly glad he had his notebook in his lap. There was something about her that made him feel like rolling over and wagging his tail when she scratched his stomach. "Now, uh, about the fall . . ."

"Actually, we didn't see anything."

"Nothing?"

"We were busy."

"Busy?" He felt himself redden again. "Oh."

He left soon after; envying the detective his relationship and hoping the old boy's heart was up to it.

"The whole world is getting younger," Celluci growled

when the door closed behind the irritating young punk in the blue uniform. "I can't say that I like it much."

Vicki put her arms around his waist and leaned into his chest. "For what it's worth, you're not getting older, you're getting better."

"Spare me," he snorted tilting her chin up so he could look into her face.

"What?"

You've always been a lousy liar, but that constable believed everything you told him.

"Mike?"

"Nothing." Sighing, he rested his cheek on the top of her head. "Just feeling old."

She pressed herself closer until she resonated with his heartbeat.

"So, you and Henry are, uh . . ." Celluci looked down at his spinach salad and found no answers, so he looked back up at Tony to find the younger man smiling. "What?"

"You're living with a vampire, Celluci. Why do two men cause you so much trouble?"

"We're not exactly living together, but I take your point. I guess it is a little ridiculous." He speared something green he couldn't identify. Why the hell couldn't he have fries with his burger? Everything in Vancouver was too goddamned healthy; he'd be glad to leave. "But you didn't answer my question."

"I'm moving out. But we'll still be friends."

"So you're staying here in Vancouver?"

Tony shrugged. "My life is here. I have a job, I have friends, I'm going to school; why would I leave?"

"*He's* here." Resting his forearms on the table, Celluci leaned forward. "You'll never be free of him, you know. You'll expect to see him in every shadow. Separating your life from his won't be that easy."

"He doesn't own me, Detective, no matter what it might have seemed like. It was time for me to leave, and we both knew it." Tony toyed with his salad a moment, started to speak, stopped, then finally said, the words spilling over each other in the rush, "And it's not that hard. You could leave, too."

After a moment, Celluci smiled and shook his head, remembering all the days and all the nights that had followed. "No. I couldn't."

"They didn't even come back to say thank you?"

"If it's all the same to you, I'm just as glad that they're gone." The dead had stopped shrieking when the doctor's heart had stopped beating. And only the doctor's heart. This time, in spite of the heightened intensity, no one else had died. In the end, vengeance, or justice, had been surgically precise. Henry, whether from proximity or awareness, had been the only other casualty. Retching and trembling, he'd had to force himself to walk out of the closet—he'd wanted to crawl. He completely understood why the doctor had gone eleven stories straight down to get away from the sound.

Vicki read some of that time on his face and reached out. Just for an instant, her hand covered his.

Henry stared down at his hand, then up at her. Less than a week ago, he'd have wanted to kill her for that. Now he regretted the touch could last so short a time. Six days out of four hundred and fifty years and they'd changed the way he defined what he was. "Do you always rewrite the rules?"

"If they're bad rules."

He shook his head. "I wonder how we managed for all those years before you came along?"

Vicki snorted. "You and me both. Most of our kind changes for passion's sake, Henry—you told me that yourself—and no one does passion like a teenager. You were seventeen. How old were the rest? I could be the first adult to come along in centuries."

"You're still a child to this life."

She grinned. "Don't sulk, Henry. It's unattractive in a mortal man and *really* unattractive in one of the immortal undead."

"Centuries of tradition," he began, but she cut him off.

"Haven't changed that much. We're still solitary predators, but now we know why. The scent of *another's* blood drives us dangerously out of control. We'd kill so indiscriminately we'd be impossible to ignore. In time, we'd be hunted down and destroyed, our strength no defense against their numbers. For the safety of all of us, we have to Hunt apart. But we don't have to be apart. Given enough time, territorial imperatives can be overcome."

Henry raised his hand, palm up toward her. When she mirrored the motion, he moved his hand toward hers. They never touched. "Mostly overcome," he said with a sad smile, letting his arm drop down to his side.

Vicki nodded, her smile perhaps more rueful than sad. "Mostly," she agreed. "Before Mike gets back, I want to thank you for what you did in that clearing." Her expression changed as she looked back at that night, back at what she'd almost destroyed. "I couldn't stop myself. I *was* going to kill Sullivan no matter how much Mike would have hated me for it."

"I know. You may have been an adult when you came to this life, but you're still a child in it. Greater control will come in time. It's the hardest thing our kind has to learn." Looking down at the lights of the city, his city, he listened for a moment to its heartbeat. "That, and how to hide what we are without becoming less than we are." He paused again, then continued gravely. "You can't let the detective know what you're capable of, Vicki. He won't be able to stand it."

"What are you talking about? He knows . . ."

"No. He thinks he knows. It's not the same thing. Tell me, how did you feel that night in the warehouse?"

"You ought to know, your hands were doing the feeling."

"Vicki!"

Arms folded across her chest, she shook her head. "I don't like to think about it."

He turned to face her, and his eyes were dark. "How did you feel?"

"I don't know."

"Yes, you do."

After a moment of facing herself in his gaze, she said quietly, "Free. I felt free."

The darkness lifted. "Can he ever know that?" Henry didn't wait for her to answer. "There are very few we can trust with what we are and fewer still of them with all we are."

"You were Mystery to me . . ." The memory came out of her mortal life.

"Then be Mystery to him."

"You're not going to walk us to the van?" Vicki asked as Celluci lifted his hockey bag onto his shoulder.

Henry shook his head, glancing around the borrowed condo. "No, I don't think so. I'll say good-bye here and start cleaning up."

"Hey! I cleaned up!"

"Who cleaned up?" Celluci grunted.

Vicki elbowed him in the ribs, careful of her strength but hard enough that he felt it. "I helped."

"I'm sure you did," Henry broke in before they started fighting. "I merely want to be sure that there are no questions left behind."

"You can't trust me to have taken care of that?"

"It's not a matter of trust, Vicki. It's a matter of responsibility. My territory, my responsibility. If I visit you in Toronto, it will be your responsibility."

Celluci started. "You're not serious, Fitzroy? I mean, good God, she was territorial before she changed!"

"Calm down, Mike, you'll burst something. He was making a joke." Her expression dared Henry to challenge that assessment. "Good-bye, old man, I'll call when I get home."

Henry nodded and matched her tone—better to keep it light. There was, after all, no need for maudlin farewells. "Take care, kid, and try to remember you don't know everything."

Vicki grinned. "Yet. Come on, Mike."

"In a minute. I want to talk to Fitzroy." When she paused, he gave her a shove toward the door. "Alone."

"Guy talk?" She glanced between them. Henry looked enigmatic, but that was hardly surprising. Celluci looked belligerent, and that was no more surprising. If she couldn't trust them alone together, then she and Henry hadn't actually accomplished anything. Just because Mike couldn't trust her and Henry alone . . . "Okay." It didn't sound okay, but she got the word out and that was what mattered. "I'll meet you at the van."

When the door closed behind her, neither man spoke. After a few moments Henry said, "She's on the elevator."

"Let's make sure she stays on." After a moment, when Henry nodded, he said, "There was just one thing I wanted to ask you. That night in the clearing, why did you kill Sullivan?"

"If Sullivan had lived, what would we have done with him?"

"You didn't have to do anything with him. The worst he could've done was tell the doctor I'd escaped—something she found out anyway when Swanson found the body."

"And without that body, Ms. Chou would never have gotten the footage for her exposé."

"After the fact," Celluci pointed out grimly. "Why did you kill him?"

"That's not the question you want to ask me, Detective." Abruptly, he dropped the Prince-of-Man manner. Michael Celluci deserved more honesty than that. "I won't give you the answer you're looking for, Mike. You'll have to ask her."

"Will she tell me?"

"She is Vampire. Nightwalker."

"Like you."

Henry almost smiled, would have had Celluci not

sounded so painfully serious. "No," he said gently. "Not like me. In fact, I'd be willing to believe she is not like any of us. But she is still the woman you fell in love with."

"And the woman you fell in love with?"

"The emotional bond, the love, if you will, that causes us to offer our blood to a mortal never survives the change." They were his words to Vicki during their first conversation. He opened his mouth to repeat them and found himself saying, "Yes," instead.

To Henry's surprise, Celluci held out his hand. "Good-bye, Fitzroy. Thank you."

Henry took it, released it, and stood alone a moment later in the empty condo, Vicki's scent surrounding him. He missed her already, but the future that he'd thought would be as unchanging as four hundred and fifty years of the past stretched out before him suddenly filled with infinite possibilities.

It had taken her seven nights—*Only seven?* He counted back and shook his head. *Just one short week*—to completely overturn something that had been considered from the beginning of their kind an immutable part of their nature.

Seven nights.

He couldn't wait to see what she'd do with eternity.

They talked about nothing much until they were outside the city heading up into the mountains listening to a local easy listening station. The news was over, the police had discovered four bodies buried in the clearing where Ronald Swanson had been found, and teams were continuing to search. Dr. Mui's finances had come to light and Patricia Chou was piecing the story together for network television. The weather was expected to be clear and hot for the next few days without the ubiquitous showers.

Celluci leaned back in the passenger seat and stared out the open window at the shadows of trees flicking by in the night. As usual, she was driving too fast.

"Vicki?" *I won't give you the answer you're looking for, Mike. You'll have to ask her.* "If Henry hadn't killed Sullivan, were you going to?"

The road seemed impossibly narrow. Vicki's eyes locked on the yellow line as the night outside the fragile barrier of the headlights closed in. The memory of rage tightened her fingers around the steering wheel.

"Vicki?"

He didn't want the truth. Not really. She hadn't actually needed Henry to tell her that. She could feel him waiting for her answer. She could smell his fear. "No. Of course not. You asked me not to."

Vampire. Nightwalker.

"She is still the woman you fell in love with. . . ."

"Mike?" Her turn to throw a question down between them. "You believe me, don't you?"

"Yeah, of course I believe you." He turned to touch her shoulder, uncertain if he was comforting or reassuring or if it mattered. "You've always been a lousy liar."

On the radio, the sports report ended, Seattle having beaten the Jays nine to three at the Skydome.

"You're listening to CHQM." The DJ could've been any one of a hundred DJs they'd heard across the country. "And here's a song for all you starcrossed lovers . . ."

Be Mystery to him. No, that wasn't how it worked with Mike. Glancing away from the road, Vicki grinned at him. "You think this one's for us?"

". . . their love may not be paying the rent, but they've still got each other. Yes, it's Sonny and Cher and 'I Got You, Babe.' "

Mike grabbed Vicki's wrist as she reached forward to turn off the radio. "No. Leave it. I think I'm starting to like it." He wrapped his warm fingers around her cool ones and brought them to his lips. "Which just goes to prove that you can get used to anything in time."

A moment later, he tightened his grip and growled, "Almost anything. Don't. Sing. Along."

BLOOD BANK

———

This Town Ain't
Big Enough

"Ow! Vicki, be careful!"

"Sorry. Sometimes I forget how sharp they are."

"Terrific." He wove his fingers through her hair and pulled just hard enough to make his point. "Don't."

"Don't what?" She grinned up at him, teeth gleaming ivory in the moonlight spilling across the bed. "Don't forget or don't . . ."

The sudden demand of the telephone for attention buried the last of her question.

Detective-Sergeant Michael Celluci sighed. "Hold that thought," he said, rolled over, and reached for the phone. "Celluci."

"Fifty-two division just called. They've found a body down at Richmond and Peter they think we might want to have a look at."

"Dave, it's . . ." He squinted at the clock. ". . . one twenty-nine in the A.M. and I'm off duty."

On the other end of the line, his partner, theoretically off duty as well, refused to take the hint. "Ask me who the stiff is."

Celluci sighed again. "Who's the stiff?"

"Mac Eisler."

"Shit."

"Funny, that's exactly what I said." Nothing in Dave Graham's voice indicated he appreciated the joke. "I'll be there in ten."

"Make it fifteen."

"You in the middle of something?"

Celluci watched as Vicki sat up and glared at him.
"I was."

"Welcome to the wonderful world of law enforcement."

Vicki's hand shot out and caught Celluci's wrist before he could heave the phone across the room. "Who's Mac Eisler?" she asked as, scowling, he dropped the receiver back in its cradle and swung his legs off the bed.

"You heard that?"

"I can hear the beating of your heart, the movement of your blood, the song of your life." She scratched the back of her leg with one bare foot. "I should think I can overhear a lousy phone conversation."

"Eisler's a pimp." Celluci reached for the light switch, changed his mind, and began pulling on his clothes. Given the full moon riding just outside the window, it wasn't exactly dark, and given Vicki's sensitivity to bright light, not to mention her temper, he figured it was safer to cope. "We're pretty sure he offed one of his girls a couple of weeks ago."

Vicki scooped her shirt up off the floor. "Irene MacDonald?"

"What? You overheard that, too?"

"I get around. How sure's pretty sure?"

"Personally positive. But we had nothing solid to hold him on."

"And now he's dead." Skimming her jeans up over her hips, she dipped her brows in a parody of deep thought. "Golly, I wonder if there's a connection."

"Golly yourself," Celluci snarled. "You're not coming with me."

"Did I ask?"

"I recognized the tone of voice. I know you, Vicki. I knew you when you were a cop, I knew you when you were a P.I. and I don't care how much you've changed physically, I know you now you're a . . . a . . ."

"Vampire." Her pale eyes seemed more silver than gray. "You can say it, Mike. It won't hurt my feelings. Bloodsucker. Nightwalker. Creature of Darkness."

"Pain in the butt." Carefully avoiding her gaze, he shrugged into his shoulder holster and slipped a jacket on over it. "This is police business, Vicki. Stay out of it. Please." He didn't wait for a response but crossed the shadows to the bedroom door. Then he paused, one foot over the threshold. "I doubt I'll back by dawn. Don't wait up."

Vicki Nelson, ex of the Metropolitan Toronto Police Force, ex-private investigator, recent vampire, decided to let him go. If he could joke about the change, he accepted it. And besides, it was always more fun to make him pay for smart-ass remarks when he least expected it.

She watched from the darkness as Celluci climbed into Dave Graham's car. Then, with the taillights disappearing in the distance, she dug out his spare set of car keys and proceeded to leave tangled entrails of Highway Traffic Act strewn from Downsview to the heart of Toronto.

It took no supernatural ability to find the scene of the crime. What with the police, the press, and the morbidly curious, the area seethed with people. Vicki slipped past the constable stationed at the far end of the alley and followed the paths of shadow until she stood just outside the circle of police around the body.

Mac Eisler had been a somewhat attractive, not very tall, white male Caucasian. Eschewing the traditional clothing excesses of his profession, he was dressed simply in designer jeans and an olive-green raw silk jacket. At the moment, he wasn't looking his best. A pair of rusty nails had been shoved through each manicured hand, securing his body upright across the back entrance of a trendy restaurant. Although the pointed toes of his tooled leather cowboy boots indented the wood of the door, Eisler's head had been turned completely around so that he stared, in apparent astonishment, out into the alley.

The smell of death fought with the stink of urine and garbage. Vicki frowned. There was another scent, a pungent predator scent that raised the hair on the back of her neck and drew her lips up off her teeth. Surprised by the strength of her reaction, she stepped silently into a deeper patch of night lest she give herself away.

"Why the hell would I have a comment?"

Preoccupied with an inexplicable rage, she hadn't heard Celluci arrive until he greeted the press. Shifting position slightly, she watched as he and his partner moved in off the street and got their first look at the body.

"Jesus H. Christ."

"On crutches," agreed the younger of the two detectives already on the scene.

"Who found him?"

"Dishwasher, coming out with the trash. He was obviously meant to be found; they nailed the bastard right across the door."

"The kitchen's on the other side and no one heard hammering?"

"I'll go you one better than that. Look at the rust on the head of those nails—they haven't *been* hammered."

"What? Someone just pushed the nails through Eisler's hands and into solid wood?"

"Looks like."

Celluci snorted. "You trying to tell me that Superman's gone bad?"

Under the cover of their laughter, Vicki bent and picked up a piece of planking. There were four holes in the unbroken end and two remaining three-inch spikes. She pulled a spike out of the wood and pressed it into the wall of the building by her side. A smut of rust marked the ball of her thumb, but the nail looked no different.

She remembered the scent.

Vampire.

". . . unable to come to the phone. Please leave a message after the long beep."

"Henry? It's Vicki. If you're there, pick up." She stared across the dark kitchen, twisting the phone cord between her fingers. "Dome on, Fitzroy, I don't care what you're doing, this is important." Why wasn't he home writing? Or chewing on Tony? Or something? "Look, Henry, I need some information. There's another one of, of us, hunting my territory and I don't know what I should do. I know what I want to do . . ." The rage remained interlaced with the knowledge of *another*. ". . . but I'm new at this bloodsucking undead stuff, maybe I'm overreacting. Call me. I'm still at Mike's."

She hung up and sighed. Vampires didn't share territory. Which was why Henry had stayed in Vancouver and she'd come back to Toronto.

Well, all right, it's not the only reason I came back. She tossed Celluci's spare car keys into the drawer in the phone table and wondered if she should write him a note to explain the mysterious emptying of his gas tank. "Nah. He's a detective, let him figure it out."

Sunrise was at five twelve. Vicki didn't need a clock to tell her that it was almost time. She could feel the sun stroking the edges of her awareness.

"It's like that final instant, just before someone hits you from behind, when you know it's going to happen, but you can't do a damn thing about it." She crossed her arms on Celluci's chest and pillowed her head on them, adding, *"Only it lasts longer."*

"And this happens every morning?"

"Just before dawn."

"And you're going to live forever?"

"That's what they tell me."

Celluci snorted. "You can have it."

Although Celluci had offered to light-proof one of the two unused bedrooms, Vicki had been uneasy about the concept. At four and a half centuries, maybe Henry Fitzroy could afford to be blasé about immolation, but Vicki still found the whole idea terrifying and had no intention of being both helpless and exposed. Anyone could walk into a bedroom.

No one would accidentally walk into an enclosed plywood box, covered in a blackout curtain, at the far end of a five-foot-high crawl space—but just to be on the safe side, Vicki dropped two by fours into iron brackets over the entrance. Folded nearly in half, she hurried to her sanctuary, feeling the sun drawing closer, closer. Somehow she resisted the urge to turn.

"There's nothing behind me," she muttered, awkwardly stripping off her clothes. Her heart slamming against her ribs, she crawled under the front flap of the box, latched it behind her, and squirmed into her sleeping bag, stretched out ready for dawn.

"Jesus H. Christ, Vicki," Celluci had said squatting at one end while she'd wrestled the twin bed mattress inside. *"At least a coffin would have a bit of historical dignity."*

"You know where I can get one?"

"I'm not having a coffin in my basement."

"Then quit flapping your mouth."

She wondered, as she lay there waiting for oblivion, where the *other* was. Did they feel the same near panic knowing that they had no control over the hours from dawn to dusk? Or had they, like Henry, come to accept the daily death that governed an immortal life? There should, she supposed, be a sense of kinship between them, but all she could feel was a possessive fury. No one hunted in *her* territory.

"Pleasant dreams," she said as the sun teetered on the edge of the horizon. "And when I find you, you're toast."

Celluci had been and gone by the time the darkness returned. The note he'd left about the car was profane and to the point. Vicki added a couple of words he'd missed and stuck it under a refrigerator magnet in case he got home before she did.

She'd pick up the scent and follow it, the hunter becoming the hunted and, by dawn, the streets would be hers again.

The yellow police tape still stretched across the mouth of the alley. Vicki ignored it. Wrapping the night around her like a cloak, she stood outside the restaurant door and sifted the air.

Apparently, a pimp crucified over the fire exit hadn't been enough to close the place and Tex Mex had nearly obliterated the scent of a death not yet twenty-four hours old. Instead of the predator, all she could smell was fajitas.

"Goddamn it," she muttered, stepping closer and sniffing the wood. "How the hell am I supposed to find . . . ?"

She sensed his life the moment before he spoke.

"What are you doing?"

Vicki sighed and turned. "I'm sniffing the door frame. What's it look like I'm doing?"

"Let me be more specific," Celluci snarled. "What are you doing *here?*"

"I'm looking for the person who offed Mac Eisler," Vicki began. She wasn't sure how much more explanation she was willing to offer.

"No, you're not. You are not a cop. You aren't even a P.I. anymore. And how the hell am I going to explain you if Dave sees you?"

Her eyes narrowed. "You don't have to explain me, Mike."

"Yeah? He thinks you're in Vancouver."

"Tell him I came back."

"And do I tell him that you spend your days in a box in my basement? And that you combust in sunlight? And what do I tell him about your eyes?"

Vicki's hand rose to push at the bridge of her glasses but her fingers touched only air. The retinitis pigmentosa that had forced her from the Metro Police and denied her the night had been reversed when Henry'd changed her. The darkness held no secrets from her now. "Tell him they got better."

"RP doesn't get better."

"Mine did."

"Vicki, I know what you're doing." He dragged both hands up through his hair. "You've done it before. You had to quit the force. You were half-blind.

So what? Your life may have changed, but you were still going to prove that you were 'Victory' Nelson. And it wasn't enough to be a private investigator. You threw yourself into stupidly dangerous situations just to prove you were still who you wanted to be. And now your life has changed again and you're playing the same game."

She could hear his heart pounding, see a vein pulsing framed in the white vee of his open collar, feel the blood surging just below the surface in reach of her teeth. The Hunger rose and she had to use every bit of control Henry had taught her to force it back down. This wasn't about that.

Since she'd returned to Toronto, she'd been drifting, feeding, hunting, relearning the night, relearning her relationship with Michael Celluci. The early morning phone call had crystallized a subconscious discontent and, as Celluci pointed out, there was really only one thing she knew how to do.

Part of his diatribe was based on concern. After all their years together playing cops and lovers, she knew how he thought: if something as basic as sunlight could kill her, what else waited to strike her down? It was only human nature for him to want to protect the people he loved—for him to want to protect her.

But that was only the basis for *part* of the diatribe.

"You can't have been happy with me lazing around your house. I can't cook and I don't do windows." She stepped toward him. "I should think you'd be thrilled that I'm finding my feet again."

"Vicki."

"I wonder," she mused, holding tight to the Hunger, "how you'd feel about me being involved in this if it wasn't your case. I am, after all, better equipped to hunt the night than, oh, detective-sergeants."

"Vicki . . ." Her name had become a nearly inarticulate growl.

She leaned forward until her lips brushed his ear. "Bet you I solve this one first." Then she was gone, moving into shadow too quickly for mortal eyes to track.

"Who you talking to, Mike?" Dave Graham glanced around the empty alley. "I thought I heard . . ." Then he caught sight of the expression on his partner's face. "Never mind."

Vicki couldn't remember the last time she felt so alive. *Which, as I'm now a card-carrying member of the blood-sucking undead, makes for an interesting feeling.* She strode down Queen Street West, almost intoxicated by the lives surrounding her, fully aware of crowds parting to let her through and the admiring glances that traced her path. A connection had been made between her old life and her new one.

"You must surrender the day," Henry had told her, *"but you need not surrender anything else."*

"So what you're trying to tell me," she'd snarled, *"is that we're just normal people who drink blood?"*

Henry had smiled. *"How many* normal *people do you know?"*

She hated it when he answered a question with a question, but now she recognized his point. Honesty forced her to admit that Celluci had a point as well. She did need to prove to herself that she was still herself. She always had. The more things changed, the more they stayed the same.

"Well, now we've got that settled—" She looked around for a place to sit and think. In her old life, that would have meant a donut shop or the window seat in a cheap restaurant and as many cups of coffee as it took. In this new life, being enclosed with humanity did not encourage contemplation. Besides, coffee, a major component of the old equation, made her violently ill, a fact she deeply resented.

A few years back, CITY TV, a local Toronto station, had renovated a deco building on the corner of Queen and John. They'd done a beautiful job and the six-story, white building with its ornately molded

modern windows had become a focal point of the
neighborhood. Vicki slid into the narrow walkway that
separated it from its more down-at-the-heels neighbor
and swarmed up what effectively amounted to a staircase for one of her kind.

When she reached the roof a few seconds later, she
perched on one crenelated corner and looked out over
the downtown core. These were her streets, not Celluci's and not some out-of-town bloodsucker's. It was
time she took them back. She grinned and fought the
urge to strike a dramatic pose.

All things considered, it wasn't likely that the Metropolitan Toronto Police Department—in the person
of Detective-Sergeant Michael Celluci—would be willing to share information. Briefly, she regretted issuing
the challenge, then she shrugged it off. As Henry said,
the night was too long for regrets.

She sat and watched the crowds jostling about on
the sidewalks below, clumps of color indicating tourists among the Queen Street regulars. On a Friday
night in August, this was the place to be as the Toronto artistic community rubbed elbows with wanna-
bes and never-woulds.

Vicki frowned. Mac Eisler had been killed before
midnight on a Thursday night in an area that never
completely slept. Someone had to have seen or heard
something. Something they probably didn't believe
and were busy denying. Murder was one thing, creatures of the night were something else again.

"Now then," she murmured, "where would a person
like that—and considering the time of day we're assuming a regular not a tourist—where would that person be tonight?"

She found him in the third bar she checked, tucked
back in a corner, trying desperately to get drunk, and
failing. His eyes darted from side to side, both hands
were locked around his glass, and his body language
screamed *I'm dealing with some bad shit here, leave
me alone*.

Vicki sat down beside him and for an instant let the Hunter show. His reaction was everything she could have hoped for.

He stared at her, frozen in terror, his mouth working, but no sound coming out.

"Breathe," she suggested.

The ragged intake of air did little to calm him, but it did break the paralysis. He shoved his chair back from the table and started to stand.

Vicki closed her fingers around his wrist. "Stay."

He swallowed and sat down again.

His skin was so hot it nearly burned and she could feel his pulse breathing against it like a small wild creature struggling to be free. The Hunger clawed at her and her own breathing became a little ragged. "What's your name?"

"Ph . . . Phil."

She caught his gaze with hers and held it. "You saw something last night."

"Yes." Stretched almost to the breaking point, he began to tremble.

"Do you live around here?"

"Yes."

Vicki stood and pulled him to his feet, her tone half command, half caress. "Take me there. We have to talk."

Phil stared at her. "Talk?"

She could barely hear the question over the call of his blood. "Well, talk first."

"It was a woman. Dressed all in black. Hair like a thousand strands of shadow, skin like snow, eyes like black ice. She chuckled, deep in her throat, when she saw me and licked her lips. They were painfully red. Then she vanished, so quickly that she left an image on the night.

"Did you see what she was doing?"

"No. But then, she didn't have be doing anything to be terrifying. I've spent the last twenty-four hours feeling like I met my death."

Phil had turned out to be a bit of a poet. *And* a bit of an athlete. All in all, Vicki considered their time together well spent. Working carefully after he fell asleep, she took away his memory of her and muted the meeting in the alley. It was the least she could do for him.

Description sounds like someone escaped from a Hammer film: The Bride of Dracula Kills a Pimp.

She paused, key in the lock, and cocked her head. Celluci was home, she could feel his life and if she listened very hard, she could hear the regular rhythm of breathing that told her he was asleep. Hardly surprising as it was only three hours to dawn.

There was no reason to wake him as she had no intention of sharing what she'd discovered and no need to feed, but after a long, hot shower, she found herself standing at the door of his room. And then at the side of his bed.

Mike Celluci was thirty-seven. There were strands of gray in his hair and although sleep had smoothed out many of the lines, the deeper creases around his eyes remained. He would grow older. In time, he would die. What would she do then?

She lifted the sheet and tucked herself up close to his side. He sighed and without completely waking scooped her closer still.

"Hair's wet," he muttered.

Vicki twisted, reached up, and brushed the long curl back off his forehead. "I had a shower."

"Where'd you leave the towel?"

"In a sopping pile on the floor."

Celluci grunted inarticulately and surrendered to sleep again.

Vicki smiled and kissed his eyelids. "I love you, too."

She stayed beside him until the threat of sunrise drove her away.

"Irene MacDonald."

Vicki lay in the darkness and stared unseeing up at the plywood. The sun was down and she was free to leave her sanctuary, but she remained a moment longer, turning over the name that had been on her tongue when she woke. She remembered facetiously wondering if the deaths of Irene MacDonald and her pimp were connected.

Irene had been found beaten nearly to death in the bathroom of her apartment. She'd died two hours later in the hospital.

Celluci said that he was personally certain Mac Eisler was responsible. That was good enough for Vicki.

Eisler could've been unlucky enough to run into a vampire who fed on terror as well as blood—Vicki had tasted terror once or twice during her first year when the Hunger occasionally slipped from her control and she knew how addictive it could be—or he could've been killed in revenge for Irene.

Vicki could think of one sure way to find out.

"Brandon? It's Vicki Nelson."

"Victoria?" Surprise lifted most of the Oxford accent off Dr. Brandon Sigh's voice. "I thought you'd relocated to British Columbia."

"Yeah, well, I came back."

"I suppose that might account for the improvement over the last month or so in a certain detective we both know."

She couldn't resist asking. "Was he really bad while I was gone?"

Brandon laughed. "He was unbearable and, as you know, I am able to bear a great deal. So, are you still in the same line of work?"

"Yes, I am." Yes, she was. God, it felt good. "Are you still the Assistant Coroner?"

"Yes, I am. As I think I can safely assume you didn't call me, at home, long after office hours, just to inform me that you're back on the job, what do you want?"

Vicki winced. "I was wondering if you'd had a look at Mac Eisler."

"Yes, Victoria, I have. And I'm wondering why you can't call me during regular business hours. You must know how much I enjoy discussing autopsies in front of my children."

"Oh, God, I'm sorry, Brandon, but it's important."

"Yes. It always is." His tone was so dry it crumbled.

"But since you've already interrupted my evening, try to keep my part of the conversation to a simple yes or not."

"Did you do a blood volume check on Eisler?"

"Yes."

"Was there any missing?"

"No. Fortunately, in spite of the trauma to the neck, the integrity of the blood vessels had not been breached."

So much for yes or no; she knew he couldn't keep to it. "You've been a big help, Brandon, thanks."

"I'd say *anytime,* but you'd likely hold me to it." He hung up abruptly.

Vicki replaced the receiver and frowned. She—the *other*—hadn't fed. The odds moved in favor of Eisler killed because he murdered Irene.

"Well, if it isn't Andrew P." Vicki leaned back against the black Trans Am and adjusted the pair of nonprescription glasses she'd picked up just after sunset. With her hair brushed off her face and the window-glass lenses in front of her eyes, she didn't look much different than she had a year ago. Until she smiled.

The pimp stopped dead in his tracks, bluster fading before he could get the first obscenity out. He swallowed, audibly. "Nelson. I heard you were gone."

Listening to his heart race, Vicki's smile broadened. "I came back. I need some information. I need the name of one of Eisler's other girls."

"I don't know." Unable to look away, he started to shake. "I didn't have anything to do with him. I don't remember."

Vicki straightened and took a slow step toward him. "Try, Andrew."

There was a sudden smell of urine and a darkening stain down the front of the pimp's cotton drawstring pants. "Uh, D . . . D . . . Debbie Ho. That's all I can remember. Really."

"And she works?"

"Middle of the track." His tongue tripped over the words in the rush to spit them at her. "Jarvis and Carlton."

"Thank you." Sweeping a hand toward his car, Vicki stepped aside.

He dove past her and into the driver's seat, jabbing the key into the ignition. The powerful engine roared to life and with one last panicked look into the shadows, he screamed out of the driveway, ground his way through three gear changes, and hit eighty before he reached the corner.

The two cops, quietly sitting in the parking lot of the donut shop on that same corner, hit their siren and took off after him.

Vicki slipped the glasses into the inner pocket of the tweed jacket she'd borrowed from Celluci's closet and grinned. "To paraphrase a certain adolescent crime-fighting amphibian, I *love* being a vampire."

"I need to talk to you, Debbie."

The young woman started and whirled around, glaring suspiciously at Vicki. "You a cop?"

Vicki sighed. "Not any more." Apparently, it was easier to hide the vampire than the detective. "I'm a private investigator and I want to ask you some questions about Irene MacDonald."

"If you're looking for the shithead who killed her, you're too late. Someone already found him."

"And that's who I'm looking for."

"Why?" Debbie shifted her weight to one hip.

"Maybe I want to give him a medal."

The hooker's laugh held little humor. "You got that right. Mac got everything he deserved."

"Did Irene ever do women?"

Debbie snorted. "Not for free," she said pointedly. Vicki handed her a twenty.

"Yeah, sometimes. It's safer, medically, you know?"

Editing out Brandon's more ornate phrases, Vicki repeated his description of the woman in the alley.

Debbie snorted again. "Who the hell looks at their faces?"

"You'd remember this one if you saw her. She's . . ." Vicki weighed and discarded several possibilities and finally settled on, ". . . powerful."

"Powerful." Debbie hesitated, frowned, and continued in a rush. "There was this person Irene was seeing a lot but she wasn't charging. That's one of the things that set Mac off, not that the shithead needed much encouragement. We knew it was gonna happen, I mean, we've all felt Mac's temper, but Irene wouldn't stop. She said that just being with this person was a high better than drugs. I guess it could've been a woman. And since she was sort of the reason Irene died, well, I know they used to meet in this bar on Queen West. Why are you hissing?"

"Hissing?" Vicki quickly yanked a mask of composure down over her rage. The other hadn't come into her territory only to kill Eisler—she was definitely Hunting it. "I'm not hissing. I'm just having a little trouble breathing."

"Yeah, tell me about it." Debbie waved a hand ending in three-inch scarlet nails at the traffic on Jarvis. "You should try standing here sucking carbon monoxide all night."

In another mood, Vicki might have reapplied the verb to a different object, but she was still too angry. "Do you know which bar?"

"What, now I'm her social director? No, I don't know which bar." Apparently they'd come to the end of the information twenty dollars could buy as Debbie turned her attention to a prospective client in a gray sedan. The interview was clearly over.

Vicki sucked the humid air past her teeth. There

weren't that many bars on Queen West. Last night she'd found Phil in one. Tonight, who knew?

Now that she knew enough to search for it, minute traces of the other predator hung in the air—diffused and scattered by the paths of prey. With so many lives masking the trail, it would be impossible to track her. Vicki snarled. A pair of teenagers, noses pierced, heads shaved, and Doc Martens laced to the knee, decided against asking for change and hastily crossed the street.

It was Saturday night, minutes to Sunday. The bars would be closing soon. If the *other* was hunting, she would have already chosen her prey.

I wish Henry had called back. Maybe over the centuries they've—we've—evolved ways to deal with this. Maybe we're supposed to talk first. Maybe it's considered bad manners to rip her face off and feed it to her if she doesn't agree to leave.

Standing in the shadow of a recessed storefront, just beyond the edge of the artificial safety the streetlight offered to the children of the sun, she extended her senses the way she'd been taught and touched death within the maelstrom of life.

She found Phil, moments later, laying in yet another of the alleys that serviced the business of the day and provided a safe haven for the darker business of the night. His body was still warm, but his heart had stopped beating and his blood no longer sang. Vicki touched the tiny, nearly closed wound she'd made in his wrist the night before and then the fresh wound in the bend of his elbow. She didn't know how he had died, but she knew who had done it. He stank of the *other*.

Vicki no longer cared what was traditionally "done" in these instances. There would be no talking. No negotiating. It had gone one life beyond that.

"I rather thought that if I killed him you'd come and save me the trouble of tracking you down. And here you are, charging in without taking the slightest

of precautions." Her voice was low, not so much
threatening as in itself a threat. "You're hunting in
my territory, child."

Still kneeling by Phil's side, Vicki lifted her head.
Ten feet away, only her face and hands clearly visible,
the other vampire stood. Without thinking—unable to
think clearly through the red rage that shrieked for
release—Vicki launched herself at the snow-white column of throat, finger hooked to talons, teeth bared.

The Beast Henry had spent a year teaching her to
control was loose. She felt herself lost in its raw power
and she reveled in it.

The *other* made no move until the last possible second then she lithely twisted and slammed Vicki to
one side.

Pain eventually brought reason back. Vicki lay panting in the fetid damp at the base of a dumpster, one
eye swollen shut, a gash across her forehead still sluggishly bleeding. Her right arm was broken.

"You're strong," the other told her, a contemptuous
gaze pinning her to the ground. "In another hundred
years you might have stood a chance. But you're an
infant. A child. You haven't the experience to control
what you are. This will be your only warning. Get out
of my territory. If we meet again, I *will* kill you."

Vicki sagged against the inside of the door and tried
to lift her arm. During the two and a half hours it had
taken her to get back to Celluci's house, the bone had
begun to set. By tomorrow night, provided she fed in
the hours remaining until dawn, she should be able to
use it.

"Vicki?"

She started. Although she'd known he was home,
she'd assumed—without checking—that because of
the hour he'd be asleep. She squinted as the hall light
came on and wondered, listening to him pad down the
stairs in bare feet, whether she had the energy to make
it into the basement bathroom before he saw her.

He came into the kitchen, tying his bathrobe belt

around him, and flicked on the overhead light. "We need to talk," he said grimly as the shadows that might have hidden her fled. "Jesus H. Christ. What the hell happened to you?"

"Nothing much." Eyes squinted nearly shut, Vicki gingerly probed the swelling on her forehead. "You should see the other guy."

Without speaking, Celluci reached over and hit the play button on the telephone answering machine.

"Vicki? Henry. If someone's hunting your territory, whatever you do, don't challenge. Do you hear me? *Don't* challenge. You can't win. They're going to be older, able to overcome the instinctive rage and remain in full command of their power. If you won't surrender the territory . . ." The sigh the tape played back gave a clear opinion of how likely he thought that was to occur. ". . . you're going to have to negotiate. If you can agree on boundaries, there's no reason why you can't share the city." His voice suddenly belonged again to the lover she'd lost with the change. "Call me, please, before you do anything."

It was the only message on the tape.

"Why," Celluci asked as it rewound, his gaze taking in the cuts and the bruising and the filth, "do I get the impression that it's 'the other guy' Fitzroy's talking about?"

Vicki tried to shrug. Her shoulders refused to cooperate. "It's my city, Mike. It always has been. I'm going to take it back."

He stared at her for a long moment then he shook his head. "You heard what Henry said. You can't win. You haven't been . . . what you are, long enough. It's only been fourteen months."

"I know." The rich scent of his life prodded the Hunger and she moved to put a little distance between them.

He closed it up again. "Come on." Laying his hand in the center of her back, he steered her toward the stairs. *Put it aside for now,* his tone told her. *We'll argue about it later.* "You need a bath."

"I need . . ."

"I know. But you need a bath first. I just changed the sheets."

The darkness wakes us all in different ways, Henry had told her. *We were all human once and we carried our differences through the change.*

For Vicki, it was like the flicking of a switch; one moment she wasn't, the next she was. This time, when she returned from the little death of the day, an idea returned with her.

Four-hundred-and-fifty-odd years a vampire, Henry had been seventeen when he changed. The *other* had walked the night for perhaps as long—her gaze had carried the weight of several lifetimes—but her physical appearance suggested that her mortal life had lasted even less time than Henry's had. Vicki allowed that it made sense. Disaster may have precipitated *her* change, but passion was the usual cause.

And no one does that kind of never-say-die passion like a teenager.

It would be difficult for either Henry or the other to imagine a response that came out of a mortal rather than a vampiric experience. They'd both had centuries of the latter and not enough of the former to count.

Vicki had been only fourteen months a vampire, but she'd been human thirty-two years when Henry'd saved her by drawing her to his blood to feed. During those thirty-two years, she'd been nine years a cop—two accelerated promotions, three citations, and the best arrest record on the force.

There was no chance of negotiation.

She couldn't win if she fought.

She'd be damned if she'd flee.

"Besides . . ." For all she realized where her strength had to lie, Vicki's expression held no humanity. ". . . she owes me for Phil."

Celluci had left her a note on the fridge.

Does this have anything to do with Mac Eisler?

Vicki stared at it for a moment then scribbled her answer underneath.

Not anymore.

It took three weeks to find where the *other* spent her days. Vicki used old contacts where she could and made new ones where she had to. Any modern Van Helsing could have done the same.

For the next three weeks, Vicki hired someone to watch the *other* come and go, giving reinforced instructions to stay in the car with the windows closed and the air-conditioning running. Life had an infinite number of variations, but one piece of machinery smelled pretty much like any other. It irritated her that she couldn't sit stakeout herself, but the information she needed would've kept her out after sunrise.

"How the hell did you burn your hand?"

Vicki continued to smear ointment over the blister. Unlike the injuries she'd taken in the alley, this would heal slowly and painfully. "Accident in a tanning salon."

"That's not funny."

She picked up the roll of gauze from the counter. "You're losing your sense of humor, Mike."

Celluci snorted and handed her the scissors. "I never had one."

"Mike, I wanted to warn you, I won't be back by sunrise."

Celluci turned slowly, the TV dinner he'd just taken from the microwave held in both hands. "What do you mean?"

She read the fear in his voice and lifted the edge of the tray so that the gravy didn't pour out and over his shoes. "I mean I'll be spending the day somewhere else."

"Where?"

"I can't tell you."

"Why? Never mind." He raised a hand as her eyes narrowed. "Don't tell me. I don't want to know.

You're going after that other vampire, aren't you? The one Fitzroy told you to leave alone."

"I thought you didn't want to know."

"I already know," he grunted. "I can read you like a book. With large type. And pictures."

Vicki pulled the tray from his grip and set it on the counter. "She's killed two people. Eisler was a scumbag who may have deserved it, but the other . . ."

"Other?" Celluci exploded. "Jesus H. Christ, Vicki, in case you've forgotten, murder's against the law! Who the hell painted a big vee on your long johns and made you the vampire vigilante?"

"Don't you remember?" Vicki snapped. "You were there. I didn't make this decision, Mike. You and Henry made it for me. You'd just better learn to live with it." She fought her way back to calm. "Look, you can't stop her, but I can. I know that galls, but that's the way it is."

They glared at each other, toe to toe. Finally Celluci looked away.

"I can't stop you, can I?" he asked bitterly. "I'm only human after all."

"Don't sell yourself short," Vicki snarled. "You're quintessentially human. If you want to stop me, you face me and ask me not to go and *then* you remember it every time *you* go into a situation that could get your ass shot off."

After a long moment, he swallowed, lifted his head, and met her eyes. "Don't die. I thought I lost you once and I'm not strong enough to go through that again."

"Are you asking me not to go?"

He snorted. "I'm asking you to be careful. Not that you ever listen."

She took a step forward and rested her head against his shoulder, wrapping herself in the beating of his heart. "This time, I'm listening."

The studios in the converted warehouse on King Street were not supposed to be live-in. A good seventy-five percent of the tenants ignored that. The studio Vicki wanted was at the back on the third floor. The heavy steel door—an obvious upgrade by the occupant—had been secured by the best lock money could buy.

New senses and old skills got through it in record time.

Vicki pushed open the door with her foot and began carrying boxes inside. She had a lot to do before dawn.

"She goes out every night between ten and eleven, then she comes home every morning between four and five. You could set your watch by her."

Vicki handed him an envelope.

He looked inside, thumbed through the money, then grinned up at her. "Pleasure doing business for you. Any time you need my services, you know where to call."

"Forget it," she told him.

And he did.

Because she expected her, Vicki knew the moment the *other* entered the building. The Beast stirred and she tightened her grip on it. To lose control now would be disaster.

She heard the elevator, then footsteps in the hall.

"You know I'm in here," she said silently, *"and you know you can take me. Be overconfident, believe I'm a fool, and walk right in."*

"I thought you were smarter than this." The *other* stepped into the apartment, then casually turned to lock the door. "I told you when I saw you again I'd kill you."

Vicki shrugged, the motion masking her fight to remain calm. "Don't you even want to know why I'm here?"

"I assume you've come to negotiate." She raised ivory hands and released thick, black hair from its bindings. "We went past that when you attacked me." Crossing the room, she preened before a large ornate mirror that dominated one wall of the studio.

"I attacked you because you murdered Phil."

"Was that his name?" The other laughed. The sound had razored edges. "I didn't bother to ask it."

"Before you murdered him."

"Murdered? You *are* a child. They are prey, we are predators—their deaths are ours if we desire them. You'd have learned that in time." She turned, the patina of civilization stripped away. "Too bad you haven't any time left."

Vicki snarled but somehow managed to stop herself from attacking. Years of training whispered, *Not yet.* She had to stay exactly where she was.

"Oh, yes." The sibilants flayed the air between them. "I almost forgot. You wanted me to ask you why you came. Very well. Why?"

Given the address and the reason, Celluci could've come to the studio during the day and slammed a stake through the *other's* heart. The vampire's strongest protection would be of no use against him. Mike Celluci believed in vampires.

"I came," Vicki told her, "because some things you have to do yourself."

The wire ran up the wall, tucked beside the surface-mounted cable of a cheap renovation, and disappeared into the shadows that clung to a ceiling sixteen feet from the floor. The switch had been stapled down beside her foot. A tiny motion, too small to evoke attack, flipped it.

Vicki had realized from the beginning that there were a number of problems with her plan. The first involved placement. Every living space included an area where the occupant felt secure—a favorite chair, a window . . . a mirror. The second problem was how to mask what she'd done. While the *other* would not be able to sense the various bits of wiring and equipment, she'd be fully aware of Vicki's scent *on* the wiring and equipment. Only if Vicki remained in the studio, could that smaller trace be lost in the larger.

The third problem was directly connected with the

second. Given that Vicki had to remain, how was she to survive?

Attached to the ceiling by sheer brute strength, positioned so that they shone directly down into the space in front of the mirror, were a double bank of lights cannibalized from a tanning bed. The sun held a double menace for the vampire—its return to the sky brought complete vulnerability and its rays burned.

Henry had a round scar on the back of one hand from too close an encounter with the sun. When her burn healed, Vicki would have a matching one from a deliberate encounter with an imitation.

The *other* screamed as the lights came on, the sound pure rage and so inhuman that those who heard it would have to deny it for sanity's sake.

Vicki dove forward, ripped the heavy brocade off the back of the couch, and burrowed frantically into its depths. Even that instant of light had bathed her skin in flame and she moaned as, for a moment, the searing pain became all she was. After a time, when it grew no worse, she managed to open her eyes.

The light couldn't reach her, but neither could she reach the switch to turn it off. She could see it, three feet away, just beyond the shadow of the couch. She shifted her weight and a line of blister rose across one leg. Biting back a shriek, she curled into a fetal position, realizing her refuge was not entirely secure.

Okay, genius, now what?

Moving very, very carefully, Vicki wrapped her hand around the one by two that braced the lower edge of the couch. From the tension running along it, she suspected that breaking it off would result in at least a partial collapse of the piece of furniture.

And if it goes, I very well may go with it.

And then she heard the sound of something dragging itself across the floor.

Oh, shit! She's not dead!

The wood broke, the couch began to fall in on itself,

and Vicki, realizing that luck would have a large part to play in her survival, smacked the switch and rolled clear in the same motion.

The room plunged into darkness.

Vicki froze as her eyes slowly readjusted to the night. Which was when she finally became conscious of the smell. It had been there all along, but her senses had refused to acknowledge it until they had to.

Sunlight burned.

Vicki gagged.

The dragging sound continued.

The hell with this! She didn't have time to wait for her eyes to repair the damage they'd obviously taken. She needed to see *now*. Fortunately, although it hadn't seemed fortunate at the time, she'd learned to maneuver without sight.

She threw herself across the room.

The light switch was where they always were, to the right of the door.

The thing on the floor pushed itself up on fingerless hands and glared at her out of the blackened ruin of a face. Laboriously it turned, hate radiating off it in palpable waves and began to pull itself toward her again.

Vicki stepped forward to meet it.

While the part of her that remembered being human writhed in revulsion, she wrapped her hands around its skull and twisted it in a full circle. The spine snapped. Another full twist and what was left of the head came off in her hands.

She'd been human for thirty-two years, but she'd been fourteen months a vampire.

"No one hunts in *my* territory," she snarled as the *other* crumbled to dust.

She limped over to the wall and pulled the plug supplying power to the lights. Later, she'd remove them completely—the whole concept of sunlamps gave her the creeps.

When she turned, she was facing the mirror.

The woman who stared out at her through bloodshot eyes, exposed skin blistered and red, was a hunter. Always had been, really. The question became, who was she to hunt?

Vicki smiled. Before the sun drove her to use her inherited sanctuary, she had a few quick phone calls to make. The first to Celluci; she owed him the knowledge that she'd survived the night. The second to Henry for much the same reason.

The third call would be to the eight hundred line that covered the classifieds of Toronto's largest alternative newspaper. This ad was going to be a little different than the one she'd placed upon leaving the force. Back then, she'd been incredibly depressed about leaving a job she loved for a life she saw as only marginally useful. This time, she had no regrets.

Victory Nelson, Investigator: Otherworldly Crimes a Specialty.

What Manner of Man

Shortly after three o'clock in the morning, Henry Fitzroy rose from the card table, brushed a bit of ash from the sleeve of his superbly fitting coat, and inclined his head toward his few remaining companions. "If you'll excuse me, gentlemen, I believe I'll call it a night."

"Well, I won't excuse you." Sir William Wyndham glared up at Fitzroy from under heavy lids. "You've won eleven hundred pounds off me tonight, damn your eyes, and I want a chance to win it back."

His gaze flickering down to the cluster of empty bottles by Wyndham's elbow, Henry shook his head. "I don't think so, Sir William, not tonight."

"You don't think so?" Wyndham half rose in his chair, dark brows drawn into a deep vee over an aristocratic arc of nose. His elbow rocked one of the bottles. It began to fall.

Moving with a speed that made it clear he had not personally been indulging over the course of the evening's play, Henry caught the bottle just before it hit the floor. "Brandy," he chided softly, setting it back on the table, "is no excuse for bad manners."

Wyndham stared at him for a moment, confusion replacing the anger on his face, instinct warning him of a danger reason couldn't see. "Your pardon," he said at last. "Perhaps another night." He watched as the other man bowed and left, then muttered, "Insolent puppy."

"Who is?" asked another of the players, dragging his attention away from the brandy.

"Fitzroy." Raising his glass to his mouth, his hand surprisingly steady considering how much he'd already drunk, Wyndham tossed back the contents. "He speaks to me like that again and he can name his seconds."

"Well, *I* wouldn't fight him."

"No one's asking you to."

"He's just the sort of quiet chap who's the very devil when pushed too far. I've seen that look in his eyes, I tell you—the very devil when pushed too far."

"Shut up." Opening a fresh deck, Wyndham sullenly pushed Henry Fitzroy from his thoughts and set about trying to make good his losses.

His curly-brimmed beaver set at a fashionably rakish angle on his head, Henry stood on the steps of his club and stared out at London. Its limits had expanded since the last time he'd made it his principal residence, curved courts of elegant townhouses had risen where he remembered fields, but, all in all, it hadn't changed much. There was still something about London—a feel, an atmosphere—shared by no other city in the world.

One guinea-gold brow rose as he shot an ironic glance upward at the haze that hung over the buildings, the smoke from a thousand chimney pots that blocked the light of all but the brightest stars. Atmosphere was, perhaps, a less than appropriate choice of words.

"Shall I get you a hackney or a chair, Mr. Fitzroy?"

"Thank you, no." He smiled at the porter, his expression calculated to charm, and heard the elderly man's heart begin to beat a little faster. The Hunger rose in response, but he firmly pushed it back. It would be the worst of bad *ton* to feed so close to home. It would also be dangerous but, in the England of the Prince Regent, safety came second to social approval. "I believe I'll walk."

"If you're sure, sir. There's some bad'uns around after dark."

"I'm sure." Henry's smile broadened. "I doubt I'll be bothered."

The porter watched as the young man made his way down the stairs and along St. James Street. He'd watched a lot of gentlemen during the years he'd worked the clubs—first at Boodles, then at Brook's, and finally here at White's—and Mr. Henry Fitzroy had the unmistakable mark of Quality. For all he was so polite and soft-spoken, something about him spoke strongly of power. It would, the porter decided, take a desperate man, or a stupid one, to put Mr. Fitzroy in any danger. *Of course, London has no shortage of either desperate or stupid men.*

"Take care, sir," he murmured as he turned to go inside.

Henry quelled the urge to lift a hand in acknowledgment of the porter's concern, judging that he'd moved beyond the range of mortal hearing. As the night air held a decided chill, he shoved his hands deep in the pockets of his many-caped greatcoat, even though it would have to get a great deal colder before he'd feel it. A successful masquerade demanded attention to small details.

Humming under his breath, he strode down Brook Street to Grosvenor Square, marveling at the new technological wonder of the gaslights. The long lines of little brightish dots created almost as many shadows as they banished, but they were still a big improvement over a servant carrying a lantern on a stick. That he had no actual need of the light, Henry considered unimportant in view of the achievement.

Turning toward his chambers in Albany, he heard the unmistakable sounds of a fight. He paused, head cocked, sifting through the lives involved. Three men beating a fourth.

"Not at all sporting," he murmured, moving forward so quickly that, had anyone been watching, it would have seemed he simply disappeared.

"Be sure that he's dead." The man who spoke held a narrow sword in one hand and the cane it had come out of in the other. The man on the ground groaned and the steel point moved around. "Never mind, I'll take care of it myself."

Wearing an expression of extreme disapproval, Henry stepped out of the shadows, grabbed the swordsman by the back of his coat, and threw him down the alley. When the other two whirled to face him, he drew his lips back off his teeth and said, in a tone of polite but inarguable menace, "Run."

Prey recognized predator. They ran.

He knelt by the wounded man, noted how the heart-beat faltered, looked down, and saw a face he knew. Captain Charles Evans of the Horse Guards, the nephew of the current Earl of Whitby. Not one of his few friends—friends were chosen with a care honed by centuries of survival—but Henry couldn't allow him to die alone in some dark alley like a stray dog.

A sudden noise drew his attention around to the man with the sword-cane. Up on his knees, his eyes unfocused, he groped around for his weapon. Henry snarled. The man froze, whimpered once, then, face twisted with fear, scrambled to his feet, and joined his companions in flight.

The sword had punched a hole high in the captain's left shoulder, not immediately fatal, but bleeding to death was a distinct possibility.

"Fitz . . . roy?"

"So you're awake, are you?" Taking the other man's chin in a gentle grip, Henry stared down into pain-filled eyes. "I think it might be best if you trusted me and slept," he said quietly.

The captain's lashes fluttered, then settled down to rest against his cheeks like fringed shadows.

Satisfied that he was unobserved, Henry pulled aside the bloodstained jacket—like most military men,

Captain Evans favored Scott—and bent his head over the wound.

"You cut it close. Sun's almost up."

Henry pushed past the small, irritated form of his servant. "Don't fuss, Varney, I've plenty of time."

"Plenty of time is it?" Closing and bolting the door, the little man hurried down the short hall in Henry's shadow. "I was worried sick, I was, and all you can say is don't fuss?"

Sighing, Henry shrugged out of his greatcoat—a muttering Varney caught it before it hit the floor—and stepped into his sitting room. There was a fire lit in the grate, heavy curtains over the window that opened onto a tiny balcony, and a thick oak slab of a door replacing the folding doors that had originally led to the bedchamber. The furniture was heavy and dark, as close as Henry could come to the furniture of his youth. It had been purchased in a fit of nostalgia and was now mostly ignored.

"You've blood on your cravat!"

"It's not mine," Henry told him mildly.

Varney snorted. "Didn't expect it was, but you're usually neater than that. Probably won't come out. Blood stains, you know."

"I know."

"Mayhap if I soak it . . ." The little man quivered with barely concealed impatience.

Henry laughed and unwound the offending cloth, dropping it over the offered hand. After thirty years of unique service, certain liberties were unavoidable. "I won eleven hundred pounds from Lord Wyndham tonight."

"You and everyone else. He's badly dipped. Barely a feather to fly with so I hear. Rumor has it, he's getting a bit desperate."

"And I returned a wounded Charlie Evans to the bosom of his family."

"Nice bosom, so I hear."

"Don't be crude, Varney." Henry sat down and

lifted one foot after the other to have the tight Hessians pulled gently off. "I think I may have prevented him from being killed."

"Robbery?"

"I don't know."

"How many did you kill?"

"No one. I merely frightened them away."

Setting the gleaming boots to one side, Varney stared at his master with frank disapproval. "You merely frightened them away?"

"I did consider ripping their throats out, but as it wasn't actually necessary, it wouldn't have been . . ." He paused and smiled. ". . . polite."

"Polite!? You risked exposure so as you can be polite?"

The smile broadened. "I am a creature of my time."

"You're a creature of the night! You know what'll come of this? Questions, that's what. And we don't need questions!"

"I have complete faith in your ability to handle whatever might arise."

Recognizing the tone, the little man deflated. "Aye and well you might," he muttered darkly. "Let's get that jacket off you before I've got to carry you in to your bed like a sack of meal."

"I *can* do it myself," Henry remarked as he stood and turned to have his coat carefully peeled from his shoulders.

"Oh, aye, and leave it lying on the floor no doubt." Folding the coat in half, Varney draped it over one skinny arm. "I'd never get the wrinkles out. You'd go about looking like you dressed out of a ragbag if it wasn't for me. Have you eaten?" He looked suddenly hopeful.

One hand in the bedchamber door, Henry paused. "Yes," he said softly.

The thin shoulders sagged. "Then what're you standing about for?"

A few moments later, the door bolted, the heavy shutter over the narrow window secured, Henry Fitzroy, vampire, bastard son of Henry the VIII, once Duke of Richmond and Somerset, Earl of Nottingham, and Lord President of the Council of the North, slid into the day's oblivion.

"My apologies, Mrs. Evans, for not coming by sooner, but I was out when your husband's message arrived." Henry laid his hat and gloves on the small table in the hall and allowed the waiting footman to take his coat. "I trust he's in better health than he was when I saw him last night?"

"A great deal better, thank you." Although there were purple shadows under her eyes and her cheeks were more than fashionably pale, Lenore Evans' smile lit up her face. "The doctor says he lost a lot of blood, but he'll recover. If it hadn't been for you . . ."

As her voice trailed off, Henry bowed slightly. "I was happy to help." Perhaps he *had* taken a dangerous chance. Perhaps he should have wiped all memory of his presence from the captain's mind and left him on his own doorstep like an oversized infant. Having become involved, he couldn't very well ignore the message an obviously disapproving Varney had handed him at sunset with a muttered, *I told you so*.

It appeared that there were indeed going to be questions.

Following Mrs. Evans up the stairs, he allowed himself to be ushered into a well-appointed bedchamber and left alone with the man in the bed.

Propped up against his pillows, recently shaved but looking wan and tired, Charles Evans nodded a greeting. "Fitzroy. I'm glad you've come."

Henry inclined his own head in return, thankful that the bloodscent had been covered by the entirely unappetizing smell of basilicum powder. "You're looking remarkably well, all things considered."

"I've you to thank for that."

"I really did very little."

"True enough, you *only* saved my life." The captain's grin was infectious and Henry found himself returning it in spite of an intention to remain aloof. "Mind you, Dr. Harris did say he'd never seen such a clean wound." One hand rose to touch the bandages under his nightshirt. "He said I was healing faster than any man he'd ever examined."

As his saliva had been responsible for that accelerated healing, Henry remained silent. It had seemed foolish to resist temptation when there'd been so much blood going to waste.

"Anyway . . ." The grin disappeared and the expressive face grew serious. "I owe you my life and I'm very grateful you came along, but that's not why I asked you to visit. I can't get out of this damned bed and I have to trust someone." Shadowed eyes lifted to Henry's face. "Something tells me that I can trust you."

"You barely know me," Henry murmured, inwardly cursing his choice of words the night before. He'd told Evans to trust him and now it seemed he was to play the role of confidant. He could remove the trust as easily as he'd placed it, but something in the man's face made him hesitate. Whatever bothered him involved life and death—Henry had seen the latter too often to mistake it now. Sighing, he added, "I can't promise anything, but I'll listen."

"Please." Gesturing at a chair, the captain waited until his guest had seated himself, then waited a little longer, apparently searching for a way to begin. After a few moments, he lifted his chin. "You know I work at the Home Office?"

"I had heard as much, yes." In the last few years, gossip had become the preferred entertainment of *all* classes, and Varney was a devoted participant.

"Well, for the last little while—just since the start of the Season, in fact—things have been going missing."

"Things?"

"Papers. Unimportant ones for the most part, until now." His mouth twisted up into a humorless grin. "I can't tell you exactly what the latest missing document contained—in spite of everything we'd still rather it wasn't common knowledge—but I can tell you that if it gets into the wrong hands, into French hands, a lot of British soldiers are going to die."

"Last night you were following the thief?"

"No. The man we think is his contact. A French spy named Yves Bouchard."

Henry shook his head, intrigued in spite of himself. "The man who stabbed you last night was no Frenchman. I heard him speak, and he was as English as you or I. English, and though I hesitate to use the term, a gentleman."

"That's Bouchard. He's the only son of an old emigre family. They left France during the revolution—Yves was a mere infant at the time, and now he dreams of restoring the family fortunes under Napoleon."

"One would have thought he'd be more interested in defeating Napoleon and restoring the rightful king."

Evans shrugged, winced, and said, "Apparently not. Anyway, Bouchard's too smart to stay around after what happened last night. I kept him from getting his hands on the document; now we have to keep it from leaving England by another means."

"We?" Henry asked, surprised into ill-mannered incredulity. "You and I?"

"Mostly you. The trouble is, we don't know who actually took the document, although we've narrowed it down to three men who are known to be in Bouchard's confidence and who have access to the Guard's offices."

"One moment, please." Henry raised an exquisitely manicured hand. "You want me to find your spy for you?"

"Yes."

"Why?"

"Because I can't be certain of anyone else in my office and because I trust you."

Realizing he had only himself to blame, Henry sighed. "And I suppose you can't bring the three in for questioning because two of them are innocent?"

Evans' pained expression had nothing to do with his wound. "Only consider the scandal. I will if I must, but as this is Wednesday and the information must be in France by Friday evening or it won't get to Napoleon in time for it to be of any use, one of those three will betray himself in the next two days."

"So the document must be recovered with no public outcry?"

"Exactly."

"I would have thought the Bow Street Runners . . ."

"No. The Runners may be fine for chasing down highwaymen and murderers, but my three suspects move in the best circles; only a man of their own class could get near them without arousing suspicion." He lifted a piece of paper off the table beside the bed and held it out to Henry, who stared at it for a long moment.

Lord Ruthven, Mr. Maxwell Aubrey, and Sir William Wyndham. Frowning, Henry looked up to meet Captain Evans' weary gaze. "You're sure about this?"

"I am. Send word when you're sure, I'll do the rest."

The exhaustion shading the other man's voice reminded Henry of his injury. Placing the paper back beside the bed, he stood. "This is certainly not what I expected."

"But you'll do it?"

He could refuse, could make the captain forget that this conversation had ever happened, but he had been a prince of England and, regardless of what he had become, he could not stand back and allow her to be betrayed. Hiding a smile at the thought of what Varney would have to say about such melodrama, he nodded. "Yes, I'll do it."

The sound of feminine voices rising up from the entryway caused Henry to pause for a moment on the landing.

". . . so sorry to arrive so late, Mrs. Evans, but we were passing on our way to dinner before Almack's and my uncle insisted we stop and see how the captain was doing."

Carmilla Amworth. There could be no mistaking the faint country accent not entirely removed by hours of lessons intended to erase it. She had enough fortune to be considered an heiress and that, combined with a dark-haired, pale-skinned, waiflike beauty, brought no shortage of admirers. Unfortunately, she also had disturbing tendency to giggle when she felt herself out of her depth.

"My uncle," she continued, "finds it difficult to get out of the carriage and so sent me in his place."

"I quite understand." The smile in the answering voice suggested a shared amusement. "Please tell your uncle that the captain is resting comfortably and thank him for his consideration."

A brief exchange of pleasantries later, Miss Amworth returned to her uncle's carriage and Henry descended the rest of the stairs.

Lenore Evans turned and leaped backward, one hand to her heart, her mouth open. She would have fallen had Henry not caught her wrist and kept her on her feet.

He could feel her pulse racing beneath the thin sheath of heated skin. The Hunger rose, and he hurriedly broke the contact. Self-indulgence, besides being vulgar, was a sure road to the stake.

"Heavens, you startled me." Cheeks flushed, she increased the distance between them. "I didn't hear you come down."

"My apologies. I heard Miss Amworth and didn't wish to break in on a private moment."

"Her uncle works with Charles and wanted to know how he was, but her uncle is *also* a dear friend of His Royal Highness and is, shall we say, less than able to climb in and out of carriages. Is Charles . . . ?"

"I left him sleeping."

"Good." Her right hand wrapped around the place where Henry had held her. She swallowed, then, as though reminded of her duties by the action, stammered, "Can I get you a glass of wine?"

"Thank you, no. I must be going."

"Good. That is, I mean . . ." Her flush deepened. "You must think I'm a complete idiot. It's just that with Charles injured . . ."

"I fully understand." He smiled, careful not to show teeth.

Lenore Evans closed the door behind her husband's guest and tried to calm the pounding of her heart. Something about Henry Fitzroy spoke to a part of her she'd thought belonged to Charles alone. Her response might have come out of gratitude for the saving of her husband's life, but she didn't think so. He was a handsome young man, and she found the soft curves of his mouth a fascinating contrast to the gentle strength in his grip.

Shaking her head in self-reproach, she lifted her skirts with damp hands and started up the stairs. "I'm beginning to think," she sighed, "that Aunt Georgette was right. Novels are a bad influence on a young woman."

What she needed now was a few hours alone with her husband but, as his wound made that impossible, she'd supposed she'd have to divert her thoughts with a book of sermons instead.

Almack's Assembly Rooms were the exclusive temple of the beau monde, and vouchers to the weekly ball on Wednesday were among the most sought-after items in London. What matter that the assembly rooms were plain, the dance floor inferior, the anterooms unadorned, and the refreshments unappetizing—this was the seventh heaven of the fashionable world, and to be excluded from Almack's was to be excluded from the upper levels of society.

Henry, having discovered that a fashionable young man could live unremarked from dark to dawn, had effortlessly risen to the top.

After checking with the porter that all three of Captain Evans' potential spies were indeed in attendance, Henry left hat, coat, and gloves and made his way up into the assembly rooms. Avoiding the gaze of Princess Esterhazy, who he considered to be rude and overbearing, he crossed the room and made his bow to the Countess Lieven.

"I hear you were quite busy last night, Mr. Fitzroy."

A little astonished by how quickly the information had made its way to such august ears, he murmured he had only done what any man would have.

"Indeed. Any *man*. Still, I should have thought the less of you had you expected a fuss to be made." Tapping her closed fan against her other hand, she favored him with a long, level look. "I have always believed there was more to you than you showed the world."

Fully aware that the Countess deserved her reputation as the cleverest woman in London, Henry allowed a little of his mask to slip.

She smiled, satisfied for the moment with being right and not overly concerned with what she had been right about. "Appearances, my dear Mr. Fitzroy, are everything. And now, I believe they are beginning a country dance. Let me introduce you to a young lady in need of a partner."

Unable to think of a reason why she shouldn't, Henry bowed again. A few moments later, as he moved gracefully through the pattern of the dance, he wondered if he should pay the Countess a visit some night, had not made a decision by the time the dance ended, and put it off indefinitely as he escorted the young woman in his care back to her waiting mama.

Well aware that he looked, at best, in his early twenties, Henry could only be thankful that a well-crafted reputation as a man who trusted to the cards for the finer things in life took him off the marriage mart. No matchmaking mama would allow her daughter to become shackled to someone with such narrow prospects. As he had no interest in giggling young damsels just out of the schoolroom, he could only be thankful. The older women he spent time with were much more . . . appetizing.

Trying not to stare, one of the young damsels so summarily dismissed in Henry's thoughts leaned foward a second and whispered, "I wonder what Mr. Fitzroy is smiling about."

The second glanced up, blushed rosily, and ducked her head. "He looks *hungry*."

The first, a little wiser in the ways of the world than her friend, sighed and laid silent odds that the curve of Mr. Henry Fitzroy's full lips had nothing to do with bread and butter.

Hearing a familiar voice, Henry searched through the moving couples and spotted Sir William Wyndham dancing with Carmilla Amworth. Hardly surprising if he'd lost as much money lately as Varney suggested. While Henry wouldn't have believed the fragile, country-bred heiress to his taste—it was a well-known secret that he kept a yacht off Dover for the express purpose of entertaining the women of easy virtue he preferred—upon reflection he supposed Sir William would consider her inheritance sufficiently alluring. And a much safer way of recovering his fortune than selling state secrets to France.

With one of Captain Evans' suspects accounted for, Henry began to search for the other two, moving quietly and unobtrusively from room to room. As dancing was the object of the club and no high stakes were allowed, the card rooms contained only dowagers and those gentlemen willing to play whist for pennies. Although he found neither of the men he looked for, he did find Carmilla Amworth's uncle, Lord Beardsley. One of the Prince Regent's cronies, he was a stout and somewhat foolish middle-aged gentleman who smelled strongly of scent and creaked alarmingly when he moved. Considering the bulwark of his stays, Henry was hardly surprised that he'd been less than able to get out of the carriage to ask after Captain Evans.

". . . cupped and felt much better," Lord Beardsley was saying as Henry entered the room. "His Royal Highness swears by cupping, you know. Must've had gallons taken out over the years."

Henry winced, glanced around, and left. As much as he deplored the waste involved in frequent cupping, he had no desire to avail himself of the Prince Regent's blood—which he strongly suspected would be better than ninety percent Madeira.

When he returned to the main assembly room, he found Aubrey on the dance floor and Lord Ruthven brooding in a corner. Sir William had disappeared, but he supposed a two-for-one trade couldn't be considered bad odds and wondered just how he was expected to watch all three men at once. Obviously, he'd have to be more than a mere passive observer. The situation seemed to make it necessary he tackle Ruthven first.

Dressed in funereal black, the peer swept the room with a somber gaze. He gave no indication that he'd noticed Henry's approach and replied to his greeting with a curt nod.

"I'm surprised to see you here, Lord Ruthven." Henry locked eyes with the lord and allowed enough power to ensure a reply. "It is well known you do not dance."

"I am here to meet someone."

"Who, if I may be so bold as to ask? I've recently come from the card rooms and may have seen him."

A muscle jumped under the sallow skin of Ruthven's cheek. To Henry's surprise, he looked away, sighed deeply, and said, "It is of no account as he is not yet here."

Impressed by the man's willpower—if unimpressed by his theatrical melancholy—Henry bowed and moved away. The man's sullen disposition and cold, corpse-gray eyes isolated him from the society his wealth and title gave him access to. Could he be taking revenge against those who shunned him by selling secrets to the French? Perhaps. This was not the time, nor the place, for forcing an answer.

Treading a careful path around a cluster of turbaned dowagers—more dangerous amass than a crowd of angry peasants with torches and pitchforks—Henry made his way to the side of a young man he knew from White's and asked for an introduction to Mr. Maxwell Aubrey.

"Good lord, Henry, whatever for?"

Henry smiled disarmingly. "I hear he's a damnably bad card player."

"He is, but if you think to pluck him, you're a year too late or two years too early. He doesn't come into his capital until he's twenty-five and after the chicken incident, his trustees keep a tight hold of the purse strings."

"Chicken incident?"

"That's right. It happened before you came to London. You see, Aubrey fell in with this fellow named Bouchard."

"Yves Bouchard?"

"That's right. Anyway, Bouchard had Aubrey wrapped around his little finger. Dared him to cluck like a chicken in the middle of the dance floor. I thought Mrs. Drummond-Burrell was going to have spasms. Neither Bouchard nor Aubrey were given vouchers for the rest of the Season."

"And this Season?"

He nodded at Aubrey who was leading his partner off the dance floor. "This Season, all is forgiven."

"And Bouchard?" Henry asked.

"Bouchard, too. Although he doesn't seem to be here tonight."

"So Aubrey was wrapped around Bouchard's little finger. *Wrapped tightly enough to spy for the French?* Henry wondered.

The return of a familiar voice diverted his attention. He turned to see Sir William once again playing court to Carmilla. When she giggled and looked away, it only seemed to inspire Sir William the more. Henry moved closer until he could hear her protests. She sounded both flattered and frightened.

Now that's a combination impossible to resist, Henry thought, watching Wyndham respond. With a predator's fluid grace, he deftly inserted himself between them. "I believe this dance is mine." When Carmilla giggled but made no objection, there was nothing Wyndham could do but quietly seethe.

Once on the floor, Henry smiled down into cornflower blue eyes. "I hope you'll forgive me for interfering, Miss Amworth, but Sir William's attentions seemed to be bothering you."

She dropped her gaze to the vicinity of his waistcoat. "Not bothering, but a bit overwhelming. I'm glad of the chance to gather my thoughts."

"I feel I should warn you that he has a sad reputation."

"He *is* a very accomplished flirt."

"He is a confirmed rake, Miss Amworth."

"Do you think he is more than merely flirting, then?" Her voice held a hint of hope.

Immortality, Henry mused, *would not provide time enough to understand women.* Granted, Sir William had been blessed with darkly sardonic good looks and an athletic build, but he was also—the possibility of his being a spy aside—an arrogant, self-serving libertine. Some women were drawn to that kind of danger; he had not thought Carmilla Amworth to be one of them. His gaze dropped to the pulse beating at an ivory temple, and he wondered just how much danger she dared to experience.

Obviously aware that she should be at least attempting conversation, she took a deep breath and blurted, "I heard you saved Captain Evans last night."

Had everyone heard about it? Varney would not be pleased. "It was nothing."

"My maid says that he was set upon by robbers and you saved his life."

"Servants' gossip."

A dimple appeared beside a generous mouth. "Servants usually know."

Considering his own servant, Henry had to admit the truth of that.

"Were they robbers?"

"I didn't know you were so bloodthirsty, Miss Amworth." When she merely giggled and shook her head, he apologized and added, "I don't know what they were. They ran off as I approached."

"Surely Captain Evans knew."

"If he did, he didn't tell me."

"It must have been so exciting." Her voice grew stronger, and her chin rose, exposing the soft flesh of her throat. "There are times I long to just throw aside all this so-called polite society."

I should have fed before I came. After a brief struggle with his reaction, Henry steered the conversation to safer grounds. It wasn't difficult as Carmilla, apparently embarrassed by her brief show of passion, answered only yes and no for the rest of the dance.

As he escorted her off the floor, Wyndham moved possessively toward her. While trying to decide just how far he should extend his protection, Henry saw Aubrey and Ruthven leave the room together. He heard the younger man say "Bouchard" and lost the rest of their conversation in the surrounding noise.

Good lord, are they both involved?

"My dance this time, I believe, Fitzroy." Shooting Henry an obvious warning, Sir William captured Carmilla's hand and began to lead her away. She seemed fascinated by him and he, for his part, clearly intended to have her.

Fully aware that the only way to save the naive young heiress was to claim her himself, Henry reluctantly went after Aubrey and Ruthven.

By the time he reached King Street, the two men were distant shadows, almost hidden by the night. Breathing deeply in an effort to clear his head of the warm, meaty odor of the assembly rooms, Henry followed, his pace calculated to close the distance between them without drawing attention to himself. An experienced hunter knew better than to spook his prey.

He could hear Aubrey talking of a recent race meeting, could hear Ruthven's monosyllabic replies, and heard nothing at all that would link them to the missing document or to Yves Bouchard. Hardly surprising. Only fools would speak of betraying their country so publicly.

When they went into Aubrey's lodgings near Portman Square, Henry wrapped himself in the darkness and climbed to the small balcony off the sitting room. He felt a bit foolish, skulking about like a common house-breaker. Captain Evans' desire to avoid a scandal, while admirable, was becoming irritating.

"Here it is."

"Are you sure?" Ruthven's heart pounded as though he'd been running. It all but drowned out the sound of paper rustling.

"Why would Bouchard lie to me?"

Why, indeed? A door opened, and closed, and Henry was on the street waiting for Ruthven when he emerged from the building. He was about to step forward when a carriage rumbled past, reminding him that, in spite of the advanced hour, the street was far from empty.

Following close on Ruthven's heels—and noting that wherever the dour peer was heading it wasn't toward home—Henry waited until he passed the mouth of a dark and deserted mews, then made his move. With one hand around Ruthven's throat and the other holding him against a rough stone wall, his lips drew back off his teeth in involuntary anticipation of the other man's terror.

To his astonishment, Ruthven merely declared with gloomy emphasis. "Come, Death, strike. Do not keep me waiting any longer."

His own features masked by the night, Henry

frowned. Mouth slightly open to better taste the air, he breathed in an acrid odor he recognized. "You're drunk!" Releasing his grip, he stepped back.

"Although it is none of your business, I am always drunk." Under his customary scowl, Ruthven's dull gray eyes flicked from side to side, searching the shadows.

That explained a great deal about Ruthven's near legendary melancholy, and perhaps it explained something else as well. "Is that why you're spying for France?"

"The only thing I do for France is drink their liquor." The peer drew himself up to his full height. "And Death or not, I resent your implication."

His protest held the ring of truth. "Then what do you want with Yves Bouchard?"

"He said he could get me . . ." All at once he stopped and stared despondently into the night. "That also is none of your business."

Beginning to grow irritated, Henry snarled.

Ruthven pressed himself back against the wall. "I ordered a cask of brandy from him. Don't ask me how he smuggles it through the blockade because I don't know. He was to meet me tonight at Almack's, but he never came."

"What did Maxwell Aubrey give you?"

"Bouchard's address." As the wine once again overcame his fear—imitation willpower, Henry realized—Ruthven's scowl deepened. "I don't believe you *are* Death. You're nothing but a common cutpurse." His tone dripped disdain. "I shall call for the Watch."

"Go right ahead." Henry's hand darted forward, patted Ruthven's vest, and returned clutching Bouchard's address. Slipping the piece of paper into an inner pocket, he stepped back and merged with the night.

Varney would probably insist that Ruthven should die, but Henry suspected that nothing he said would be believed. Besides, if he told everyone he'd met Death in an alley, he wouldn't be far wrong.

As expected, Bouchard was not in his rooms.

And neither, upon returning to Portman Square, was Maxwell Aubrey. Snarling softly to himself, Henry listened to a distant watchman announce it was a fine night. At just past two, it was certainly early enough for Aubrey to have gone to one of his clubs, or to a gaming hall, or to a brothel. Unfortunately, all Henry knew of him was that he was an easily influenced young man. Brow furrowed, he'd half decided to head back toward St. James Street when he heard the crash of breaking branches coming from the park the square enclosed.

Curious, he walked over to the wrought-iron fence and peered up into an immense old oak. Believing himself familiar with every nuance of the night, he was astonished to see Aubrey perched precariously on a swaying limb, arms wrapped tightly around another, face nearly as white as his crumpled cravat.

"What the devil are you doing up there?" Henry demanded, beginning to feel that Captain Evans had sent him on a fool's mission. The night was rapidly taking on all the aspects of high farce.

Wide-eyed gaze searching the darkness for the source of the voice, Aubrey flashed a nervous smile in all directions. "Seeber dared me to spend a night in one of these trees," he explained ingenuously. Then he frowned. "You're not the Watch, are you?"

"No, I'm not the Watch."

"Good. That is, I imagine it would be hard to explain this to the Watch."

"I imagine it would be," Henry repeated dryly.

"You see, it's not as easy as it looks like it would be." He shifted position slightly and squeezed his eyes closed as the branch he sat on bobbed and swayed.

The man was an idiot and obviously not capable of being a French spy. Bouchard would have to be a *greater* idiot to trust so pliable a tool.

"I don't suppose you could help me down."

Henry considered it. "No," he said at last and walked away.

* * *

He found Sir William Wyndham, the last name on the list, and therefore the traitor by default, at White's playing deep basset. Carefully guarding his expression after Viscount Hanely had met him in a dimly lit hall and leaped away in terror, Henry declined all invitations to play. Much like a cat at a mouse hole, he watched and waited for Sir William to leave.

Unfortunately, Sir William was winning.

At five, lips drawn back off his teeth, Henry left the club. He could feel the approaching dawn and had to feed before the day claimed him. He had intended to feed upon Sir William, leaving him weak and easy prey for the captain's men—but Sir William obviously had no intention of leaving the table while his luck held.

The porter who handed Mr. Fitzroy his greatcoat and hat averted his gaze and spent the next hour successfully convincing himself that he hadn't seen what he knew he had.

Walking quickly through the dregs of the night, Henry returned to Albany but, rather than enter his own chambers, he continued to where he could gain access to the suite on the second floor. Entering silently through the large window, he crossed to the bed and stared down at its sleeping occupant.

George Gordon, the sixth Lord Byron, celebrated author of *Childe Harold's Pilgrimage,* was indeed a handsome young man. Henry had never seen him as having the ethereal and poignant beauty described by Caroline Lamb, but then, he realized, Caroline Lamb had never seen the poet with his hair in paper curlers.

His bad mood swept away by the rising Hunger, Henry sat down on the edge of the bed and softly called Byron's name, drawing him up but not entirely out of sleep.

The wide mouth curved into an anticipatory smile, murmuring, "Incubus," without quite waking.

"I don't like you going to see that poet," Varney muttered, carefully setting the buckled shoes to one side. "You're going to end up in trouble there, see if you don't."

"He thinks I'm a dream." Henry ran both hands back through his hair and grinned, remembering the curlers. So much for Byron's claim that the chestnut ringlets were natural. "What could possibly happen?"

"You could end up in one of his stories, that's what." Unable to read, Varney regarded books with a superstitious awe that bordered on fear. "The secret'd be out and some fine day it'd be the stake sure as I'm standing here." The little man drew himself up to his full height and fixed Henry with an indignant glare. "I told you before and I'll tell you again, you got yourself so mixed up in this society thing you're forgetting what you are! You got to stop taking so many chances." His eyes glittered. "Try and remember, most folks don't look kindly on the bloodsucking undead."

"I'll try and remember." Glancing up at his servant over steepled fingers, Henry added, "I've something for you to do today. I need Sir William Wyndham watched. If he's visited by someone named Yves Bouchard, go immediately to Captain Evans; he'll know what to do. If he tries to leave London, stop him."

Brows that crossed above Varney's nose in a continuous line lifted. "How stopped?"

"Stopped. Anything else, I want to be told at sunset."

"So, what did this bloke do that he's to be stopped?" Varney raised his hand lest Henry get the wrong idea. "Not that I won't stop him, mind, in spite of how I feel about you suddenly taking it into your head to track down evil doers. You know me, give me an order and I'll follow it."

"Which is why I found you almost dead in a swamp outside Plassey while the rest of your regiment was *inside* Plassey?"

"Not the same thing at all," the ex-soldier told him, pointedly waiting for the answer to his question.

"He sold out Wellington's army to the French."

Varney grunted. "Stopping's too good for him."

"Sir William Wyndham got a message this afternoon. Don't know what was in it, but he's going to be taking a trip to the coast tonight."

"Damn him!" Henry dragged his shirt over his head. "He's taking the information to Napoleon *himself!*"

Varney shrugged and brushed invisible dust off a green-striped waistcoat. "I don't know about that, but if his coachman's to be trusted, he's heading for the coast right enough, as soon as the moon lights the road."

Henry stood on the steps of Sir William's townhouse, considered his next move and decided the rising moon left him no time to be subtle.

The butler who answered the imperious summons of the polished brass knocker opened his mouth to deny this inopportune visitor entry, but closed it again without making a sound.

"Take me to Sir William," Henry commanded.

Training held, but only just. "Very good, sir. If you would follow me." The butler's hand trembled slightly, but his carefully modulated voice gave no indication that he had just been shown his own mortality. "Sir William is in the library, sir. Through this door here. Shall I announce you?"

With one hand on the indicated door, Henry shook his head. "That won't be necessary. In fact, you should forget I was ever here."

Lost in the surprising dark depths of the visitor's pale eyes, the butler shuddered. "Thank you, sir. I will."

Three sets of branched candelabra lit the library, more than enough for Henry to see that the room held two large leather chairs, a number of hunting trophies, and very few books.

Sir William, dressed for travel in breeches and top

boots, stood leaning on the mantlepiece reading a single sheet of paper. He turned when he heard the door open and scowled when he saw who it was. "Fitzroy! What the devil are you doing here? I told Babcock I was not to be . . ."

Then his voice trailed off as he got a better look at Henry's face. There were a number of men in London he considered to be dangerous, but until this moment, he would not have included Henry Fitzroy among them. Forcing his voice past the growing panic he stammered, "W-what?"

"You dare to ask when you're holding *that*!" A pale hand shot forward to point at the paper in Wyndham's hand.

"This?" Confusion momentarily eclipsed the fear. "What has this to do with you?"

Henry charged across the room, grabbed a double handful of cloth, and slammed the traitor against the wall. "It has everything to do with me!"

"I didn't know! I swear to God I didn't know!" Hanging limp in Henry's grasp, Sir William made no struggle to escape. Every instinct screamed "RUN!" but a last vestige of reason realized he wouldn't get far. "If I'd known you were interested in her . . ."

"Who?"

"Carmilla Amworth."

Sir William crashed to his knees as Henry released him and stepped back. "So that's how you were going to hide it," he growled. "A seduction on your fabled yacht. Was a French boat to meet you in the channel?"

"A French boat?"

"Or were you planning on finding sanctuary with Napoleon? And what of Miss Amworth, compromised both by your lechery and your treason?"

"Treason?"

"Forcing her to marry you would gain you her fortune, but tossing her overboard would remove the only witness." Lips drawn back off his teeth, Henry buried his hand in Sir William's hair and forced his head back. Cravat and collar were thrown to the floor, exposing the muscular column of throat. "I don't know how you convinced her to accompany you, but it doesn't really matter now."

With the last of his strength, Sir William shoved the crumpled piece of paper in Henry's face, his life saved by the faint scent of a familiar perfume clinging to it.

Henry managed to turn aside only because he'd fed at dawn. His left hand clutching the note, his right still holding Sir William's hair, he straightened.

"*. . . I can no longer deny you but it must be tonight for reasons I cannot disclose at this time.*" It was signed, C. Amworth.

Frowning, he looked down into Sir William's face. If Carmilla had insisted that they leave for the yacht tonight, there could be only one answer. "Did Yves Bouchard suggest you seduce Miss Amworth?"

"I do not seduce young woman on the suggestion of acquaintances," Sir William replied as haughtily as possible under the circumstances. "However," he added hurriedly as the hazel eyes locked onto his began to darken, "Bouchard may have mentioned she was not only rich but ripe for the plucking."

So, there was the Bouchard connection. Caught between the two men, Carmilla Amworth was being used by both. By Bouchard to gain access to Wyndham's yacht and therefore France. By Wyndham to gain access to her fortune. And that seemed to be all that Sir William was guilty of. Still frowning, Henry stepped back. "Well, if you didn't steal the document," he growled, "who did?"

"I did." As he turned, Carmilla pointed a small but eminently serviceable pistol at him. "I've been waiting in Sir William's carriage these last few moments and when no one emerged, I let myself in. Stay right where you are, Mr. Fitzroy," she advised, no longer looking either fragile or waiflike. "I am held to be a very good shot." Her calm gaze took in the positions of the two men and she suddenly smiled, dimples appearing in both cheeks. "Were you fighting for my honor?"

Lips pressed into a thin line, Henry bowed his head. "Until I discovered you had none."

The smile disappeared. "I was raised a republican, Mr. Fitzroy, and I find the thought of that fat fool returning to the throne of France to be ultimately distasteful. In time . . ." Her eyes blazed. ". . . I'll help England be rid of her own fat fool."

"You think the English will rise and overthrow the royal family?"

"I know they will."

"If they didn't rise when m . . ." About to say, *my father,* he hastily corrected himself. ". . . when King Henry burned Catholic and Protestant indiscriminately in the street, what makes you think they'll rise now?"

Her delicate chin lifted. "The old ways are finished. It's long past time for things to change."

"And does your uncle believe as you do?"

"My uncle knows nothing. His little niece would come visiting him at his office and little bits of paper would leave with her." The scornful laugh had as much resemblance to the previous giggles as night to day. "I'd love to stand around talking politics with you, but I haven't the time." Her lavender kid glove tightened around the butt of one of Manton's finest. "There'll be a French boat meeting Sir William's yacht very early tomorrow morning, and I have information I must deliver."

"You used me!" Scowling, Sir William got slowly to his feet. "I don't appreciate being used." He took a step forward, but Henry stopped him with a raised hand.

"You're forgetting the pistol."

"The pistol?" Wyndham snorted. "No woman would have the fortitude to kill a man in cold blood."

Remembering how both his half-sisters had held the throne, Henry shook his head. "You'd be surprised. However," he fixed Carmilla with an inquiring stare, "we seem to be at a standstill as you certainly can't shoot both of us."

"True. But I'm sure both of you *gentlemen* . . ." The emphasis was less than complimentary. ". . . will cooperate lest I shoot the other."

"I'm afraid you're going to shoot no one." Suddenly behind her, Henry closed one hand around her wrist and the other around the barrel of the gun. He had moved between one heartbeat and the next; impossible to see, impossible to stop.

"What are you?" Carmilla whispered, her eyes painfully wide in a face blanched of color.

His smile showed teeth. "A patriot." He'd been within a moment of killing Sir William, ripping out his throat and feasting on his life. His anger had been kicked sideways by Miss Amworth's entrance and he supposed he should thank her for preventing an unredeemable faux pas. "Sir William, if you could have your footman go to the house of Captain Charles Evans on Charges Street, I think he'll be pleased to know we've caught his traitor."

". . . so they came and took the lady away, but that still doesn't explain where you've been 'til nearly sunup."

"I was with Sir William. We had unfinished business."

Varney snorted, his disapproval plain. "Oh. It was like that, was it?"

Henry smiled as he remembered the feel of Sir William's hair in his hand and the heat rising off his kneeling body.

Well aware of what the smile meant, Varney snorted again. "And did Sir William ask what you were?"

"Sir William would never be so impolite. He thinks we fought over Carmilla, discovered she was a traitor, drank ourselves nearly senseless, and parted the best of friends." Feeling the sun poised on the horizon, Henry stepped into his bedchamber and turned to close the door on the day. "Besides, Sir William doesn't *want* to know what I am."

* * *

"Got some news for you." Varney worked up a lather on the shaving soap. "Something happened today."

Resplendent in a brocade dressing gown, Henry leaned back in his chair and reached for the razor. "I imagine that something happens every day."

"Well *today,* that Carmilla Amworth slipped her chain and run off."

"She escaped from custody?"

"That's what I said. Seems they underestimated her, her being a lady and all. Still, she's missed her boat, so even if she gets to France, she'll be too late. You figure that's where she's heading?"

"I wouldn't dare to hazard a guess." Henry frowned and wiped the remaining lather off his face. "Is everyone talking about it?"

"That she was a French spy? Not likely, they're all too busy talking about how she snuck out of Lady Glebe's party and into Sir William's carriage." He clucked his tongue. "The upper classes have got dirty minds, that's what I say."

"Are you including me in that analysis?"

Varney snorted. "Ask your poet. All I say about you is that you've got to take more care. So you saved Wellington's army. Good for you. Now . . ." he held out a pair of biscuit-colored pantaloons. ". . . do you think you could act a little more suitable to your condition?"

"I don't recall ever behaving *unsuitably.*"

"Oh, aye, dressing up so fine and dancing and going to the theater and sitting about playing cards at clubs for *gentlemen.*" His emphasis sounded remarkably like that of Carmilla Amworth.

"Perhaps you'd rather I wore grave clothes and we lived in a mausoleum?"

"No, but . . ."

"A drafty castle somewhere in the mountains of eastern Europe?"

Varney sputtered incoherently.

Henry sighed and deftly tied his cravat. "Then let's hear no more about me forgetting who and what I am. I'm very sorry if you wanted someone a little more darkly tragic. A brooding, mythic persona who only emerges to slake his thirst on the fair throats of helpless virgins . . ."

"Here now! None of that!"

"But I'm afraid you're stuck with me." Holding out his arms, he let Varney help him into his jacket. "And I am almost late for an appointment at White's. I promised Sir William a chance to win back his eleven hundred pounds."

His sensibilities obviously crushed, Varney ground his teeth.

"Now, what's the matter?"

The little man shook his head. "It just doesn't seem right that you, with all you could be, should be worried about being late for a card game."

His expression stern, Henry took hold of Varney's chin, and held the servants' gaze with his. "I think *you* forget who I am." His fingertips dimpled stubbled flesh. "I am a Lord of Darkness, a Creature of the Night, an Undead Fiend with Unnatural Appetites, indeed a *Vampyre;* but all of that . . ." His voice grew deeper and Varney began to tremble. ". . . is no excuse for bad manners."

Author's Note:

The real Henry Fitzroy, Duke of Richmond, bastard son of Henry VIII, died at seventeen on July 22nd, 1536, of what modern medicine thinks was probably tuberculosis. Modern medicine, however, has no explanation for why the Duke of Norfolk was instructed to smuggle the body out of St. James's Palace and bury it secretly.

All things considered, who's to say he stayed buried?

The Cards Also Say

Surveying Queen Street West from her favorite perch on the roof of the six-story CITY TV Building, Vicki Nelson fidgeted as she watched the pre-theater crowds spill from trendy restaurants. Usually able to sit, predator-patient, for hours on end, she had no idea why she was suddenly so restless.

Old instincts honed by eight years with the Metropolitan Toronto Police and two years on her own as a PI suggested there was something wrong, something she'd seen or heard. Something was out of place, and it nagged at her subconscious, demanding first recognition then action.

Apparently, observation wouldn't tell her what she needed to know; she had to participate in the night.

Crossing to the rear of the building, she climbed swiftly down the art deco ornamentation until she could drop the last ten feet into the alley below. Barely noticing the familiar stink of old urine, she straightened her clothes and stepped out onto John Street.

A dark-haired young man who'd been leaning on the side of the building straightened and turned toward her.

Hooker, Vicki thought, then, as she drew closer and realized there was nothing of either sex or commerce in the young man's expression, revised her opinion.

"My grandmother wants to see you," he said matter-of-factly as she came along beside him.

Vicki stopped and stared. "To see me?"

"Yeah. You." Running the baby fingernail on his right hand over the fuzzy beginning of a mustache, he avoided her gaze and in a bored tone recited, "Tall, fair, dressed like a man . . ."

Brows raised, Vicki glanced down at her black corduroy jacket, faded jeans, and running shoes.

". . . coming out of the alley behind the white TV station." Finished, he shrugged and added, "Looks like you. Looks like the place. You coming or not?" His posture clearly indicated that he didn't care either way. "She says if you don't want to come with me, I've got to say night walker."

Not night walker as he pronounced it, two separate words, but Nightwalker.

Vampire.

"Do you have a car?"

In answer, he nodded toward an old Camaro parked under the NO PARKING sign, continuing to avoid her gaze so adroitly, it seemed he'd been warned.

They made the trip up Bathurst Street to Bloor in complete silence. Vicki waited until she could ask her questions of someone more likely to know the answers. The young man seemed to have nothing to say.

He stopped the car just past Bloor and Euclid and, oblivious to the horns beginning to blow behind him, jerked his head toward the north side of the street. "In there."

At the other end of the gesture was a small storefront. Painted in brilliant yellow script over a painting of a classic horse-drawn Gypsy caravan were the words: *Madame Luminitsa, Fortune Teller. Sees Your Future in Cards, Palms, or Tea Leaves.* Behind the glass, a crimson curtain kept the curious from attempting to glimpse the future for free.

The door was similarly curtained and held a sign that listed business hours as well as an explanation that Madame Luminitsa dealt only in cash, having seen too many bad credit cards. As Vicki pushed it open and stepped into a small waiting room, she heard a buzzer sound in the depths of the building.

The waiting room reminded her of a baroque doctor's office, with, she noted, glancing down at the glass-topped coffee table, one major exception—the magazines were current. The place was empty not only of customers but also of the person who usually sat behind the official-looking desk in the corner of the room. There were two interior doors: one behind the desk, one in the middle of the back wall. Soft background music with an Eastern European sound, combined with three working incense burners, set the mood.

Vicki sneezed and listened for the nearest heartbeat.

A group in the back of the building caught her attention but couldn't hold it when she became aware of the two lives just behind the back wall. One beat slowly and steadily, the other raced, caught in the grip of some strong emotion. As Vicki listened, the second heartbeat began to calm.

It sounded very nearly post-coital.

"Must've got good news," she muttered, crossing to the desk.

The desktop had nothing on it but a phone and half a pad of yellow legal paper. About to start searching the drawers, Vicki moved quickly away when she heard the second door begin to open.

A slim man with a distinctly receding hairline and slightly protuberant eyes emerged first, a sheet of crumpled yellow paper clutched in one hand. "You don't know what this means to me," he murmured.

"I have a good idea." The middle-aged woman behind him smiled broadly enough to show a gold-capped molar. "I'm pleased that I could help."

"Help?" he repeated. "You've done more than help. You've opened my eyes. I've got to get home and get started."

He rushed past Vicki without seeing her. As the outer door closed behind him, she took a step forward. "Madame Luminitsa, I presume?"

Flowered skirt swirling around her calves, the

woman strode purposefully toward the desk. "Do you have an appointment?"

Vicki shook her head. Under other circumstances, she'd have been amused by the official trappings to what was, after all, an elaborate way to exploit the unlimited ability of people to be self-deluded. "Someone's grandmother wants to see me."

"Ah. So you're the one." She showed no more interest than the original messenger had. "Wait here."

Since it seemed to be the only way she'd find out what was going on, Vicki dropped down onto a corner of the desk and waited while Madame Luminitsa went back into the rear of the building. Although strange things seemed to be afoot, she'd learned to trust her instincts and she didn't think she was in danger.

The Romani, as a culture, were more than willing to exploit the greed and/or stupidity of the *gadje,* or non-Rom, but they were also culturally socialized to avoid violence whenever possible. During the eight years she'd spent on the police force, Vicki had never heard of an incident where one of Toronto's extensive Romani communities had started a fight. Finished a couple, yes, but never started one.

Still, someone here had named her Nightwalker.

When the door opened again, the woman framed within it bore a distinct family resemblance to Madame Luminitsa. There were slight differences in height and weight and coloring—a little shorter, a little rounder, a little grayer—but a casual observer would have had difficulty telling them apart. Vicki was not a casual observer, and she slowly stood as the dark gaze swept over her. The Hunger rose in recognition of a challenging power.

"Good. Now we know who we are, we can put it aside and get on with things." The woman's voice held a faint trace of Eastern Europe. "You'd best come in." She stepped aside, leaving the way to the inner room open.

Curiosity overcoming her instinctive reaction, Vicki

slipped a civilized mask back into place and did as suggested.

The inner room was a quarter the size of the outer. The ceiling had been painted navy blue and sprinkled with day-glo stars. Multicolored curtains fell from the stars to the floor and on each wall an iron bracket supporting a round light fixture thrust through the folds. In the center of the room, taking up most of the available floor space, was a round table draped in red between two painted chairs. Shadows danced in every corner and every fold of fabric.

"Impressive," Vicki acknowledged. "Definitely sets the mood. But I'm not here to have my fortune told."

"We'll see." Indicating the second chair, the woman sat down.

Vicki sat as well. "Your grandson neglected to give me your name."

"You can call me Madame Luminitsa."

"Another one?"

The fortune teller shrugged. "We are all Madame Luminitsa if business is good enough. My sister, our daughters, their daughters . . ."

"You?"

"Not usually."

"Why not?" Vicki asked dryly. "Your predictions don't come true?"

"On the contrary." She folded her hands on the table, the colored stones in the rings that decorated six of eight fingers flashing in the light. "Some people can't take a dump without asking advice—Madame Luminitsa gives them a glimpse of the future they want. I give them the future they're going to get."

Arms crossed, Vicki snorted. "You're telling me you can really see the future?"

"I saw you, Nightwalker. I saw where you'd be this evening. I sent for you and you came."

Which was, undeniably, unpleasantly, true. "For all that, you seem pretty calm about what I am."

"I'm used to seeing what others don't." Her expression darkened again for a moment as though she were gazing at a scene she'd rather not remember, then she shook her head and half-smiled. "If you know your history, Nightwalker—my people and your people have worked together in the past."

Vicki had a sudden vision of Gypsies filling boxes of dirt to keep their master safe on his trip to England. The memory bore the distinctive stamp of an old Hammer film. She returned the half-smile, another fraction of trust gained. "The one who changed me said that Bram Stoker was a hack."

"He got a few things right. The Romani were enslaved in that part of the world for many years and we had masters who made Bram Stoker's count seem like a lovely fellow." Her voice held no bitterness at the history. It was over, done; they'd moved on and wouldn't waste the energy necessary to hold a grudge. "I've seen you're no danger to me, Nightwalker. As for the others . . ." The deliberate pause held a clear warning. ". . . they don't know."

"All right." It was an acknowledgment more than agreement. "So why did you send for me?"

"I saw something."

"In my future?"

"Yes."

Vicki snorted, attempting to ignore the hair lifting off the back of h er neck. "A tall, dark stranger?"

"Yes."

Good cops learned to tell when people were lying. It wasn't a skill vampires needed; no one lied to them. So far, Vicki had been told only the truth—or at least the truth as Madame Luminitsa believed it. Unfortunately, truth tended to be just a tad fluid when spoken Romani to *gadje*.

The other woman sighed. "Would you feel better if I said that I saw a short, fair stranger?"

"Did you?"

"No. The stranger that I saw was tall and dark, and he is dangerous. To you and to my family."

Now this meeting began to make sense. Intensely loyal to their extended families and clans, the Romani would never go to this much trouble for a mere *gadje,* even, or especially, if that *gadje* was a member of the bloodsucking undead. Self-interest, however, Vicki understood. "I'm listening."

"It isn't easy to always see, so I look only enough to keep my family safe. This afternoon I laid out the cards, and I saw you and I saw danger approaching as a tall, dark man. Cliché," she shrugged, "but true. If you fall, this stranger will grow so strong that when he turns his hate on other targets, he will be almost invincible."

"And the danger to you?"

"He hates you because you're different. You haven't hurt him or anyone near him, but neither are you like him." Madame Luminitsa paused, glanced around the room, and spread her hands. "We are also different, and we work hard at keeping it that way. In the old days, we could have taken to the roads, but now we, as much as you, are sitting targets."

"You're sure he's just a man?" Vicki asked, twisting a pinch of the tablecloth between thumb and forefinger. She'd met a demon once and didn't want to again.

"*Just* a man? Men do by choice what demons do by nature."

Vicki'd spent too much time in Violent Crimes to argue with that. "You've got to give me more to go on than tall, dark, and male."

From a pocket in her skirt or perhaps a shelf under the table, Madame Luminitsa pulled out a deck of tarot cards. "I can."

"Oh, come on . . ."

Shuffling the cards with a dexterity that spoke of long practice, the older woman ignored her. She placed the shuffled deck in the center of the table. "With your left hand, cut the cards into three piles to your left," she said.

Vicki stared down at the cards, then up at the fortune teller. "I don't think so."

"Cut the cards if you want to live."

Put like that, it was pretty hard to refuse.

Tarot cards had made a brief surge into popular culture while Vicki'd been a university student. A number of the girls she knew laid out patterns at every opportunity. Vicki'd considered it more important to maintain her average than to take the time to learn the symbolism. She also considered most of the ker-chiefed, sandaled, skirted amateur fortune tellers to be complete flakes. As a history major, she was fully aware of the persecutions the Romani had gone through for centuries, persecutions that had started up with renewed vigor after the fall of the Iron Curtain, and she was at a loss to understand why anyone would consider the life of the caravans to be romantic.

The pattern Madame Luminitsa laid out was a fa-miliar one. "Aren't you supposed to start by picking a card out to stand for me?"

"Do I tell you your business?"

"Uh, no."

"Then don't tell me mine." She laid down the tenth card, set the unused part of the deck carefully to one side, and sat back in her chair, her eyes never leaving the brightly colored rectangles spread out in front of her. "The Three of Swords sets an atmosphere of loss. Reversed, the Emperor covers it; a weak man but one who will take action. In his past, the star reversed; physical or mental illness."

"Wait a minute, I thought this was my reading."

"It's a reading to help you find the stranger before he can strike."

"Oh." Vicki reached into the inside pocket of her jacket for the small notebook and pen. She carried the old massive shoulder bag less and less these days. Somehow a purse, even one of luggage dimensions, just didn't seem vampiric. "Maybe I should be writing this down."

Madame Luminitsa waited until the first three cards had been recorded and then went on. "He has just set aside his material life."

"Fired from his job?"

"I don't know, but now he does other, more spiritual things."

"How can destroying me be spiritual?"

"He believes he's removing evil from the world."

"And what will he believe when he goes after your people?"

"For some, different is enough to be considered evil. He's about to come to a decision; you haven't much time."

"Or much information."

"You're here, in his recent past. I suspect you took his blood and the mental illness kept the shadows you command from blotting the memory. The Page of Swords—here—means he's watching you. Spying, learning your patterns before he strikes."

She remembered the feeling that something was wrong, out of place. "Great. Like I've only ever fed off one tall dark man, unstable and unemployed."

"There's only one watching you."

"That makes me feel so much better."

"Ace of Wands, reversed. He's likely to make one unsuccessful attempt before you're in any actual danger. He's afraid of being alone, and he's created this purpose to fill the void. He has no family. No friends. But look here . . ."

Vicki obediently bent forward.

". . . the Nine of Wands. He has prepared for this. In the final outcome, he is dead to reason. Don't argue with him, stop him."

"Kill him?"

Madame Luminitsa shuffled the cards back into the deck. "That's up to you, Nightwalker."

Tapping her pen against the paper, Vicki glanced over her list. "So I'm looking for a tall, dark, unstable, unemployed, lonely man with sawdust in his cuffs from sharpening stakes, who remembers me feeding from him and has been spying on me ever since. He'll make an attempt he won't carry through all the way, but when push comes to shove, I won't be able to talk him out of destroying me and may have to destroy him first." When she looked up, her eyes had silvered slightly. "How do I know you're not setting me up to destroy an enemy of yours?"

"You don't."

"How do I know you didn't deliberately mislead me so that you can destroy me yourself?"

"You don't."

"So, essentially, what you're saying is, I have to trust that you, and this whole fortune-telling thing, are on the level."

The Romani's eyes reflected bits of silver; the physical manifestation of Vicki's power stopped at the surface. "Yes."

"Vicki, get real! These are Gypsies, they live for the elaborate scam."

"Not this time, Mike." Swiveling out into the room, she tipped back her desk chair and frowned up at him. "Even if your stereotyping was accurate, this wasn't a scam. Madame Luminitsa needs me to protect her family. That's the only possible reason strong enough for her to even deal with me. If my danger wasn't her danger as well, I'd be facing it on my own."

"So she wants something from you."

Beginning to wish she'd never told him how she'd spent her evening, Vicki closed her eyes and counted to ten. "Yes, she does. And so she's no different than any of my other clients who want something from me except that she's paid in full, in advance, by warning me of the danger that I'm in."

"You want to know what danger you're in?" Detective-Sergeant Michael Celluci stopped pacing and turned to glare at the woman in the chair. He'd loved her when they'd been together on the police force, he'd loved her when a degenerative eye disease had forced her to quit a job she'd excelled at and start over as a private investigator, and he'd continued to love her even after she'd become an undead, blood-sucking creature of the night—*but* there were times, and this was one of them, when he wanted to wring her neck. "This fortune teller knows what you are, and what one Gypsy knows, they all do."

"Romani."

"What?"

"Most prefer to be called Romani, not Gypsy."

He threw up his hands. "What difference does that make?"

"Well, let's see . . ." Her voice dripped sarcasm. "How would you like to be called a dumb, bigoted wop?"

Celluci's eyes narrowed and, over the angry pounding of his heart, Vicki could hear him breathing heavily through his nose. "Fine. Romani. Whatever. They still know what you are, and therefore they know you're completely helpless during the day. I want you to move back in with me."

"So you can protect me?"

"Yes!" He spat out the word, defying the reaction he knew she'd have.

To his surprise, there was no explosion.

As much touched as irritated by his concern, Vicki sighed impatiently and said, "Mike, do you honestly think that a plywood box in your basement is safer than this apartment?" The converted warehouse space boasted a barred window, a steel door, industrial strength locks, and an enclosed loft with an access so difficult even Celluci didn't attempt it on his own. The safety features had been designed by a much older vampire who'd made one fatal error— she hadn't realized that the territory was already taken.

Slowly, Celluci sank down onto the arm of the sofa. "No. I don't."

"And it's not like you're home all day."

"I know. It's just . . ."

Vicki rolled her office chair out from under the edge of the loft, stopping only when they were knee to knee. She reached out and pushed an over-long curl of hair back off his face. "I'm not saying that I won't ever move back, Mike, just not now. Not because a mentally unstable, unemployed blood donor thinks he's a modern Van Helsing."

He caught her hand, the skin cool against his palm. "And the Gy . . . the Romani?"

"From what I understand about their culture, Madame Luminitsa's abilities make her a bit of an outsider already, and she won't risk being named *marhime* . . . a kind of social/cultural exile," she added when Mike's brows went up, "by telling her family she's dealing with a vampire."

"All right." Releasing his grip, he pushed her chair far enough away to give him room to stand. "So how do we stop this Van Helsing of yours?"

"I love it when you get all macho," she purred, rubbing her foot up his inseam. Before he could react, she scooted back to the office, the chair's wheels protesting her speed. "According to the cards, he's prepared. You could check with the B&E guys to see if anyone's reported stolen holy water."

"Holy water?"

"Madame Luminitsa said he thinks of me as evil and holy water is one of the traditional, albeit ineffectual, ways to melt a vampire."

"How the hell would someone steal holy water?"

"Don't you ever watch movies, Mike?" She mimed filling a water pistol. "Ask them about communion wafers, too."

"Communion wafers?" He sighed and looked at his watch. "Fine. Whatever. Patterson's on evenings this week and he owes me a favor. It's only a quarter past eleven, so if I leave in the next few minutes, I'll catch him at Headquarters before he heads home."

"Great—I'll make this next bit quick. Since the cards also pointed out that our stalker's recently unemployed, a homicide detective with an open case involving the shooting of two counselors at a Canada Manpower center last month would have a reason to ask for a printout of everyone who'd recently applied for unemployment insurance."

"The guy who did the shooting could've been unemployed for years."

"You don't know that."

"Okay, let's say I come up with a plausible story and get the list—would you recognize the name of a . . ." He paused. This aspect of her life wasn't something they spoke about. Intellectually, Celluci knew he couldn't fulfill all her needs, but he chose to ignore what that actually meant. ". . . dinner companion."

"I don't know. Do you remember what you had for dinner every night for the last month?"

His lip curled into an expression approximating a smile. "Any other time, I'd be pleased you thought so little of them; this time, it's damned inconvenient. If you won't recognize his name, why do you want to see the list?"

"I *might* recognize his name," Vicki corrected. "But mostly I want to see the list to compare it to . . ." She paused and decided Detective-Sergeant Michael Celluci would be happier not knowing about the list she planned on comparing it to.

Unlike the unemployment office, the Queen Street Mental Health Center was open more or less twenty-four hours a day—recent government cutbacks having redefined the word open.

Vicki watched from the shadows as the old woman wearing a plastic hospital bracelet shuffled into the circle of light by the glass doors, cringed as the streetcar went by, pushed a filthy palm against the buzzer, and left it there. She'd been easy enough to find—this part of the city had an embarrassment of riches when it came to the lost—but less than easy to control. Those parts of the human psyche that responded to the danger, to the forbidden sensuality that the vampire represented, were so inaccessible they might as well not have existed. Vicki'd finally given her ten bucks and told her, in words of one syllable, what she needed done.

Sometimes, the old ways worked best.

Eventually, an orderly appeared, shaking his head as if the motion would disconnect the incessant buzzing. Peering through the wired glass, his frown segued into annoyed recognition. "Damn it, Helen," he muttered as he opened the door. "Stop leaning on the fucking buzzer."

Vicki slipped inside while he dealt with the old woman.

When he turned, the door closing behind him, she was there: her eyes silver, her smile very white, the Hunger rising.

"I need you to do me a favor," she said.

He swallowed convulsively as she ran her thumb lightly down the muscles of his throat.

Sometimes, the new ways worked best.

When the approaching dawn drove her home, Vicki carried a list of recent discharges from Queen Street and a similar list from the Clark Institute. All she needed was Celluci's list from UIC to make comparisons. With luck there'd be names in common, names with addresses she could visit until she recognized the distinctive signature of a life she'd fed on.

Her pair of lists were depressingly long and, given the current economic climate in Mike Harris' Ontario, she expected the third to be no shorter. Searching them would take most of a night and checking the names in common could easily take another two or three nights after that.

Unlocking her door, Vicki hoped they'd have the time. Madame Luminitsa had seemed convinced the wacko in the cards was about to make his move.

The apartment was dark, but the shadows were familiar. Nothing lurked in the corners except dust bunnies not quite big enough to be a danger.

After locking and then barring the door with a two by four painted to match the wall—unsophisticated safety measures were often the most effective—Vicki hurried toward the loft, fighting to keep her shoulders from hunching forward as she felt the day creep up behind her. Almost safe within her sanctuary, she looked down and saw the light flashing on her answering machine. She hesitated. The sun inched closer toward the horizon.

"Oh, damn." Unable to let it go, she swung back down to the floor.

"Vicki, Mike. St. Paul's Anglican on Bloor reported a break-in last Tuesday afternoon. The only thing missing was a box of communion wafers. If he drained the holy water as well, they didn't bother reporting it. Looks like you were right." His sigh seemed to take up a good ten seconds of tape. "There's no point in telling you to be careful but could you please . . ."

She couldn't wait for the end of the message. The sun was too close. Throwing herself up and into the loft, she barred that door as well and sank back onto the bed.

The seconds, moving so quickly a moment before, slowed.

There were sounds, all around her, Vicki couldn't remember ever hearing before. Outside, in the alley— was that someone climbing toward her window?

No. Pigeons.

That vibration in the wall—a drill?

No. The distant ring of a neighbor's alarm.

In spite of her vulnerability, she had never faced the dawn wondering if she'd see the dusk—until today. She didn't like the feeling.

"Maybe I *should* move back into Celluci's ba . . ."

Vicki hated spending the day in her clothes. She had a long hot shower to wash away the creases and listened to another message from Celluci suggesting she check out the church as he'd be at work until after midnight. ". . . and don't bother feeding, you can grab a bite when I get there."

"Like *that's* going to spend things up?" she muttered, shrugging into her jacket as the tape rewound. "Feeding from you isn't exactly fast food."

Quite the contrary.

Deciding to grab a snack on the street, or they'd never get to those lists, Vicki set aside the two by four and opened her door. Out in the hallway, key in hand, she stared down at the lower of the two locks. It smelled like latex. Like a glove intended to hide fingerprints.

She jumped as the door opened across the hall.

"Hey, sweetie. Did he scratch the paint?"

"Did who scratch the paint, Lloyd?"

"Well, when I got home this P.M. I saw some guy on his knees foolin' with your lock. I yelled, and he fled." Ebony arms draped in a blue silk kimono, crossed over a well-muscled chest. "I knocked, but you didn't wake up."

"I've told you before, Lloyd, I work nights and I'm a heavy sleeper." It seemed that pretty soon she'd have to reinforce the message. "Can you tell me what this guy looked like?"

Lloyd shrugged. "White guy. Tall, dark, dressed all in black, but not like he was makin' a fashion statement, you know? I didn't get a good look at his face, but I can tell you, I've never seen him before." He paused and suddenly smiled. "I guess he was a tall, dark stranger. Pretty funny, eh?"

"Not really."

"He's likely to make one unsuccessful attempt before you're in any actual danger."

He'd made his attempt.

"The Page of Swords—here—means he's watching you."

He knew what she was, and he knew where she lived.

"Well, that sucks," Vicki muttered, standing on the front step of the converted factory, scanning the street.

Something was out of place, and it nagged at her subconscious, demanding first recognition then action.

At some point during the last few nights, she'd seen him, or been aware of him watching her. A little desperately, she searched for the touch of a life she'd shared, however briefly, but the city defeated her. There were a million lives around and such a tenuous familiarity got lost in the roar.

Another night, she'd have walked to St. Paul's. To-night, she flagged a cab and hoped her watching stranger had to run like hell to keep up.

It had been some years since churches in the city had been able to leave their doors unlocked after dark; penitent souls looking for God had to make do with twenty-four-hour donut shops. Ignoring the big double doors that faced the bright lights of Bloor Street, Vicki slipped around to the back of the old stone building and one of the less obvious entrances. To her surprise, the door was unlocked.

When she pulled it open, she realized why. Choir practice. Keeping to the shadows, she made her way up and into the back of the church. There were bodies in the pews, family and friends of those singing, and, standing off to one side, an elderly minister—or per-haps St. Paul's was high enough Anglican that they called him a priest.

Vicki waited until the hymn ended, then tapped the minister on the shoulder and asked if she could have a quiet word. She used only enough power to get the information she wanted—when he assumed she was with the police, she encouraged him to think it.

The communion wafers had been kept in a locked cupboard in the church office. Time and use had erased any scent Vicki might have recognized.

"No, nothing else," the minister said confidently when she asked if anything else had been taken.

"What about holy water?"

He glanced up at her in some surprise. "Funny you should mention that." Relocking the cupboard, he led the way out of the office. "We had a baptism on Thursday evening—three families, two babies and an adult—or I might never have noticed. When I took the lid off the font, just before the service, the water level was lower than it should have been—I knew because I'd been the one to fill it, you see—and I found a cuff button caught on the lip." Opening the door to his own office, he crossed to the desk. "It's a heavy lid and anyone trying to scoop the water out, for heaven only knows what reason, would have to hold it up one-handed. Easy enough to get your shirt caught, I imagine. Ah, here it is."

Plucking a white button out of an empty ashtray, he turned and dropped it in Vicki's palm. "The sad thing is, you know, this probably makes the thief one of ours."

"Why?"

"Well, the Catholics keep holy water by the door; it's a whole lot easier to get to. If he went to all this trouble, he was probably on familiar ground. Will that button help you catch him, do you think?"

Vicki smiled, forgetting for a moment the effect it was likely to have. "Oh, yes, I think it will."

She had the cab wait out front while she ran into her apartment for the pair of lists, then had it drop her off in front of Madame Luminitsa's.

Which was closed.

Fortunately, there were lights on upstairs and there could be no mistaking the unique signature of the fortune teller's life. Fully aware she was not likely to be welcomed with open arms and not really caring, Vicki went around back.

She'd never seen so many large cars in so many states of disrepair as were parked in the alley that theoretically provided delivery access for the stores. Squeezing between an old blue delivery van and a cream-colored caddy, she stood at the door and listened: eight heartbeats, upstairs and down, three of them children, one of them the woman she was looking for. There were a number of ways she could gain an audience—Stoker had been wrong about that, she no more needed to be invited in than an encyclopedia salesman—but, deciding it might be best to cause the least amount of offense, she merely knocked on the door.

The man who opened it was large. Not tall exactly, nor exactly fat—large. A drooping mustache, almost too black to be real, covered his upper lip and he stroked it with the little finger of his right hand as he looked her up and down, waiting for her to speak.

"I'm looking for Madame Luminitsa," Vicki told him, masks carefully in place. "It's very important."

"Madame Luminitsa is not available. The shop is closed."

She could feel the Hunger beginning to rise, remembered she'd intended to feed and hadn't. "I saw her last night; she sent for me."

"Ah. You." His expression became frankly speculative, and Vicki wondered just how much Madame Luminitsa *had* told her family. Without turning his head, he raised his voice. "One of you, fetch your grandmother."

Vicki heard a chair pushed out and the sound of small feet running up a flight of stairs. "Thank you."

He shrugged. "She may not come. In the meantime, do you own a car?"

"Uh, no."

"Then I can sell you one of these." An expansive gesture and a broad smile reserved for prospective customers indicated the vehicles crowding the alley. "You won't find a better price in all of Toronto, and I will personally vouch for the quality of each and every one." A huge hand reached out and slapped the hood of the blue van. "Brand new engine, eight cylinders, more power than . . ."

"Look, I'm not interested." Not unless that tall, dark stranger gave her a chance to run him over.

"Later then, after the cards have been played out."

A small, familiar hand covered in rings reached out into the doorway and shoved the big man aside. He glanced down at the woman Vicki knew as Madame

Luminitsa and hurriedly stepped back into the building, closing the door behind him.

"You haven't stopped him," the fortune teller said bluntly.

"Give me a break," Vicki snorted. "I have to find him first. And I think you can help me with that."

"The cards . . ."

"Not the cards." She pulled the lists from her shoulder bag and fished the button out of a pocket. "This was his. If his name's here, shouldn't it help you find him?"

The dark brows rose. "You watch too much television, Nightwalker." But she took the pile of fanfold and the button. "Has he made his first attempt?"

"Yeah. He has."

"Then there's a need to hurry."

"No shit, Sherlock," Vicki muttered as the fortune teller slipped back inside.

She acted as though she hadn't heard, declaring imperiously as the door closed, "I'll let you know what I find."

The door was unlocked, but since Vicki could hear Celluci's heartbeat inside her apartment, she wasn't concerned. She *was* surprised to hear another life besides his, both hearts beating hard and fast. They'd obviously been arguing; not an unusual occurrence around the detective.

He'd probably pulled a late duty and, when she hadn't answered his calls, had thought she was in trouble and brought his partner in with him for backup, just in case. It wasn't hard for Vicki to follow his logic. If they were too late to save her, explanations wouldn't matter. If they were in time, she could easily clear up the confusion he'd caused poor Detective-Sergeant Graham.

Stepping into the apartment, she froze just over the threshold, eyes widening in disbelief. "You've got to be kidding."

"Snuck up on me in the parking lot," Celluci growled, glaring up at the man holding his own gun to his head. "Shoved a pad of chloroform under my nose and jabbed me with a pin so I'd inhale." Muscles strained as he fought to free his hands from the frame of the chair. "Used my own goddamed handcuffs, too."

"Shut up! Both of you!" He was probably in his midforties, with short black hair and a beard lightly dusted with gray, tall enough from the fortune teller's point of view. White showed all around the brown eyes locked on Vicki's face. His free hand pointed toward the door, trembling slightly with the effect of strong emotions. "Close it."

Without turning, she pushed it shut, gently so that the latch didn't quite catch; then she let the Hunger rise. He'd made a big mistake not attacking her in the day when she was vulnerable. Her eyes grew paler than his, and her voice went past command to compulsion. "Let him go."

Celluci shuddered, but the man with the gun only laughed shrilly. "You have no power over me! You never have! You never will!" He met her gaze and, even through the Hunger, she saw that he was right. Like the woman she'd used to gain access to Queen Street, he had no levels of darkness or desire she could touch. Everything inside his head had been locked tightly away, and she didn't have the key. She couldn't command him, so in spite of Madame Luminitsa's belief that she couldn't reason with him, she reined in the Hunger and let the silver fade from her eyes.

"Let him go," she said again. "You have me."

"But I can't keep you without him." The muzzle of the gun dug a circle into Celluci's cheek. "You can't leave, or I'll blow his freakin' head off."

She'd forgotten that she had another vulnerability besides the day. "If you kill him, I'll rip your living heart out of your chest, and I'll make you eat it while you . . ."

"Vicki."

He laughed again as Celluci protested. "You can't get to me, before I can pull the trigger. As long as I have him, I have you."

"So we have a standoff," she said. The silver rose unbidden to her eyes. " Do you think you can out-wait me?"

His teeth flashed in the shadow of his beard. "I know I can. I only have to wait until dawn."

And he would, too. It was the one certainty Vicki could read in his eyes. She took an involuntary step forward.

He lifted a bright green water pistol. "Hold it right there, or I'll shoot."

"I don't think so." She took another step.

The holy water hit her full in the face. He was a good shot, she had to give him that— although under the circumstances, there wasn't much chance of him missing the target that mattered. Wiping the water from her eyes, she growled, "If this is how you plan to kill me, there's a flaw in the plan."

Appalled that the water hadn't had its intended ef-fect, he recovered quickly. Throwing the plastic pistol onto the sofa, he reached down beside him and brought up a rough-hewn wooden stake. "The water was only intended to slow you down. This is what I'll kill you with."

Celluci cursed and began to struggle again.

The man with the gun ignored him, merely keeping the muzzle pressed tight into his face.

Vicki had no idea of how much damage she could take and survive but a stake through the heart had to count as a mortal wound, especially since he seemed to be the type to finish the job with a beheading and a mouthful of garlic. "What happens *after* I'm dead?"

"After?" He looked confused. "Then you'll be dead. And it'll be over." He checked his watch. "Less than five hours."

Desperately trying to remember everything she'd ever learned about defusing a hostage situation, Vicki took a deep breath and spread her arms, trying to appear as nonthreatening as possible. "Since we're going to be together for those five hours," she said quietly, forcing her lips down over her teeth, "why don't you explain why you've decided to kill me? I've never hurt you."

"You don't remember me, do you?"

"Not remember as such, no." She could tell that she'd fed from him and how long ago, but that was all.

"Do you spread your evil over so many?"

"What evil?" Vicki asked, trying to keep her tone level. It wasn't easy when all she could think of was rushing forward and ripping the hand holding the gun right off the end of his arm.

"You are evil by existing!" Tears glimmered against his lower lids and spilled over to vanish in his beard. "You mock their deaths by not dying."

"The Three of Swords sets an atmosphere of loss."

"Whose deaths?"

"My Angela, my Sandi."

Vicki exchanged a puzzled look with Celluci. "Whoever they are, I'm sorry for your loss, but I didn't kill them."

"Of course you didn't kill them." He had to swallow sobs before he could go on. In spite of his anguish, the hand holding the gun never wavered. "It was a car accident. They died and were buried, and now the worms devour their flesh. But you!" His voice rose to a shriek. "You live on, mocking their death with infinity. You will never die." Drawing in a long shuddering breath, he checked his watch again. "God sent you to me and gave me the power to resist you, so I could kill you and set things right."

"God doesn't work that way," Celluci objected.

His smile was almost beatific. "Mine does."

Uncertain of where to go next, Vicki was astonished to hear footsteps stop outside her door. A soft touch eased it open just enough for a breath to pass through.

"Nightwalker, his name is James Wause."

Then the footsteps went away again.

There was power in a name. Power enough to reach

through the madness? Vicki didn't know, but it was their only chance. She let the Hunger rise again, this time let it push away the masks of civilization, and when she spoke, her voice had all the primal cadences of a storm.

"James Wause."

He jerked and shook his head. "No."

She caught his gaze with hers, saw the silver reflected in the dilated pupils as his madness kept her out, then saw it abruptly vanish as she called his name again, and it gave her the key to the locked places inside. The cards had said she couldn't reason with him, so she stopped trying. She called his name a third and final time. When he crumpled forward, she caught him. When he lifted his chin, she brought her teeth down to his throat.

"Vicki."

There was power in a name.

But his blood throbbed warm and red beneath his skin, and sobbing in a combination of sorrow and ecstasy, he was begging her to take him.

"Vicki, no."

More importantly, he had threatened one of hers.

"Vicki! Hey!" Celluci head-butted her in the elbow, about all the contact the handcuffs allowed. "Stop it! Now."

There was also power in the sheer pigheaded unwillingness that refused to allow her to lose the humanity she had remaining. Forcing the Hunger back under fingertip control, she dropped the man she held and turned to the one beside her. The cards hadn't counted on Detective-Sergeant Michael Celluci.

Ignoring the Hunger still in her expression, he snorted. "Nice you remembered I'm here. Now do you think you could do something about the nine millimeter automatic—with, I'd like to add, the safety off— that Mr. Wause dropped into my lap?"

Later, after Celluci had been released and James Wause laid out on the sofa, put to sleep by a surprisingly gentle command, Vicki leaned against the loft support and tried not think of how close it had all come to ending.

When Celluci picked up the phone, she reached out and closed her hand around his wrist. "What are you doing?"

He looked at her, sighed, and set the receiver back in its cradle. "No police, right?"

"Would the courts understand what I am any better than he did?" She nodded toward Wause who stirred in his sleep as though aware of her regard.

Celluci sighed again and gathered her into the circle of his arms. "All right," he said, resting his cheek against her hair. "What do we do with him?"

"I've got an idea."

This time the back door was locked, but Vicki quickly picked the lock, slung James Wause over her shoulder, and carried him into the church. Celluci had wanted to come, but she'd made him wait in the car.

Laying him out in a front pew, she tucked the box of unused communion wafers under his hands and stepped back. His confession would be short a few details—this time she'd successfully removed all memory of her existence from his mind—but she hoped she'd opened the way for him to get the help he needed to cope with his grief.

"The vampire as therapist," she sighed. She nodded toward the altar as she passed. "If he's one of yours, you deal with him."

It didn't surprise her to see the beat-up old Camaro out in the church parking lot when she emerged. Lifting a hand to let Celluci know he should stay where he was, she walked over to the passenger side door.

"Did the cards tell you I'd be here?"

Madame Luminitsa nodded toward the church. "You gave him to God?"

"Seems like it."

"Alive."

"Didn't the cards say?"

"The cards weren't sure."

On the other side of the car, the grandson snorted. Both women ignored him.

"Did the cards tell you where I lived?" Vicki asked.

"If they did, are you complaining?"

Without his name, she'd have never stopped him. "No. I guess I'm not."

"Good. You've less blood on your hands than I feared," the fortune teller murmured, taking Vicki's hands in hers and turning them. "Some day, I'll have to read your palms."

Vicki glanced over at Celluci, who was making it plain he wasn't going to wait patiently much longer. "I'll bet I have a really long life line."

An ebony brow rose as, across the parking lot, the car door opened. "How much?"

The Vengeful Spirit of Lake Nepeakea

"Camping?"

"Why sound so amazed?" Dragging the old turquoise cooler behind her, Vicki Nelson, once one of Toronto's finest and currently the city's most successful paranormal investigator, backed out of Mike Celluci's crawlspace.

"Why? Maybe because you've never been camping in your life. Maybe because your idea of roughing it is a hotel without room service. Maybe . . ." He moved just far enough for Vicki to get by then followed her out into the rec room. ". . . because you're a . . ."

"A?" Setting the cooler down beside two sleeping bags and a pair of ancient swim fins, she turned to face him. "A *what*, Mike?" Gray eyes silvered.

"Stop it."

Grinning, she turned her attention back to the cooler. "Besides, I won't be on vacation, I'll be working. You'll be the one enjoying the great outdoors."

"Vicki, my idea of the great outdoors is going to the Skydome for a Jays game."

"No one's forcing you to come." Setting the lid to one side, she curled her nose at the smell coming out of the cooler's depths. "When was the last time you used this thing?"

"Police picnic, 1992. Why?"

She turned it up on its end. The desiccated body of a mouse rolled out, bounced twice, and came to rest with its sightless little eyes staring up at Celluci. "I think you need to buy a new cooler."

"I think I need a better explanation than *'I've got a great way for you to use up your long weekend,'* " he sighed, kicking the tiny corpse under the rec room couch.

"So this developer from Toronto, Stuart Gordon, bought an old lodge on the shores of Lake Nepeakea and he wants to build a rustic timeshare resort so junior executives can relax in the woods. Unfortunately, one of the surveyors disappeared and local opinion seems to be that he's pissed off the lake's protective spirit . . ."

"The what?"

Vicki pulled out to pass a truck and deftly reinserted the van back into her own lane before replying. "The protective spirit. You know, the sort of thing that rises out of the lake to vanquish evil." A quick glance toward the passenger seat brought her brows in. "Mike, are you all right? You're going to leave permanent finger marks in the dashboard."

He shook his head. The truckload of logs coming down from northern Ontario had missed them by inches. Feet at the very most. *All right, maybe meters but not very many of them.* When they'd left the city, just after sunset, it had seemed logical that Vicki, with her better night sight, should drive. He was regretting that logic now, but realizing he didn't have a hope in hell of gaining control of the vehicle, he tried to force himself to relax. "The speed limit isn't just a good idea," he growled through clenched teeth, "it's the law."

She grinned, her teeth very white in the darkness. "You didn't use to be this nervous."

"I didn't use to have cause." His fingers wouldn't release their grip so he left them where they were. "So this missing surveyor, what did he . . ."

"She."

". . . she do to piss off the protective spirit?"

"Nothing much. She was just working for Stuart Gordon."

"The same Stuart Gordon you're working for."

"The very one."

Right. Celluci stared out at the trees and tried not to think about how fast they were passing. *Vicki Nelson against the protective spirit of Lake Nepeakea. That's one for pay per view . . .*

"This is the place."

"No. In order for this to be 'the place' there'd have to be something here. It has to be *'a place'* before it can be *'the place'.*"

"I hate to admit it," Vicki muttered, leaning forward and peering over the arc of the steering wheel, "but you've got a point." They'd gone through the village of Dulvie, turned right at the ruined barn and followed the faded signs to The Lodge. The road, if the rutted lanes of the last few kilometers could be called a road, had ended, as per the directions she'd received, in a small gravel parking lot—or more specifically in a hard-packed rectangular area that could now be called a parking lot because she'd stopped her van on it. "He said you could see the lodge from here."

Celluci snorted. "Maybe *you* can."

"No. I can't. All I can see are trees." At least she assumed they were trees; the high contrast between the area her headlights covered and the total darkness beyond made it difficult to tell for sure. Silently calling herself several kinds of fool, she switched off the lights. The shadows separated into half a dozen large evergreens and the silhouette of a roof steeply angled to shed snow.

Since it seemed they'd arrived, Vicki shut off the engine. After a heartbeat's silence, the night exploded into a cacophony of discordant noise. Hands over sensitive ears, she sank back into the seat. "What the hell is that?"

"Horny frogs."

"How do you know?" she demanded.

He gave her a superior smile. "PBS."

"Oh." They sat there for a moment, listening to the frogs. "The creatures of the night," Vicki sighed, "what music they make." Snorting derisively, she got out of the van. "Somehow, I expected the middle of nowhere to be a lot quieter."

Stuart Gordon had sent Vicki the key to the lodge's back door; once she switched on the main breaker, they found themselves in a modern stainless steel kitchen that wouldn't have looked out of place in any small, trendy restaurant back in Toronto. The sudden hum of the refrigerator turning on momentarily drowned out the frogs and both Vicki and Celluci relaxed.

"So now what?" he asked.

"Now we unpack your food from the cooler, we find you a room, and we make the most of the short time we have until dawn."

"And when does Mr. Gordon arrive?"

"Tomorrow evening. Don't worry, I'll be up."

"And I'm supposed to do what, tomorrow in the daytime?"

"I'll leave my notes out. I'm sure something'll occur to you."

"I thought I was on vacation."

"Then do what you usually do on vacation."

"Your footwork." He folded his arms. "And on my last vacation—which was also your idea—I almost lost a kidney."

Closing the refrigerator door, Vicki crossed the room between one heartbeat and the next. Leaning into him, their bodies touching between ankle and chest, she smiled into his eyes and pushed the long curl of hair back off of his forehead. "Don't worry, I'll protect you from the spirit of the lake. I have no intention of sharing you with another legendary being."

"Legendary?" He couldn't stop a smile. "Think highly of yourself, don't you?"

*   *   *

"Are you sure you'll be safe in the van?"

"Stop fussing. You know I'll be fine." Pulling her jeans up over her hips, she stared out the window and shook her head. "There's a whole lot of nothing out there."

From the bed, Celluci could see a patch of stars and the top of one of the evergreens. "True enough."

"And I really don't like it."

"Then why are we here?"

"Stuart Gordon just kept talking. I don't even remember saying yes but the next thing I knew, I'd agreed to do the job."

"He pressured you?" Celluci's emphasis on the final pronoun made it quite clear that he hadn't believed such a thing was possible.

"Not pressured, no. Convinced with extreme prejudice."

"He sounds like a prince."

"Yeah? Well, so was Machiavelli." Dressed, she leaned over the bed and kissed him lightly. "Want to hear something romantic? When the day claims me, yours will be the only life I'll be able to feel."

"Romantic?" His breathing quickened as she licked at the tiny puncture wounds on his wrist. "I feel like a box luuu . . . ouch! All right. It's romantic."

Although she'd tried to keep her voice light when she'd mentioned it to Celluci, Vicki really *didn't* like the great outdoors. Maybe it was because she understood the wilderness of glass and concrete and needed the anonymity of three million lives packed tightly around hers. Standing by the van, she swept her gaze from the first hints of dawn to the last lingering shadows of night and couldn't help feeling excluded, that there was something beyond what she could see that she wasn't a part of. She doubted Stuart Gordon's junior executives would feel a part of it either and wondered why anyone would want to build a resort in the midst of such otherness.

The frogs had stopped trying to get laid and the silence seemed to be waiting for something.

Waiting . . .

Vicki glanced toward Lake Nepeakea. It lay like a silver mirror down at the bottom of a rocky slope. Not a ripple broke the surface. Barely a mile away, a perfect reflection brought the opposite shore closer still.

Waiting . . .

Whippor-will!

Vicki winced at the sudden, piercing sound and got into the van. After locking both outer and inner doors, she stripped quickly—if she were found during the day, naked would be the least of her problems—laid down between the high, padded sides of the narrow bed and waited for the dawn. The birdcall, repeated with Chinese water torture frequency, cut its way through special seals and interior walls.

"Man, that's annoying," she muttered, linking her fingers over her stomach. "I wonder if Celluci can sleep through . . ."

As soon as he heard the van door close, Celluci fell into a dreamless sleep that lasted until just past noon. When he woke, he stared up at the inside of the roof and wondered where he was. The rough lumber looked like it'd been coated in creosote in the far distant past.

"No insulation, hate to be here in the winter . . ."

Then he remembered where *here* was and came fully awake.

Vicki had dragged him out to a wilderness lodge, north of Georgian Bay, to hunt for the local and apparently homicidal protective lake spirit.

A few moments later, his sleeping bag neatly rolled on the end of the old iron bed, he was in the kitchen making a pot of coffee. That kind of a realization upon waking needed caffeine.

On the counter next to the coffeemaker, right where he'd be certain to find it first thing, he found a file

labeled LAKE NEPEAKEA in Vicki's unmistakable
handwriting. The first few pages of glossy card stock
had been clearly sent by Stuart Gordon along with the
key. An artist's conception of the timeshare resort,
they showed a large L-shaped building where the
lodge now stood and three dozen "cottages" scattered
through the woods, front doors linked by broad gravel
paths. Apparently, the guests would commute out to
their personal chalets by golf cart.

"Which they can also use on . . ." Celluci turned
the page and shook his head in disbelief. ". . . the
nine-hole golf course." Clearly, a large part of Mr.
Gordon's building plan involved bulldozers. And right
after the bulldozers would come the cappuccino. He
shuddered.

The next few pages were clipped together and
turned out to be photocopies of newspaper articles
covering the disappearance of the surveyor. She'd
been working with her partner in the late evening,
trying to finish up a particularly marshy bit of shore
destined to be filled in and paved over for tennis
courts, when, according to her partner, she'd stepped
back into the mud, announced something had moved
under her foot, lost her balance, fell, screamed, and
disappeared. The OPP, aided by local volunteers, had
set up an extensive search but she hadn't been found.
Since the area was usually avoided because of the
sinkholes, sinkholes a distraught Stuart Gordon swore
he knew nothing about—"Probably distraught about
having to move his tennis courts," Celluci muttered—
the official verdict allowed that she'd probably stepped
in one and been sucked under the mud.

The headline on the next page declared *DEVEL-
OPER ANGERS SPIRIT,* and in slightly smaller type,
Surveyor Pays the Price. The picture showed an elderly woman with long gray braids and a hawklike
profile staring enigmatically out over the water. First
impressions suggested a First Nations elder. In actually
reading the text, however, Celluci discovered that
Mary Joseph had moved out to Dulvie from Toronto

in 1995 and had become, in the years since, the self-proclaimed keeper of local myth. According to Ms. Joseph, although there had been many sightings over the years, there had been only two other occasions when the spirit of the lake had felt threatened enough to kill. *"It protests the lake,"* she was quoted as saying, *"from those who would disturb its peace."*

"Two weeks ago," Celluci noted, checking the date. "Tragic but hardly a reason for Stuart Gordon to go to the effort of convincing Vicki to leave the city."

The final photocopy included a close-up of a car door that looked like it had been splashed with acid. *SPIRIT ATTACKS DEVELOPER'S VEHICLE.* During the night of May 13th, the protector of Lake Nepeakea had crawled up into the parking lot of the lodge and secreted something corrosive and distinctly fishy against Stuart Gordon's brand new Isuzu Trooper. *A trail of dead bracken, a little over a foot wide and smelling strongly of rotting fish, leads back to the lake.* Mary Joseph seemed convinced it was a manifestation of the spirit, the local police were looking for anyone who might have information about the vandalism, and Stuart Gordon announced he was bringing in a special investigator from Toronto to settle it once and for all.

It was entirely probable that the surveyor had stepped into a mud hole and that local vandals were using the legends of the spirit against an unpopular developer. Entirely probable. But living with Vicki had forced Mike Celluci to deal with half a dozen improbable things every morning before breakfast so, mug in hand, he headed outside to investigate the crime scene.

Because of the screen of evergreens—although given their size barricade was probably the more descriptive word—the parking lot couldn't be seen from the lodge. Considering the impenetrable appearance of the overlapping branches, Celluci was willing to bet that not even light would get through. The spirit could have done anything it wanted to, up to and including changing the oil, in perfect secrecy.

Brushing one or two small insects away from his face, Celluci found the path they'd used the night before and followed it. By the time he reached the van, the one or two insects had become twenty-nine or thirty and he felt the first bite on the back of his neck. When he slapped the spot, his fingers came away dotted with blood.

"Vicki's not going to be happy about that," he grinned, wiping it off on his jeans. By the second and third bites, he'd stopped grinning. By the fourth and fifth, he really didn't give a damn what Vicki thought. By the time he'd stopped counting, he was running for the lake, hoping that the breeze he could see stirring its surface would be enough to blow the little bastards away.

The faint but unmistakable scent of rotting fish rose from the dead bracken crushed under his pounding feet and he realized that he was using the path made by the manifestation. It was about two feet wide and lead down an uncomfortably steep slope from the parking lot to the lake. But not exactly all the way to the lake. The path ended about three feet above the water on a granite ledge.

Swearing, mostly at Vicki, Celluci threw himself backwards, somehow managing to save both his coffee and himself from taking an unexpected swim. The following cloud of insects effortlessly matched the move. A quick glance through the bugs showed the ledge tapering off to the right. He bounded down it to the water's edge and found himself standing on a small, man-made beach staring at a floating dock that stretched out maybe fifteen feet into the lake. Proximity to the water *had* seemed to discourage the swarm, so he headed for the dock, hoping that the breeze would be stronger fifteen feet out.

It was. Flicking a few bodies out of his coffee, Celluci took a long grateful drink and turned to look back up at the lodge. Studying the path he'd taken, he was amazed he hadn't broken an ankle and had to admit a certain appreciation for who or what had created it.

A graying staircase made of split logs offered a more conventional way to the water and the tiny patch of gritty sand, held in place by a stone wall. Stuart Gordon's plans had included a much larger beach and had replaced the old wooden dock with three concrete piers.

"One for papa bear, one for mama bear, and one for baby bear," Celluci mused, shuffling around on the gently rocking platform until he faced the water. Not so far away, the far shore was an unbroken wall of trees. He didn't know if there *were* bears in this part of the province, but there was certainly bathroom facilities for any number of them. Letting the breeze push his hair back off his face, he took another swallow of rapidly cooling coffee and listened to the silence. It was unnerving.

The sudden roar of a motorboat came as a welcome relief. Watching it bounce its way up the lake, he considered how far the sound carried and made a mental note to close the window should Vicki spend any significant portion of the night with him.

The moment distance allowed, the boat's driver waved over the edge of the cracked windshield and, in a great, banked turn that sprayed a huge fantail of water out behind him, headed toward the exact spot where Celluci stood. Celluci's fingers tightened around the handle of the mug, but he held his ground. Still turning, the driver cut his engines and drifted the last few meters to the dock. As empty bleach bottles slowly crumpled under the gentle impact, he jumped out and tied off his bowline.

"Frank Patton," he said, straightening from the cleat and holding out a callused hand. "You must be the guy that developer's brought in from the city to capture the spirit of the lake."

"Detective Sergeant Mike Celluci." His own age or a little younger, Frank Patton had a workingman's grip that was just a little too forceful. Celluci returned pressure for pressure. "And I'm just spending a long weekend in the woods."

Patton's dark brows drew down. "But I thought . . ."

"You thought I was some weirdo psychic you could impress by crushing his fingers." The other man looked down at their joined hands and had the grace to flush. As he released his hold, so did Celluci. He'd played this game too often to lose at it. "I suggest, if you get the chance to meet the actual investigator, you don't come on quite so strong. She's liable to feed you your preconceptions."

"She's . . ."

"Asleep right now. We got in late and she's likely to be up . . . investigating tonight."

"Yeah. Right." Flexing his fingers, Patton stared down at the toes of his workboots. "It's just, you know, we heard that, well . . ." Sucking in a deep breath, he looked up and grinned. "Oh hell, talk about getting off on the wrong foot. Can I get you a beer, Detective?"

Celluci glanced over at the styrofoam cooler in the back of the boat and was tempted for a moment. As sweat rolled painfully into the bug bites on the back of his neck, he remembered just how good a cold beer could taste. "No, thanks," he sighed with a disgusted glare into his mug. "I've, uh, still got coffee."

To his surprise, Patton nodded and asked, "How long've you been dry? My brother-in-law gets that exact same look when some damn fool offers him a drink on a hot almost-summer afternoon," he explained as Celluci stared at him in astonishment. "Goes to AA meetings in Bigwood twice a week."

Remembered all the bottles he'd climbed into during those long months Vicki had been gone, Celluci shrugged. "About two years now—give or take."

"I got generic cola . . ."

He dumped the dregs of cold, bug-infested coffee into the lake. The Ministry of Natural Resources could kiss his ass. "Love one," he said.

"So essentially everyone in town and everyone who owns property around the lake and everyone in a

hundred-kilometer radius has reason to want Stuart
Gordon gone."

"Essentially," Celluci agreed, tossing a gnawed
chicken bone aside and pulling another piece out of
the bucket. He'd waited to eat until Vicki got up,
maintaining the illusion that it was a ritual they continued to share. "According to Frank Patton, he hasn't
endeared himself to his new neighbors. This place
used to belong to an Anne Kellough who . . . What?"

Vicki frowned and leaned toward him. "You're covered in bites."

"Tell me about it." The reminder brought his hand
up to scratch at the back of his neck. "You know
what Nepeakea means? It's an old Indian word that
translates as 'I'm fucking sick of being eaten alive by
black flies; let's get the hell out of here.' "

"Those old Indians could get a lot of mileage out
of a word."

Celluci snorted. "Tell me about it."

"Anne Kellough?"

"What, not even one 'poor sweet baby'?"

Stretching out her leg under the table, she ran her
foot up the inseam of his jeans. "Poor sweet baby."

"That'd be a lot more effective if you weren't wearing hiking boots." Her laugh was one of the things
that hadn't changed when she had. Her smile was
too white and too sharp and it made too many new
promises, but her laugh remained fully human. He
waited until she finished, chewing, swallowing, con-
gratulating himself for evoking it, then said, "Anne
Kellough ran this place as sort of a therapy camp.
Last summer, after ignoring her for 13 years, the
Ministry of Health people came down on her kitchen.
Renovations cost more than she thought, the bank
foreclosed, and Stuart Gordon bought it twenty minutes later."

"That explains why she wants him gone—what
about everyone else?"

"Lifestyle."

"They think he's gay?"

"Not his, theirs. The people who live out here, down in the village and around the lake—while not adverse to taking the occasional tourist for everything they can get—like the quiet, they like the solitude and, God help them, they even like the woods. The boys who run the hunting and fishing camp at the west end of the lake . . ."

"Boys?"

"I'm quoting here. The boys," he repeated, with emphasis, "say Gordon's development will kill the fish and scare off the game. He nearly got his ass kicked by one of them, Pete Wegler, down at the local gas station and then got tossed out on said ass by the owner when he called the place quaint."

"In the sort of tone that adds, 'and a Starbucks would be a big improvement'?" When Celluci raised a brow, she shrugged. "I've spoken to him, it's not that much of an extrapolation."

"Yeah, exactly that sort of tone. Frank also told me that people with kids are concerned about the increase in traffic right through the center of the village."

"Afraid they'll start losing children and pets under expensive sport utes?"

"That, and they're worried about an increase in taxes to maintain the road with all the extra traffic." Pushing away from the table, he started closing plastic containers and carrying them to the fridge. "Apparently, Stuart Gordon, ever so diplomatically, told one of the village women that this was no place to raise kids."

"What happened?"

"Frank says they got them apart before it went much beyond name calling."

Wondering how far "much beyond name calling" went, Vicki watched Mike clean up the remains of his meal. "Are you sure he's pissed off more than just these few people? Even if this was already a resort and he didn't have to rezone, local council must've agreed to his building permit."

"Yeah, and local opinion would feed local council

to the spirit right alongside Mr. Gordon. Rumor has it, they've been bought off."

Tipping her chair back against the wall, she smiled up at him. "Can I assume from your busy day that you've come down on the mud hole/vandals' side of the argument?"

"It does seem the most likely." He turned and scratched at the back of his neck again. When his fingertips came away damp, he heard her quick intake of breath. When he looked up, she was crossing the kitchen. Cool fingers wrapped around the side of his face.

"You didn't shave."

It took him a moment to find his voice. "I'm on vacation."

Her breath lapped against him, then her tongue.

The lines between likely and unlikely blurred.

Then the sound of an approaching engine jerked him out of her embrace.

Vicki licked her lips and sighed. "Six cylinder, sport utility, four wheel drive, *all* the extras, black with gold trim."

Celluci tucked his shirt back in. "Stuart Gordon told you what he drives."

"Unless you think I can tell all that from the sound of the engine."

"Not likely."

"A detective sergeant? I'm impressed." Pale hands in the pockets of his tweed blazer, Stuart Gordon leaned conspiratorially in toward Celluci, too many teeth showing in too broad a grin. "I don't suppose you could fix a few parking tickets."

"No."

Thin lips pursed in exaggerated reaction to the blunt monosyllable. "Then what do you *do,* detective sergeant?"

"Violent crimes."

Thinking that sounded a little too much like a suggestion, Vicki intervened. "Detective Celluci has agreed to assist me this weekend. Between us, we'll be able to keep a 24-hour watch."

"Twenty-four hours?" The developer's brows drew in. "I'm not paying more for that."

"I'm not asking you to."

"Good." Stepping up onto the raised hearth as though it were a stage, he smiled with all the sincerity of a television infomercial. "Then I'm glad to have you aboard Detective, Mike—can I call you Mike?" He continued without waiting for an answer. "Call me Stuart. Together we'll make this a safe place for the weary masses able to pay a premium price for a premium week in the woods." A heartbeat later, his smile grew strained. "Don't you two have detecting to do?"

"Call me Stuart?" Shaking his head, Celluci followed Vicki's dark-on-dark silhouette out to the parking lot. "Why is he here?"

"He's bait."

"Bait? The man's a certified asshole, sure, but we are *not* using him to attract an angry lake spirit."

She turned and walked backward so she could study his face. Sometimes he forgot how well she could see in the dark and forgot to mask his expressions. "Mike, you don't believe that call-me-Stuart has actually pissed off some kind of vengeful spirit protecting Lake Nepeakea?"

"You're the one who said bait . . ."

"Because we're not going to catch the person, or persons, who threw acid on his car unless we catch them in the act. He understands that."

"Oh. Right."

Feeling the bulk of the van behind her, she stopped. "You didn't answer my question."

He sighed and folded his arms, wishing he could see her as well as she could see him. "Vicki, in the last four years I have been attacked by demons, mummies, zombies, werewolves . . ."

"That wasn't an attack, that was a misunderstanding."

"He went for my throat, I count it as an attack. I've

offered my blood to the bastard son of Henry VIII and I've spent two years watching you hide from the day. There isn't anything much I don't believe in anymore."

"But . . ."

"I believe in you," he interrupted, "and from there, it's not that big a step to just about anywhere. Are you going to speak with Mary Joseph tonight?"

His tone suggested the discussion was over. "No, I was going to check means and opportunity on that list of names you gave me." She glanced down toward the lake, then up at him, not entirely certain what she was looking for in either instance. "Are you going to be all right out here on your own?"

"Why the hell wouldn't I be?"

"No reason." She kissed him, got into the van, and leaned out the open window to add, "Try and remember, Sigmund, that sometimes a cigar is just a cigar."

Celluci watched Vicki drive away. Then he turned on his flashlight and played the beam over the side of Stuart's car. Although it would have been more helpful to have seen the damage, he had to admit that the body shop had done a good job. And to give the man credit, however reluctantly, developing a wilderness property did provide more of an excuse than most of his kind had for the four-wheel drive.

Making his way over to an outcropping of rock where he could see both the parking lot and the lake but not be seen, Celluci sat down and turned off his light. According to Frank Patton, the black flies only fed during the day and the water was still too cold for mosquitoes. He wasn't entirely convinced, but since nothing had bitten him so far, the information seemed accurate. "I wonder if Stuart knows his little paradise is crawling with blood suckers." His right thumb stroking the puncture wound on his left wrist, he turned toward the lodge.

His eye widened.

Behind the evergreens, the lodge blazed with light.

Inside lights. Outside lights. Every light in the place. The harsh yellow-white illumination washed out the stars up above and threw everything below into such sharp relief that even the lush spring growth seemed manufactured. The shadows under the distant trees were now solid, impenetrable sheets of darkness.

"Well, at least Ontario Hydro's glad he's here." Shaking his head in disbelief, Celluci returned to his surveillance.

Too far away for the light to reach it, the lake threw up shimmering reflections of the stars and lapped gently against the shore.

Finally back on the paved road, Vicki unclenched her teeth and followed the southern edge of the lake toward the village. With nothing between the passenger side of the van and the water but a whitewashed guardrail and a few tumbled rocks, it was easy enough to look out the window and pretend she was driving on the lake itself. When the shoulder widened into a small parking area and a boat ramp, she pulled over and shut off the van.

The water moved inside its narrow channel like liquid darkness, opaque and mysterious. The part of the night that belonged to her ended at the water's edge.

"Not the way it's supposed to work," she muttered, getting out of the van and walking down the boat ramp. Up close, she could see through four or five inches of liquid to a stony bottom and the broken shells of fresh water clams, but beyond that, it was hard not believe she couldn't just walk across to the other side.

The ubiquitous spring chorus of frogs suddenly fell silent, drawing Vicki's attention around to a marshy cove off to her right. The silence was so complete she thought she could hear a half a hundred tiny amphibian hearts beating. One. Two . . .

"Hey, there."

She'd spun around and taken a step out into the lake before her brain caught up with her reaction. The feel of cold water filling her hiking boots brought her back to herself and she damped the hunter in her eyes before the man in the canoe had time to realize his danger.

Paddle in the water, holding the canoe in place, he nodded down at Vicki's feet. "You don't want to be doing that."

"Doing what?"

"Wading at night. You're going to want to see where you're going; old Nepeakea drops off fast." He jerked his head back toward the silvered darkness. "Even the ministry boys couldn't tell you how deep she is in the middle. She's got so much loose mud on the bottom it kept throwing back their sonar readings."

"Then what are you doing here?"

"Well, I'm not wading, that's for sure."

"Or answering my question," Vicki muttered stepping back out on the shore. Wet feet making her less than happy, she half hoped for another smartass comment.

"I often canoe at night. I like the quiet." He grinned at her, clearly believing he was too far away and there was too little light for her to see the appraisal that went with it. "You must be that investigator from Toronto. I saw your van when I was up at the lodge today."

"You must be Frank Patton. You've changed your boat."

"Can't be quiet in a 50-horsepower Evenrud, can I? You going in to see Mary Joseph?"

"No. I was going in to see Anne Kellough."

"Second house past the stop sign on the right. Little yellow bungalow with a carport." He slid backward so quietly even Vicki wouldn't have known he was moving had she not been watching him. He handled the big aluminum canoe with practiced ease. "I'd offer you a lift but I'm sure you're in a hurry."

Vicki smiled. "Thanks anyway." Her eyes silvered. "Maybe another time."

She was still smiling as she got into the van. Out on the lake, Frank Patton splashed about trying to retrieve the canoe paddle that had dropped from nerveless fingers.

"Frankly, I hate the little bastard, but there's no law against that." Anne Kellough pulled her sweater tighter and leaned back against the porch railing. "He's the one who set the health department on me, you know."

"I didn't."

"Oh yeah. He came up here about three months before it happened looking for land and he wanted mine. I wouldn't sell it to him so he figured out a way to take it." Anger quickened her breathing and flared her nostrils. "He as much as told me, after it was all over, with that big shit-eating grin and his, 'Rough, luck, Ms. Kellough, too bad the banks can't be more forgiving.' The patronizing asshole." Eyes narrowed, she glared at Vicki. "And you know what really pisses me off? I used to rent the lodge out to people who needed a little silence in their lives; you know, so they could maybe hear what was going on inside their heads. If Stuart Gordon has his way, there won't *be* any silence and the place'll be awash in brand names and expensive dental work."

"*If* Stuart Gordon has his way?" Vicki repeated, brows rising.

"Well, it's not built yet, is it?"

"He has all the paperwork filed; what's going to stop him?"

The other woman picked at a flake of paint, her whole attention focused on lifting it from the railing. Just when Vicki felt she'd have to ask again, Anne looked up and out toward the dark waters of the lake. "That's the question, isn't it," she said softly, brushing her hair back off her face.

The lake seemed no different to Vicki than it ever had. About to suggest that the question acquire an answer, she suddenly frowned. "What happened to your hand? That looks like an acid burn."

"It is." Anne turned her arm so that the burn was more clearly visible to them both. "Thanks to Stuart fucking Gordon, I couldn't afford to take my car in to the garage and I had to change the battery myself. I thought I was being careful . . ." She shrugged.

"A new battery, eh? Afraid I can't help you miss." Ken, owner of Ken's Garage and Auto Body, pressed one knee against the side of the van and leaned, letting it take his weight as he filled the tank. "But if you're not in a hurry, I can go into Bigwood tomorrow and get you one." Before Vicki could speak, he went on. "No wait, tomorrow's Sunday, place'll be closed. Closed Monday too, seeing as how it's Victoria Day." He shrugged and smiled. "I'll be open but that won't get you a battery."

"It doesn't have to be a new one. I just want to make sure that when I turn her off on the way home I can get her started again." Leaning back against the closed driver's side door, she gestured into the work bay where a small pile of old batteries had been more or less stacked against the back wall. "What about one of them?"

Ken turned, peered, and shook his head. "Damn but you've got good eyes, miss. It's dark as bloody pitch in there."

"Thank you."

"None of them batteries will do you any good though, cause I drained them all a couple of days ago. They're just too dangerous, eh? You know, if kids get poking around?" He glanced over at the gas pump and carefully squirted the total up to an even thirty-two dollars. "You're that investigator working up at the lodge, aren't you?" he asked as he pushed the bills she handed him into a greasy pocket and counted out three loonies in change. "Trying to lay the spirit?"

"Trying to catch whoever vandalized Stuart Gordon's car."

"He, uh, get that fixed then?"

"Good as new." Vicki opened the van door and paused, one foot up on the running board. "I take it he didn't get it fixed here?"

"Here?" The slightly worried expression on Ken's broad face vanished to be replaced by a curled lip and narrowed eyes. "My gas isn't good enough for that pissant. He's planning to put his own tanks in if he gets that god damned yuppie resort built."

"If?"

Much as Anne Kellough had, he glanced toward the lake. "If."

About to swing up into the van, two five-gallon glass jars sitting outside the office caught her eye. The lids were off and it looked very much as though they were airing out. "I haven't seen jars like that in years," she said, pointing. "I don't suppose you want to sell them?"

Ken turned to follow her finger. "Can't. They belong to my cousin. I just borrowed them, eh? Her kids were supposed to come and get them but, hey, you know kids."

According to call-me-Stuart, the village was no place to raise kids.

Glass jars would be handy for transporting acid mixed with fish bits.

And where would they have gotten the fish, she wondered, pulling carefully out of the gas station. *Maybe from one of the* boys *who runs the hunting and fishing camp.*

Pete Wegler stood in the door of his trailer, a slightly confused look on his face. "Do I know you?"

Vicki smiled. "Not yet. Aren't you going to invite me in?"

Ten to twelve. The lights were still on at the lodge. Celluci stood, stretched, and wondered how much longer Vicki was going to be. *Surely everyone in Dul-vie's asleep by now.*

Maybe she stopped for a bite to eat.

The second thought followed the first too quickly for him to prevent it so he ignored it instead. Turning his back on the lodge, he sat down and stared out at the lake. Water looked almost secretive at night, he decided as his eyes readjusted to the darkness.

In his business, secretive meant guilty.

"And if Stuart Gordon has gotten a protective spirit pissed off enough to kill, what then?" he wondered aloud, glancing down at his watch.

Midnight.

Which meant absolutely nothing to that ever-expanding catalog of things that went bump in the night. Experience had taught him that the so-called supernatural was just about as likely to attack at two in the afternoon as at midnight, but he couldn't not react to the knowledge that he was as far from the dubious safety of daylight as he was able to get.

Even the night seemed affected.

Waiting . . .

A breeze blew in off the lake and the hair lifted on both his arms.

Waiting for *something* to happen.

About fifteen feet from shore, a fish broke through the surface of the water like Alice going the wrong way through the looking glass. It leapt up, up, and was suddenly grabbed by the end of a glistening, gray tube as big around as his biceps. Teeth, or claws, or something back inside the tube's opening sank into the fish and together they finished the arch of the leap. A hump, the same glistening gray, slid up and back into the water, followed by what could only have been the propelling beat of a flat tail. From teeth to tail the whole thing had to be at least nine feet long.

"Jesus H. Christ." He took a deep breath and added, "On crutches."

* * *

"I'm telling you, Vicki, I saw the spirit of the lake manifest."

"You saw something eat a fish." Vicki stared out at the water but saw only the reflection of a thousand stars. "You probably saw a bigger fish eat a fish. A long, narrow pike leaping up after a nice fat bass."

About to deny he'd seen any such thing, Celluci suddenly frowned. "How do you know so much about fish?"

"I had a little talk with Pete Wegler tonight. He provided the fish for the acid bath, provided by Ken the garageman, in glass jars provided by Ken's cousin, Kathy Boomhower—the mother who went much beyond name calling with our boy Stuart. Anne Kellough did the deed—she's convinced Gordon called in the Health Department to get his hands on the property— having been transported quietly to the site in Frank Patton's canoe." She grinned. "I feel like Hercule Poirot on the Orient Express."

"Yeah? Well, I'm feeling a lot more Stephen King than Agatha Christie."

Sobering, Vicki laid her hand on the barricade of his crossed arms and studied his face. "You're really freaked by this, aren't you?"

"I don't know exactly what I saw, but I didn't see a fish get eaten by another fish."

The muscles under her hand were rigid and he was staring past her, out at the lake. "Mike, what is it?"

"I told you, Vicki. I don't know exactly what I saw." In spite of everything, he still liked his world defined. Reluctantly transferring his gaze to the pale oval of her upturned face, he sighed. "How much, if any, of this do you want me to tell Mr. Gordon tomorrow?"

"How about none? I'll tell him myself after sunset."

"Fine. It's late, I'm turning in. I assume you'll be staking out the parking lot for the rest of the night."

"What for? I guarantee the vengeful spirits won't be back." Her voice suggested that in a direct, one-on-one confronttation, a vengeful spirit wouldn't stand a chance. Celluci remembered the thing that rose up out of the lake and wasn't so sure.

"That doesn't matter, you promised 24-hour protection."

"Yeah, but . . ." His expression told her that if she wasn't going to stay, he would. "Fine, I'll watch the car. Happy?"

"That you're doing what you said you were going to do? Ecstatic." Celluci unfolded his arms, pulled her close enough to kiss the frown lines between her brows, and headed for the lodge. *She had a little talk with Pete Wegler, my ass.* He knew Vicki had to feed off others, but he didn't have to like it.

Should never have mentioned Pete Wegler. She settled down on the rock, which was still warm from Celluci's body heat, and tried unsuccessfully to penetrate the darkness of the lake. When something rustled in the underbrush bordering the parking lot, she hissed without turning her head. The rustling moved away with considerably more speed than it had used to arrive. The secrets of the lake continued to elude her.

"This isn't mysterious, it's irritating."

As Celluci wandered around the lodge, turning off lights, he could hear Stuart snoring through the door of one of the two main floor bedrooms. In the few hours he'd been outside, the other man had managed to leave a trail of debris from one end of the place to the other. On top of that, he'd used up the last of the toilet paper on the roll and hadn't replaced it, he'd put the almost empty coffee pot back in the coffeemaker with the machine still on so that the dregs had baked onto the glass, and he'd eaten a piece of Celluci's chicken, tossing the gnawed bone back into the bucket. Celluci didn't mind him eating the piece of chicken, but the last thing he wanted was Stuart Gordon's spit over the rest of the bird.

Dropping the bone into the garbage, he noticed a crumpled piece of paper and fished it out. Apparently the resort was destined to grow beyond its current boundaries. Destined to grow all the way around the lake, devouring Dulvie as it went.

"Which would put Stuart Gordon's spit all over the rest of the area."

Bored with watching the lake and frightening off the local wildlife, Vicki pressed her nose against the window of the sports ute and clicked her tongue at the dashboard full of electronic displays, willing to bet that call-me-Stuart didn't have the slightest idea of what most of them meant.

"Probably has a trouble light if his air freshener needs . . . hello."

Tucked under the passenger seat was the unmistakable edge of a laptop.

"And how much to you want to bet this thing'll scream bloody blue murder if I try and jimmy the door . . ." Turning toward the now dark lodge, she listened to the sound of two heartbeats. To the slow, regular sound that told her both men were deeply asleep.

Stuart slept on his back with one hand flung over his head and a slight smile on his thin face. Vicki watched the pulse beat in his throat for a moment. She'd been assured that, if necessary, she could feed off lower lifeforms—pigeons, rats, developers—but she was just as glad she'd taken the edge off the Hunger down in the village. Scooping up his car keys, she went out of the room as silently as she'd come in.

Celluci woke to a decent voice belting out a Beatles tune and came downstairs just as Stuart came out of the bathroom fingercombing damp hair.

"Good morning, Mike. Can I assume no vengeful spirits of Lake Nepeakea trashed my car in the night?"

"You can."

"Good. Good. Oh, by the way . . ." His smile could have sold attitude to Americans. ". . . I've used all the hot water."

"I guess it's true what they say about so many of our boys in blue."

"And what's that?" Celluci growled, fortified by two cups of coffee made only slightly bitter by the burned carafe.

"Well, you know, Mike." Grinning broadly, the developer mimed tipping a bottle to his lips. "I mean, if you can drink that vile brew, you've certainly got a drinking problem." Laughing at his own joke, he headed for the door.

To begin with, they're not your boys in blue and then, you can just fucking well drop dead. You try dealing with the world we deal with for a while, asshole, it'll chew you up and spit you out. But although his fist closed around his mug tightly enough for it to creak, all he said was, "Where are you going?"

"Didn't I tell you? I've got to see a lawyer in Bigwood today. Yes, I know what you're going to say, Mike; it's Sunday. But since this is the last time I'll be out here for a few weeks, the local legal beagle can see me when I'm available. Just a few loose ends about that nasty business with the surveyor." He paused, with his hand on the door, voice and manner stripped of all pretensions. "I told them to be sure and finish that part of the shoreline before they quit for the day—I know I'm not, but I feel responsible for that poor woman's death and I only wish there was something I could do to make up for it. You can't make up for someone dying though, can you, Mike?"

Celluci growled something noncommittal. Right at the moment, the last thing he wanted was to think of Stuart Gordon as a decent human being.

"I might not be back until after dark, but hey, that's when the spirit's likely to appear so you won't need me until then. Right, Mike?" Turning toward the screen where the black flies had settled, waiting for their breakfast to emerge, he shook his head. "The first thing I'm going to do when all this is settled is drain every stream these little blood suckers breed in."

The water levels in the swamp had dropped in the two weeks since the death of the surveyor. Drenched in the bug spray he'd found under the sink, Celluci followed the path made by the searchers, treading carefully on the higher hummocks no matter how solid the ground looked. When he reached the remains of the police tape, he squatted and peered down into the water. He didn't expect to find anything, but after Stuart's confession, he felt he had to come.

About two inches deep, it was surprisingly clear.

"No reason for it to be muddy now, there's nothing stirring it . . ."

Something metallic glinted in the mud.

Gripping the marsh grass on his hummock with one hand, he reached out with the other and managed to get thumb and forefinger around the protruding piece of . . .

"Stainless steel measuring tape?"

It was probably a remnant of the dead surveyor's equipment. One end of the six inch piece had been cleanly broken, but the other end, the end that had been down in the mud, looked as though it had been dissolved.

When Anne Kellough had thrown the acid on Stuart's car, they'd been imitating the spirit of Lake Nepeakea.

Celluci inhaled deeply and spit a mouthful of suicidal black flies out into the swamp. "I think it's time to talk to Mary Joseph."

"Can't you feel it?"

Enjoying the first decent cup of coffee he'd had in days, Celluci walked to the edge of the porch and stared out at the lake. Unlike most of Dulvie, separated from the water by the road, Mary Joseph's house was right on the shore. "I can feel *something*," he admitted.

"You can feel the spirit of the lake, angered by this man from the city. Another cookie?"

"No, thank you." He'd had one and it was without question the worst cookie he'd ever eaten. "Tell me about the spirit of the lake, Ms. Joseph. Have you seen it?"

"Oh yes. Well, not exactly it, but I've seen the wake of its passing." She gestured out toward the water but, at the moment, the lake was perfectly calm. "Most water has a protective spirit, you know. Wells and springs, lakes and rivers; it's why we throw coins into fountains, so that the spirits will exchange them for luck. Kelpies, selkies, mermaids, Jenny Greenteeth, Peg Powler, the Fideal . . . all water spirits."

"And one of them, is that what's out there?" Somehow he couldn't reconcile mermaids to that toothed trunk snaking out of the water.

"Oh no, our water spirit is a New World water spirit. The Cree called it a mantouche— surely you recognize the similarity to the word Manitou or Great Spirit? Only the deepest lakes with the best fishing had them. They protected the lakes and the area around the lakes and, in return . . ."

"Were revered?"

"Well, no, actually. They were left strictly alone."

"You told the paper that the spirit had manifested twice before?"

"Twice that we know of," she corrected. "The first recorded manifestation occurred in 1762 and was included in the notes on native spirituality that one of the exploring Jesuits sent back to France."

Product of a Catholic school education, Celluci wasn't entirely certain the involvement of the Jesuits added credibility. "What happened?"

"It was spring. A pair of white trappers had been at the lake all winter, slaughtering the animals around it. Animals under the lake's protection. According to the surviving trapper, his partner was coming out of a highwater marsh, just after sunset, when his canoe suddenly upended and he disappeared. When the remaining man retrieved the canoe, he found that bits had been burned away without flame and it carried the mark of all the dead they'd stolen from the lake."

"The mark of the dead?"

"The record says it stank, Detective. Like offal." About to eat another cookie, she paused. "You do know what offal is?"

"Yes, ma'am. Did the survivor see anything?"

"Well, he said he saw what he thought was a giant snake except that it had two stubby wings at the upper end. And you know what that is."

. . . *a glistening, gray tube as big around as his biceps.* "No."

"A wyvern. One of the ancient dragons."

"There's a dragon in the lake."

"No, of course not. The spirit of the lake can take many forms. When it's angry, those who facing its anger see a great and terrifying beast. To the trapper, who no doubt had northern European roots, it appeared as a wyvern. The natives would have probably seen a giant serpent. There are many so-called serpent mounds around deep lakes."

"But it couldn't just *be* a giant serpent?"

"Detective Celluci, don't you think that if there was a giant serpent living in this lake that someone would have gotten a good look at it by now? Besides, after the second death the lake was searched extensively with modern equipment—and once or twice since then as well—and nothing has ever been found. That trapper was killed by the spirit of the lake and so was Thomas Stebbing."

"Thomas Stebbing?"

"The recorded death in 1937. I have newspaper clippings . . ."

According to the newspaper, in the spring of 1937, four young men from the University of Toronto came to Lake Nepeakea on a wilderness vacation. Out canoeing with a friend at dusk, Thomas Stebbing saw what he thought was a burned log on the shore and they paddled in to investigate. As his friend watched in horror, the log "attacked" Stebbing, left him burned and dead, and "undulated into the lake" on a trail of dead vegetation.

The investigation turned up nothing at all, and the eyewitness account of a "kind of big worm thing" was summarily dismissed. The final, official verdict was that the victim had indeed disturbed a partially burnt log, and as it rolled over him was burned by the embers and died. The log then rolled into the lake, burning a path as it rolled, and sank. The stench was dismissed as the smell of roasting flesh and the insistence by the friend that the burns were acid burns was completely ignored—in spite of the fact he was a chemistry student and should therefore know what he was talking about.

"The spirit of the *lake* came up on *land,* Ms. Joseph?"

She nodded, apparently unconcerned with the contradiction. "There were a lot of fires being lit around the lake that year. Between the wars this area got popular for a while and fires were the easiest way to clear land for summer homes. The spirit of the lake couldn't allow that, hence its appearance as a burned log."

"And Thomas Stebbing had done what to disturb its peace?"

"Nothing specifically. I think the poor boy was just in the wrong place at the wrong time. It is a vengeful spirit, you understand."

Only a few short years earlier, he'd have understood that Mary Joseph was a total nutcase. But that was before he'd willingly thrown himself into the darkness that lurked behind a pair of silvered eyes. He sighed and stood; the afternoon had nearly ended. It wouldn't be long now until sunset.

"Thank you for your help, Ms. Joseph. I . . . what?"

She was staring at him, nodding. "You've seen it, haven't you? You have that look."

"I've seen something," he admitted reluctantly and turned toward the water. "I've seen a lot of thi . . ."

A pair of jet skis roared around the point and drowned him out. As they passed the house, blanketing it in noise, one of the adolescent operators waved a cheery hello.

Never a vengeful lake spirit around when you really need one, he thought.

"He knew about the sinkholes in the marsh and he sent those surveyors out anyway." Vicki tossed a pebble off the end of the dock and watched it disappear into the liquid darkness.

"You're sure?"

"The information was all there on his laptop and the file was dated back in March. Now, although evidence that I just happened to have found in his computer will be inadmissible in court, I can go to the Department of Lands and Forests and get the dates he requested the geological surveys."

Celluci shook his head. "You're not going to be able to get him charged with anything. Sure, he should've told them, but they were both professionals, they should've been more careful." He thought of the crocodile tears Stuart had cried that morning over the death and his hands formed fists by his side. Being an irresponsible asshole was one thing; being a manipulative, irresponsible asshole was on another level entirely. "It's an ethical failure," he growled, "not a legal one."

"Maybe I should take care of him myself, then." The second pebble hit the water with considerably more force.

"He's your client, Vicki. You're supposed to be working for him, not against him."

She snorted. "So I'll wait until his check clears."

"He's planning on acquiring the rest of the land around the lake." Pulling the paper he'd retrieved from the garbage out of his pocket, Celluci handed it over.

"The rest of the land around the lake isn't for sale."

"Neither was this lodge until he decided he wanted it."

Crushing the paper in one hand, Vicki's eyes silvered. "There's got to be something we can . . . Shit!" Tossing the paper aside, she grabbed Celluci's arm as the end of the dock bucked up into the air and leapt back one section, dragging him with her. "What the fuck was that?" she demanded as they turned to watch the place they'd just been standing rock violently back and forth. The paper she'd dropped into the water was nowhere to be seen.

"Wave from a passing boat?"

"There hasn't been a boat past here in hours."

"Sometimes these long narrow lakes build up a standing wave. It's called a seiche."

"A seiche?" When he nodded, she rolled her eyes. "I've got to start watching more PBS. In the meantime . . ."

The sound of an approaching car drew their attention up to the lodge in time to see Stuart slowly and carefully pull into the parking lot, barely disturbing the gravel.

"Are you going to tell him who vandalized his car?" Celluci asked as they started up the hill."

"Who? Probably not. I can't prove it after all, but I will tell him it wasn't some vengeful spirit and it definitely won't happen again." At least not if Pete Wegler had anything to say about it. The spirit of the lake might be hypothetical, but she wasn't.

"A group of villagers, Vicki? You're sure?"

"Positive."

"They actually thought I'd believe it was an angry spirit manifesting all over the side of my vehicle?"

"Apparently." Actually, they hadn't cared if he believed it or not. They were all just so angry, they needed to do something, and since the spirit was handy . . . She offered none of that to call-me-Stuart.

"I want their names, Vicki." His tone made it an ultimatum.

Vicki had never responded well to ultimatums. Celluci watched her masks begin to fall and wondered just how far his dislike of the developer would let her go. He could stop her with a word, he just wondered if he'd say it. Or when.

To his surprise, she regained control. "Check the census lists, then. You haven't exactly endeared yourself to your neighbors."

For a moment, it seemed that Stuart realized how close he'd just come to seeing the definition of his own mortality but then he smiled and said, "You're right, Vicki, I haven't endeared myself to my neighbors. And do you know what; I'm going to do something about that. Tomorrow's Victoria Day, I'll invite them all to a big picnic supper with great food and fireworks out over the lake. We'll kiss and make up."

"It's Sunday evening and tomorrow's a holiday. Where are you going to find food and fireworks?"

"Not a problem, Mike. I'll email my caterers in Toronto. I'm sure they can be here by tomorrow afternoon. I'll pay through the nose but hey, developing a good relationship with the locals is worth it. You two will stay, of course."

Vicki's lips drew back off her teeth but Celluci answered for them both. "Of course."

"He's up to something," he explained later, "and I want to know what that is."

"He's going to confront the villagers with what he knows, see who reacts, and make their lives a living hell. He'll find a way to make them the first part of his expansion."

"You're probably right."

"I'm always right." Head pillowed on his shoulder, she stirred his chest hair with one finger. "He's an unethical, immoral, unscrupulous little asshole."

"You missed annoying, irritating, and just generally unlikeable."

"I could convince him he was a combination of Mother Theresa and Lady Di. I could rip his mind out, use it for unnatural purposes, and stuff it back into his skull in any shape I damn well chose, but I can't."

Once you start down the dark side, forever will it dominate your destiny. But he didn't say it aloud because he didn't want to know how far down the dark side she'd been. He was grateful that she'd drawn any personal boundaries at all, that she'd chosen to remain someone who couldn't use terror for the sake of terror. "So what are we going to do about him?"

"I can't think of a damned thing. You?"

Suddenly he smiled. "Could you convince him that *you* were the spirit of the lake and that he'd better haul his ass back to Toronto unless he wants it dissolved off?"

She was off the bed in one fluid movement. "I knew there was a reason I dragged you out here this weekend." She turned on one bare heel then turned again and was suddenly back in the bed. "But I think I'll wait until tomorrow night. He hasn't paid me yet."

"Morning, Mike. Where's Vicki?"

"Sleeping."

"Well, since you're up, why don't you help out by carrying the barbecue down to the beach. I may be willing to make amends but I'm not sure they are, and since they've already damaged my car, I'd just as soon keep them away from anything valuable. Particularly when in combination with propane and open flames."

"Isn't Vicki joining us for lunch, Mike?"

"She says she isn't hungry. She went for a walk in the woods."

"Must be how she keeps her girlish figure. I've got to hand it to you, Mike, there aren't many men your age who could hold onto such a woman. I mean, she's really got that independent thing going, doesn't she?" He accepted a tuna sandwich with effusive thanks, took a bite and winced. "Not light mayo?"

"No."

"Never mind, Mike. I'm sure you meant well. Now, then, as it's just the two of us, have you ever considered investing in a timeshare . . ."

Mike Celluci had never been so glad to see anyone as he was to see a van full of bleary eyed and stiff caterers arrive at four that afternoon. As Vicki had discovered during that initial phone call, Stuart Gordon was not a man who took no for an answer. He might have accepted "Fuck off and die!" followed by a fast exit, but since Vicki expected to wake up on the shores of Lake Nepeakea, Celluci held his tongue. Besides, it would be a little difficult for her to chase the developer away if they were halfway back to Toronto.

Sunset.

Vicki could feel maybe two dozen lives around her when she woke, and she laid there for a moment reveling in them. The last two evenings she'd had to fight the urge to climb into the driver's seat and speed toward civilization.

"Fast food."

She snickered, dressed, and stepped out into the parking lot.

Celluci was down on the beach talking to Frank Patton. She made her way over to them, the crowd opening to let her pass without really being aware she was there at all. Both men nodded as she approached and Patton gestured toward the barbecue.

"Burger?"

"No thanks, I'm not hungry." She glanced around. "No one seems to have brought their kids."

"No one wants to expose their kids to Stuart Gordon."

"Afraid they'll catch something," Celluci added.

"Mike here says you've solved your case and you're just waiting for Mr. Congeniality over there to pay you."

Wondering what Mike had been up to, Vicki nodded.

"He also says you didn't mention any names. Thank you." He sighed. "We didn't really expect the spirit of the lake thing to work but . . ."

Vicki raised both hands. "Hey, you never know. He could be suppressing."

"Yeah, right. The only thing that clown suppresses is everyone around him. If you'll excuse me, I'd better go rescue Anne before she rips out his tongue and strangles him with it."

"I'm surprised she came," Vicki admitted.

"She thinks he's up to something and she wants to know what it is."

"Don't we all," Celluci murmured as he walked away.

The combined smell of cooked meat and fresh blood making her a little light-headed, Vicki started Mike moving toward the floating dock. "Have I missed anything?"

"No, I think you're just in time."

As Frank Patton approached, Stuart broke off the conversation he'd been having with Anne Kellough— or more precisely, Vicki amended, *at* Anne Kellough— and walked out to the end of the dock where a number of large rockets had been set up.

"He's got a permit for the damned things," Celluci muttered. "The son of a bitch knows how to cover his ass."

"But not his id." Vicki's fingers curved cool around Mike's forearm. "He'll get his, don't worry."

The first rocket went up, exploding red over the lake, the colors muted against the evening gray of sky and water. The developer turned toward the shore and raised both hands above his head. "Now that I've got your attention, there's a few things I'd like to share with you all before the festivities continue. First of all, I've decided not to press charges concerning the damage to my vehicle, although I'm aware that . . ."

The dock began to rock. Behind him, one of the rockets fell into the water.

"Mr. Gordon." The voice was Mary Joseph's. "Get to shore, now."

Pointing a finger toward her, he shook his head. "Oh no, old woman, I'm Stuart Gordon . . ."

No *call-me-Stuart*, tonight, Celluci noted.

". . . and you don't tell me what to do, I tell . . ."

Arms windmilling, he stepped back, once, twice, and hit the water. Arms and legs stretched out, he looked as though he was sitting on something just below the surface. "I have had enough of this," he began . . .

. . . and disappeared.

Vicki reached the end of the dock in time to see the pale oval of his face engulfed by dark water. To her astonishment, he seemed to have gotten his cell phone out of his pocket and all she could think of was that old movie cut line, *Who you gonna call?*

One heartbeat, two. She thought about going in after him. The fingertips on her reaching hand were actually damp when Celluci grabbed her shoulder and pulled her back. She wouldn't have done it, but it was nice that he thought she would.

Back on the shore, two dozen identical wide-eyed stares were locked on the flat, black surface of the lake, too astounded by what had happened to their mutual enemy, Vicki realized, to notice how fast she'd made it to the end of the dock.

Mary Joseph broke the silence first. "Thus acts the vengeful spirit of Lake Nepeakea," she declared. Then as heads began to nod, she added dryly, "Can't say I didn't warn him."

Mike looked over at Vicki, who shrugged.

"Works for me," she said.

Someone to Share
the Night

You write for a living, Henry reminded himself, staring at the form on the monitor. *A hundred and fifty thousand publishable words a year. How hard can this be?* Red-gold brows drawn in, he began to type.

"Single white male seeks . . . no . . ." The cursor danced back. "Single white male, mid-twenties, seeks . . ." That wasn't exactly his age, but he rather suspected that personals ads were like taxes, everybody lied. "Seeks . . ."

He paused, fingers frozen over the keyboard. *Seeks what?* he wondered, staring at the five words that, so far, made up the entire fax. Then he sighed and removed a word. He had no real interest in spending time with those who used race as a criteria for friendship. Life was too short. Even his.

"Single male, mid-twenties, seeks . . ." He glanced down at the tabloid page spread out on his desk searching for inspiration. Unfortunately, he found wishful thinking, macho posturing, and, reading between the lines, a quiet desperation that made the hair rise off the back of his neck.

"What am I doing?" Rolling his eyes, he shoved his chair away from the desk. "I could walk out that door and have anyone I wanted."

Which was true.

But it wouldn't *be* what he wanted.

This is not an act of desperation, he reminded himself. Impatient, perhaps. Desperate, no.

"Single male, mid-twenties, not into the bar scene . . ." The phrase *meat market* was singularly apt in his case. ". . . seeks . . ."

What he'd had.

But Vicki was three thousand odd miles away with a man who loved her in spite of changes.

And Tony, freed from a life of mere survival on the streets, had defined himself and moved on.

They'd left a surprising hole in his life. Surprising and painful. Surprisingly painful. He found himself unwilling to wait for time and fate to fill it.

"Single male, mid-twenties, not into the bar scene, out of the habit of being alone, seeks someone strong, intelligent, and adaptable."

Frowning, he added, "Must be able to laugh at life." Then he sent the fax before he could change his mind. The paper would add the electronic mailbox number when they ran it on Thursday.

Late Thursday or early Friday depending how the remaining hours of darkness were to be defined, Henry picked a copy of the paper out of a box on Davie Street and checked his ad. In spite of the horror stories he'd heard to the contrary, they'd not only gotten it right but placed it at the bottom of the first column of Alternative Lifestyles, where it had significantly more punch than if it had been buried higher up on the page.

Deadlines kept him from checking the mailbox until Sunday evening.

There were thirty-two messages. Thirty-two.

He felt flattered until he actually listened to them and then, even though no one else knew, he felt embarrassed about feeling flattered.

Twenty, he dismissed out of hand. A couple of the instant rejects had clearly been responding to the wrong mailbox. A few sounded interesting but had a change of heart in the middle of the message and left no actual contact information. The rest seemed to be laughing just a little *too* hard at life.

But at the end of a discouraging half an hour, he still had a dozen messages to choose from; seven women, five men. It wasn't thirty-two, but it wasn't bad.

Eleven of them had left him e-mail addresses.

One had left him a phone number.

He listened again to the last voice in the mailbox, the only one of the twelve who believed he wouldn't abuse the privilege offered by the phone company.

"Hi. My name is Lilah. I'm also in my mid-twenties—although which side of the midpoint I'd rather not say."

Henry could hear the smile in her voice. It was a half smile, a crooked smile, the kind of smile that could appreciate irony. He found himself smiling in response.

"Although I can quite happily be into the bar scene, I do think they're the worst possible place to meet someone for the first time. How about a coffee? I can probably be free any evening this week."

And then she left her phone number.

Still smiling, he called it.

If American troops had invaded Canada during the War of 1812 with half the enthusiasm Starbucks had exhibited when crossing the border, the outcome of the war would have been entirely different. While Henry had nothing actually against the chain of coffee shops, he found their client base to be just a little too broad. In the café on Denman that he preferred, there were never any children, rushing junior executives, or spandex shorts. Almost everyone wore black and, in spite of multiple piercings and overuse of profanity, the younger patrons were clearly imitating their elders.

Their elders were generally the kind of artists and writers who seldom made sales but knew how to look the part. They were among the very few in Vancouver without tans.

Using the condensation on a three-dollar bottle of water to make rings on the scarred tabletop, Henry watched the door and worried about recognizing Lilah when she arrived. Then he worried a bit that she wasn't going to arrive. Then he went back to worrying about recognizing her.

You are way too old for this nonsense, he told himself sternly. *Get a . . .*

The woman standing in the doorway was short, vaguely Mediterranean with thick dark hair that spilled halfway down her back in ebony ripples. If she'd passed her mid-twenties it wasn't by more than a year or two. She'd clearly ignored the modern notion that a woman should be so thin she looked like an adolescent boy with breasts. Not exactly beautiful, something about her drew the eye. Noting Henry's regard, she smiled, red lips parting over very white teeth and it was exactly the expression that Henry had imagined. He stood as she walked to his table, enjoying the sensual way she moved her body across the room and aware that everyone else in the room was enjoying it, too.

"Henry?" Her voice was throatier in person, almost a purr.

"Lilah." He gave her name back to her as confirmation.

She raised her head and locked her dark gaze to his. They blinked in unison.

"Vampire."

Henry Fitzroy, bastard son of Henry VIII, once Duke of Richmond and Somerset, dropped back into his chair with an exhalation halfway between a sigh and a snort. "Succubus."

"So are you saying you *weren't* planning to feed off whoever answered your ad?"

"No, I'm saying it wasn't the primary reason I placed it."

The overt sexual attraction turned off, Lilah swirled a finger through a bit of spilled latté and rolled her eyes. "So you're a better man than I am, Gunga Din, but I personally don't see the difference between us. You don't kill anymore, I don't kill anymore."

"I don't devour years off my . . ." He paused and frowned, uncertain of how to go on.

"Victims? Prey? Quarry? Dates?" The succubus sighed. "We've got to come up with a new word for it."

Recognizing she had a point, Henry settled for the lesser of four evils. "I don't devour years off my date's life."

"Oh, please. So they spend less time having their diapers changed by strangers in a nursing home, less time drooling in their pureed mac and cheese. If they knew, they'd thank me. At least I don't violate their structural integrity."

"I hardly think a discreet puncture counts as a violation."

"Hey, you said puncture, not me. But . . ." She raised a hand to stop his protest. ". . . I'm willing to let it go."

"Gracious of you."

"Always."

In spite of himself, Henry smiled.

"You know, hon, you're very attractive when you do that."

"Do what?"

"When you stop looking so irritated about things not turning out the way you expected. Blind dates *never* turn out the way you expect." Dropping her chin she looked up at him through the thick fringe of her lashes. "Trust me, I've been on a million of them."

"A million?"

"Give or take."

"So you're a pro . . ."

A sardonic eyebrow rose. "A gentleman wouldn't mention that."

"True." He inclined his head in apology and took the opportunity to glance at his watch. "*Run Lola Run* is playing at the Caprice in ninety minutes; did you want to go?"

For the first time since entering the café, Lilah looked startled. "With you?"

A little startled himself, Henry shrugged, offering the only reason that explained the unusually impulsive invitation. "I'd enjoy spending some time just being myself, without all the implicit lies."

Dark brows drew in and she studied him speculatively. "I can understand that."

An almost comfortable silence filled the space between them.

"Well?" Henry asked at last.

"My German's a little rusty. I haven't used it for almost a century."

Henry stood and held out his hand. "There're subtitles."

Shaking her head, she pushed her chair out from the table and laid her hand in his. "Why not."

Sunset. A slow return to awareness. The feel of cotton sheets against his skin. The pulse of the city outside the walls of his sanctuary. The realization he was smiling.

After the movie, they'd walked for hours in a soft mist, talking about the places they'd seen and when they'd seen them. A primal demon, the succubus had been around for millennia but politely restricted her observations to the four and a half centuries Henry could claim. Their nights had been remarkably similar.

When they parted as friends about an hour before dawn, they parted as friends although it would never be a sexual relationship; sex was too tied to feeding for them both.

"World's full of warm bodies," Lilah had pointed out, *"but how many of them saw Mrs. Siddon play Lady Macbeth at Covent Garden Theater on opening night* and *felt the hand washing scene was way, way over the top?"*

How many indeed, Henry thought, throwing back the covers and swinging his legs out of bed. Rather than deal with the balcony doors in the master suite, he'd sealed the smallest room in the three bedroom condo against the light. He'd done the crypt thing once, and didn't see the attraction.

After his shower, he wandered into the living room and picked up the remote. With any luck he could catch the end of the news. He didn't often watch it but last night's . . . date? . . . had left him feeling reconnected to the world.

". . . when southbound travelers waited up to three hours to cross the border at the Peace Arch as US customs officials tightened security checks as a precaution against terrorism."

"Canadian terrorists." Henry frowned as he toweled his hair. "Excuse me while I politely blow up your building?"

"Embarrassed Surrey officials had to shut down the city's Web site after a computer hacker broke into the system and rewrote the greeting, using less-than-flattering language. The hacker remains unknown and unapprehended.

"And in a repeat of our top story, police have identified the body found this morning on Wreck Beach as Taylor Johnston, thirty-two, of Haro Street. They still have no explanation for the condition of the body although an unidentified constable commented that 'it looked like he had his life sucked out of him.'

"And now to Rajeet Singh with our new product report."

Jabbing at the remote, Henry cut Rajeet off in the middle of an animated description of a battery-operated cappuccino frother. Plastic cracked as his fingers tightened. A man found with the life sucked out of him. He didn't want to believe. . . .

As part of an ongoing criminal investigation, the body was at the City Morgue in the basement of Vancouver General Hospital. The previous time Henry'd made an after hours visit, he'd been searching for information to help identify the victim. This time, he needed to identify the murderer.

He walked silently across the dark room to the
drawer labeled TAYLOR JOHNSTON, pulled it
open, and flipped back the sheet. LEDs on various
pieces of machinery and the exit sign over the door
provided more than enough light to see tendons and
ligaments standing out in sharp relief under desiccated, parchment-colored skin. Hands and feet looked
like claws and the features of the skull had overwhelmed the features of the face. The unnamed constable had made an accurate observation; the body
did, indeed, look as if all the life had been sucked out
of it.

Henry snarled softly and closed the drawer.

"You don't kill anymore, I don't kill anymore . . ."

He found the dead man's personal effects in a manila envelope in the outer office. A Post-it note suggested that the police should have picked the envelope
up by six PM. The watch was an imitation Rolex—but
not a cheap one. There were eight keys on his key
ring. The genuine cowhide wallet held four high end
credit cards, eighty-seven dollars in cash, a picture of
a golden retriever, and half a dozen receipts. Three
were out of bank machines. Two were store receipts.
The sixth was for a credit card transaction.

Henry had faxed in both his personal ad and his
credit information. It looked as though Taylor Johnston had dropped his off in person.

*"Blind dates never turn out the way you expect. Trust
me, I've been on a million of them."*

In a city the size of Vancouver, a phone number
and a first name provided no identification at all. Had
Lilah answered when he called, Henry thought he'd
be able to control his anger enough to arrange another
meeting but she didn't, and when he found himself
snarling at her voice mail, he decided not to leave
a message.

"Although I can quite happily be into the bar scene . . ."

She'd told him she liked jazz. It was a place to start.

*   *   *

She wasn't at O'Doul's, although one of the waiters recognized her description. From the strength of his reacton, Henry assumed she'd fed—but not killed. Why kill Johnston and yet leave this victim with only pleasant memories? Henry added it to the list of questions he intended to have answered.

A few moments later, he parked his BMW, illegally, on Abbot Street and walked around the corner to Water Street, heading for The Purple Onion Cabaret. There were very few people on the sidewalks—a couple, closely entwined, a small clump of older teens, and a familiar form just about to enter the club.

Henry could move quickly when he needed to and he was in no mood for subtlety. He was in front of her before she knew he was behind her.

An ebony brow rose, but that was the only movement she made. "What brings you here, hon? I seem to recall you saying that jazz made your head ache."

He snarled softly, not amused.

The brow lowered, slowly. "Are you Hunting me, Nightwalker? Should I scream? Maybe that nice young man down the block will disentangle himself from his lady long enough to save me."

Henry's lips drew up off his teeth. "And who will save him as you add another death to your total?"

Lilah blinked, and the formal cadences left her voice. "What the hell are you talking about?"

Demons seldom bothered lying; the truth caused more trouble.

She honestly didn't know what he meant.

"You actually saw this body?" When Henry nodded, Lilah took a long swallow of mocha latte, carefully put the cup down on its saucer, and said, "Why do you care? I mean, I know why you cared when you thought it was me," she added before he could speak. "You thought I'd lied to you and you didn't like feeling dicked around. I can understand that. But it's not me. So why do you care?"

Henry let the final mask fall, the one he maintained

even for the succubus. "Someone, something, is hunting in my territory."

Across the café, a mug slid from nerveless fingers and hit the Italian tile floor, exploding into a hundred shards of primary-colored porcelain. There was nervous laughter, scattered applause, and all eyes thankfully left the golden-haired man with the night in his voice.

Lilah shrugged. "There's millions of people in the Greater Vancouver area, hon. Enough for all of us."

"It's the principle of the thing," he muttered, a little piqued by her lack of reaction.

"It's not another vampire."

It was almost a question so he answered it. "No. The condition of the corpse was classic succubus."

"Or incubus," she pointed out. "You don't know for certain those men weren't gay, and I sincerely doubt that you and I alone were shopping from the personals."

"I wasn't looking to feed," Henry ground out through clenched teeth.

"That's right. You were looking for a victimless relationship and . . ." Lilah spread her hands, fingernails drawing glistening scarlet lines in the air. ". . . ta dah, you found me. And if I'm not what you were looking for, then you were clearly planning to feed—if not sooner, then later—so you can just stop being so 'more ethical than thou' about it." She half turned in her chair, turning her gesture into a wave at the counter staff. "Sweetie, could I have another of these and a chocolate croissant? Thanks."

The café didn't actually have table service. Her smile created it.

Henry's smile sent the young man scurrying back behind the counter.

"Is there another succubus in the city?" He demanded.

"How should I know? I've never run into one, but that just means I've never run into one." The pointed tip of a pink tongue slowly licked foam off her upper lip.

Another mug shattered.

"Incubus?"

She sighed and stopped trying to provoke a reaction from the vampire. "I honestly don't know, Henry. We're not territorial like your lot, we pretty much keep racking up those frequent flyer miles—town to town, party to party . . ." Eyebrows flicked up then down. ". . . man to man. If this is your territory, can't *you* tell?"

"No. I can recognize a demon if I see one, regardless of form, but you have no part in the lives I Hunt or the blood I feed from." He shrugged. "A large enough demon might cause some sort of dissonance, but . . ."

"But you haven't felt any such disturbance in the Force."

"What?"

"You've got to get out to more movies without subtitles, hon." She pushed her chair out from the table and stood, lowering her voice dramatically. "Since you've been to the morgue, there's only one thing left for us to do."

"Us?" Henry interrupted, glancing around with an expression designed to discourage eavesdroppers. "This isn't your problem."

"Sweetie, it became my problem when you showed me your Prince of Darkness face."

He stood as well; she had a point. Since he'd been responsible for involving her, he couldn't then tell her she wasn't involved. "All right, what's left for us to do?"

Her smile suggested that a moonless romp on a deserted beach would be the perfect way to spend the heart of the night. "Why, visit the scene of the crime, of course."

Traffic on the bridge slowed them a little and it was almost two AM by the time they got to Wreck Beach.

Taylor Johnston's body had been found on the north
side of the breakwater at Point Grey. Henry parked
the car on one of the remaining sections of Old Marine Drive but didn't look too happy about it.

"Campus security," he replied when Lilah inquired.
"This whole area is part of the University of British
Columbia's endowment lands and they've really been
cracking down on people parking by the side of the
road."

"*You're* worried about campus security?" The succubus shook her head in disbelief as they walked away
from the car. "You know, hon, there are times when
you're entirely too human for a vampire."

He supposed he deserved that. "The police have
been all over this area; what are we likely to find that
they missed?"

"Something they weren't looking for."

"Ghoulies and ghosties and things that go bump in
the night?"

"Takes one to know one." She stepped around the
tattered end of a piece of yellow police tape. "Or in
this case, takes two."

For a moment, Henry had the weirdest sense of déjà
vu. It could have been Vicki he was following down
to the sand, their partnership renewed. Then Lilah
half turned, laughingly telling him to hurry, and she
couldn't have been more different than his tall, blonde
ex-lover.

*Single male, mid-twenties, seeks someone to share
the night.*

So what if it was a different someone. . . .

He knew when he stood on the exact spot the body
had been found; the stink of the dying man's terror
was so distinct that it had clearly been neither a fast
nor a painless death.

"Not an incubus, then," Lilah declared dumping
sand out of an expensive Italian pump. "We may like
to take our time, but no one ever complains about
the process."

Henry frowned and turned his face into the breeze coming in off the pacific. There was no moon and except for the white lines of breakers at the seawall, the waves were very dark. "Can you smell the rot?"

"Sweetie, there's a great big dead fish not fifteen feet away. I'd have to be in the same shape as Mr. Johnston not to smell it."

"Not the fish." It smelled of the crypt. Of bones left to lie in the dark and damp. "There." He pointed toward the seawall. "It's in there."

Lilah looked up at Henry's pale face, then over at the massive mound of rock jutting out into the sea. "What is?"

"I don't know yet." Half a dozen paces toward the rock, he turned back toward the succubus. "Are you coming?"

"No, just breathing hard."

"Pardon?"

He looked so completely confused, she laughed as she caught up. "You really don't get out much, do you, hon?"

The night was no impediment to either of them, but the entrance was well hidden. If it hadn't been for the smell, they'd never have found it.

Dropping to her knees beside him, Lilah handed Henry a lighter. He stretched his arm to its full length under a massive block of stone, the tiny flame shifting all the shadows but one.

"You can take the lighter with you." Lilah rocked back onto her heels, shaking her head. "I, personally, am not going in there."

Henry understood. Succubi were only slightly harder to kill than the humans they resembled. "I don't think it's home," he muttered dropping onto his stomach and inching forward into the black line of the narrow crevice.

Lilah's voice drifted down to him. "Not a problem, hon, but I'd absolutely ruin this dress. Not to mention my manicure."

"Not to mention," Henry repeated, smiling in spite

of the conditions. There was an innate honesty in the succubus he like. A lot.

Twice his body-length under the stone, after creeping through a puddle of salt water at least an inch deep, the way opened up and, although he had to keep turning his shoulders, he could move forward in a crouch. The smell reminded him of the catacombs under St. Mark's Square in Venice where the sea had permeated both the rock and the ancient dead.

Three or four minutes later, he straightened cautiously as the roof rose away and drew Lilah's lighter out of his pocket, expecting to see bones piled in every corner. He saw, instead, a large crab scuttling away, a filthy nest of clothing, and a dark corner where the sucking sound of water moving up and down in a confined space overlaid the omnipresent roar of the sea. A closer inspection showed an almost circular hole down into the rock and, about ten or twelve feet away, the moving water of the Pacific Ocean. A line of moisture showed the high tide mark and another large crab peered out of a crevice just below it. It was obvious where the drained bodies were dumped and what happened to them after dumping.

The scent of death, or rot, hadn't come from the expected cache of corpses, so it had to have come from the creature who laired here.

Which narrows it down considerably, Henry thought grimly as he closed the almost unbearably hot lighter with a snap.

Lilah and a young man were arranging their clothes as he crawled out from under the seawall. The succubus, almost luminescent by starlight, waved when she saw him.

"Hey, sweetie, you might want to hear this."

"Hear what?" The smell of sex and a familiar pungent smoke overlaid the smell of death.

The young man smiled in what Henry could only describe as a satiated way and said, "Like you know the dead guy they found here this morning, eh? I sort of like saw it happen.''

Henry snarled. "Saw what?"

"Whoa, like what big teeth you have, Grandma. Anyway, I've been crashing on the beach when the weather's good, you know, and like last night I'm asleep and I hear this whimpering sort of noise and I think it's a dog in trouble, eh? But it's not. It's like two guys. I can't see them too good but I think, 'hey, go for the gusto, guys,' but one of them seems really pissed 'cause like the tide's really high and I guess he can't go to his regular nooky place in the rocks and he sort of throws himself on the other guy so I stop looking, you know."

"Why didn't you tell this to the police?"

The young man giggled. "Well, some mornings you don't want to talk to the police, you know. And I was like gone before they arrived anyhow. So, like, is this your old lady, 'cause she's one prime piece of . . . OW!"

Henry tightened his grip on the unshaven chin enough to dimple the flesh. He let the Hunter rise, and when the dilated pupils finally responded by dilating further, he growled, "Forget you ever saw us."

"Dude . . ."

"It's a wight," Henry said when they were back in the car. "From the pile of clothing, it looks like it's been there for a while. It probably lives on small animals most of the time, but every now and then people like your friend go missing off the beach or students disappear from the campus, but since they never find a body, no one ever goes looking for a killer.

"Last night, it went hunting a little farther from home only to get back and find the tide in and over the doorway. Which answers the question of why it left the body on the beach. It must've had to race the dawn to shelter."

"Wait a minute." Lilah protested, pausing in her

dusting of sand from crevices. "A wight wouldn't care about going through salt water. Salted holy water, yes, but not just the sea."

"If it tried to drag its victim the rest of the way, he'd drown."

"And no more than the rest of us, wights don't feed from the dead," Lilah finished. "And all the pieces but one fall neatly into place. You don't honestly think a wight would pick its victim from the personal ads, do you, hon?"

Unclean creature of darkness seeks life essence to suck.

"I don't honestly think it can read," Henry admitted. "That whole personals thing had to have been a coincidence."

"And now that we've answered that question, why don't we head for this great after-hours club I know?"

"I don't have time for that, Lilah. I have a silver letter opener at home I can use for a weapon."

"Against?"

She sounded so honestly confused he turned to look at her. "Against the wight. I can't let it keep killing."

"Why not? Why should you care? Curiosity is satisfied, move on."

Traffic on Fourth Avenue turned his attention back to the road. "Is that the only reason you came tonight? Curiosity?"

"Of course. When a life gets sucked and it's not me doing the sucking, I like to know what is. You're not really . . . ?" He could feel the weight of her gaze as she studied him. "You're not seriously . . . ? You are, aren't you?"

"Yes, I am. It's getting careless."

"Good. Someday, it'll get caught by the dawn, problem solved."

"And when some forensic pathologist does an autopsy on the remains, what then?"

"I'm not a fortune-teller, hon. The only future I can predict is who's going to get lucky."

"Modern forensics will find something that shouldn't

exist. Most people will deny it, but some will start thinking."

"You do know that they moved *The X-Files* out of Vancouver?"

Henry kept his eyes locked on the taillights in front of him. The depth of his disappointment in her reaction surprised him. "Our best defense is that no one believes we exist so they don't look for us. If they start looking . . ." His voice trailed off into mobs with torches and laboratory dissection tables.

They drove in silence until they crossed the Burrard Bridge, then Lilah reached over and laid her fingers on Henry's arm. "That's a nice, pragmatic reason you've got there," she murmured, "but I don't believe you for a moment. You're going to destroy this thing because it's killing in your territory. But it has nothing to do with the territorial imperatives of a vampire," she added before he could speak. "Your territory. Your people. Your responsibility." She dropped her hand back onto her lap. "Let me out here, hon. I try to keep my distance from the overly ethical."

His fingers tightened on the steering wheel as he guided the BMW to the curb. "You *weren't* what I was looking for when I placed that ad," he said as she opened the door. "But I thought we . . ." Suddenly at a low for words, he fell back on the trite. ". . . had a connection."

Leaning over she kissed his cheek. "We did." Stepping out onto the sidewalk, she smiled back in through the open door. "You'll find your Robin, Batman. It just isn't me."

Henry returned to the beach just before high tide, fairly certain the wight hadn't survived so long by making the same mistake twice. He blocked the entrance to the lair with a silver chain and waited.

The fight didn't last long. Henry felt mildly embarrassed by taking his frustrations out on the pitiful creature, but he'd pretty much gotten over it by the time he fed the desiccated body to the crabs.

He broke a number of traffic laws getting home before dawn. Collapsing inside the door to his sanctuary, he woke at sunset stiff and sore from a day spent crumpled on a hardwood floor. He tried to call Lilah and tell her it was over, but whatever connection there'd been between them was well and truly broken. Her phone number was no longer in service.

The brief, aborted companionship made it even harder to be alone.

For two nights, he Hunted and fed and wondered if Lilah had been right and he should have been more specific.

Overly ethical creature of the night seeks sidekick.

The thought of who'd answer something like that frightened him the way nothing else had frightened him over the last four and a half centuries.

Finally, he picked up the list of e-mail addresses and started alphabetically.

The man who came in the door of the café was tall and dark and muscular. Shoulder-length hair had been caught back in a gold clasp. Gold rings flashed on every finger and dangled from both ears. He caught Henry's eye and strode across the café toward him, smiling broadly.

Stopped on the other side of the table.

Stopped smiling.

"Henry?"

"Abdula?"

They blinked in unison.

"Vampire."

Henry dropped back into his chair. "Djinn."

Perhaps he ought to have his ad placed somewhere *other* than Alternative Lifestyles.

Another Fine Nest

There were three other people in the small bookstore.
Vicki hesitated to call them customers, since in the
ten minutes she'd been standing in front of the new
releases shelf ostensibly reading the staff reviews—her
favorite the succinct *Trees died for this?*—none of
them had given any indication they were planning to
actually buy a book. Two were reading, the third attempting to engage the young woman behind the cash
register in conversation but succeeding only in
monologue.

Without ever having seen him before, Vicki easily
identified her contact. Male Caucasian, five eight, dark
hair and beard, carrying a good twenty kilos more
than was healthy; she could hear his heart pounding
as he stared down at the pages of the novel he held.
Since he was holding it upside down, it seemed highly
unlikely his growing excitement had anything to do
with what he wasn't reading. He smelled strongly of
garlic.

He was clearly waiting for the other two customers
to leave before approaching her. *"They mustn't find
out I've called you."*

"Who?"

"Them."

Screw that. Suddenly tired of amateur cloak and
dagger theatrics, she walked deeper into the narrow
store until she stood directly behind him. Unfortunately, a massive sneeze derailed the impression she'd

intended to make. Up close, the smell of garlic was nearly overpowering.

He spun around, dark eyes wide, the heavy gold cross he wore bouncing between the open wings of his jacket.

"Hey." She rummaged in her pocket for a tissue. "Vicki Nelson. You have a job for me?"

Sitting at one of the coffee shop's small tables, Vicki took a drink from her bottle of water and waited for Duncan Travis to pull himself together. His hands, clasped reverently around the paper curves of his triple/triple, were still trembling. She stared at her reflection in the glass, beyond that to the bookstore now across the street, and wished he'd get to the freakin' point.

"I could see your reflection in the glass!"

So could she, but since the glass and her reflection were behind him . . .

"I checked everyone out as they came into the store."

Oh. Her reflection in the glass at the store. That made a little more sense.

"That's why I didn't know you were you."

"You didn't?"

"No." Duncan detached one hand from the papercup just long enough to sketch a quick emphasis in the air. "I know, you know."

"You know what?"

"About you. What you are."

"I kind of assumed you did, since you called me." Her emphasis on the last three words didn't seem to make the intended impression.

"Not that! People talk, you know. And there's stuff, on the Web . . ." Grabbing the base of the cross, he thrust it toward her, the chain biting deep into the folds of his neck.

Vicki sighed. "People say I'm Catholic? Religious? What?"

"Vampire!" He dropped his voice as heads turned. "Nosferatu. A member of the bloodsucking undead."

"I knew what you meant." She sighed again. Maybe keeping a lower profile over the last couple of years *would* have been a good idea. "I was just messing with your head. You've got garlic in your pockets, don't you?"

"I am not so desperate that I'd trust you not to drain me and cast my body aside. I have taken precautions." From his expression, Duncan clearly believed his tone sounded threatening. He was wrong.

"Okay." Vicki leaned back in her chair and massaged the bridge of her nose, attempting to forestall a burgeoning headache. "A quick lesson in reality as opposed to the vast amounts of television I suspect you watch. One. Garlic, crosses, holy water—not repelling. Except for maybe the garlic, because frankly, you reek. Two. A biological change does not suddenly start reversing the laws of physics. I had a reflection before I changed, I still have one now. Three. If that's a stake in your pocket and, trust me, I'd much prefer it to be a stake 'cause I don't want you that happy to see me, have you considered the actual logistics of using it? You'll be trying to thrust a not very sharp hunk of wood through clothing, skin, muscle, and bone before you get to the meaty bits. I have no idea what you expect I'll be doing while you make the attempt, but let me assure you that I'll be doing it faster and more violently than you can imagine. Four. Unless you immediately tell me why you called and said you had a job only I could do—giving me, by the way, your credit card number—not very smart, Duncan—I will make you forget you ever saw me." Dropping her hand to the tabletop, she leaned forward, her eyes silvering slightly. "Eternity is too short for all this screwing around. Start talking."

Duncan swallowed, blinked, and wet his lips. "Wow."

"Thank you. The job?"

"King-tics."

"What?"

"We don't know if they're alien constructs or if they've risen from one of the hell dimensions . . ."

Oh yeah, way too much Buffy, Vicki acknowledged silently.

". . . but they're infesting the city. Their nest has to be found and taken out."

"Okay. We?"

"My group."

"AD&D?"

"Third edition."

"Right. Nest?"

"They're insectoids. The ones we've seen seem to be sexless workers, therefore they're likely hive-based. That means a queen and a nest."

"You guys seem to have a pretty good grasp of the situation; why not take them out yourselves?"

Duncan snorted. "In spite of what you seem to think, Ms. Nelson, our grip on reality is fairly firm. Three of us are computer programmers, two work retail, and one is a high school math teacher. We know when we're out of our depth. You turned up on an Internet search—you were local and certain speculations made us think you'd believe us."

"About King-tics?"

"Yeah."

"So let's say I do. Let's say, hypothetically, I believe there's a new kind of something infesting the city. Why is that a problem? Toronto's already ass deep in cockroaches and conservatives; what's one more lower life form?"

"King-tics are smarter than either. And they drink blood." Confident that he now had her full attention, Duncan stretched out one leg and tugged his pants up from his ankle.

Vicki stared at the dingy gray sweat sock and contemplated beating someone's head—hers, his, she wasn't sure which—against the table. "Try using hot water and adding a little bleach."

"What?" He glanced down and flushed. "Oh."

A quick adjustment later and Vicki found herself studying two half-healed puncture wounds just below the curve of Duncan's ankle. Slightly inflamed and about an inch apart, they were right over a vein that ran close to the surface. "Big bug."

"Yeah. But they move really, really fast. They use the crowds in the subway stations as cover. Bite. Drink. Scuttle away. Who's going to notice a couple of little pricks when we're surrounded by bigger pricks every day of our lives?"

"Cynical observation?" Vicki asked the expectant silence.

"Uh, yeah."

"Okay." He'd probably been saving it up too. "You didn't feel the bite?"

"No. I'd have never noticed anything except that my shoe was untied and I knelt to do it up and I . . ."

Screamed like a little girl?

". . . saw this bug. It looked at me, Ms. Nelson. I swear it looked at me . . ."

She believed him, actually. She could hear the before and after in his voice.

". . . and then it disappeared. I sort of saw it moving but it was just so fast. We started looking for them after that and well, once you know what you're looking for . . ." He paused then and his gaze skittered off hers but she had to give him credit for trying. "Once you *admit* what you're looking for, it becomes a lot easier to see."

Yeah. Yeah. You know what I am. I got that twenty minutes ago. "Go on."

"I told the group what had happened and we started looking for the bugs. The King-tics. I mean, we spotted them so we figured we should get to name them, right?" When she didn't answer, he sighed, shrugged, and continued. "At first we only saw them at Bloor and Yonge, at the Bloor Station, probably because it's lower. More subterranean. But then, we saw a few on the upper level, you know, the Yonge line. Yesterday, I saw three at Wellsley."

Vicki fought the urge to turn her head. Wellsley Station was a short block south of the coffee shop.

"Thing is," Duncan laughed nervously, "they saw me too. They were watching me from the shadows. First time I'd ever seen them still. Usually you catch a sort movement out of the corner of one eye but this . . . It was creepy. Anyway, we talked it over and decided to call you."

"So I can . . . ?"

"I told you. Destroy the nest and the queen. One way or another the subway system hooks up to every major building in the downtown core. The whole city could become a giant banquet hall for these things."

Vicki sat back in her chair and thought about giant intelligent bloodsucking bugs in the subway for a moment. When Duncan opened his mouth to . . . well, she didn't know what he was planning to do because she cut him off with a finger raised in silent warning. Giant, intelligent bloodsucking bugs in the subway. Feeding off the ankles of Toronto. Another predator—predators—feeding in her territory, true, but it was somehow hard to get worked up about something called a King-tic.

Giant, intelligent bloodsucking bugs in the subway.

She couldn't believe she was even considering taking the job.

Still, that sort of thing always ended badly in the movies, didn't it?

The Wellsley platform was empty except for a clump of teenagers at the far end discussing the appalling news that N'Sync would be on the Star Wars Episode II DVD. On the off chance that the six simultaneous rants would suddenly stop and silence fall, Vicki pitched her voice too low to be overheard. "That's where you saw them?"

Duncan nodded. "Yeah. Right there. In the corner. In the shadows. Three of them. Staring at me."

"If you're talking like a character in a Dashiell

Hammett novel on purpose, you should know I find it really annoying."

"Sorry."

"Just don't do it again." Stepping closer, Vicki examined the grey tiled corner for webs or egg casings or marks against the fine patina of subway station grime and came up empty. Sighing, she turned her attention back to Duncan. "What were you doing while the bugs—the King-tics—were staring at you?"

He shrugged. "I stared at them for a while."

"And then?"

"They left." He pointed up the tunnel toward Bloor.

"Right."

His expectant silence took her to the edge of the platform. A train had gone by just before they'd entered the station. She could hear the next one a station, maybe a station and a half away. Plenty of time. "You wouldn't have a . . . *artist's conception* of these things, would you?"

"Not with me. I could fax it to you when I get home."

"You do that. Go now."

"What are you going to do?"

"What you're paying me to do."

"You're going into the tunnel!"

He sounded so amazed, she turned to look at him. "It's where the bugs are, Duncan. What did you expect me to do?"

"Go into the tunnels," Duncan admitted. "It's just . . ." He shifted his weight from foot to foot and flashed her an admiring smile. ". . . well, you're actually doing it. And it's so dangerous."

"Because of the bugs?"

"No. Because of the subway trains."

"Trust me, trains aren't a problem."

Behind the beard, his jaw dropped. "You turn into mist?"

Vicki sighed. "I step out of the way."

*   *   *

There were bugs in the subway tunnels. There were also rats, mice, fast food wrappers, used condoms, and a pair of men's Y-front underwear, extra large. The bugs were not giants, not bloodsucking, and, although one of the cockroaches gave her what could only be interpreted as a dirty look just before she squashed it flat, not noticeably intelligent. The rats and mice avoided her, but then, so did pretty much all mammals except humans and cats. The fast food wrappers and used condoms were the expected debris of the twenty-first century. Vicki didn't waste time speculating about the underwear because she really, *really* didn't want to know.

At Yonge and Bloor she crossed the station and slipped down to the lower tracks, easily avoiding the security cameras and the weary curiosity of late commuters.

There were maybe—possibly—fewer rats and mice scrabbling out of her way.

Maybe—possibly—sounds that didn't quite add up to the ambient noise she remembered from other trips.

It depressed her just a little that she'd been down in these tunnels often enough to remember the ambient noise.

When the last train of the night went by, she fought the urge to brace herself against the sides of the workman's niche, rise up to window height, and give any passengers a flickering, strobelike look at what haunted the dark places of the city. *Something about being an immortal, undead creature of the night really changes the things you find funny,* she sighed, allowing the rush of wind to hold her in place as the squares of light flashed by.

The maintenance workers traveled in pairs, but it wasn't hard to separate the younger of the two from his companion. A crescent of white teeth in the darkness. A flash of silver eyes. A promise of things forbidden in the light.

Like shooting fish in a barrel. Grabbing a fistful of

his overalls, Vicki dragged him into a dark corner, stiffened her arm to keep him there, and locked her gaze with his. "Giant intelligent bloodsucking bugs."

He looked confused. "Okay."

"Seen any?"

"Down here?"

"Anywhere."

Dark brows drew in. "The cockroaches seem to be getting smarter."

"I noticed that too. Anything else?"

Broad shoulders shrugged. "Sometimes I think I'm hearing things, but the other guys say it's just me."

If they're really intelligent and nesting in the tunnels, they wouldn't want the maintenance workers to find them, would they? Even if they did cross over from some television-inspired hell dimension, a couple of TTC-issue flame-throwers would still take them out. They'd wait, hiding quietly, feeding where it wouldn't be noticed until . . .

Until what?

Until there were enough to them to . . . to . . .

The heat under her hand and the thrum of blood so close weren't making it any easier to think. Not that she'd ever thought well on an empty stomach.

Later, when she lifted her mouth from an open vein in the crook of a sweaty elbow, she had the strangest feeling of being watched. Watched in an empty section of tunnel with no feel of another life anywhere near.

Watched and weighed.

Mike Celluci was asleep when Vicki got home an hour or so before dawn. He was lying on his back, one arm under the covers, one flung out over the empty half of the bed. She slipped in beside him and snuggled up against his shoulder, still damp and warm from the shower, knowing this was how she felt the most human—body temperature almost normal, skin flushed. She felt him wake, felt his arm tighten around her.

"So how'd the job work out?"

"Giant intelligent bloodsucking bugs in the subway." She was beginning to enjoy saying it.

"Seriously?"

"Well, so far I'm pretty much taking the word of my employer. I had a look around the tunnels in question and saw sweet FA but he truly believes there's something nasty down there and I think he may be right."

"There's a lot of nasty in the tunnels."

Memory called up the underwear. Vicki winced. "Yeah. I know." After a moment, spent pushing back against the large hand stroking her back, she sighed and murmured, "Any rumors going around Toronto's finest about strange shit in the subway?"

"Sweet talker."

"Just answer the question."

"No one's said anything to me but I'll ask around. You should probably talk to TTC security."

"Tomorrow. Well, technically, later today."

"You . . . hungry?"

Which wasn't really what he was asking her but feeding had gotten so tied up with other things it had become impossible to separate them. They'd tried. It hadn't worked.

"I could eat."

She only took a mouthful or two from him these days. Enough for mutual sensation, not enough to worry about bleeding him dry over time. Every relationship had to make compromises—she never told him she when she got a bite downtown, he didn't die.

Tonight was . . . different.

Sitting up, sheet folding across her lap, she rolled the taste of his blood around in her mouth.

Sharp. A little bitter.

Like something had been . . . added?

"S'matter?" he asked sleepily, rubbing the toes of one foot against the ankle of the other.

"Mike, have you been in a subway station lately?" She crawled to the end of the bed.

"Sure."

"Bloor and Yonge?"

"Yeah."

Two half healed puncture wounds under the outside curve of his left ankle.

Her eyes silvered.

The job had just gotten personal.

The sun set at 6:03 PM.

Vicki blinked at the darkness, back in the world between one instant and the next.

The phone rang at 6:04.

Pulling it out of the adapter, she flipped it open and snapped, "What?"

"Ms. Nelson. I saw another one!"

"Duncan?" The reception inside a plywood box wrapped in a blackout curtain inside Mike Celluci's crawl space wasn't the best.

"This one didn't just stare at me, Ms. Nelson. It started walking toward me. It knew who I was!"

"Maybe it remembers how you taste." The words were out of her mouth before she could consider their effect.

"OHGODOHGODOHGOD . . ."

"Duncan, calm down. Now." A sort of whimper and then ragged breathing.

"St. George station. University line. They're spreading, aren't they?"

"So it seems."

"What should I *do*?"

"Do?" Vicki paused, half folded around, reaching for the folded pile of clean clothes by her feet. "You should stay out of subway stations." She snagged a pair of socks and began pulling them on. "What blood type are you?"

"What?"

Shimmying underwear up over her hips, she repeated the question.

"O—positive . . ."

She cut him off before he could ask why she wanted to know, told him she'd be in touch, and hung up.

Type O blood could be given to anyone because its erythrocytes contained no antigens, making it compatible with any plasma. Knowledge from before the change. After, well, blood was blood was blood; hot and sweet and the type, so not relevant.

A lot of people were type O.

Mike Celluci was type O.

The faxed sketch of the King-tic was lying on the kitchen table under an old bank envelope. On the back of the envelope, Celluci's dark scrawl: "If this isn't a joke, TRY to be careful. Better yet, catch one, use it to convince the city they have a problem, and let them deal with the rest. Call me."

Someone in Duncan's group had talent. Drawn on graph paper, the bug was almost three dimensional. Six legs but grouped around a single, spiderlike body. Feathery antennae, like on a moth, two eyes on short stalks, four darker areas against the front of the body that could be more eyes. It had a *face,* which was just creepy. Notes under the drawing described the color as urban camouflage, black and grey, different on every bug they'd seen. The size . . .

Vicki blinked and looked again.

Giant intelligent bloodsucking bugs.

Still, she hadn't expected them to be so big.

A foot across and another six to eight inches on either side for the legs.

Leaving the sketch on the table, she crossed the kitchen and peered into the cupboard under the sink. Picked up a package of roach motels, put it down again. Grabbed instead for the can of bug spray, guaranteed to work on roaches, earwigs, flies, millipedes, and all other invading insects.

All other?

Probably not, but it never hurt to be prepared.

"Mike? What've you got for me?" Had she still been able to blush, she would have at his response, but since she couldn't, she just grinned. "Stop being smutty and answer the question. Because I'm on the subway and do not need that image in my head."

Feeling the weight of regard, Vicki lifted her chin and caught the eye of the very bleached blond young man sitting directly across the train and let just a little of the Hunger show. He froze, fingernails digging into the red fuzz on the front curve of the seat. When she released him, he ran for the other end of the car.

She really hated eavesdroppers.

"Yeah, I'm listening."

An old woman had collapsed at the Bay Street station and died later in hospital. Police were investigating because according to witnesses she'd cried out in pain just before she fell. According to the medical report she'd died of anaphylactic shock.

"An allergic reaction to something in her blood? What type? Yeah, yeah, I know you told me what type of reaction, what blood type?"

Type O.

"This isn't the actual size, right?"

"Of course not." Vicki smiled down at the TTC security guard and took comfort in the knowledge that she wasn't, in fact, lying. Not her fault if he assumed the bugs were smaller than drawn.

"I'm afraid I can't help you. I mean, Joe Public hasn't complained about anything like this and none of my people have said anything either." He handed back the sketch, smiling broadly, willing to share the joke. "You've *seen* one of these?"

"Not me. Like I said, I'm working on a case and my client thinks he's seen one of these."

"And you get paid if they're real or not?"

"Something like that."

"Not a bad gig."

"Pays the bills. What's wrong?"

"What? Oh, just an itchy ankle."

"Let me see." Not a request. No room for refusal. She loved the social shortcuts that came with the whole bloodsucking undead thing.

Two holes. Just below the ankle.

"Do you know your blood type?"

"Uh . . . A?"

More people knew their astrological sign than their blood type—useful if they were in an accident and the paramedics needed to read their horoscope.

She moved so that her body blocked the view of anyone who might be looking through into the security office—although most of them were trying to see themselves on the monitors. "Give me your hand."

He shuddered slightly as she wrapped cool fingers around heated skin, shuddered a little harder as her teeth met through the dark satin of his wrist. A long swallow for research purposes, another because it was so good, one more just because. A lick against the wound and a moment waiting to be sure the coagulants in her saliva had worked.

Lowering his hand carefully to the arm of his chair, Vicki smiled down into his eyes.

"Thank you for help, Mr. Allan. Is that someone pissing against the wall in the outside stairwell?"

His attention back on the monitors, she slipped out of the room.

There was nothing in his blood, type A blood, that wasn't supposed to be there.

The old woman, type O, had died from an allergic reaction to a foreign substance in her blood.

Mike, type O, had a foreign substance in his blood.

If Duncan Travis also had a foreign substance in his blood then it would safe to assume the King-tics were specifically making specific blood types. She should check Duncan for markers, find a B and an AB who'd been bitten and . . .

Screw it. Discovering if they were only marking Os or marking everything but As wouldn't help her find the bugs any faster. The fact that they were marking at all and that she couldn't think a good reason why, but could think of several bad reasons was enough to propel her into the crowd of commuters and down into the Bloor station.

The fastest way to find something? Go to where it is. *National Geographic* didn't set up all those cameras around water holes because they liked the way the light reflected off the surface.

If the King-tics fed off subway station crowds, then Vicki'd stand in crowded subway stations until she spotted one, no matter how much the press of humanity threatened to overwhelm her. At least at the end of the day, they all smelled like meat rather than the nasal cacophony that poured out of the trains every morning.

Oh, great. Now I'm hungry.

Everyone standing within arm's reach shuffled nervously away.

Oops.

Masking the Hunger, she ran through her list of mental appetite suppressants.

Homer Simpson, Joan Rivers, Richard Simmons, pretty much anyone who'd ever appeared on the Jerry Springer Show . . .

Her mouth flooded with saliva as the rich scent of fresh blood interrupted her litany. A train screamed into the station, the crowd surged forward, and Vicki used the Hunger to cut diagonally across the platform, less aware of the mass of humanity moving around her than she was of the black and grey shadow scuttling across the ceiling. With the attention of any possible witnesses locked on the interior of the subway cars and their chances of actually boarding, she dropped down off the end of the platform and began to run, just barely managing to keep the bug in sight.

Duncan was right. For a big bug, the thing could really motor.

Then it turned sideways and was gone.

Gone?

Rocking to a stop, Vicki flung herself back against the tunnel wall as another train came by, the roar of steel wheels against steel rails covering some much-needed venting. Eleven years on the police force had given her a vocabulary most sailors would envy. She got through about half of it while the train passed.

In the sudden silence that followed the fading echoes of profanity, she heard the faint skittering sound of six fast moving legs. A sound that offered its last skitter directly over her head. All she had to do was look up.

Unlike the King-tic in the drawing, this one had a membranous sac bulging out from the lower curve of its body. Inside the sac, about an ounce of blood.

Vicki's snarl was completely involuntary.

Both eyestalks pointing directly at her, the bug brought one foreleg up and rubbed at its antennae.

Again the feeling of being weighed.

And wanted.

The eyestalks turned and it flattened itself enough to slip through a crack between the wall and the ceiling.

Easy to find handholds in the concrete since the city had trouble finding money to repair the infrastructure people could see. Anything tucked away underground could be left to rot. Pressed as flat as possible against the wall—*What good is saving the world if you lose your ass to a passing subway?*—Vicki tucked her head sideways and peered through the crack at what seemed to be another tunnel identical to the one she was in. In the dim glow of the safety lights, it looked as though the shadows were in constant movement.

King-tics.

Lots and lots of them.

Probably nesting in an old emergency access tunnel, she decided as something poked her in the back of the head.

Turning she came eye to eye to eye with another bug. After she got the girly shriek out of the way, she realized it didn't seem upset to find her there, it just wanted her to move. Backing carefully down two handholds, she watched it slide sideways through the crack, briefly flashing its sac of blood.

Hard not to conclude that they were feeding something.

She slid the rest of the way to the tunnel floor, waited for a train to pass, and began working her way carefully up the line. If the bugs were using that crack as their primary access, that suggested the main access had been sealed shut. Twenty paces. Twenty-five. And her fingertips caught a difference in the wall.

The TTC had actually gone to the trouble of parging over the false wall, most likely in an attempt to hide it—or more specifically what was behind it—from street people looking for a place to squat. The faint outline of a door suggested they hadn't originally wanted to hide it from themselves. Forcing her fingers through the thin layer of concrete, Vicki hooked them under the nearest edge and pulled, the *crack* hidden in the roar of a passing train.

Under the concern, plywood and a narrow door nailed shut.

The nails parted faster than the concrete had.

Feeling a little like Sigourney Weaver and a lot like she should have her head examined, Vicki pushed into the second tunnel.

It wasn't very big; a blip in the line between Yonge and University swinging around to the north of the Bay Street station, probably closed because it came too close to any number of expensive stores. Although the third rail was no longer live, it seemed everything else had just been sealed up and forgotten. The place reeked of old blood and sulfur.

Well, they certainly smell like they came from a hell dimension.

Closing the door behind her, Vicki waded carefully toward what seemed to be the quiet center in the mass of seething bugs.

The bugs ignored her.

They can't feed from me, so they ignore me. I've

done nothing to harm them, so they ignore me. I also feed on blood so they . . . Holy shit.

Duncan Travis and his group had been certain there'd be a queen in the nest. They were just a bit off. There were three queens. Well, three great big scary somethings individually wrapped in pulsing gelatinous masses being fed by the returning blood carrying—no, harvesting—bugs.

You guys haven't missed a cliché, have you?

Sucker bet that the blood being drained down between three frighteningly large pairs of gaping mandibles was type O. The workers could probably feed on any type—since they seemed to be biting across the board—but they needed that specific universal donor thing to create a queen.

Like worker bees feeding a larva royal jelly.

And Mike laughed at me for watching "The Magic School Bus."

As she shifted her weight forward, a double row of slightly larger King-tics moved into place between her and the queens. Apparently, their tolerance stopped a couple of meters out. Not a problem; Vicki didn't need to get any closer. Didn't actually want to get any closer. Like recognized like and she knew predators when she saw them. The queens would not be taking delicate bites from the city's ankles, they'd be biting the city off at the ankles and feeding on the bodies as they fell.

A sudden desire to whip out the can of bug spray and see just how well it lived up to its advertising promise was hurriedly squashed. As was Mike's idea of grabbing a bug and presenting it to the proper authorities—whoever the hell they were. Somehow it just didn't seem smart—or survivable—to piss them off while she was standing in midst of hundreds of them. Barely lifting her feet from the floor, she shuffled back toward the door, hurrying just a little when she saw that all three queens had turned their eyestalks toward her.

Odds were good they weren't going to be confined by that gelatinous mass much longer.

So. What to do?

Closing the door carefully behind her, she waited, shoulder blades pressed tight against the wood as another train went by. Options? She supposed she could always let the TTC deal with it. It would be as easy for her to convince the right TTC official to come down to the tunnels for a little look as it would be for her to convince him to expose his throat. Not as much fun, but as easy. Unfortunately, years of experience had taught her that the wheels of bureaucracy ran slowly, even given a shove, and her instincts—new and old—were telling her they didn't have that kind of time to waste.

Still, given that the King-tics were nesting in the subway system, it seemed only right that the TTC deal with it.

Vicki picked up the garbage train at Sherbourne. There were no security cameras in the control booth and coverage on the platform didn't extend to someone entering the train from the tracks. Tucking silently in behind the driver, Vicki tapped him on the shoulder and dropped her masks.

And sighed at the sudden pervasive smell of urine.

"Your hands! Blood all over your hands!"

"It's not blood," she sighed, scrubbing her palms against the outside of her thighs. "It's rust. Now concentrate, I need you to tell me how to start this thing."

"Union rules . . ."

Her upper lip curled.

". . . have no relevance here. Okay. Sure. Push this."

"And to go faster?"

"This. To stop . . ."

"Stopping won't be a problem." She leaned forward, fingers gently gripping his jaw, her eyes silver. "Go join your coworkers on the platform. Be surprised when the train starts to move. Don't do *any-thing* that might stop it or cause it to be stopped. Forget you ever saw me."

"Saw who?"

*   *   *

Mike was watching the news when Vicki came upstairs the next evening. "Here's something you might be interested in. Seems a garbage train went crashing into an access tunnel and blew up—which they're not wont to do—but unfortunately a very hot fire destroyed all the evidence."

"Did you just say *wont*?"

"Maybe. Why?"

Just wondering." Leaning over the back of his chair, she kissed the top of his head. "Anyone get hurt?"

"No. And, fortunately, the safety protocols activated in time to save the surrounding properties."

"Big words. You quoting?"

"Yes. You crazy?"

She thought about it for a minute but before she could answer, her phone rang. Stepping away from the chair, she flipped it open. "Good evening, Duncan."

"How did you know it was me?"

"Call display."

"Oh. Right. But yesterday . . . ?"

"You called before I was up. It's pretty damned dark inside a coffin."

"You sleep in a coffin!?"

"No, I'm messing with your head again. I expect you've seen the news?"

"It's the only thing that's been on all day. You did that, didn't you? That was you destroying the nest! Did you get them all?"

"Yes."

"Are you sure?"

"They shit sulfur, Duncan. They were pretty flammable."

"But what if some of them were out, you know, hunting?"

"They hunt on crowded subway platforms. No crowds in the wee smalls."

"Oh. Okay. Did you find out where they came from?"

"No. It didn't seem like a good idea to sit down

and play twenty questions with them. And besides, they just seemed to be intelligent because they were following pretty specific programming. They were probably no smarter than your average cockroach."

"But giant and bloodsucking?"

"Oh, yeah."

Vicki had no idea what he was thinking about during the long pause that followed; she didn't *want* to know.

"So it's safe for me to go back on the subway?"

"You and three million other people."

"About your bill . . ."

"We'll talk about it tomorrow in the coffee shop— we should be able to get into the area by then." She looked a question at Mike, now standing and watching her. He nodded reluctantly. "Seven thirty. Good night, Duncan."

Mike shook his head as she powered off the phone and holstered it. "You're actually going to charge him?"

"Well, I'd send a bill to the city but I doubt they'd pay it—given that there's no actual evidence I just saved their collective butts. Again." Demons, mummies, King-tics—it was amazing how fast that sort of thing got old. She followed Mike into the kitchen and watched a little jealously as he poured a cup of coffee. She missed coffee.

"Speaking of no actual evidence; how did you get the garbage train to blow?"

Vicki grinned. "Not that I'm admitting anything, detective-sergeant, but *if* I wanted top blow up a garbage train in a specific giant bloodsucking bug-infested place, I'd probably use a little accelerant and a timer, having first switched the rails and cleared the tunnels of all mammalian life forms."

"You closed down the entire system, Vicki."

"Giant bloosucking bugs, Mike."

"I'm not saying you didn't have a good reason," he sighed, leaning against the counter. "But don't you think your solution was a little extreme?"

"Not really, no."

"What aren't you telling me?"

Moving into his arms, she bit him lightly on the chin. "I'm not telling you I blew up that garbage train."

"Good point."

"I'm not telling you what I really think of people who watch golf."

"Thank you."

She could feel his smile against the top of her head, his heart beating under her cheek, his life in her hands. Nor was she telling him that people like him, with type O blood, had been tagged so they'd be easier to find. Why bother with random biting when it was possible to go straight to the blood needed to create new queens? Even if they'd been harmless parasites, she'd have blown them up for that alone.

Mike Celluci was hers and she didn't share.

"Vicki, you going to tell me what you're snarling about?"

"Just thinking of something that really bugs me . . ."

Sceleratus

"Man, this whole church thing just freaks me right out." Tony came out of the shadows where the street-lights stopped short of Holy Rosary Cathedral and fell into step beside the short, strawberry blond man who'd just come out of the building. "I mean, you're a member of the bloodsucking undead for Christ's sa . . . Ow!" He rubbed the back of his head. "What was that for?"

"I just came from confession. I'm in a mood."

"It's going to pass, right?" In the time it took him to maneuver around three elderly Chinese women, his companion had made it almost all the way to the parking lot and he had to run to catch up. "You know, we've been together what, almost two years, and you haven't been in church since last year around this time and . . ."

"Exactly this time."

"Okay. Is it like an anniversary or something?"

"Exactly like an anniversary." Henry Fitzroy, once Duke of Richmond and Somerset, bastard son of Henry VIII, fished out the keys to his BMW and unlocked the door.

Tony studied Henry's face as he got into his own seat, as he buckled his seat belt, as Henry pulled out onto Richards Street. "You want to tell me about it?" he asked at last.

They'd turned onto Smithe Street before Henry answered. . . .

*   *   *

Even after three weeks of torment, her body burned and broken, she was still beautiful to him. He cut the rope and caught her as she dropped, allowing her weight to take him to his knees. Holding her against his heart, rocking back and forth in a sticky pool, he waited for grief.

She had been dead only a few hours when he'd found her, following a blood scent so thick it left a trail even a mortal could have used. Her wrists had been tightly bound behind her back, a coarse rope threaded through the lashing and used to hoist her into the air. Heavy iron weights hung from burned ankles. The Inquisitors had begun with flogging and added more painful persuasions over time. Time had killed her; pain layered on pain until finally life had fled.

They'd had a year together, a year of nights since he'd followed her home from the Square of San Marco. He'd waited until the servants were asleep and then slipped unseen and unheard into her father's house, into her room. Her heartbeat had drawn him to the bed, and he'd gently pulled the covers back. Her name was Ginevra Treschi. Almost thirty, and three years a widow, she wasn't beautiful but she was so alive—even asleep—that he'd found himself staring. Only to find a few moments later that she was staring back at him.

"I don't want to hurry your decision," she'd said dryly, "but I'm getting chilled and I'd like to know if I should scream."

He'd intended to feed and then convince her that he was a dream but he found he couldn't.

For the first time in a hundred years, for the first time since he had willingly pressed his mouth to the bleeding wound in his immortal lover's breast, Henry Fitzroy allowed someone to see him as he was.

All he was.

Vampire. Prince. Man.

Allowed love.

Ginevra Treschi had brought light back into a life spent hiding from the sun.

Only one gray eye remained beneath a puckered lid and the Inquisitors had burned off what remained of the dark hair—the ebony curls first shorn in the convent that had been no protection from the Hounds of God. In Venice, in the year of our Lord 1637, the Hounds hunted as they pleased among the powerless. First, it had been the Jews, and then the Moors, and then those suspected of Protestantism until finally the Inquisition, backed by the gold flowing into Spain from the New World, began to cast its net where it chose. Ginevra had been an intelligent woman who dared to think for herself. In this time, that was enough.

Dead flesh compacted under his hands as his grip tightened. He wanted to rage and weep and mourn his loss, but he felt nothing. Her light, her love, had been extinguished and darkness had filled its place.

His heart as cold as hers, Henry kissed her forehead and laid the body gently down. When he stood, his hands were covered in her blood.

There would be blood enough to wash it away.

He found the priests in a small study, sitting at ease in a pair of cushioned chairs on either side of a marble hearth, slippered feet stretched out toward the fire, gold rings glittering on pale fingers. Cleaned and fed, they still stank of her death.

". . . confessed to having relations with the devil, was forgiven, and gave her soul up to God. Very satisfactory all around. Shall we return the body to the Sisters or to her family?"

The older Dominican shrugged. "I cannot see that it makes any difference, she . . . Who are you?"

Henry lifted his lip off his teeth in a parody of a smile. "I am vengeance," he said, closing and bolting the heavy oak door behind him. When he turned, he saw that the younger priest, secure in the power he wielded, blinded by that security, had moved toward him.

Their eyes met. The priest, who had stood calmly by while countless *heretics* found their way to redemption on paths of pain, visibly paled.

Henry stopped pretending to smile. "And I am the devil Ginevra Treschi had relations with."

He released the Hunger her blood had called.

They died begging for their lives as Ginevra had died.

It wasn't enough.

The Grand Inquisitor had sent five other Dominicans to serve on his Tribunal in Venice. Three died at prayer. One died in bed. One died as he dictated a letter to a novice who would remember nothing but darkness and blood.

The Doge, needing Spain's political and monetary support to retain power, had given the Inquisitors a wing of his palace. Had given them the room where the stone walls were damp and thick and the screams of those the Hounds brought down would not disturb his slumber.

Had killed Ginevra as surely as if he'd used the irons.

With a soft cry, Gracia la Valla sat bolt upright in the Doge's ornate bed clutching the covers in both hands. The canopy was open and a spill of moonlight pattered the room in shadows.

She heard a sound beside her and, thinking she'd woken her lover, murmured, as she reached out for him, "Such a dark dream I had."

Her screams brought the household guard.

He killed the Inquisition's holy torturer quickly, like the animal he was, and left him lying beside the filthy pallet that was his bed.

It still wasn't enough.

*　　*　　*

In the hour before dawn, Henry carried the body of Ginevra Treschi to the chapel of the Benedictine Sisters who had tried to shelter her. He had washed her in the canal, wrapped her in linen, and laid her in front of their altar, her hands closed around the rosary she'd given him the night they'd parted.

Her lips when he kissed them were cold.

But so were his.

Although he had all but bathed in the blood of her murderers, it was her blood still staining his hands.

He met none of the sisters and, as much as he could feel anything, he was glad of it. Her miraculous return to the cloister would grant her burial in their consecrated ground—but not if death returned with her.

Henry woke the next night in one of the vaults under San Marco, the smell of her blood all around him. It would take still more blood to wash it away. For all their combined power of church and state, the Inquisition did not gather their victims randomly. Someone had borne witness against her.

Giuseppe Lemmo.

Marriage to him had been the alternative to the convent.

He had a large head, and a powdered gray wig, and no time for denial. After Henry had drunk his fill, head and wig and the body they were more or less attached to slid silently into the canal.

As Lemmo sank beneath the filthy water, the sound of two men approaching drove Henry into the shadows. His clothing stank of new death and old, but it was unlikely anyone could smell it over the stink of the city.

"No, no, I say the Dominicans died at the hand of the devil rising from hell to protect one of his own."

Henry fell silently into step behind the pair of merchants, the Hunger barely leashed.

"And I say," the second merchant snorted, "that the Holy Fathers called it on themselves. They spend so much time worrying about the devil in others, well, there's no smoke without fire. They enjoyed their work too much for my taste and you'll notice, if you look close, that most of their *heretics* had a hefty purse split between the Order and the Doge after their deaths."

"And more talk like that will give them *your* purse to split, you fool."

Actually, it had saved them both, but they would never know it.

"Give who my purse? The Hounds of God in Venice have gone to their just reward." He turned his head and spat into the dark waters of the canal. "And I wish Old Nick the joy of them."

His companion hurriedly crossed himself. "Do you think they're the only dogs in the kennel? The Dominicans are powerful; their tribunals stretch all the way back to Spain and up into the northlands. They won't let this go unanswered. I think you will find before very long that Venice will be overrun by the Hounds of God."

"You think? Fool, the One Hundred will be too busy fighting over a new Doge to tell His Holiness that some of his dogs have been put down."

Before they could draw near the lights and crowds around the Grand Canal, Henry slipped into the deeper darkness between two buildings. The Dominican's Tribunals stretched all the way back to Spain. He looked down at Ginevra's blood on his hands.

"Drink, signore?"

Without looking at either the bottle or the man who offered it, Henry shook his head and continued staring out over the moonlit water toward the lights of Sicily. Before him, although he could not tell which lights they were, were the buildings of the Inquisition's largest tribunal outside of Spain. They had their own courthouse, their own prison, their own chapel, their own apartments where half of every *heretic's* possessions ended up.

It was entirely possible they knew he was coming or that *something* was coming. Rumor could travel by day and night while he could move only in darkness.

Behind him stretched a long line of the dead. He had killed both Dominicans and the secular authorities who sat with them on the tribunals. He had killed the lawyers hired by the Inquisition. He had killed those who denounced their neighbors to the Inquisition and those who lent the Inquisition their support. He had killed those who thought to kill him.

He had never killed so often or been so strong. He could stand on a hill overlooking a village and know how many lives were scattered beneath him. He could stand in shadow outside a shuttered building and count the number of hearts beating within. He could stare into the eyes of the doomed and be almost deafened by the song of blood running through their veins. It was becoming hard to tell where he ended and the Hunger began.

The terrified whispers that followed him named him demon, so, when he fed, he hid the marks that would have shown what he truly was. There were too many who believed the old tales and he was far too vulnerable in the day.

"Too good to drink with me, signore?" Stinking of wine, he staggered along the rail until the motion of the waves threw him into Henry's side. Stumbling back, he raised the jug belligerently. "Too good to . . ."

Henry caught the man's gaze with his and held it. Held it through the realization, held it through the terror, held it as the heart began to race with panic, held it as bowels voided. When he finally released it, he caught the jug that dropped from nerveless fingers and watched the man crawl whimpering away, his mind already refusing to admit what he had seen.

It had been easy to find a ship willing to cross the narrow strait at night. Henry had merely attached himself to a party of students negotiating their return to the university after spending the day in the brothels of Reggio and the exotic arms of mainland whores. Although the sky was clear, the moon full, and the winds from the northwest, the captain of the schooner had accepted their combined coin so quickly he'd probably been looking for an excuse to make the trip. No doubt, his hold held some of the steady stream of goods from France, Genoa, and Florence that moved illegally down the western coast to the Spanish-controlled kingdom of Naples and then to Sicily.

The smugglers would use the students as Henry intended, as a diversion over their arrival in Messina.

They passed the outer arm of the sickle-shaped harbor, close enough that the night no longer hid the individual buildings crouched on the skirts of Mount Etna. He could see the spire of the cathedral, the Abbey of Santa Maria della Valle, the monastery of San Giorgio, but nothing that told him where the Dominicans murdered in the name of God.

No matter.

It would be easy enough to find what he was looking for.

They could lock themselves away, but Henry would find them. They could beg or plead or pray, but they would die. And they would keep dying until enough blood had poured over his hands to wash the stain of Ginevra's blood away.

Messina was a port city and had been in continuous use since before the days of the Roman Empire. Beneath its piers and warehouses, beneath broad avenues and narrow streets, beneath the lemon trees and the olive groves, were the ruins of an earlier city. Beneath its necropolis were Roman catacombs.

As the students followed their hired torchbearer from the docks to the university, Henry followed the scent of death through the streets until he came at last to the end of the Via Annunziata to the heavy iron gates that closed off the Piazza del Dominico from the rest of the city. The pair of stakes rising out of the low stone dais in the center of the square had been used within the last three or four days. The stink of burning flesh almost overwhelmed the stink of fear.

Almost.

"Hey! You! What are you doing?"

The guard's sudden roar out of the shadows was intended to intimidate.

"Why the gates?" Henry asked without turning. The Hounds preferred an audience when they burned away heresy.

"You a stranger?"

"I am vengeance," Henry said quietly, touching the iron and rubbing the residue of greasy smoke between two fingers. As the guard reached for him, he turned and closed his hand about the burly wrist, tightening his grip until bones cracked and the man fell to his knees. "Why the gates?" he repeated.

"Friends. Oh, God, please . . ." It wasn't the pain that made him beg but the darkness in the stranger's eyes. "Some of the heretics got friends!"

"Good." He had fed in Reggio, so he snapped the guard's neck and let the body fall back into the shadows. Without the guard, the gates were no barrier.

"You said he was ready to confess." Habit held up out of the filth, The Dominican stared disapprovingly at the body on the rack. "He is unconscious!"

The thin man in the leather apron shrugged. "Wasn't when I sent for you."

"Get him off that thing and back into the cell with the others." Sandals sticking to the floor, he stepped back beside the second monk and shook his head. "I am exhausted and his attorney has gone home. Let God's work take a break until morning, for pity's . . ."

The irons had not been in the fire, but they did what they'd been made to do. Even as the Hunger rose to answer the blood now turning the robe to black and white and red, Henry appreciated the irony of the monk's last word. A man who knew no pity had died with pity on his tongue. The second monk screamed and choked on a crimson flood as curved knives, taken from the table beside the rack, hooked in under his arms and met at his breastbone.

Henry killed the jailer as he'd killed the guard. Only those who gave the orders paid in blood.

Behind doors of solid oak, one large cell held half a dozen prisoners and two of the smaller cells held one prisoner each. Removing the bars, Henry opened the doors and stepped back out of sight. He had learned early that prisoners would rather remain to face the Inquisition than walk by him, but he always watched them leave, some small foolish part of his heart hoping he'd see Ginevra among them, free and alive.

The prisoner from one of the small cells surged out as the door was opened. Crouched low and ready for a fight, he squinted in the torchlight searching for an enemy. When he saw the bodies, he straightened and his generous mouth curved up into a smile. Hair as red-gold as Henry's had begun to gray, but in spite of approaching middle-age, his body was trim and well built. He was well-dressed and clearly used to being obeyed.

On his order, four men and two women shuffled out of the large cell, hands raised to block the light, bits of straw clinging to hair and clothing. On his order, they led the way out of the prison.

He was using them to see if the way was clear, Henry realized. Clever. Ginevra had been clever, too.

Murmured Latin drew his attention back to the bodies of the Dominicans. Kneeling between them, a hand on each brow, the elderly Franciscan who'd emerged from the other cell performed the Last Rites.

"In nominee Patris, et Filii, et Spiritus Sancti. Amen." One hand gripping the edge of the rack, he pulled himself painfully to his feet. "You can come out now. I know what you are."

"You have no idea, monk."

"You think not?" The old man shrugged and bent to release the ratchet that held the body on the rack taut. "You are the death that haunts the Inquisition.

You began in Venice, you finally found your way to us here in Messina."

"If I am death, you should fear me."

"I haven't feared death for some time." He turned and swept the shadows with a rheumy gaze. "Are you afraid to face *me,* then?"

Lips drawn back off his teeth, Henry moved into the light.

The Franciscan frowned. "Come closer."

Snarling, Henry stepped over one of the bodies, the blood scent wrapping around him. Prisoner of the Inquisition or not, the monk would learn fear. He caught the Franciscan's gaze with his but, to his astonishment, couldn't hold it. When he tried to look away, he could not.

After a long moment, the old monk sighed, and released him. "Not evil, although you have done evil. Not anger, nor joy in slaughter. I never knew your kind could feel such pain."

He staggered back, clutching for the Hunger as it fled. "I feel nothing!"

"So you keep telling yourself. What happened in Venice, vampire? Who did the Inquisition kill that you try to wash away the blood with theirs?"

Over the roaring in his head, Henry heard himself say, "Ginevra Treschi."

"You loved her."

It wasn't a question. He answered it anyway. "Yes."

"You should kill me, you know. I have seen you. I know what you are. I know what is myth . . ." He touched two fingers to the wooden cross hanging against his chest. ". . . and I know how to destroy you. When you are helpless in the day, I could drag your body into sunlight; I could hammer a stake through your heart. For your own safety, you should kill me."

He was right.

What was one more death? Henry's fingers, sticky with blood already shed, closed around the old man's skinny neck. He would kill him quickly and return to the work he had come here to do. There were many, many more Dominicans in Messina.

The Franciscan's pulse beat slow and steady.

It beat Henry's hand back to his side. "No. I do not kill the innocent."

"I will not argue original sin with you, vampire, but you're wrong. Parigi Carradori, the man from the cell next to mine, seeks power from the Lord of Hell by sacrificing children in dark rites."

Henry's lip curled. "Neither do I listen to the Inquisition's lies."

"No lie; Carradori admits it freely without persuasion. The demons hold full possession of his mind, and you have sent him out to slaughter the closest thing to innocence in the city."

"That is none of my concern."

"If that is true, then you really should kill me."

"Do not push me, old man!" He reached for the Hunger but for the first time since Ginevra's death it was slow to answer.

"By God's grace, you are being given a chance to save yourself. To find, if you will, redemption. You may, of course, choose to give yourself fully to the darkness you have had wrapped about you for so many months, allowing it, finally, into your heart. Or you may choose to begin making amends."

"Amends?" He stepped back slowly so it wouldn't look so much like a retreat and spat into the drying blood pooled out from the Dominicans' bodies. "You want me to feel sorrow for the deaths of these men?"

"Not yet. To feel sorrow, you must first feel. Begin by stopping Carradori. We will see what the Lord has in mind for you after that." He patted the air between them, an absentminded benediction, then turned and began to free the man on the rack, working the leather straps out of creases in the swollen arms.

Henry watched him for a moment, then turned on one heel and strode out of the room.

He was not going after Carradori. His business was with the Inquisition, with those who had slowly murdered his Ginevra, not with a man who may or may not be dealing with the Dark One.

". . . you have sent him out to slaughter the closest thing to innocence in the city."

He was not responsible for what Carradori chose to do with his freedom. Stepping out into the square, he listened to the sound of Dominican hearts beating all around him. Enough blood to finally *be* enough.

". . . seeks power from the Lord of Hell by sacrificing children in dark rites."

Children died. Some years, more children died than lived. He could not save them all even were he willing to try.

"You may choose to give yourself fully to the darkness. Or you may choose to begin making amends."

"Shut up, old man!"

Torch held high, head cocked to better peer beyond its circle of light, a young monk stepped out of one of the other buildings. "Who is there? Is that you, Brother Pe . . . ?" He felt more than saw a shadow slip past him. When he moved the torch forward, he saw only the entrance to the prison. A bloody handprint glistened on the pale stone.

The prisoners had left the gate open. Most of them had taken the path of least resistance and stumbled down the Via Annunziata, but one had turned left, gone along the wall heading up toward the mountain.

Carradori.

Out away from the stink of terror that filled the prison, Henry could smell the taint of the Dark One in his blood.

The old man hadn't lied about that, at least.

Behind him, a sudden cacophony of male voices suggested his visit had been discovered. It would be dangerous to deal further with the Inquisition tonight. He turned left.

He should have caught up to Carradori in minutes, but he didn't and he found himself standing outside a row of tenements pressed up against the outer wall of the necropolis with no idea of where the man had gone. Lip drawn up off his teeth, he snarled softly and a scrawny dog, thrown out of sleep by the sound, began to howl. In a heartbeat, a dozen more were protesting the appearance of a new predator on their territory.

The noise the monks had made was nothing in comparison.

As voices rained curses down from a dozen windows, Henry ran for the quiet of the necropolis.

The City of the Dead had tenements of its own; the dead had been stacked in this ground since the Greeks controlled the strait. Before Venice, before Ginevra, Henry had spent very little time with the dead—his own grave had not exactly been a restful place. Of late, however, he had grown to appreciate the silence. No heartbeats, no bloodsong, nothing to call the Hunger, to remind him of vengeance not yet complete.

But not tonight.

Tonight he could hear two hearts and feel a life poised on the edge of eternity.

The houses of the dead often became temples for the dark arts.

Warding glyphs had been painted in blood on the outside of the mausoleum. Henry sneered and passed them by. Blood held a specific power over him, as specific as the power he held over it. The dark arts were a part of neither.

The black candles, one at either end of the skinny child laid out on the tomb, shed so little light Henry entered without fear of detection. To his surprise, Carradori looked directly at him with wild eyes.

"And so the agent of my Dark Lord comes to take his place by my side." Stripped to the waist, he had cut more glyphs into his own flesh, new wounds over old scars.

"I am no one's agent," Henry spat, stepping forward.

"You set me free, vampire. You slaughtered those who had imprisoned me."

"You may choose to give yourself fully to the darkness."

"That had nothing to do with you."

Holding a long straight blade over the child, Carradori laughed. "Then why are you here?"

"Or you may choose to begin making amends."

"I was curious."

"Then let me satisfy your curiosity."

He lifted the knife and the language he spoke was neither Latin nor Greek, for Henry's father had seen that he was fluent in both. It had hard consonants that tore at the ears of the listener as much as at the throat of the speaker. The Hunger, pushed back by the Franciscan, rose in answer.

This would be one way to get enough blood.

Then the child turned her head.

Gray eyes stared at Henry past a fall of ebony curls. One small, dirty hand stretched out toward him.

But the knife was already on its way down.

He caught the point on the back of his arm, felt it cut through him toward the child as his fist drove the bones of Carradori's face back into his brain. He was dead before he hit the floor.

The point of the blade had touched the skin over the child's heart but the only blood in the tomb was Henry's.

He dragged the knife free and threw it aside, catching the little girl up in his arms and sliding to his knees. The new wound in his arm was nothing to the old wound in his heart. It felt as though a glass case had been shattered and now the shards were slicing their way out. Rocking back and forth, he buried his face in the child's dark curls and sobbed over and over, "I'm sorry, I'm sorry, I'm sorry."

". . . confessed to having relations with the devil, was forgiven, and gave her soul up to God."

"And I am the devil Ginevra Treschi had relations with."

Loving him had killed her.

*   *   *

When he woke the next evening the old Franciscan was sitting against the wall, the shielded lantern at his feet making him a gray shadow in the darkness.

"I thought you'd bring a mob with stakes and torches."

"Not much of a hiding place, if that's what you thought."

Sitting up, Henry glanced around the alcove and shrugged. He had left the girl at the tenements, one grimy hand buried in the ruff of the scrawny dog he'd wakened and then, with dawn close on his heels, he'd gone into the first layer of catacombs and given himself to the day.

"Why didn't you?"

"'Vengeance is mine,' sayeth the Lord. And besides . . ." Clutching the lantern, he heaved himself to his feet. ". . . I hate to lose a chance to redeem a soul."

"You know what I am. I have no soul."

"You said you loved this Ginevra Treschi. Love does not exist without a soul."

"My love killed her."

"Perhaps." Setting the lantern on the tomb, he took Henry's left hand in his and turned his palm to the light. The wound began to bleed sluggishly again, the blood running down the pale skin of Henry's forearm to pool in his palm. "Did she choose to love you in return?"

His voice less than a whisper. "Yes."

"Then don't take that choice away from her. She has lost enough else. You have blood on your hands, vampire. But not hers."

He stared at the crimson stains. "Not hers."

"No. And you can see whose blood is needed to wash away the rest." He gently closed Henry's fingers.

"Mine . . ."

The smack on the back of the head took him by surprise. He hadn't even seen the old monk move.

"The Blood of the Lamb, vampire. Your death will

not bring my brother Dominicans back to life, but your life will be long enough to atone."

"You are a very strange monk."

"I wasn't always a monk. I knew one of your kind in my youth and perhaps by redeeming you, I redeem myself for the mob and the stakes I brought to him."

Henry could see his own sorrow mirrored in the Franciscan's eyes. He knew better than to attempt to look beyond it.

"Why were you a prisoner of the Inquisition?"

"I'm a Franciscan. The Dominicans don't appreciate our holding of the moral high ground."

"The moral high ground . . ."

"Christ was poor. We are poor. *They* are not. Which does not mean, however, that they need to die."

"I didn't . . ."

"I know." He laid a warm palm against Henry's hair. "How long has it been since your last confession . . . ?"

"The Tribunal's buildings were destroyed in an earthquake in 1783. They were never rebuilt. When I went back to Messina in the 1860s, even I couldn't find the place they'd been."

Tony stared out into the parking garage. They'd been home for half an hour, just sitting in the car while Henry talked. "Did you really kill all those people?"

"Yes."

"But some of them were bad people, abusing their power and . . . that's not the point, is it?"

"No. They died because I felt guilty about what happened to Ginevra, not because the world would have been a better place without them in it, not because I had to kill to survive." His lips pulled back off his teeth. "I have good reasons when I kill people now."

"Speaking as people," Tony said softly, "I'm glad to hear that."

His tone drew Henry's gaze around. "You're not afraid?"

"Because you vamped out three hundred and fifty years ago?" He twisted in the seat and met Henry's eyes. "No. I know you *now*." When Henry looked away, he reached out and laid a hand on his arm. "Hey, I got a past, too. Not like yours, but you can't live without having done things you need to make up for. Things you're sorry you did."

"Is being sorry enough?"

"I haven't been to Mass since I was a kid, but isn't it supposed to be? I mean, if you're *really* sorry? So what kind of penance did he give you?" Tony asked a few moments later when it became obvious Henry wasn't going to elaborate on how sorry he was.

"Today?"

"No, three hundred and fifty years ago. I mean, three Hail Marys aren't gonna cut it after, well . . ."

"He made me promise to remember."

"That's all?" When it became clear Henry wasn't going to answer that either, he slid out of the car and leaned back in the open door. "Come on, TSN's got Australian rugger on tonight. You know you love it."

"You go. I'll be up in a few minutes."

"You okay?"

"Fine."

"I could . . ."

"Tony."

"Okay. I could go upstairs." He straightened, closed the car door, and headed across the parking garage to the elevator. When he reached it, he hit the call button and waited without turning. He didn't need to turn. He knew what he'd see.

Henry.

Still sitting in the car.

Staring at his hands.

Critical Analysis

"You! You're a police officer, aren't you?"

Detective Sergeant Michael Celluci stared down at the pale, long-fingered hand clutching his arm and then up at the tall, unshaven, young man who'd stopped him on the steps of police headquarters and asked the question. "I am."

Pink-rimmed, bloodshot eyes locked onto Celluci's face. "I need your help."

"With what?"

"Someone's going to kill me."

"Uh-huh." The man was sincerely frightened. Celluci'd seen frightened often enough to know it. Sincere . . . well, not so much. Not in his line of work. He nodded toward the doors where condensation beaded the glass barrier between warmth and January in downtown Toronto. "You want to talk about this inside?"

"His name is Raymond Carr and it started with threatening e-mail." Celluci passed Vicki the file folder and headed over to the coffeemaker. "It escalated to someone hacking his system and sticking the threats into his work."

"What's he do?"

"He's a writer. Did you make this when you got up, or is it sludge left over from this morning?" The mug of coffee he'd just poured stalled halfway to his mouth.

"What do you care? You'd drink the sludge anyway. What's he write?"

"Pretty much anything people will pay him for. Of course, people are paying him a lot less when their ad copy comes complete with death threats."

"You'll save, save, save while we beat in your head with a bat?"

"Less wordy. Oh, and he's working on a book."

"Yeah, isn't everyone." She frowned at the top printout. "I assume the word *die* isn't meant to be in here?" A few more pages in. "Or here? Actually, since it's repeated about a dozen times, forget I asked. What did he do and who did he do it to?"

"He doesn't know."

"Well, he clearly pissed off someone with some hacking abilities," she muttered, scanning the rest of the file.

Celluci pulled out a chair and sat down on the other side of the kitchen table. "He says he didn't."

Fingertips against the edge of the table, she leaned back, balancing on two legs of her chair. "So you think it's some kind of a sick joke? Just some bored tech-nonerd getting his jollies by screwing with a stranger?"

"That's possible. Point is, Carr's terrified. We wrote him up, but there's not much we can do until we have more to go on than electronic threats."

"Don't you guys have techno-nerds of your own now?" She beat out a drum roll. "Several someones who can trace an e-mail like this back to the sender?"

"Apparently, we can't do squat without Carr's computer and he won't hand it over. Says his whole life is on that machine."

"Really? I hope he remembers to do backups." She flipped the folder closed and let her chair drop flat. "What does he expect you—where 'you' refers to Toronto's finest, not you personally—to do?"

"Protect him."

"I think I just figured out where this is going."

Cellcui smiled and drained his mug. "Carr's address

is on the outside of the folder. I told him you'd be by this evening."

"Mike, I'm not hired muscle."

"Did I say you were? You have special abilities."

"Special abilities?" Her smile was both threat and invitation.

He cleared his throat. "And," He continued emphatically, ignoring the invitation and disregarding the threat, "you may be an undead creature of the night, but you were a cop, and a good one, for years. Use *those* skills for a change. Find out who's threatening him. Do some detecting. While you're there, see that no one beats his head in with a bat."

Raymond Carr lived on Bloor Street in a third-floor flat over the Korona Restaurant. As Vicki made her way up the steep, narrow stairs, she avoided touching the grimy banister and wondered if he could afford her services. Mike sometimes forgot she wasn't on the public payroll anymore. Or he was indulging in some weird passive-aggressive "let me take care of you" macho thing. She wasn't sure which.

The apartment door had been painted a deep blue sometime in the distant past. It wore a grimy patina of hand-shaped smudges fading down into black scuff marks probably caused by shoving it open with a booted foot.

Hand raised to knock, Vicki paused and frowned. With millions of lives surrounding her—and, more specifically, with the half a dozen lives close at hand behind inadequate walls of ancient plaster and lathe— it was difficult to separate out the sounds coming from inside Carr's apartment. Sifting sound, disregarding everything that wasn't life, focusing, she picked out a heartbeat. It was slower than it should be. Struggling.

Not even burning onions on the second floor could mask the smell of blood.

The door had a deadbolt on it and a security chain. Both were screwed into a doorframe that had proba-

bly been installed at the turn of the century. The wood
gave way with a sound like a dry cough. The mulitiple
layers of cheap paint hung on a moment longer, then
Vicki was in the apartment and racing down the long
hall toward the front room, following her nose.

This door was also locked.

And was unlocked just as quickly.

A young man—blond hair, pale skin, late-twenties,
approximately six feet tall and a hundred and seventy
pounds—lay sprawled on the linoleum, blood spreading out from under his head along the artificial water-
shed of the uneven floor. He was alone in the room.

Between one heartbeat and the next, Vicki knelt
beside him, his head cradled in one hand, a folded
towel from the bathroom in the other. Had any assail-
ants still been around, they might have wondered
when she'd had time to get back down the hall but
had they still been around, she'd have dealt with them
first, so the question would have been moot. The room
was empty except for the injured man. No one was
hiding under the desk. No one lurked in the tiny turn-
of-the-century closet.

A couple of mouthfuls of spit on the towel—easy
enough to work up under the circumstances, the smell
of blood was making her mouth water—and then both
spit and towel applied to the wound. As the coagulant
in her saliva went to work, she pulled her cell phone
from her pocket, flipped it open, and dialed one-
handed.

"So you broke down the door?"

"That's right."

"Because you could smell the blood?"

"Yes."

"From out in the hall?"

"That's what I said."

"Just trying to get my facts straight, Ms. Nelson."

Vicki forced her lips back down over her teeth as
the earnest young constable went over her statement
for the fourth time.

"And then you broke down the inner door as well?"

"Yes."

He gave her what he probably considered an intimidating stare. "You forced the lock right out of the wood. Splintered the wood. So not only do you have a rather unbelievable sense of smell, you're unusually strong."

"I work out." While she appreciated he was just doing his job, enough was enough. Locking her eyes on his, she smiled. "Now go away," she said softly, "and stop bothering me."

"I . . . I think that's all I need to know."

"Good." A more normal tone. A slightly more normal smile.

He backed up two steps, then turned and scuttled down the hall toward the apartment door, nearly bouncing off Mike Celluci.

"Vicki . . ."

"I was cooperating."

"You terrified him."

"So? Back in the day, I used to terrify the uniforms all the time." She sighed as they fell into step heading toward Carr's tiny office. "When did they start hiring children?"

"About the time I started going gray."

They paused to allow the crime scene team to leave, and Vicki reached up to push the curl of hair back off his face. She'd gotten rather sentimental about his scattering of gray hair—after she stopped being furious at it. Raging at the years that took him farther and farther away from her. She would age, but slowly. She'd changed at thirty-four. It would be centuries before she saw forty.

Sunlight and the occasional idiot Van Helsing clone allowing.

She stepped aside so the head of the crime scene unit could have a talk with Celluci and, well beyond normal eavesdropping distance, eavesdropped shamelessly.

"So," she said when they were finally alone in the

apartment. "The door was locked from the inside, the window was painted shut, and they think they've only got one person's prints, although they'll have to get back to you on that. Didn't I once read a Miss Marple book with this plot?"

"You read a book?"

"Funny man."

Celluci shoved his hands in the pockets of his overcoat and scowled at the room. A battered office chair, more duct tape than upholstery, lay on its side against the outside wall. "He could have just tipped over backward and hit his head."

"With the chair over there and this kind of a spatter pattern? Stop playing idiot's advocate, Mike. Looks to me like he pushed away from the desk, spun the chair around . . ." Vicki sketched the arc in the air. ". . . leaped out of it, and was on his feet when he was hit. Whoever it was came in through the door . . ."

"The locked door."

"We don't know for certain that the door was locked when the assailant *arrived*. Came in through the door," she repeated when Mike nodded reluctantly. "Walked very, very quietly around to about here . . ." She indicated a spot by the desk.

"It didn't have to be that quiet. If Carr was writing, he could have been distracted. Lost in his own world."

"Fair enough. But the assailant didn't just sneak in and attack him from behind, or he'd have fallen forward, over the keyboard. He got Carr's attention first. There must have been a fight. Maybe the neighbors heard something."

"Gosh, Vicki." Celluci's voice dripped heavy, obvious sarcasm. "I would never have thought to ask the neighbors if they heard anything. It's a good thing you're here. And frankly, I'm more concerned with how the guy got out, not in." A long stride took him to the other side of the red-brown puddle. He frowned at the window and the layers of paint that had clearly not been cracked. "Last time this was opened, Trudeau was Prime Minister."

"No one here but Raymond Carr when I broke in. No one passed me on the stairs, and no one came out of the building with a bloody weapon while I was close enough to see the door."

"Would you have seen the weapon under a winter coat?"

She smiled at him. "If it was bloody, I'd have known it was there."

"If. He could have left before you got close."

"Not at the rate Carr was bleeding out. It had to have happened just before I got here or the coroner'd be slabbing him right about now."

He shrugged, accepting her explanation. "Don't these apartments have a back exit into a courtyard?"

"The uniforms checked it. Locked. Three bolts thrown. Impossible to do from outside. And the window in the kitchen has as much paint on it as this one. Plus a layer of grease."

"I hate this kind of shit." Celluci dragged both hands back through his hair, dropping the curl over his forehead again. "I don't suppose our perp turned to mist or smoke, or there's a bat hiding out in a dark corner that we missed?"

"Don't be ridiculous."

"You telling me vampires don't exist?"

"I'm telling you that even if Hollywood didn't have its collective head up its ass, we wouldn't have wasted the blood." Carefully avoiding the splatter trail, she moved to the desk and looked down at the monitor. It was a new model, one of the liquid crystal screens made by a company she didn't recognize. From across the room, it had looked blank. Up close, there was one word, dead center on the screen.

"Mike."

He leaned in for a closer look. "Die."

"It's not an e-mail. They had to have typed it when they were in the room."

"I'll make sure they dust the keyboard when they bring the machine in. What are you doing?"

She frowned at an oval of drying blood nearly invisi-

ble on the black plastic of the monitor housing. It
was shaped like a thumbprint, but she couldn't see
a pattern.

"So you're eyeballing hills and valleys now?" he
snorted when she pointed it out to him. "Good work,
Vicki, we've got the son of a bitch. Our bad guy had
to have left it there when he was typing. Left hand
holding the monitor, typing with his right. If you can
find another one of these, we might be able to piece
together how the fuck he got out of the room."

"If I can find another one?"

"You know, sniff it out."

"Sniff it out?"

He turned to scowl at her. "Would you quit repeating everything I say?"

"I'm not repeating everything," she told him, "just
the stupid parts. This room is saturated in blood scent,
Mike. And before you ask," she cautioned, "I can't
track the bad guy. I'm not a bloodhound."

One dark brow rose.

"Not funny."

"You're right. I'm sorry." Hands shoved deep in his
pockets, he looked around the room. "So, what do
we have?"

"You have an unsolved assault. And I have to find
another client."

"He's not dead."

"You want me to guard him in the hospital?"

"That's up to you."

"I hate hospitals."

Vicki'd disliked hospitals before she changed and
she'd started disliking them even more after. Light-
sensitive eyes found them far too bright and no
amount of disinfectant could keep them from reeking
of death. That they also reeked of disinfectant was not
a selling point.

Raymond Carr was in a private room at the far end
of a quiet corridor, the room the hospital unofficially

kept for ongoing criminal cases. Sometimes it held the criminals. Sometimes the cases. With budgets cut and then cut again, the police department hadn't the manpower to guard an unsuccessful writer from an unknown enemy. They'd do their best to turn the unknown to a known, but as long as Carr seemed safe in the hospital, he'd remain unguarded.

Vicki stood in the room's darkest corner and watched the pale man on the bed draw in one short, shallow breath after another. He was sleeping—not entirely peacefully. Long fingers twitched against the covers and his eyeballs bounced behind his lids. Vicki wondered what he was dreaming about.

He'd told the police he couldn't remember what had happened. That one moment he'd been writing and the next he was in the back of an ambulance staring up at a pair of EMTs. It was all still in there, though. Trapped in the dark places.

Vicki did some of her best work in dark places. Unfortunately, Carr was wired—she wouldn't be able to question him without setting off the bells and whistles.

"Who's there?"

Might as well try it the old-fashioned way. The Hunter carefully masked, she stepped out of the shadows. "My name's Vicki Nelson. Detective Sergeant Celluci told you I was coming over tonight."

"What happened to me?"

"You got hit on the head."

His eyes widened and he stared up at her with dawning comprehension. "You're the one he was sending to protect me!"

"Sorry; I got there a little late." And anyone else would have knocked and gone away. "For what it's worth, I kept you from bleeding to death."

"My computer!"

Apparently, it wasn't worth much. "The police have it."

"My book! My God, they have my book!"

"Calm down." A quick glance at the monitors showed a rise in heart rate. "You'll get it back when they finish the investigation."

"It'll never be finished."

She wasn't entirely certain if he meant the investigation or the book. "You must have back-up copies."

"It's on disk." The bandage whispered against the pillowcase as he rocked his head from side to side. "I meant to burn it, but . . ." The rocking stopped. His pupils were so dilated his irises had nearly disappeared. "Why do you want my copy?"

"I don't. I was just reassuring . . ."

"You're trying to steal it!"

"No, I'm not." She let her eyes silver just enough to force him calm.

He panicked instead. The heart-rate monitor screamed as he tried to scramble back through the head of the bed.

Vicki was in the stairwell before the nurses left their station. She waited, the door open a crack, listening as they tranquilized him and strapped him down. He kept yelling that his book was in danger.

"Quite the imagination on him," one nurse muttered to the other as they left the room, her tone suggesting that "quite the imagination" could be translated as "total paranoid nutcase."

As Vicki slipped away, she thought it might be time to find out what else "quite the imagination" might mean.

The yellow crime scene tape remained across the door, but in the still, dark hours of the morning when Vicki returned to Raymond Carr's apartment, the police were long gone. Because of the manner of Vicki's original entrance, the apartment couldn't be secured, so they'd taken the trouble to put a padlock in place— a lot cheaper than keeping a uniform around until the landlord could arrive and make repairs. It was a good lock. It took Vicki about two minutes to pop it.

As well as the computer, the police had cleared

Carr's desktop and taken all the drawers, hoping for a clue amid the debris. While she appreciated their thoroughness, she was a little annoyed by the need to pry a copy of the book out of official channels. Official channels were notoriously narrow.

And speaking of narrow . . . Since she was there, she leaned her laptop case against the wall and stepped into the closet to check the ceiling for trapdoors leading to a closed-off and forgotten attic. Nothing. The cheap linoleum was solidly attached in all four corners, so there was no chance of a trapdoor to the apartment below.

On her hands and knees, peering under the desk at a floor unmarked by secret passageways, she snickered, "Who's the paranoid nutcase now?"

Paranoid nutcase . . .

Carr had thought she was going to steal his book. Had believed it so strongly, the hysterics had protected him from her ability to get into his head.

Vicki twisted and looked up at the bottom of the keyboard slide.

The masking tape that attached the square mailing envelope was almost the same color as the pale wood of the desk. The label on the single disk inside simply said, *Book.*

"The blood on the monitor wasn't a print."

Vicki glanced up from her laptop as Celluci came into the living room and dropped down beside her on the couch. "I'm sorry, Mike."

He grunted a noncommittal response to her sympathy. "What are you reading?"

"Raymond Carr's book. It's weirdly good. He starts off by massacring almost an entire village just so the hero—Harticalder—can go off and kick ass, so the plot's mostly a series of violent encounters strung together on a less-than-believable travelogue, but even doing the most asinine things, the characters are strangely believable. These guys read like real people."

His hand closed around her shoulder, warm even through the fleece of her sweatshirt. "Where did you get that?"

"Calm down, I left the original where it was." She popped the disk out of the side of her computer. "*This* is a copy." Pushing it back into the drive, she set the machine aside and pivoted in place until she faced him. "There's something else."

"What do you mean?"

"I know that look. It's your *I've come to a conclusion* expression."

He sighed and ran his hand back up through his hair. "The lab says there's no weapon, that the floor was the point of impact. One bang."

Vicki snorted. "No one hits their head that hard on a floor. It's a flat surface. Essentially flat," she amended, remembering how the blood had spread.

"And there's no indication of anyone else ever being in that room."

"Except for the blood on the monitor," she pointed out, poking him in the thigh with her bare foot.

"A random splatter. Raymond Carr got tangled up in his chair, fought to get free, and fell. That's why the chair was over by the window. No one pushed him, no one slammed his head down—there isn't another mark on his body."

Carr's skin was so pale that bruises would show almost instantly, blood from crushed capillaries pooling under the surface. "What about the threats?"

"We did a little background check, and it turns out that Raymond Carr is a paranoid schizophrenic. If he was off his medication, the odds are good he was writing the threats to himself."

"And?" Vicki asked pointedly.

"And what?" His hand closed around her ankle before she could poke him again. They both knew he couldn't hold her, but that wasn't the point.

"And you've had all day; is he off his medication?"

"Doesn't seem to have been. But . . ." He sketched uncertainties in the air with his free hand.

"But even paranoids have enemies."

He smiled then and pulled her close enough to kiss. "I knew you were going to say that."

"What about the blood on the monitor?" she asked when they pulled apart.

Celluci's turn to snort. "You know as well as I do that sometimes not all the pieces fit. You know better than I do that weird happens."

That was an impossible point to argue with, so she didn't bother and later, after he fell asleep, she checked that the bite on his wrist had closed over and slid out of bed to finish the book. Or at least to finish all of the book there was.

The fight scenes continued to be contrived, but the dialogue rang true and as she closed the last file, Vicki had to admit she believed in ol' Harticalder and his people. Almost buried under the preposterous plot, Carr had real talent.

On a whim, she went online and ran a search on the brand of monitor on Carr's desk. Her laptop was almost five years old and, even with the monitor dimmed down as far as it would go, it was still hard on light-sensitive eyes. Odds were good that new ones like Carr's had new features.

According to the official Web site, they did everything but make toast.

It seemed that Quinct, the company, had developed an amazing new technology for manufacturing the liquid crystal screens. They'd produced them for almost a year, claiming the new screens provided a viewing surface a minimum sixty percent sharper than the competition. And then, they'd gone bankrupt.

A bankruptcy sale explained how Raymond Carr had managed to afford one.

The site gave no reasons for the company's fall, and the best Vicki managed to find elsewhere on the Web was a Livejournal thread discussing the monitors. Apparently, they weren't just sixty percent sharper—according to the half-dozen people in the thread who'd owned them, they made images so clear new details came into focus in the background and even the written word seemed somehow real.

Real. There was that word again.

As she shut down her machine, she decided not to repeat the word to Mike. Although forced to become more open-minded than he'd been, speculation outside the boundaries covered by the crime lab and some good old-fashioned legwork still annoyed him, and an annoyed Mike Celluci was no fun to live with.

Besides, no one knew better than she did that reality came with qualifiers.

But she popped the copy of the book out of her laptop just to be on the safe side.

No one attacked Raymond Carr in the hospital, and the day he was released, the police handed back his computer.

"There was no crime committed," Celluci explained that evening when Vicki commented on the speedy return. "Just a man who slipped off his meds and had an accident."

"You told me it looked like he was taking his meds."

"Let it go, Vicki." Elbows braced on the kitchen table, he rubbed his temples. "I've got two teenagers dead because some asshole in a car thought it would be fun to shoot at strangers. I don't have time to protect Raymond Carr from himself. You think he needs supervision, you do it."

She thought it wouldn't hurt to drop by.

This time the door was unlocked and the blood scent was stronger.

Carr hadn't had time to put a new lock on his office door and his landlord's rudimentary repairs hadn't included replacing the latch mechanism. When Vicki laid her palm against it, it swung open, unresisting.

The only light in the room came from the monitor, but even before the change that allowed her to miss his heartbeat and the song of his blood, she would have known Raymond Carr was dead. The living were never so completely still.

His chair had been tipped back—flung back considering the distance from the desk. He was still in it, his arms outstretched, fingers curled. His feet in old-fashioned, scuffed, leather slippers were in the air, his head rested in a puddle beginning to dry to a brackish brown around the edges. It was difficult to tell for certain without moving the body, but the back of his head looked flat and there were three distinct points of impact.

The police would assume they'd been wrong. That there'd been an assailant the first time. That this mysterious assailant had somehow gotten into and then out of a locked room in a locked apartment and that today—late afternoon by the smell—he or she returned and finished the job. If they'd found no evidence of a second person in the room, they had to have missed something and, blaming themselves for Raymond Carr's death, they'd work like hell to make up for their mistake.

Except . . .

Vicki pulled a latex glove out of her pocket—even the bloodsucking undead left fingerprints—and walked to the desk. There was a single word in the center of the monitor.

Dead.

She moved the cursor down to the next line and typed *Harticalder?*

Then she felt a little foolish when nothing happened.

"Right," she muttered, deleting the name and snapping off the glove. "Vampires exist, werewolves exist, wizards exist, so therefore it's logical that characters can be made so real that they climb out of a new and improved monitors and bash the brains in of the bastard who put them through so much shit. Which is not to say," she added to Raymond Carr, "that you didn't deserve it. You slaughterd the entire village, for Christ's sake!"

Then she frowned as his eyes flared silver for an instant, reflecting the light of the monitor.

When she turned, there was still only one word on the screen.

Dead.

There'd be no marks on Carr's body because no matter how real they seemed, imaginary characters didn't leave marks. Or fingerprints. Or worry about locked doors. Or climb out of monitors and take vengeance on the creator who killed their wives and children to make a plot point.

Vicki pulled the glove back on and reformatted the hard drive. Pulled the plug on the machine, then took a cheap pen from the desk and drove a hole into the corner of the monitor. The part of her that had been a good cop for all those years hated the thought of compromising a crime scene. The rest of her slid the book's backup disk out of its hidden sleeve, snapped it in half, and put the pieces into her pocket.

Half a block away, from the pay phone inside the front door of the Brunswick Hotel, she made an anonymous phone call.

"Obviously, it had to do with the book. This time the hard drive was reformatted—not just erased but re-fucking formatted—and the copy taken. Carr must have written something that really pissed someone off. I guess it's a good thing you made that illegal . . ." Celluci paused in his pacing to stress the word, ". . . copy, or we'd have nothing."

"Sorry, Mike." Vicki moved a red queen onto a black king and looked up from the laptop. "I copied my notes from the voodoo case onto the disk."

"You what?"

"Well, how would I know you'd need it? You said the lab determined he fell. That it was an accident."

She could hear his teeth grinding. "The evidence at the time . . ."

"Except for the missing book," she interrupted.

"And the destroyed monitor!" he interrupted in turn.

They stared at each other for a long moment.

"You never mentioned a destroyed monitor," Vicki sighed at last. "Fine, except the missing book *and* the destroyed monitor, what evidence do you have this time? Prints? Witnesses? Fibers? Anything?"

"Vicki, no one accidentally slams their own head into the floor three times with force enough to flatten the back of their own skull!"

The volume as much as the content of his protest answered her question; he had nothing. The police had nothing. She set the laptop to one side, stood, and crossed the room to lay a sympathetic hand on Mike's arm. "I'm not saying it was an accident. Maybe he destroyed his own book and then killed himself."

He caught up her hand in his and pulled her around to face him. "No one kills themselves by slamming their own head into the floor three times! Where the hell did you get that idea?"

"I don't know." Raymond Carr had created a village filled with amazingly real characters and then slaughtered almost all of them to make a plot point. Harticalder had ridden away to wreak vengeance on those who'd done the slaughtering. Maybe he'd traveled a little farther than planned. And if not him, well, there'd still been half a dozen other characters left behind to mourn.

"Vicki?"

She shrugged. "I guess I read it in a book."

So This Is Christmas

"So what do you think? The blue or the black?"

Vicki Nelson turned to stare at her companion in some confusion. "The blue or the black what?"

"Scarf." Detective-Sergeant Mike Celluci held up the articles in question. "Last time I saw Angela she was doing a sort of goth-lite, so the black might work better, but I like the blue."

"Who is Angela?"

"My sister Marie's oldest girl." he grinned and pulled a virulently fuchsia scarf from the pile. "Maybe I should get her this just to hear her scream."

Vicki rolled her eyes and fought the urge to do a little screaming of her own. She wondered what had possessed her to accompany Mike to a suburban mall on Christmas Eve. At the time, concerned about how little they'd seen each other lately, going with him as he finished his shopping had seemed like the perfect solution. Now, not so much. "Maybe you should do something about the earrings those teenagers have just slipped into their pockets. Over there," she added, when it was clear she had his attention. "Blonde girl in the short red jacket and the dark-haired girl in brown."

"You're sure?"

Her eyes silvered faintly. "I'm sure."

As he walked across the store, she fought down the Hunger that had risen with even such a small display of power. Being stuck in an enclosed space with hundreds of people all sweating inside heavy winter coats as they rushed frantically from one store to another was like sitting a dieter down next to an enormous plate of shortbread cookies. The urge to nibble was nearly overwhelming.

She snarled slightly as someone careened into her, stepped back into the shelter of the scarf display as a harried looking young woman rushed by pushing a stroller piled high with packages, and turned to find Celluci back by her side. "Well?"

"They both think I should get the black scarf." He put the blue scarf back on the pile. Apparently he'd taken them with him.

"And earrings?"

"They put them back."

"Then you left them with store security."

"I gave them a warning and sent them home."

"You what?"

"Oh come on, Vicki, it's Christmas." Angela's gift in hand, he started toward the nearest cash register.

"What the hell does Christmas have to do with it?" she demanded, falling into step by his side. "It's not like they were stealing a fruitcake for their dear old mom. They'd have lifted those earrings if it was Easter or the first of July. Are you going to let them off because the baby Jesus died for their sins? Or because they're wearing red and white for Canada Day? Or . . ."

"I get it." He stopped at the end of a long line and sighed. "This is going to take a while."

"I could move things along." She smiled, her upper lip rising off her teeth.

"No."

"Fine." Hands shoved into her pockets, she turned the smile on the young man crowding into the line behind her. He paled, dropped his penguin-imprinted fleece throw, and raced away. Vicki snorted as she watched him go. Running screaming from the mall seemed like a good idea to her.

* * *

She liked to watch Mike eat, so the trip to the food court wasn't quite as bad as it could have been. Screaming, tired, overstimulated children—more perceptive than their parents—fell silent around her and not even Mike had objected when she'd leaned toward the two very loud young men at the next table and softly growled, "Shut up."

One of them had whimpered but they hadn't said anything since.

"There's definitely things I love about this time of the year," she said watching Mike lick a bit of ketchup from the corner of his mouth. "Hard to complain about an early sunset and a late sunrise."

He swallowed and grinned. "Here I thought you meant Christmas."

"What this?" One hand waved at the red velvet bows wrapped around every stationary surface and a few that hadn't been stationary until they'd been tied down. "Or maybe," she added scornfully, "you mean the hordes of happy shoppers panicked they won't buy the right piece of name brand garbage, running up their credit cards so far they miss a few payments, lose their house, and end up living with their kids in the back of a van." She paused long enough to duck under a heavily laden tray passing a little too closely. "Next thing you know, Dad's doing five to ten for taking a swing at the cop who ran him in for pissing behind a dumpster, Mom's turning tricks on Jarvis, and the kids are in juvie. All because of Christmas."

Mike started at her in astonishment. "Who stole your ho ho ho?"

"I'm a realist," she told him. "You do remember that violent crimes increase over the holiday season? A little too much alcohol, a little too much family . . ."

"I have a great family. Which you'd know if you'd come with me tomorrow."

"Mike."

"I love you, I love them. At Christmas you should be with the people you love. I get home from work, you eat, then we spend the evening with them. And don't say you won't go because they'll expect you to eat. Dinner will be long over and I know you're fast enough to fake snacks. You could always fake a food allergy."

"It won't work."

"Why not?" He brushed the graying curl of hair off his forehead and glared at her over the cardboard edge of his coffee cup.

"It's not who I am."

"It's not who you choose to be," he snapped, tossed the empty cup down on his tray and stood. Vicki beat him to the garbage cans. "You're taking too many chances," he grunted, glancing around the food court. "Cut it out. This could be the day some twenty-first century Van Helsing came to the mall to buy his kid Baby's First Vampire Staking kit."

"You're babbling."

The muscle jumping in his jaw suggested he was aware of it. "If you can function here, you can function at my mother's house."

"Is *that* why we're here?" she asked as they headed toward the exit. "To prove I don't lose control in crowds?"

"I talked to Fitzroy. He said you can handle it."

"You called Henry?" Astonishment brought her to a full stop by the fence separating Santa's Workshop from the food court. "You actually called Henry?"

"He thinks you should come with me tomorrow."

And astonishment gave way to pique. "I don't care what he thinks!"

"Come on, Vicki, it's Christmas."

"I know." The warmth in Mike's brown eyes was *not* going to get to her. "And Christmas is a . . ." A screaming child about to be lifted onto Santa's lap cut her off. "Can you believe that," she demanded as Santa settled back and adjusted his beard. "You spend all year trying to street-proof kids and all of a sudden their parents are shoving them onto the lap of some strange old man and paying an arm and a leg for a fuzzy picture that costs about eight cents to produce."

"Who crapped in your stocking?"

The voice came from about waist level. Vicki peered over the fence and into the face of one of Santa's elves—although given his height, the breadth of his shoulders, and the beaded braids in his beard, this one looked more like a dwarf in spite of green tights and red pointy-toed shoes.

"Take a picture," he snarled. "It'll last longer."

"Sorry."

"Yeah, like that sounded sincere." He crossed heavily muscled arms over a barrel chest and glared up at her from under bushy brows. "So what's your problem?"

"With what?"

"With Christmas, for crying out loud. Come on. I haven't got all night."

She glanced up at Mike, who was staring in dopey fascination as a laughing older woman wrestled a pink and frilly little girl back into her snowsuit.

The elf pointedly cleared his throat.

"Look, I have no problem with Christmas. You want to dress up and play Santa's Workshop, that's fine with me. Someone else wants to go into debt until next November, their choice. I just want to be left alone to celebrate Christmas my way."

"Bet you don't."

"Don't what?"

"Celebrate Christmas."

"Maybe I'm Jewish. You ever think of that?"

"Are you?"

"No, but . . ." She waved at hand at Mike, suddenly wanting the elf's too-penetrating gaze pointed somewhere else. "He's working all day."

Dark eyes remained locked on her face. "So the cops with families can have the day off and then I betcha he's spending the evening with about sixty people from nine to ninety who'll be glad to see him. Big Italian-Canadian family. Lot of hugging. You should go with him."

"You should mind your own business."

"Except we're not talking about me," he snorted. "We're talking about you."

"You don't know anything about me." She let the Hunter rise enough to silver her eyes.

To her surprise, the elf met her gaze. "All right, you're not so tough," he muttered after a long moment. "And you need to get moving, lady. The mall's about to close."

Vicki blinked, looked around, and realized that a number of the stores had already pulled down their security grids and the food court was rapidly emptying. Santa had disappeared and his helpers were packing things up.

"I forgot things closed so early on Chrismas Eve," Mike said as he wrapped her hand in his and continued their interrupted walk to the exit. "I hope you didn't still have shopping to do."

A little unsettled, she let him pull her along. "No, I'm good."

"I've always thought so."

His tone of voice made her feel warm, wanted, and unworthy all at once but she recovered enough to snarl at a group of carolers outside the doors. "God Rest Ye Merry Gentlemen" went up an octave and changed key twice.

It wasn't until they got to the car that she thought to wonder how the elf had known Mike was a cop.

Mike was working a twelve-hour shift—six AM to six PM—so Vicki woke him up at five with lips and teeth and kept him distracted for long enough that he had no time to do anything but throw on clothes and race out the door. No time to start in on it being Christmas Day. Time enough to say, "Think about tonight, that's all I'm asking," as he left.

She'd thought about it. She thought it was a bad idea, her mingling with Mike's extended family as if they were a couple like any other.

"And what does your girlfriend do, Michael?"

"Well, Mom, Vicki spends her days unconscious in

a lightproof packing crate in my crawl space and after sunset she works as a private investigator."

"That sounds interesting."

"Have her tell you about the reanimated Egyptian wizard who tried to take over the world sometime. Oh, and did I mention she's a vampire?"

Okay, not likely, but still not a good idea. Besides, with luck she had a couple of hundred Christmases to look forward to. She needed to pace herself.

"A couple of hundred years of Chia pets, dogs in antlers, and 'Rockin' Around the Christmas Tree,' " she muttered, sitting down at her laptop. "I can't wait."

At fifteen minutes to sunrise, she shut down, took her cell phone from the charger, and headed for the crawl space only to find that Mike had hung a wreath on the end of the crate that opened.

"You'd think I could get away from the whole Christmas thing down here," she sighed as she stripped. Sinking into the slab of memory foam, she locked up, slipped under the duvet, and turned off the flashlight.

By sunset, Christmas would be nearly over.

Vampires don't dream.

"All right, if I'm not dreaming, what the hell is going on?" Vicki got out of the enormous wingback chair and peered around the room. There was a window and door and a fireplace, but beyond that, the room seemed a bit undefined—as though only the essentials were in place. There had to be walls, hard to have either a window or a door without them, but they were present more by inference than actuality.

The chair felt real. The green and blue checked dressing gown felt real. The sound of heavy footsteps dragging chains up a flight of stairs, however . . .

She turned as a familiar translucent figure burst through the door.

"In life," he howled, approaching the chair, "I was your informant Tony Foster!"

Because it seemed like the safest reaction, Vicki sat back down. "You're not dead, Tony."

Tony stopped and pulled a script from the pocket of his *Darkest Night* show jacket. "I'm sure that was my line," he muttered, flipping pages. "It's not like I ever wanted to be in front of the cameras, oh, no, I want to direct but what do I get . . . Ah. Here it is. In life I was your informant, Tony Foster. That's what it says." He shoved the script back in his pocket and grinned at her. "Can I go on?"

"Why not?" Eventually, there'd be a punchline and maybe then she'd figure out what was happening.

"I have come from beyond the grave to warn you."

Now they were getting somewhere. "Warn me of what?"

He held up the end of the chain wrapped around his body. About every fifteen centimeters was a classic lunch box. Although it was hard to see them clearly, Vicki recognized *Bewitched, The Brady Bunch,* and *Starsky and Hutch* as well as assorted *Star Wars, Star Treks,* and superheroes. "The chain you bear was as long and heavy as this when I left Toronto and it has grown longer and heavier since."

"I'm dragging lunch boxes?"

"They're metaphors. Each box represents—Hey!" Tony pulled a bit of the chain around to look more closely at the lunch box. "Cool. The old *Batman* television show. Do you know how much one of these things is worth, mint?"

"Do I care?"

"Right. Do you care? That's the problem." He cleared his throat and took up his declamation posture again. "Each box represents a family commitment you blew off."

"Okay." Vicki folded her arms and frowned. "My mother died, was brought back to life, and died again. That's about all the family commitment I've had in the last few years."

"And what about Mike Celluci? I mean, he's not my first choice, but you two are tight."

"How tight Mike and I are is none of your business."

"Friends are my business!"

"I thought you were a TAD on a crappy television show?'

Tony threw back his head and howled. Lights flashed. Thunder crashed. Omnious music played. "Why do you not believe in me, O Woman of the Worldly Mind?"

Still frowning, Vicki stared at him. The music stopped. The thunder faded. The ambient light steadied. After a long moment, Tony shrugged, looking sheepish.

"Listen, Vicki . . ." Adjusting his chain, he sat down on a second chair that had appeared as his butt descended. ". . . sometimes you get family, sometimes you make family; you know what I mean? Like Neil Simon said, no man is an island . . ."

"*Paul* Simon. And that's not what he said."

"Whatever. What I'm getting at is even Dracula had those babes in the basement. Just because you're a member of the bloodsucking undead doesn't mean you should cut yourself off from human intercourse." He paused. Frowned. Started to snicker.

"You're laughing because you said intercouse, aren't you?" When Tony nodded, she rolled her eyes. "What are you, twelve?"

"Sorry."

"Just get on with it."

"Fine." Standing, he drew himself up to his full height and pointed. "You have one chance to escape my fate."

Vicki opened her mouth and closed it again, strongly suspecting that any questions about said fate wouldn't be answered anyway. At least not coherently.

Tony stared at her suspiciously for a moment then continued, "You will be visited by three ghosts . . ."

"You have got to be kidding me."

His shrug set the lunch boxes clanking. "Yeah, surprised me too. I'd have bet you were more the *It's a Wonderful Life* type."

"Get out."

"Expect the first when the bell tolls one!"

Before she could ask *What bell?* or even *What part of get out do you not understand?* he was gone.

Wondering just how high Mike's blood alcohol level had been and how he'd gotten it there before she fed on him this morning, Vicki blinked and found herself in an entirely different scene, lying inside the closed red brocade curtains of a huge four-poster bed. A quick glance under the covers. She was wearing blue flannel pajamas printed with dancing polar bears. Since she didn't own pajamas matching that description, or any pajamas at all for that matter, she was beginning to get a little concerned about just who was supplying the imagery.

A bell, and it sounded like a big one, tolled once.

All things considered, the sudden soft illumination through the red brocade wasn't much of a surprise.

"I can't believe I'm doing this," she muttered, sitting up and pulling the curtain back. On the far side of the room, she could just barely make out a figure in the center of a blazing circle of light. "Turn it down!" she snarled, one hand raised to protect sensitive eyes.

The light dimmed. "Better?"

"Henry?"

Glowing only slightly, Henry Fitzroy, bastard son of Henry VIII, once Duke of Richmond and Somerset, romance writer, ex-lover, and vampire walked toward the bed. He was wearing . . .

"What the hell are you wearing?"

Henry glanced down and smoothed the velvet skirt of his coat. "These are my Garter Robes. I have to say that I'm impressed by the condition they're in given that I haven't worn them in four hundred and seventy years."

"You look like . . ."

He bowed, right leg to the front, ass in the air, and his poofy hat nearly sweeping the floor. "A Tudor prince?"

"Yeah all right, that too." She sighed and dragged a pillow up against the headboard so she could lean back in comfort. "So what's going on? Tony told me I'd be visited by three ghosts."

"I am the first."

"No way."

"I am the Ghost of Christmas Past."

Vicki snorted. "Well, they got the past part right."

"Not my past, your past."

She snorted again. "Then you should be wearing a mullet and leg warmers. Either way, I'm not playing."

"This isn't a game, Vicki."

"And it isn't a dream." Arms folded over the dancing polar bears, she scowled up at him. "Because we don't dream. So what is it?"

"That's not for me to say. I'm here as a guide, nothing more."

"And if I refuse to be guided?"

His eyes darkened and his smile became a scimitar slash across his face.

She felt her own Hunter rise to answer his. Lips drawn back, she threw herself out of the bed, propelled by the territorial imperative that declared vampires hunted alone. How dare Henry show up in her subconscious—or wherever the fuck they were—and challenge? "You think so? Bring it on!"

Henry stepped forward to meet her and, as they made contact, the room and the bed swirled away. When their surroundings came back into focus, they were standing on one side of a familiar room, tucked in between a green vinyl recliner and an artificial Christmas tree. A little girl, about five years old, sat cross-legged on the floor gleefully cheering on the battling plastic robots set up on the coffee table.

"Oh, my God, that's me!"

Henry pulled his cloak from Vicki's loosened grasp. "I told you—Christmas past."

"I loved those robots!" Stepping forward, she knelt at the end of the table. "Now this is what I call a toy with no socially redeeming value."

"Vicki! Uncle Stan's here."

The young Vicki jumped to her feet shrieking, "Grandma!" and raced for the kitchen leaving the red robot lying on its side, fists flailing, plastic feet paddling the air. Unopposed, the blue robot headed for the edge of the table.

"My grandmother always stayed with Uncle Stan's family at Christmastime," Vicki explained. She could almost hear Henry wondering how she'd gotten from her uncle to her grandmother. "If Uncle Stan's here, Grandma's here." She reached for the blue robot only to have it fall through her palm and bounce under the couch.

"This is the past," Henry reminded her. "Shadows of things that were; you can't affect it."

"Which makes me think we're here in order for it to affect me." Still on her knees, she twisted around to face him. "If I'm supposed to get in touch with my inner child, you might as well take me back right now. My inner child is at a boarding school in Uruguay."

"Ah." He nodded as if that made perfect sense. "Well, we can't go back until we've seen everything. There are rules."

"Rules? You tricked me to get me here." Rolling up onto her feet, she took a step toward him.

Henry shrugged. "You're a little predictable."

"And you're a . . ."

A babble of voices cut her off. Her mother led the group into the living room, closely followed by her Aunt Connie holding baby Susie and trying to keep three-year-old Steve from racing straight for the tree. The last time Vicki'd seen her mother, she'd been a rotting reanimated corpse, murdered and brought back to life as part of an insane science experiment. Infinitely preferable to see her young and laughing, even if the home highlight job made her hair look horribly striped.

Young Vicki came next, walking backward, holding her grandmother's hand and listing everything Santa had brought her.

"Oh, my God, I'm wearing a Partridge Family sweatshirt."

"You're very cute."

"I'm five," Vicki snorted. "Even I could manage cute at five."

Last into the room came her dad and her Uncle Stan, conducting a spirited argument about hockey in general and the recent Toronto/Boston game in particular. Her dad, lifelong Black Hawks fan, was loudly declaring that the Leafs' recent win had been pure luck. Her Uncle Stan, who really didn't care either way but liked to wind her dad up, was declaiming the superior firepower of the Toronto team.

"Weird," she said softly as her father scooped up her cousin Steve just as he was about to climb the tree, "I thought he was taller."

"You were five."

"I haven't been five for a long time, Henry."

Time kindly compressed opening yet more presents and the singing of Christmas carols led by Vicki's no longer decomposing mother. As the sun set, the whole family sat down to a dinner of turkey, stuffing, mashed potatoes, frozen peas, and brown-and-serve buns.

"Good lord," Vicki muttered as the canned cranberry sauce was passed around the table, "could we have been any more middle class?"

"You look happy."

Waving an enormous drumstick, young Vicki was teaching her younger cousin how to make a dam out of potatoes so the gravy didn't touch the vegetables. She did look happy, older Vicki had to admit, but then, it didn't take much at five. "Are we finished here?"

Henry nodded. "Here, yes. Time to move on." He raised a hand and their surroundings wobbled slightly, then came back into focus.

Vicki rolled her eyes. "Wow. They clearly spent a

fortune on the special effects. And in case you didn't notice . . ." She waved a dismissive hand at the table. ". . . we didn't go anywhere."

"We moved two years forward."

"Golly gee. Nothing's changed."

And then she noticed the empty place at the table. "My grandmother . . ."

"Died," Henry said softly.

"She was old. People get old and they die." Even to her own ears, she sounded angry.

"She was surrounded by people who loved her, right to the end. There are worse ways to die."

Vicki remembered the way flesh felt tearing under her teeth, the rush of blood into her mouth, the feel of a life as it fled. "Yeah, well, you should know."

Henry made no response, but then what could he say? *Takes one to know one.* Too trite, however true.

The scene shifted again. This time, although the food hadn't changed, there were only two people sitting at the table.

"Your Uncle Stan just didn't feel right coming this year," Vicki's mother said as she spooned mashed potatoes onto a plate. "Not with your father so recently . . . gone."

Ten-year-old Vicki muttered something that may have been, "Sure," and slapped margarine onto a bun.

"Wow. You lose one, you lose them all." Vicki folded her arms.

"They were the closest family your mother had and they never came back for Christmas after your father . . ."

". . . ran off with the whore half his age. Yeah, tell me something I don't know, Henry, or move on, because if you're the only thing around here I can affect, I'm about to."

His eyes darkened but before Vicki could react, the scene shifted.

There wasn't anything especially Christmas-like about Linda Ronstadt except that "Desperado" was blasting from the speakers at the police Christmas

party. This was the party after the family party—a
staff sergeant from 52 Division sat slumped in a chair
wearing the bottom half of a Santa suit, three couples
shuffled around the dance floor, a group of old-timers
were scaring the piss out of a rookie with exaggerated
stories of Christmas suicides, and everyone had been
drinking. Heavily.

"You're on the dance floor," Henry shouted over
the music, breaking into her search.

"Oh, no . . ."

It was *that* Christmas party.

Grabbing Henry's arm, she leaned toward his ear.
"Let's go."

"Oh, come on, you look cute. Both of you."

Unable to help herself, she followed his gaze to one
of the three dancing couples. Her younger self wore
a navy blue sweater with white snowflakes embroi-
dered onto it over a very tight pair of acid wash jeans
with ankle zippers tucked into a pair of black and
silver ankle boots. Fashion being slightly kinder to
men, Mike wore black jeans, a black dress shirt, and
a red lamé tie.

"Oh, my God."

"At least you weren't in leg warmers. I remember
the 80s," Henry added when she shot him a warning
glare. "And trust me, the 1780s were worse."

Both younger Vicki and younger Mike were obviously drunk. He leaned forward and murmured something into her ear. She leaned back, one hand slipped
between their bodies, then she grinned and mouthed,
"Where?"

"Forget it." A hand against his chest kept Henry
from following the couple off the dance floor. "I know
how this ends and we're not watching."

One red-gold eyebrow rose. "Why not? Are you
ashamed?"

"For Christ's sake, Henry, we had sex in a stall in
the women's can. I'm not proud of it." But she
couldn't stop herself from grinning at the memory.

"Okay, I'm not ashamed of it either but we're still not watching."

"We could . . ."

"No."

"Fine." Linda Ronstadt gave way to ABBA. "It seems that after the disappointment of your childhood, you learned how to celebrate Christmas."

She stared at him in disbelief. "Is that why we're here?" When his eyebrow rose again, she started to snicker. "This is the best whoever is in charge of this farce could come up with? I get drunk and done up against some badly spelled graffiti? That's their idea of a merry Christmas?"

"You didn't have a good time?"

"I had a great time." Laughing now, full out. She hadn't laughed like this in . . . actually, she couldn't remember the last time she'd laughed like this. A quick sidestep took her out of the path of the staff sergeant in the Santa suit as he staggered off to empty his bladder, bang on the wall between the cans, and yell at the younger them to keep it the hell down. "I had a great time at least twice," she gasped, forcing the words through the laughter. "I always have a great time with Mike if you must know, but that's not the point."

Henry was looking a little pouty and that was funny too. "Then what is the point?"

"That this is stupid." Wiping her eyes with one hand, she waved the other at the cheesy decorations and the drunk cops. "If you've got nothing better than this, you might as well call it a night! Oh, my God . . ." She'd almost got herself under control but the opening bars of the DJ's latest choice set her off again. ". . . he's going to play 'The Time Warp'!"

Snarling softly, Henry raised a hand, the party faded, and they were back in the bedroom again.

Vicki collapsed on the bed. "Thank you. I don't think I was up to watching that." After a few final snickers, she took a deep breath and sat up to find Henry staring down at her. "You're not finished?"

"Just one more thing." His eyes darkened. "Michael Celluci was the best thing that ever happened to you, as much as it pains me to admit it. He has always accepted you for what you are—opinionated, obnoxiously competitive, and emotionally defensive—and has loved you anyway. He has given you a place in his home and his heart without ever asking that you cease to walk the night. All he asks is that you spend Christmas with his family and yet your fear continually denies him this one thing."

"And it's going to keep denying him." Gripping the comforter with both hands, she kept herself from rising to answer the challenge in his eyes. "That way there's no danger of my skipping the shortbread and snacking on Aunt Louise."

"That's not what you fear."

"Cousin Jeffrey then."

"I have seen four hundred and seventy Christmases, Vicki. I know your fear."

"You know Cousin Jeffrey?"

"Vicki . . ."

She snorted. "You know your fears, Henry. You don't know mine."

"I know . . ."

"No, you don't."

"Our kind . . ."

"Nope."

He was going to lose control any minute, she could see it in the way he'd subtly shifted his weight. His age made the whole one-vampire-to-a-territory imperative—not to mention the one-vampire-to-a-completely-cracked-fantasy—both easier and harder to overcome. "You can be the most irritating person I have ever met," he snarled and vanished.

Vicki pulled her fingers out of the holes in the comforter and the mattress beneath and raised them over her head. "I win."

Although it didn't, unfortunately, appear that she could go home yet.

Three spirits, Tony had said.

"Next," she sighed.

Right on cue, lights blazed under the door in the wall to the left of the bed. She could hear music. Pink. "Get the Party Started."

"I wonder what happens if I just sit here?" she asked no one in particular, folding her arms and shifting her weight more definitively onto the bed.

The music got louder, the world blurred, and Vicki found herself standing in the open doorway. Across the room, sitting in a familiar tacky Santa's Workshop, wearing a familiar tacky red velvet suit, nearly buried under piles of brightly wrapped packages, was Detective Sergeant Michael Celluci.

Vicki sighed. "The Ghost of Christmas Presents, I presume?"

"That's Ghost of Christmas Present," Mike told her, tugging down the ratty beard, "as in not past or future."

"Then you might want to shuffle your playlist, because this song . . ." She paused just long enough to allow the music to rise to the foreground. ". . . is very 2001."

"The music is not important." Tossing the beard over a sixty-inch, flat screen TV, Mike beckoned her forward. "Come in and know me better!"

"If I knew you any better, we'd be breaking a few laws." But since she didn't seem to have a choice in the matter, she walked toward him. Away from the door, she could see that besides the workshop and the presents there were also tables laid out with roast turkey and torteire and mashed potatoes and roast squash with a maple sugar glaze and bear claws and a steaming carafe of coffee and, yes, the party-size box of assorted Tim Bits. It all looked great but her appreciation was aesthetic only—these days she had no visceral reaction to food she had loved for over thirty-four years. She remembered enjoying them but the desire was gone. *Mostly gone,* she amended silently with a last look at the coffee.

"Just what exactly is a room full of food I can't eat

suppose to be teaching me?'' she asked as she turned toward the workshop.

Mike stood and closed the remaining distance between them. When he was close enough that Vicki could feel the warmth coming off his body, he unbuttoned Santa's jacket and slipped it off his shoulders, standing before her in a tight white tank and the bottom of the costume. She could hear his heart beating, the blood moving through his veins. His scent threatened to overwhelm her.

Ah, yes. *There* was desire.

"The food is for me," he said, holding out one bare, muscular arm. "I need to keep up my strength."

Vicki stared at the inside of his wrist, mesmerized by the pulse throbbing under the soft, pale skin. Between one heartbeat and the next her teeth could be in his flesh, his blood running warm and salty down her throat . . .

"Vicki?"

"No, thanks, I'm not hungry." As she spoke, she realized it was true. Taking a deep breath, more for emotional grounding than physical necessity, she lifted her head and met his eyes.

He smiled. "You know that I am always here for you."

"Yeah. I know."

Given the theme of Henry's segment, she expected Mike to ask why she wasn't then there for him in turn, but all he said was, "Come on, there's some things you need to see."

"Families celebrating . . ." The scene changed. ". . . Christmas?" The last word was a near growl as Vicki adjusted to being suddenly perched on a snowbank in a pair of pajamas. "You know that's really fucking annoying! Where are we?"

"Don't you recognize this place?" Mike asked, buttoning the Santa jacket.

They were standing on the edge of a farmyard looking in at a red brick house and a long low barn. It looked familiar but . . .

Just then the door to the house slammed open and a very large black dog charged outside followed by a pair of white, half-grown puppies.

"It's the Heerkens farm." Vicki grinned as she watched the black dog allow himself to be caught and tumbled in the snow. "The big willow tree's gone but they . . ." She waved a hand at the two pups barking like crazy as they leaped around their companion. ". . . are unmistakable."

The door opened again, a little less violently this time, and a very pregnant young woman with silver-blonde hair leaned out into the yard. "Come on you three, back inside! Breakfast is ready!" When no one started toward the house, she shook her head and growled, "Shadow!"

Black ears went up.

"Shadow?" Vicki felt her jaw drop.

"It's been a few years since you've been by," Mike pointed out. He sounded amused but Vicki decided she'd let that go for now. The last time she'd seen Shadow, he'd been a half grown pup, not this danger-ous looking animal whose head probably came higher than her hip. "The mother-to-be?"

"Rose. The little ones are hers too."

"Impossible." Rose had been a teenager the last time Vicki'd seen her, all teasing and tossed hair.

Two steps forward took Vicki inside the farmhouse kitchen—an impossible distance covered but then, nothing much about this night had been particularly possible. The shabby kitchen was comfortingly famil-iar, the same oversized furniture, the same drifts of dog hair, the same piles of clothing tossed haphazardly about. The man sitting at the end of the table but-tering a huge pile of toast was obviously Stuart Heerkins-Wells, Rose's uncle and the old dominant male. A new scar ran from his throat along the top of his shoulder—new in that Vicki hadn't seen it be-fore, but actually about six or seven years old.

The outside door slammed back against the kitchen wall, and as Shadow herded the two younger animals in from outside, he changed to become a not-very-tall but heavily muscled, dark-haired young man. Daniel. The fact that he was naked was less disconcerting than the undeniable fact he was no longer the cheerful ten-year-old she'd known. The pups charged across the room to leap up and down around Rose's legs, becoming, as they leaped, boys around six or eight years old with their mother's white-blonde hair.

"Hey!" Rose expertly smacked a reaching hand away from the large pan of sausages on the stove. "Why don't you two do something useful and go get your father. He's in the living room."

"After breakfast can we take the toboggan Santa gave us out to the hill?"

"Only if your father goes with you."

"But, Mom . . . !"

"Or your Uncle Daniel."

From the whoops of glee and the clatter of eight sets of toenails against the worn linoleum as the two pups raced around Daniel before heading into the living room, they considered their uncle a soft touch. Or at least more likely to agree to a Christmas Day spent out in the snow than their father. It was as impossible not to smile as they passed as it had been not to smile at a much younger Shadow.

As Rose slapped Daniel's hand away from the sausages in exactly the same way she'd discouraged her son, a full choral rendition of "Joy to the World" exploded out of the living room. "Oh, no, if they start singing I'll never get them to eat!"

"I'll go." Stuart pushed the plate of toast into the center of the table and stood, smiling fondly at his niece. "Get my lazy son to help you with that pan. You need to start being careful about heavy lifting or we're going to end up with a Christmas baby." He kissed the top of her head as he passed.

"I have done this before, you know," she muttered as Daniel took the pan and started transferring the sausages to a platter. "Why don't I . . ."

"Answer the phone," Daniel suggested with a grin

as the old black plastic phone still hanging on the wall by the ratty sofa started to ring.

She rolled her eyes but she went to answer it anyway. "Good morning and Merry Christmas! Peter? Where are you? Of course I expected you to call, but it's early." With one hand cupping the curve of her belly, she leaned against the wall and smiled as she listened to her twin.

Shoving a basket of oranges to one side, Daniel set the sausages on the table, then bent and took a pan of home fries from the oven where they'd been keeping warm. As he worked, he hummed a baseline to the multipart harmonies pouring out of the living room.

Vicki felt a hand close over her shoulder.

"Although they live separately from a society that would fear and destroy them, although their lives are often violent and the space they need grows less with every passing year, still they celebrate Christmas."

Vicki frowned as the music changed. "They're singing 'Don't Cry for me Argentina.' "

"So werewolves are fans of Andrew Lloyd Webber, that's not the point." Celluci's fingers tightened. "The point is . . ."

She turned inside his grip and looked up at him. "The point is that they manage to celebrate Christmas, so why can't I? Right?" when he nodded, she smiled. "Subtlety has never been your strong point and whoever is arranging this . . ." She patted him gently on the Santa suit. ". . . is playing to your strengths. So let's go."

"Go?"

"Unless this is it?"

Shaking his head, he took her hand. "You're taking this better then I expected."

"I'm bowing to the inevitable." His fingers were warm around hers and she took a moment to enjoy it before nudging him with her free hand and saying, "Well?"

The kitchen, Daniel, the sausages disappeared.

Another kitchen reappeared around them.

"You know, I'm not really a big kitchen person anymore," Vicki sighed, looking around and recognizing Mike's parents' huge Mississauga kitchen. "Actually, I never was. You might have more success it you took me someplace I enjoyed."

"Like the roof of police headquarters?"

"That is not what I meant by *took*," Vicki muttered. "And your mother is sitting right over there."

"She can't hear us. We are but shadows." His voice faded as his mother's rose. A little overly dramatic as far as Vicki was concerned but it did make for a faster segue. Just because she was the next thing to immortal didn't mean she wanted to hang around indefinitely.

"He says he'll come without her, but if she makes him choose. . . ." Mrs. Celluci shook her head, curls tumbling much as her son's did.

Another woman, who looked so much like Mike she had to be his sister, set her mug on the counter and patted their mother on the arm. "He loves us. He'll always come."

"He loves her and if she says stay . . . Another Christmas, Marie, and we may not see him here. . ."

Vicki stared up at Mike in disbelief. "Oh, give me a break; you're also playing the part of Tiny Tim?"

His cheeks flushed.

"She used to come here with him sometimes, when they were both in the police, I don't know why she stopped . . ."

Marie shrugged philosophically. "People change."

That was an understatement.

"But to separate a man from his family . . . What kind of a change does that?"

With any luck, she'd never know.

"She is the kind of woman who wants everything her way."

"Selfish," agreed Marie.

"I am not," Vicki snapped. "You don't understand."

"They can't hear you," Mike reminded her quietly.

"She wants him to live with her wrapped in a co-coon. Like a bug."

"Like a spider," Mike's sister declared with relish. "Wrapping him in her web."

Mrs. Celluci rolled her eyes. "She doesn't want to eat him, Marie. She just wants to keep him with only her. I wonder . . ." A long swallow of coffee. "I wonder what she is afraid of."

"Okay." Vicki's eyes silvered as she turned away from the conversation. "That's enough pop psychology for one day. Wrap it up, Santa."

"There's more you should hear."

"Wrap it up now!"

"Or?"

Her answer was a low, warning growl.

Mike's gaze flicked over to the two women leaning on the counter. "We're shadows here, remember? You can't hurt them."

Vicki wrapped her fingers around his throat, resting them gently against the heated skin, feeling his life pulse past. "You're flesh and blood."

"Yes."

The sorrow in his response stopped the Hunter cold. Unable to look away, Vicki watched as he faded within her grip, growing fainter and fainter until she held only the memory of his warmth. Her heart pounded faster than it had since the night Mike had cradled her in his arms while Henry pressed a bleeding wrist to her lips. She swallowed with a mouth gone dry.

Then she frowned, pivoted on one heel, and grabbed a double handful of black fabric draped over the figure that had appeared suddenly behind her. "Fuck that," she snarled. "It stops right here." A vicious yank dragged the fabric clear of whoever gave it shape. Vicki tossed it aside, expected to see the elf from the mall, and saw instead . . .

Nothing.

The fabric she'd tossed aside stood beside her now, a hint of features under the drape.

"Well, nice to see the Nazgul are getting work. Missed the casting call for Dementors, did you?" She kept her tone flip, but power recognized power. Whatever had plunged her into this insane tour of reworked Victorian cliché was under that fabric. Vampires didn't dream, but that hadn't stopped it. It had plundered her memories, exposed her feelings, and . . .

Shown her things she hadn't known which, if true, proved it was operating outside of her psyche. Whatever it was, it wasn't all in her head. Something had gone to a lot of trouble to get her to celebrate Christmas.

So what? She really hated being manipulated.

"All right." Her lips drew up off her teeth. "Now you show me that no one cares when I die."

Under the fabric, power shifted so that it seemed to be pointing into the fog.

Fog? "Interesting weather patterns." Vicki took a step forward and the fog cleared. She blinked as lightning flashed. "That's um . . ." Another look. "That's a mob with torches and stakes attacking Cinderella's castle."

When she turned to face the fabric again, she sensed it was waiting expectantly.

"I get staked at Disney World?"

The fabric had no eyes to roll no arms to fold but Vicki still had the unmistakable feeling that time was running out.

"Okay. Fine." She folded her arms, since it seemed someone had to. "Torches and stakes are historic ways of dealing with a vampire. Historically, vampires kept to themselves, creating fear and distrust in the general population. If I don't learn from history, I'm doomed to repeat it." To sum up, she added sound effects to a mimed rim-shot.

Another power shift and the fabric pointed into a new section of fog.

Under the circumstances, the misty outline of gravestones wasn't unexpected.

"If there was enough to bury, I guess that kills the vampires turn to dust theory," she muttered, walking forward. "I'm not afraid of dying," she added in a slightly louder voice, "so I doubt we're going to have any major breakthrough here."

But it wasn't her name on the stone. The grave hadn't been filled in. The coffin hadn't been closed.

She stared down at Mike, watched silently as he slowly rotted, ignoring the pain from the half moon cuts her fingernails gouged into her palms. When bone finally turned to dust, her eyes flashed silver and with bloody hands she ripped the fabric into so many pieces they fell into the open grave like black snow.

The sun set.

Vicki fumbled her cell phone up from the blankets beside her, flipped it open and blinked at the display. Four forty-eight PM, December 25th. In the faint blue light, she could see four semicircular cuts on each palm, the deepest still seeping blood.

Vampires didn't dream.

Nothing she could do would keep Michael Celluci from dying. If she left now, if she dressed and threw everything she had in her van and drove until sunrise and made sure he never found her and if she stopped seeing age overtake him, he'd still die.

And rot.

People died. But before they died, they should get a chance to spend time with people they loved.

"You didn't tell me anything I didn't already know," she snarled at the darkness.

The darkness felt smug.

"Bite me."

As it happened, it wasn't about Christmas at all.

She was wrapping the last 500 gram package of organic free-traded Mexican coffee when Mike got home from work. He stared at the presents on the table, at the ceramic candy canes dangling from Vicki's ears, and shook his head.

"What the hell is going on here?"

"I could hardly go to your parents on Christmas Day without presents."

"You're going to my parents?"

"We're going to your parents."

"Yeah, that's sweet. I repeat, what the hell is going on?"

She sighed and stuck a bow down over the mess she'd made of one end of the package. Considering what she'd paid for the wrapping paper, it was crap. "I want to be with you, you want to be with your family—you're the detective, connect the dots."

His smile almost wiped out the memory of teeth in a crumbling skull. "Where did you get all this stuff?"

"Toronto's a big, multicultural city, Mike. Not everyone celebrates Christmas. You'd be amazed at what's open."

"I thought you'd stopped celebrating Christmas?"

She snorted. "Not likely."

"And the vampire thing?"

"Isn't going away. But neither is the human thing." She stood and pulled him toward her. "Just keep me away from your cousin Jeffrey."

"I don't have a cousin named Jeffrey."

Mouth pressed to the warm column of his throat, she felt his confusion and smiled. "Good."

Acknowledgments

"This Town Ain't Big Enough" originally published in VAMPIRE DETECTIVES, edited by Martin H. Greenberg (DAW Books, 1995).

"What Manner of Man" originally published in TIME OF THE VAMPIRES, edited by P. N. Elrod and Martin H. Greenberg (DAW Books, 1996).

"The Cards Also Say" originally published in THE FORTUNE TELLER, edited by Lawrence Schimel and Martin H. Greenberg (DAW Books, 1997).

"The Vengeful Spirit of Lake Nepeaka" originally published in WHAT HO, MAGIC!, by Tanya Huff (Meisha Merlin Publishing, Inc, 1999).

"Someone to Share the Night" originally published in SINGLE WHITE VAMPIRE SEEKS SAME, edited by Martin Greenberg and Brittany A. Koren (DAW Books, 2001).

"Another Fine Nest" originally published in THE BAKKA ANTHOLOGY, edited by Kristen Pederson Chew (Bakka Books, 2002)

"Scleratus" originally published in THE REPENTANT, edited by Brian M. Thomsen and Martin H. Greenberg (DAW Books, 2003).

"Critical Analysis" originally published in SLIPSTREAMS, edited by Martin H. Greenberg and John Helfers (DAW Books, 2006.)

Tanya Huff

The Finest in Fantasy

SING THE FOUR QUARTERS   0-88677-628-7
FIFTH QUARTER   0-88677-651-1
NO QUARTER   0-88677-698-8
THE QUARTERED SEA   0-88677-839-5

The Keeper's Chronicles
SUMMON THE KEEPER   0-88677-784-4
THE SECOND SUMMONING   0-88677-975-8
LONG HOT SUMMONING   0-7564-0136-4

Omnibus Editions:
WIZARD OF THE GROVE   0-88677-819-0
(Child of the Grove & The Last Wizard)
OF DARKNESS, LIGHT & FIRE   0-7564-0038-4
(Gate of Darkness, Circle of Light & The Fire's Stone)

To Order Call: 1-800-788-6262